Veil of Shadows III

Omnibus Special Edition

M. R. Pritchard

MIDNIGHT
LEDGER

Second Edition
December 2024
Midnight Ledger
Paperback ISBN: 978-1-957709-55-0
Hardcover ISBN: 978-1-957709-59-8

VEIL OF SHADOWS III

About Veil of
Shadows III

A collection of the Veil of Shadows Series Books 7-10.

———

This omnibus edition begins with "Etched in Darkness", book 7 in the Veil of Shadows Series. You can start here if books 1-6 are not your jam. The next few books in this series will focus on Jed and Shay's relationship and can be read without books 1-6. We will go back in time and revisit old friends. Then catch up with Sparrow and Meg's timeline.

———

If you want to immerse yourself further in the Veil of Shadows, visit the blog for Veil of Shadows discussions, previews, and spoilers.

———

Etched in Darkness (Veil of Shadows 7)

When darkness beckons and love defies the unknown, destiny takes an unexpected turn.

Before Shay got her blowtorch blue hair, she was just an ordinary Montana cowgirl, raised by prepper parents on a remote ranch. But everything shifted one fateful day when a ranch hand struck a perilous bargain with a Crossroads Demon, unleashing chaos that forever altered Shay's existence.

Amidst the turmoil, Jed, a mysterious man with a past intertwined with the supernatural, arrives in town, becoming Shay's unexpected ally. As the eerie consequences of the unholy pact unfold, Shay finds herself at a crossroads, torn between the safety of her familiar ranch life and the allure of a journey into the unknown alongside Jed.

Haunted by newfound powers and grappling with the weight of an otherworldly destiny, Shay must navigate treacherous landscapes—both within and outside herself. Will she embrace the unknown, embarking on an adventure fraught with danger and desire, or choose the familiar comforts of her home despite the looming darkness?

In a tale woven with dark enchantment and the whispered promises of forbidden love, Shay must confront her deepest fears and make a choice that will alter not just her fate but the destiny of those entwined with her.

———

Embrace the Night (Veil of Shadows Book 8)

Haunted by shadows, Bound by fate.

As Jed and Shay embark on their journey to California, the path ahead is fraught with peril. Angels, hell-bent on Jed's demise, and Demons coveting Shay for their own sinister purposes, shadow their every step.

All seems to be progressing smoothly until a heartbroken ghost intervenes, diverting their course and leading to Shay's abduction. With each twist in the road, danger emerges anew, compelling Jed to contemplate the solitary and perilous route to ruin.

In a relentless pursuit against supernatural forces and unforeseen threats, Jed must navigate a treacherous landscape where allies are scarce, and the odds of survival grow slimmer. Will he defy the odds to rescue Shay, or will the Demons of their journey propel him toward a desolate path of self-destruction? The road to California unfolds as a haunting odyssey, where every turn unearths not only the perils of the present but also the ghosts of Jed's past.

————

Shadows of Destiny (Veil of Shadows Book 9)

A journey of darkness and despair: Will Jed defy fate to save Shay, or succumb to his own ruin?

If looks could kill, Alastor would raze all of Hell in retribution. He didn't appreciate being sent home in a blast of light with everything he'd built destroyed, and he's going to do everything in his power to hunt down the half-breed who did it.

For Jed and Shay, Hell is filled with challenges, from hiding a stolen Angel baby to being a body double for the Queen, these two have their work cut out for them. Yet, beneath the surface, Jed wrestles with the guilt of upending Shay's once-normal existence.

Jed and Shay must navigate a perilous path, where the line between savior and destroyer blurs, and the consequences of their choices echo through the infernal corridors.

———

Midnight Serenade (Veil of Shadows Book 10)

Trapped between Heaven and Hell, Jed faces his demons while Shay's fate hangs in the balance.

Jed finds himself ensnared in a perilous web of darkness and despair as he confronts his inner demons. Shay's fate teeters on the edge of oblivion, her very existence hanging in the balance.

Meanwhile, amidst the chaos of the infernal realm, Alastor, driven by a thirst for vengeance, searches for a means to infiltrate the castle and unleash his wrath upon those who have wronged him. But his path is fraught with danger, and the shadows of betrayal lurk around every corner.

As if the looming threat of Alastor's vengeance weren't enough, Nero's transformation into a monstrous entity sends shockwaves through the kingdom, casting a pall of fear and uncertainty over all who dwell within its walls. Outside the castle, a malevolent presence lurks, waiting to unleash its fury upon any who dare to cross its path.

In this dark and twisted tale of betrayal, redemption, and the struggle for survival, Jed and Shay must navigate a treacherous landscape where the line between friend and foe blurs and the consequences of their choices echo through the halls of Hell itself. Will they find the strength to overcome the darkness that threatens to consume them, or will they be lost to its unforgiving embrace?

———

Love and Destiny Collide in a World Where Darkness Knows No Rest.

"Veil of Shadows" delivers a riveting blend of Supernatural & Constantine with the pulse-pounding tension of The Walking Dead, unveiling an unrelenting battle between good and evil. Delve into a realm of fated mates entwined in a deadly dance, where bad omens are a harbinger of darkness. As lovers turn to foes and friendships are tested, join the struggle against demons and the living dead. Brace yourself for an action-packed, paranormal romantic dark fantasy you won't be able to put down.

———

I was hooked from the get-go..." -ABNA Expert Reviewer

"It's unfortunate that one can't predict or be a part of aiding which books go viral, as Sparrow Man by M.R. Pritchard is certainly worthy of such reward ... this novel took me by complete surprise. What I thought was a simple zombie story morphed into something wild and completely unforeseen. Yet it fit perfectly within the world Pritchard has created, mysteries unfolding into fantastical developments. The eclectic characters were a joy to follow and the romance unfolded without being forced."-TheBehrg, KindleScout winning author of Housebroken

"Whoever thought a trip to Hell could be so interesting! Pritchard does a good job balancing humor and thrills—hell, it's mostly funny—and delivering the reader a cast of characters so unbelievable that you can't help but love them." - Charles, Vine Voice

"Another great fantasy ... with humor, edginess, childlike joy, and the frailty of love. Pritchard reminds us to nurture those we hold dear as

we root for her characters to have a happily ever after." - Muddy Rose Reviews

"This is the story of being there for someone who is going through a tough time, of love and trauma with strong characters that you can't help but like. Meg, and Sparrow, stand out in a well told tale. I am not normally into fantasy but this one grabbed me as it is so much more." - Misfits Reviewer

ETCHED IN DARKNESS

ONE

RUNNING FOR YOUR LIFE WASN'T A SPORT ON THE Earthen plane, but for Jed, it was survival. Jed had been on the run since he could walk on two legs and finally escape the creatures that came for him day and night. Since he was Nephilim, this was the way it would always be. He'd been around for a while. He'd been hunted for a while. He knew this from the few others he'd met that were like him. They didn't last long, but they traded stories and methods to stay alive. Jed tapped his pocket, feeling the notebook of spells that was left to him by the last Nephilim he'd come across decades ago. Declan wasn't much older that Jed, but he'd lasted by way of spells and runes carved into every flat surface of his house and belongings. Jed took it one step further and carved those runes into his skin. It was good practice since now he could make a living with the tattoo gun. But, every so often, a creature would walk through the doors of his shop that didn't belong. Like Meg did that one day. Meg, with her dark energy and light eyes. There was something about her he didn't understand. She paid in full and held conversation while he tattooed the watercolor sparrow over her heart. He revealed little about himself. It was when she came back again and brought that fallen-Angel Hellion Sparrow that she wound up ruining the pleasant spot he was at in life. Sparrow was all kinds of cursed. Jed could see it the moment he laid eyes on the guy. Worse was that Meg was head over heels in love. He helped them, tattooed them with runes of protection. And all it got him was noticed.

Jed touched the mark on his neck. He also lost a little blood when Meg bit him. Jed tried to shake away the feelings. Lust and heat had filled his body. He remembered touching her waist before he passed out. Whatever she was, he wanted more but he also wanted to never see her again. Meg was trouble. Trouble he didn't have time for if he wanted to stay alive.

Now here he was on the run again, making his way toward the rural towns of the Midwest, away from the crowded cities of the Northeast. With any hope, he'd avoid the dead until someone else took care of them and he'd avoid Angels and Demons and dead things as well. He'd find food and shelter and hunker down until it was safe again.

Jed stopped under the awning of an empty gas station. The dead hadn't been walking for long, a few months at least, but the destruction and abandon was rapid. Jed glanced through the glass of the gas station and auto shop to see if there was anything inside worth investigating. His pack was heavy with clothes and food, his water jug half-full. He focused on the shelves behind the counter. He could use a smoke. It had been a long time since he set a cancer stick to his lips. He gave up the dirty habit when New York State outlawed them. It surprised him Indiana hadn't outlawed them too.

The sound of shuffling feet broke the afternoon silence. On this daily trek from Walkerton to Kingsbury, Jed hadn't seen much life. He was sure the dead were making their way to nearby Chicago. They always seemed to move with purpose, clustering in small groups. Something drove them to move and follow as one.

A man's voice startled Jed. "A large herd of zombies are making their way through California."

Jed walked to the door of the gas station and found the television mounted in the far corner of the waiting area. A map of the U.S. replaces the reporter's image; the movement of the dead is illustrated with green blobs like weather radar. There's a large area of green over southern California, moving north. They color the area south of the green zone black. A dead zone. A universal warning. Do not go there.

"If you're still in northern California and you're hearing this message, evacuate. Evacuate now! The Coast Guard has abandoned the west coast. The National Guard has declared California a complete loss."

Jed focused on the spattering of green where he was traveling. The Midwest wasn't overly populated, it would be easier to hunker down. His gaze went to the west coast again. The green blob travelled along a main highway. He found that interesting. The dead didn't care about roads, they moved through forests just as haphazardly. It was almost like they were following something.

The news reporter rubbed his face and looked thoroughly terrified. There were loud thuds from the television and a light fell over and hit the desk where the reporter sat. The reporter stood. "Evacuate now!" he shouted one last time before picking up his chair and throwing it. A dead woman walked across the News set before the screen turned to static.

Jed glanced at the shelves and noticed some of the snack foods hadn't been completely pillaged. There was a handful of Slim Jims, Oreos, and a few tins of Spam. Jed went for the protein. The sugary cookies might taste good, but he knew he'd be feeling like crap the next day.

There was a change in the air. Something like mild electricity popping. Turning, he noticed a figure walking down the street.

Jed paused, crouched, and watched the tall man walking down the road. Angel wings were invisible on this plane, but he could see their transparent glimmer. He always knew when they were near; feathered or leathered, he could see the wings in the right light.

This was an Angel. Come to put an end to his life, since he was forbidden and all. They never stopped. Jed traced his footsteps in his mind and tried to think of any clues he could have left behind. He'd been careful on his travels. He was always careful. Never left a trail or a crumb or much of a memory. He was good at being invisible. He was beige in an ochre world, blending in with vacant faces and warm bodies. He tipped his hat lower to hide his face. A shuffling sound echoed.

Jed whispered a spell of glamour and his fingers tapped gently in spellcasting. He leaned to the side and didn't see his reflection in the glass window of the gas station. He scooted forward, careful not to step on any debris that would make the Angel walking down the road notice him. He made his way out the door, keeping to the shadows. He stopped once he got around the corner of the building.

The shuffling sound got louder. It didn't seem to bother the Angel walking down the street. He was tall, lithe with muscle, a blade drawn. His clothing was similar to what most wore on the Earthen plane; leathers and linen or jeans and a T-shirt. A Demon he'd be able to spot based on clothing alone. They were always in full leather. Dark leather, black or deep red like a kidney bean. The Angel gripped his blade and walked with purpose. Jed wiped sweat from his brow, worried the glamour wasn't doing its job.

The wind blew.

Jed sneezed.

Shit.

The Angel picked up his pace and began running in Jed's direction. The shuffling sound got even louder as five of the dead broke onto the street and went after the Angel.

Jed ran. He wasn't a coward; he just knew it was easier to avoid the creatures that came for him than expend the energy needed to kill them. He needed to save his energy for the important battles.

Two

Shay counted the supplies that lined the root cellar. It was deep underground and cold. She stepped on a hole near the wall, grinding her foot until the soil collapsed inward. Sometimes small animals or bugs dug their way into the cellar. Usually they left empty handed because the food was sealed and packaged to last years. There were root vegetables in bins. Shay opened the lid on one to make sure whatever came through the hole hadn't made a home here. This food needed to last them.

She twisted the lid on the wooden barrel and lifted. The soil covered potatoes looked undisturbed. She closed the lid and rotated the barrel as best she could. There weren't any chew marks or holes. She moved on to the barrel of carrots, another of onion, and lastly the beets. Everything looked undamaged. She swiped at her hair, wishing for a hot shower sometime soon.

"Everything good down here?" a familiar voice asked.

Shay's spine went straight, and her heart picked up a few beats. "All good," she replied, turning to face the man who'd entered the cellar. It was Clyburn.

Shay took the laminated list out of her pocket and held it out.

"Everything's stocked." She sidestepped to avoid him. "I'm headed up to help with dinner."

"Whoa," Clyburn said, holding out his hand. "Where ya going so fast, little lady?"

"I have things to do." She avoided his hand and glanced at the door. The man was obstructing her way out. "I don't have time for this."

He settled his thumbs in the belt loops of his jeans and looked down. "Why you always avoiding me, Shay?" He sounded dejected.

She took a few more steps, wishing he'd move the hell out of her way. "I have to go."

Clyburn took a few steps. He was toying with her.

Shay didn't like the feeling of being trapped. Hated it more and more each day. Hated that Clyburn felt the need to find and harass her. Shay took her chance at the unobstructed passage and ran for the door of the root cellar.

Clyburn was faster, grabbing her around the waist and pulling her back against his chest. He laughed and tightened his arm around her middle.

"Let go of me." Shay struggled, wanting to scream.

Clyburn pressed his cheek against the side of her head. His scruffy beard scratched at her face. Shay could smell the sweet and earthy scent of his chewing tobacco. "Mmm. You smell good," Clyburn said, his voice deep and low.

Shay scrabbled at his arms, hoping to leave marks under the flannel shirt he wore. She wanted him to let go.

"My father is expecting me. He'll be here any minute." Shay was unsuccessful in stomping his foot since Clyburn wore steel toed boots.

"Maybe I want to invite you to the square dance on Friday."

"Doubt they'll still be having it." Shay didn't stop struggling.

"They will. Going to be a powwow too."

"If we're all still alive by then." She knocked her head against his and saw stars.

Clyburn finally released her. "We'll definitely be alive," he said.

Shay ran out the door and up the uneven steps of the root cellar entrance. She slammed the door closed and ran as far from the cellar as she could.

Shay passed a stockpile of logs, the gardens, the barns where the chickens and pigs and goats stayed. She ran past the houses and the rusted tractors. She ran past the tall Ponderosa Pine that set their property apart and made it easy to find if you got turned around in the beyond. Shay finally stopped at the horse barn. Out of breath, she gripped the wooden stall door. A black stallion wandered over and nuzzled her head.

Shay's heart was beating fast, and she wanted nothing more than to melt to the ground. The stallion could tell she was upset and nuzzled harder against her shoulders.

"You're such a gentleman, Nero." Shay patted the stallion's neck. "More so than anyone else here."

Shay hid in the horse barn until her father came looking for her.

———

"Shay-baby," Nicholas called. "I know you're in here."

Shay heard the enclosure open and looked up from where she was sitting in Nero's corral. Sweet hay crunched under her feet as she stood. Nero whinnied and walked closer. Ready to protect.

"It's okay," Shay said as she reached out and patted Nero on his flank. "It's just dad."

Nicholas took up the doorway to the paddock, a giant man dressed in dusty jeans and a rugged button-up shirt stained with dirt. He tucked a pair of gloves into his pocket and brushed his hands off on his pants. The man was part cowboy, part prepper, and he had been wrapped around Shay's finger since the day she was born.

Shay's father taught her everything she knew: how to grow a garden, how to store food, how to ride a horse, shoot a gun, hunt a bison. Most importantly, he'd taught her how to survive the apocalypse she never thought would come. It came. Headfirst, the apocalypse rammed through their Montana ranch with death and destruction. It had only been a few months, but many had died. They hadn't lost a soul on the ranch and there was enough food and supplies to keep them going for years. But Shay didn't intend to stay holed up on the ranch for years. She'd had plans. They involved seeing the world. She'd been accepted to Brigham Young University in Utah on a scholarship. She wasn't sure where the biological sciences would take her but she knew it was a good starting point. It would've taken her places. But now she was stuck. She'd probably never see the rest of Montana, let alone college in Utah, or anything else. Shay was having a hard time accepting that she was stuck on this ranch, only to be pursued by Clyburn, probably for the rest of her life. She figured she still had plenty of living to do before settling down and couldn't accept the idea of it right now.

"Why are you hiding out in here?" her father asked.

"Nero was lonely. I brought him some carrots." Shay didn't like lying, but she also didn't want to admit that her father's favorite ranch hand had been after her for months now. Clyburn wanted a relationship. Shay wanted nothing to do with the man. He was strong and handsome and capable, but Shay was simply not interested. They were only a few months into the apocalypse. Things could change. The dead could drop and leave humanity alone. If nothing she had hope for something better than their current situation. It couldn't get worse, could it?

"You got a good girl here, Nero," her father laughed as he patted the horse, then brought Shay in for a hug. He kissed the top of her head. "Momma made chicken and dumplings. Come on." He tugged at a piece of hair that had fallen out of her ponytail.

Shay left the horse corral, only feeling safe now that her father was there. They walked out of the barn, the heat of summer cooling as evening came. In the light, Shay noticed blood on her father's boot. She'd seen a lot of blood lately. More gore and brain matter than she ever expected to see in her life. She didn't take pride in it.

Slamming a poker through a walking corpse's head to get it off the fence was a necessary evil these days.

"Did they get in?" she asked.

"No." His voice was grim. "There was a lone one walking across the fields. Must've heard the animals. The fence kept it out, but we put an end to it and burned the body." He pointed to black smoke rising in the distance. "Damned soul bought himself a six-foot deep oven to have its last rest in."

"Will they ever stop coming?" Shay asked.

"Never know." He pulled her shoulders against him in a brief hug. "Don't worry, Shay-baby, I'll protect you."

Shay nodded, and Clyburn's actions made more sense now. He'd been high on adrenaline after killing one of the walking dead. He was looking for another rush involving her, of course. Shay needed to carry a concealed weapon. Clyburn thought she was easy prey, but she wasn't. Eventually, she'd have to unleash on him.

THREE

JED MADE IT PAST THE OUTLYING CITIES OF CHICAGO unharmed. He'd hitchhiked through Iowa, surprised that people stopped to give him a ride. He assumed everyone was a little more forgiving now that most were running for their lives on a daily basis. But Jed had that effect on people. They were eager to help him, eager to listen, eager to offer food and drink. He figured it had something to do with him being a Nephilim. Whatever energy he carried, the people of the Earthen plane were willing to assist him. Especially the women. Jed did his best to hide his face with messy hair and a base-ball cap pulled low. He could hide with his magic, but his face was easily identifiable and easily remembered. He hid from cameras. Preferred small towns with limited infrastructure. Big brother wouldn't keep his secrets. If a traffic camera caught his image, the Angels and Demons would come soon after. They always did. It was a hard lesson that led Jed to a simpler life.

The Angel was still hunting him. Jed could sense it. He couldn't stay glamoured invisible forever. The spell would drain his reserves. He had to be smart, calculated, careful. His fingers lingered over the fresh spell of protection he'd inked on his skin. It burned and he didn't have a tegaderm to cover it with. First world problems. There was a time when fresh tattoos were never covered. They were left out to weep and crust until the image broke through like an egg hatching.

His back thudded against the rusted metal of the truck bed as it drove over a few potholes. The cab was full. A father named Bill, a young mother named Laura, and two little girls. He took one glance at them and volunteered to ride in the truck bed. The mother sighed in relief after taking in the tattoos covering his arms. The little girls glanced out the window at him every so often. He didn't ask their names, didn't want to know. He didn't want to make connections and remember. He'd learned the hard way.

They stopped at a rest stop near the South Dakota border just past a road sign for *Meckling: Population 2,500*. Bill got out, shotgun in hand. He passed Jed a baseball bat.

"Girls have to use the bathroom," Bill said.

Jed stood and jumped out of the truck bed. He weighed the baseball bat in his hand, liking the feel. He had a few weapons tucked away. Knives that were carved with spells, a small handgun with not nearly enough bullets. Jed preferred a blunt object to swing. The baseball bat was perfect.

They walked toward the rest stop building slowly, taking in their surroundings. Bill skirted across the flowerbeds to get a good look behind the building. It was mostly glass with two doors. If anyone was there, they'd see. The enclosed bathrooms made Jed's body tense with anticipation. He didn't like killing things, but the walking dead were already... dead. They were just stuck on the wrong plane. Their souls should've gone to Hell for sorting, but something was happening between the realms. Something dark was walking the Earthen plane, disrupting the natural order of things. Hence the apocalypse and the zombies. Jed was trying his best not to get caught up in it, but since Meg was the last to visit him before all Hell broke loose, he figured he was slightly involved already.

Jed gripped the baseball bat as Bill opened the door to the rest stop lobby. They listened. There were no noises. No smells. No grunts or groans or shuffling feet.

Bill pointed to the lights. At least this place still had electricity. It was out most places. But Jed knew the rural areas would still have men and women with purpose, doing their best to hold humanity together as long as they could. He was sure they'd come across some open restaurants, maybe even a hotel with hot water.

Bill motioned to the women's room and Jed walked closer to back him up. Bill pushed open the door, crouching to look under the stalls. As Jed followed behind, Bill walked through the bathroom, using the barrel of his shotgun to push open the stall doors. When he got to the fourth and final one, he turned to Jed with a look of relief.

"All clear?" Jed asked.

"Yup," Bill replied. "Let's check the men's room."

They passed two vending machines filled with snacks and soda. Bill pointed. "We need to empty those before we leave."

"Good idea." Jed pushed open the door to the men's room. He paused, crouching. There was a set of boots in the last stall. Jed held a finger to his lips and gripped the bat like he was about to hit a home run on the bottom of the ninth.

Bill readied his shotgun.

Jed sidestepped to the last stall and prodded the door with the toe of his boot. "Come out."

There was a noise from inside, a gurgling and a grunt.

Jed kicked the door as hard as he could.

A dead man hissed. His hair was ragged and half fallen out, teeth rotten and putrid.

"I got it," Bill said, moving into place.

The dead man stumbled forward.

Jed hit up with the bat, knocking the dead man in the chest and forcing him to stand up straight.

Bill blew off its head in one shot.

The carcass fell backward onto the toilet and the door closed.

"Watched all those movies about zombies my whole life and I'll still never get over it." Bill shivered. "God save us all."

Jed headed for the door. "You should get the girls."

They'd cleared the building in less than ten minutes. Still, Jed didn't like the idea of leaving Laura and the girls alone in the truck. Surprise was a battle tactic and, as far as Jed was concerned, every moment was an opportunity to die, especially so these days.

FOUR

SHAY WOKE TO A SCRATCHING SOUND OUTSIDE HER window. She sat up, hurried, rolled out of bed, and grabbed the flashlight from her nightstand as she dropped to the floor. The old farmhouse was two stories but the roof to the covered porch was outside her window. It was easy to access if anyone wanted to. As a teenager, she'd snuck out to watch the stars on the rooftop enough times to know someone was there now.

There was a hunting knife under her mattress. Shay reached for it and sat up just far enough to get a good view of the window and a man-sized shadow.

Shay froze and watched. It took a few moments before she recognized the figure.

Clyburn.

He tugged at the window, trying to open it.

Shay flattened herself to the floor, waiting until the noise stopped and she recognized the sound of him climbing down from the roof.

Shay finally stood and checked the locks on the window. Thankful she'd remembered to lock them before falling asleep.

Clyburn approached her in the morning, a steaming cup of

coffee in one hand and a piece of paper in his other. He walked toward Shay, looking tired, smiling when her eyes didn't look away.

"You dropped this." He held out the root cellar list.

Shay reached for it but Clyburn moved the paper once, twice, three times before she plucked it from his fingers.

"Thanks." Shay tucked the list in her back pocket and stepped down off the front porch.

"Where are you going?" Clyburn asked.

"Wherever I want." Shay headed for the horse barn.

"They're fed already." Clyburn sipped at his coffee.

Shay stopped walking, turned to look through the kitchen window at her mother and father talking as they washed dishes together. She wished her father would walk through that door so Clyburn would go away.

"You should stop avoiding me." Clyburn said. "I'm perfect for you. Your father agrees."

Shay made a face. "Nero is perfect for me. I don't need a man."

Clyburn laughed and kicked at the dirt. "I know the ranch. I can keep you safe." He looked past the fence surrounding their ranch. "I can protect you from what's out there."

"I don't need protecting." Shay said. "And don't try to break into my bedroom window again." Shay tapped the small hunting knife she'd tucked into her cargo pocket of her pants. She wanted to whip it out and stab him in the shoulder. She could do it too, she knew it would only take her about five seconds. Shay took a deep breath. She wasn't the maiming type, at least not yet.

Clyburn crossed his arms, resting his wrist and coffee mug in the crook of his arm. He smiled. "Thought you heard me."

"Be lucky my father didn't. He'd have shot you dead on the spot."

Clyburn stuck out a finger to point at her. "That's where you're wrong. If he kills me, I turn into one of those walking corpses." He snapped his jaw, straight teeth clanking together. "Then I bite, and everyone turns." He leaned closer. "He won't shoot me dead. He wouldn't risk your life. Be happy I'm not some city boy from back east with no sense of survival. Cowgirl up, this is happening."

"Over my dead body." Shay waved. "Nice speakin' atcha." Shay headed for the horse stall, not trusting Clyburn to have actually fed Nero. There were plenty of lies she'd caught him in, which is why she didn't trust the man. She was sure that Nero's stall would have an empty oat bucket and yesterday's water.

Shay was thankful that Clyburn didn't follow. She'd had enough of his nonsense. There was no way in Hell she'd carry on with him. No sense in it. She couldn't believe her father would even consider it.

"You know I won't be living forever." Her father's voice called from the wraparound porch as he stepped down the stairs to follow her.

"Yes, you will, daddy," Shay said. "You're the heartiest survivor I've ever known."

"Why don't you go to the square dance with Clyburn?" he asked.

Shay sighed loudly. "I'm not going. It's not safe."

"We have to have some fun. I'll bring momma. We can double date." He smiled but Shay could tell it was forced.

"I'd rather dye my hair blue." Shay looked up at her father. "Daddy, I don't need a man to take care of me. You taught me everything I need to know to survive. Momma read me all the books. Heck, I reread all the books."

Her father reached out and touched her hair. "This might look nice blue. I just want someone to take care of you."

"I don't need anyone like that. Definitely not a ranch hand." Shay shivered, wishing she'd put on her jacket.

"There aren't many options these days, darlin'."

"We'd have to leave the ranch to know." Shay pointed toward town. "My knight in shining armor could be waiting for me over yonder."

Her father laughed, then coughed. "Maybe we'll go check then."

Shay's brows rose in interest. Her father hadn't let her leave the ranch since the dead walking had spread to Montana. She didn't really want to go anywhere now. She was safe here, but she knew she needed to get out in the real world eventually. She needed to put her skills to use. She needed to... do something else.

———

THERE WERE two other ranch hands; Clyde and James, who stayed on the property. They were old and had no interest in Shay. They simply wanted to survive. James was one-hundred percent Northern Cheyenne Indian and left on the weekends to see his family on the reservation.

Clyde was an old friend of Nicholas' who had gotten into enough trouble throughout his life. He spent most of his time smoking on the porch and watching old movies on the television. Clyde watched the news every day and updated them all. He told Shay's father where the walking corpses were heading, where they'd been, where the National Guard was headed–it was nowhere near Colstrip, Montana.

When Friday came, James was packed and ready to head to the reservation.

"What about the powwow?" Clyburn asked.

"No." James shook his head. "Not a good time." He looked up at the sky. "There are evil spirits nearby."

"Maybe you should stay another day," her father suggested.

James tightened a strap on his horse and patted his saddlebags. "I have to see how they are. I've been here long enough. Telephone lines are out. Cell phone service is down." James pointed to Clyde. "Old man says the television is mostly static, all week long. I have to go." James fitted his foot in a stirrup and launched himself onto the horse's back. "I'll be back Monday." He tipped his hat.

Clyburn opened the front gate and let James go. They all stood and watched him ride the horse across the prairie. A few little birds fluttered out of his way.

James had planned his route during dinner. He was going to stay on the outskirts of Colstrip, head south avoiding route 39, and stick to the valleys between the mountains. He'd travel around Lame Deer, cross US-212 just west of the casino and enter the reservation from there. Nicholas had asked a few questions to verify James's route.

"I've done it plenty of times," James reminded him. "Decades worth."

"The dead didn't walk then," her father reminded James.

Shay had a bad feeling in her stomach. The towns weren't highly populated, but she didn't think James could protect himself if too many of the walking dead came after him. He could go into the mountains and lose them in the rough terrain, but it was risky. There were snakes and elk and bears that wouldn't be afraid to go after him.

FIVE

Bill and his family were headed to Saskatchewan. He'd told Jed they had more family there, and the Canadians weren't having as much of a crisis as the U.S. They were taking Montana Highway 59 north. Jed needed to take US-212 West.

"Good luck, man," Bill said with a firm handshake.

"You too," Jed said, securing his pack.

"You should stop at one of these stores and get some new gear." Bill pointed to a shop down the road. "No one will care these days."

"Sure will." Jed patted the side of the truck as Bill got behind the wheel. He waved to Laura and the little girls, hoping they wouldn't remember his face.

Jed hit the road walking, thankful that the family had driven him across a few states without getting harmed. The Angel that was tracking him outside Chicago must've lost his trail.

Mountains flanked US-212 on each side. He could see far in the distance. He figured he'd make it to Ashland by nightfall. As he walked, he practiced minor spells. He stretched and exercised his fingers so they'd bend and tap in awkward positions during spell-casting.

One truck drove by him and slammed on the brakes.

Jed saw the man looking in his rearview mirror.

The driver put the red truck in reverse, moved to the middle of the road, and stopped next to Jed.

"Whatcha doin out here?" asked the driver. He was young but missing a few teeth. There was a rifle propped between the seats.

"Just passing through," Jed said.

"Well, you wanna ride?"

Jed didn't really want a ride. He wanted to walk and clear his mind and keep up his stamina. He looked toward the mountain. There was nothing out here. He was more likely to die by wild elk attack out here than zombie bite.

"Sure, man," Jed reached for the passenger door.

"Name's Dan," the driver said. "You?"

"Jed."

"I can drop you in Lame Deer. I'm headed up to Nichols. Unless you want to go that way." Dan hit the windshield wiper button and blood smeared across the windshield. "Sorry about that. Hit one of those walking dead people."

"I'm headed west." Jed adjusted his pack between his feet.

"Welp, Lame Deer has a casino that's still up and running. I can drop you there. I drove by yesterday and it still had the lights on."

"Thanks," Jed said.

Dan drove fast. The speedometer hovered around one-hundred miles per hour. There was nothing else on the road, so Jed didn't complain. He was just happy to be riding shotgun and not in the truck bed.

Jed studied Dan from his periphery. It was odd, the guy showing up out of nowhere. Jed didn't trust. He didn't trust miracles and he didn't trust help that was too good to be true. He couldn't see any wings or horns. He rubbed a rune on his hand, considered casting a spell right here in front of a stranger.

Dan slammed on the brakes. The truck skidded to a stop.

Jed reached for his gun, ready to fight in close quarters. He noticed the bite mark on Dan's arm. Shit.

"Whoa, chill out, pal." Dan pointed across the street. "Casino."

Jed sighed a breath of relief, feeling like an idiot. "Thanks." He said as he opened the door and got out.

Dan took off before Jed could get a good grip on his pack. "Hey! My bag!" Panic flashed through Jed's body. Everything important for staying alive was in that pack. Dan stopped the truck and shoved the pack into the street.

Jed jogged after his belongings as Dan's truck accelerated down the road before turning sharply right.

"Asshole," Jed muttered, picking up his bag. Jed didn't curse him much, Dan wouldn't need it. He'd be dead soon; a walking bag of flesh like the others, lost and wandering the Earthen plane, his soul in unrest. Jed should've killed the guy. He should have prevented Dan from hurting others. God forbid the guy turned while he was driving. He shook his head, knowing better. Can't save them all. Jed knew he could only save himself. This life was meant to be lived alone. Letting someone get close to him meant they would only end up on the run forever or dead. Jed wouldn't do that to another soul.

Jed took in his surroundings. The casino was tiny but offered lodging and food. Jed had been traveling nonstop for weeks. He was ahead of schedule and didn't want to show up in California too early. He headed for the casino.

Six

James never came back. By Tuesday, Clyburn and Nicholas were packing up the horses to go find him.

"I want to go," Shay said, holding Nero's harness.

"No," Clyburn said first.

"Daddy," Shay stared at her father.

"Who will take care of momma while I'm gone?" her father asked.

"Momma is a strong woman who can take care of herself," Shay said.

"You packed that horse?" her father asked.

"Yes." Shay tipped her chin up. "I got my firearms, extra bullets, hunting knives, water, snacks, and a change of underwear."

Clyburn chuckled.

Shay's eyes threw daggers.

"You might as well let the lady tag along," Clyburn said.

Shay could barely believe it. After all of his jabs about her needing protection, he was going to be on her side in this argument. Maybe he wasn't a total tool. Shay glanced at the bulge in his lip from packed chewing tobacco. Nope. Still a tool.

"Go tell momma goodbye," her father said. "That woman will tan my hide if you leave without kissing her cheek."

Shay ran into the house to speak with her mother before leaving. Then, the horses were trotting through the gate of the ranch and Clyde was locking it behind them.

"Bring James home," Clyde said, as they galloped away.

———

SHAY'S HORSE followed her father. Clyburn was a few yards behind them. They traveled parallel to Highway 34 and stopped briefly at Castle Rock Lake for the horses to drink. There were figures wandering around the Colstrip Inn & Suites hotel in the distance. Their clothing looked ragged, their skin pale and sallow, they barely lifted their feet while walking.

"You think they're dead?" Shay asked.

"Most likely," Clyburn replied, studying the lake water as though he could see something beneath the surface.

"They won't come," Nicholas said, patting his horse and leading it away from the lake. "As long as we are quiet."

Shay opened her water and took a drink before following her father.

"Let's get out of here," Clyburn said as he mounted his horse. Shay and her father did the same.

They traveled past the Lake and around the sandy runoff from the abandoned mines.

"There won't be much past here," her father said. "Until we get to Lame Deer."

They followed the path James said he'd take. There were tracks from his horse and his boots, and broken stalks of bramble.

Out here in the valleys of Montana, all seemed normal. There were rabbits and snakes, a chilled breeze blowing in from the west that promised winter would be on its way soon. Shay zipped her jacket.

The squealing of rubber tires on the road and a revving engine broke through their silent trek. "Wait," Nicholas held up his hand.

Shay reigned in Nero. Clyburn stopped his horse next to Shay.

"Don't look good," Nicholas said.

There was a red truck driving erratically. The windshield wipers swiped back and forth across a blood smeared window.

"We should go," Clyburn said.

Shay watched the truck weave all over the road. It accelerated abruptly before turning sharply to the left, hitting a narrow embankment, and rolling.

"Shouldn't we help them?" Shay asked. She knew better than to ask but it was the human thing to do. She'd want someone to help her if someone injured her in a car accident.

"We don't help the damned," her father said. "Let's get out of here before the corpse crawls out and comes after us."

Shay clicked her tongue and Nero picked up speed.

The three travelers rode south at a fast pace. They didn't see James, but they followed the tracks of his horse until they stopped at US-212. There were no tracks on the opposite side of the pavement.

They rode east, toward Lame Deer center.

"He wouldn't have gone towards town," Clyburn said.

"Right about that," Nicholas said, inspecting the tree line for clues.

"This isn't the route he told us he'd take," Shay reminded the men.

SEVEN

Jed pushed open the door to Lame Deer casino. It was single story, more of a glorified motel than a hotel. The carpet was emerald green, the walls gold and burgundy. It smelled like cigarette smoke, but underneath there was a stench he couldn't put his finger on, musky and dirty. Something he didn't like lingered.

He walked to the front desk and reserved a room for the night.

"Checkout is at eleven in the morning," the young guy with a goatee said as he searched for the room key.

Jed paid and took the key with the number nine on it. "The sign said there's a buffet." He hadn't eaten a proper meal in days.

The desk guy pointed to the other side of the room. "Closes at nine tonight."

"Thanks." Jed walked through the casino toward the rooms. He opened the door to room nine and threw his bag on the bed. Jed pulled the knife out of his pocket and etched a rune of protection into the doorframe. Jed pulled back the covers on the bed and checked for things normal people would never look for: runes of blood, clasps of hair, piles of ash or sand, hex bags. He found nothing, but left his own mark for safety.

43

Jed made his way to the buffet after locking his belongings in the room. The casino looked to be about three-quarters full. There were security guards watching everyone closely. They would ask to check arms, wrists, and necks for bite marks. Jed rubbed his neck where Meg had bitten him. Thankfully the scar was small. He adjusted his shirt so the guards wouldn't see.

The buffet wasn't much to write home about. There was over-cooked steak, soggy broccoli, and a cheesy pasta dish that had congealed on the serving spoon. He filled his plate with all of it. The food might not be top tier but it was warm. A young woman at the bar offered him a pale lemonade or water. Jed took one of each. He sat near the window in an empty booth and watched out it as he ate. He glanced out the window multiple times to ensure that Angel didn't drop out of the sky to continue his hunt.

The smell of smoke lingered in the dining room along with the musky smell from before. There was something dead here. A rat in the walls, a possum in the ceiling, or a human in a closet somewhere.

Jed finished his meal and walked through the casino. He fished a coin out of his pocket and sat down to play the slots for a few minutes. He won ten dollars. Played it all and lost it. It was a decent way to kill fifteen minutes; made him appear human, just like the rest of the casino guests. Most of the workers had tanned skin and pitch-black hair. If he had to guess, Lone Deer was owned and run by local Native Americans. He made a mental note to do some research on the area. He went to the lobby for some reading material. There was a shelf with an array of pamphlets. Jed took a handful. He wouldn't be going to any museums or on any recreational day trips to the reservation, but he could read about it before continuing on to California in the morning. Last, he grabbed a map of the west. He already had a path planned out, but he wanted to make sure he wasn't missing anything.

Stomach full and showered clean, Jed relaxed on the bed. He'd pushed a dresser in front of the door, just in case. The bathroom window was big enough for him to crawl out of if needed. There was never a moment he wasn't planning. He was sure it was the only way he'd survived this long: have a defense plan and an escape plan for every moment.

He fell asleep reading about the Northern Cheyenne Indian Reservation.

EIGHT

SHAY WOKE BEFORE THE SUN. NERO WAS NUDGING HER. She sat up and inched herself away from Clyburn. He'd snuck too close to her during the night. She smoothed her palm over Nero's cheek.

"Good boy." She patted him and took in their surroundings. They'd stopped to camp just outside of Lame Deer. There was a campsite near the waste station. It smelled just bad enough that no one in their right mind would bother them.

Shay got up and started getting ready for the day. She rolled up her sleeping bag and packed it. She took the horses to wander, eat the sweet grass, and drink from the trickling stream nearby. Nicholas and Clyburn had taken turns staying awake and watching over camp during the night. Nothing had disturbed them, only the chill on the wind.

Nicholas and Clyburn woke and packed up their things.

"We'll head for Lame Deer. Should be there before brunch," Nicholas said.

The crew made their way to the road, grateful that they no longer smelled the waste station fumes. An SUV drove by with two women inside. They looked scared, their faces pale and eyes wide. They didn't stop. The driver gave them a wide berth as she sped by.

"You think something happened here?" Shay asked.

"Probably," Nicholas said.

There was a sound in the trees nearby. A whinny, the clopping of hooves. A horse galloped out of the tree line headed for them. Dappled brown and white, they all recognized the horse.

"That's James's horse." Clyburn reached for the reins and brought him in.

There was blood on the saddle.

"Where'd he go?" Nicholas asked the horse.

Shay knew a bystander might think of them as nuts for asking a horse a question, but horses were smart. They knew things. They loved their humans just as much as humans loved them.

The horse huffed and shook his head toward Lame Deer.

"Show us," Nicholas said as he took the horse's reins and headed toward town.

"Stay close," Clyburn warned.

Shay swallowed the lump that was growing in her throat. Whatever happened to James could not be good. He was rarely without his horse, especially while traveling. They'd gone from the ranch to the reservation hundreds of times over the years.

More cars sped out of Lame Deer. Soon there was a line of cars and trucks leaving, while they were the only ones headed to town. A few beeped their horns and waved, warning them.

"Turn around," they shouted out the window.

The last car simply blessed themselves, forehead, chest, shoulder to shoulder and whispered a prayer as they went by.

———

LAME DEER WAS A STEAMING pile of dung. Cars were burning. The Dollar Tree was burning. WinCo foods was burning. James's horse led them straight to the Casino.

"Of course," Clyburn muttered in disgust.

Shay knew James liked to gamble, but she barely believed he'd run off to the casino in the middle of all this.

"None of us are without our faults," Nicholas said, clicking his tongue at the horse.

They all had guns ready but the sounds of screams and crashing directed the attention of the dead elsewhere. Through some miracle, they made it to the casino parking area unscathed.

James's horse huffed and nodded his head toward the casino door.

"We know," Nicholas patted the horse. "We'll go get him."

"Do you think anyone is alive in there?" Shay asked.

"It's not on fire, so I have some hope," Nicholas said. "Stick together."

They tied up the horses under a sprawling oak and headed for the front entrance to the casino.

NINE

JED WOKE TO THE SMELL OF SMOKE, ACRID AND unpleasant. He jerked upright and looked at the door. The smell was faint-maybe not coming from the casino?

Jed got out of bed and dressed in a hurry. There were strange noises outside his door; thuds as something heavy knocked against the wall. He hurried to get dressed and shove his belongings into his bag. Tying his boots, he heard faraway screams and shouting. Shit. This couldn't be good. He grabbed the pamphlets off the nightstand and shoved them in his pocket, then moved the dresser away from the door and looked out the peephole. The pale eye of a dead woman looked back.

"Shit," Jed muttered to himself. He reached for the fixed-blade machete knife secured to the side of his bag. It was the best weapon for fighting the living dead. A gun was too loud and brought more. And his magic didn't protect him well from souls that were trapped on the wrong plane. They existed in some strange way. He'd yet to find a spell or rune that would take care of them. Jed looked out the window to get a good idea of what he was up against.

Suddenly, a man in dusty jeans and a button-up shirt was striding down the hall, past the window, and struck the dead woman in the head with a sickening *thwack*.

The man knocked on his door with two pounds of his fist.

Jed opened it and did his best not to look at the brain matter that was dripping down the door.

"Hey. I'm looking for James Crow. Indian looking guy with black hair down to here." The man motioned to his shoulder.

"Not here." Jed adjusted his pack. "How bad is it?" he asked.

"Town is gone. This place will be done for soon." The man moved on and knocked on the door next to Jed's room.

Jed stepped into the hallway. Doors were opening up and plenty of people were still alive. Under the scent of smoke, he smelled breakfast.

Jed made his way to the lobby. Two men were dragging a dead body out the back door. From what he could see, there was already a small pile of bodies. There was no sense of chaos or panic so he turned in his room key.

"What's going on here?" Jed asked the goateed guy at the desk.

The guy moved slowly as he picked up the key and found the hook where it hung until the next guest. "Dead overtook Lame Deer during the night. Most of the town is on fire. We're holding down the fort here." He motioned to the door. "Already had armed guards employed. A few of the dead got in but they took care of them."

"That's good," Jed said.

"Sure you don't want to stay? Few stragglers have come in and said it's terrible out there. You could stay here until it clears up."

"I need to be getting on," Jed said as he tapped the counter. "Thanks though."

Jed went to the dining room. There was bacon, eggs, and French toast. He piled his plate high, not knowing when he'd eat like this again. He grabbed two cups of coffee and sat near a window in the corner. He didn't want any surprises. As he ate, he watched the smoke billow out of the buildings about a half a mile away in the center of town.

He shifted to the side and pulled out the pamphlet with the town map and studied it. Last night he'd planned on walking straight through town. Now he needed to avoid it. US 212 was the quickest route; going south would bring him past more shopping and houses. To the north, there was less in terms of people clustering, but he'd have to trek through a lot of rugged, elevated terrain.

Jed thought of the waterways of the Great Lakes region he'd already traversed. So many times he had to make his way around the little finger lakes and canals. Some elevated terrain would be nothing in comparison. The canopy of trees would hide him from anything flying overhead, hunting him.

Jed ate the eggs first. He added too much salt and pepper, but he didn't care. Seasoned food would be scarce soon enough. The bacon was a little soggy but dipped in syrup tasted just fine. He glanced at the buffet, wondering if it would be selfish to get another plate and two more coffees. He watched the door and tried to get an idea of how many guests were out there. He checked the clock. Since it was nearly ten and only a few tables were occupied and there were mounds of food, he went up to the buffet for more.

Long ago, Jed worked as a line cook in a small diner. It wasn't hard work and he'd learned a lot. Butter is your friend, salt the fries before the grease dried, melt all the cheese with a little steam. The bacon could have been left on the griddle for another two minutes, then it would be crispy. Jed took six slices. They overcooked the eggs. Jed knew the eggs should've been set in the serving pan when they were three-quarters of the way done because they'd continue to cook as they sat. He took four slices of French toast and the two coffees. Returning to his seat, he piled the dirty plates together so the staff wouldn't have to. It was a slight gesture to let them know he wasn't a total heathen.

Voices were shouting in the lobby.

Jed leaned to the side to get a look as he shoved food in his mouth and chewed.

The guy in the button up and dusty jeans was at the lobby desk. The guards were fighting at the door.

Jed ate faster figuring he was going to have to leave soon. He shoveled the eggs into his mouth and considered tucking the French toast into his bag for later. There was a crashing sound, followed by growling: inhuman noises that Jed knew only came from walking corpses. He stood, swallowing a cup of coffee in three gulps. Glancing to the back of the room, he looked for a door that might let him out. There was only a door that led to the kitchen. In the back of the kitchen there'd be a door to the outside, but he wasn't sure he wanted to venture through any rooms he couldn't get a good look at. He didn't want to be a sitting duck. He reached forward and inspected the window where he'd eaten. It didn't open.

Jed headed to the threshold to the lobby, French toast in hand. He took a bite as he walked, wishing he had slathered it in butter before leaving.

The lobby had a front door that was currently under siege. The opposite side of the lobby had a patio with seating and a growing pile of bodies. Directly across from him was the casino floor with guests still playing the slots and cards as though the apocalypse wasn't taking place around them. The man in the dusty jeans was asking the goateed guy behind the desk about someone named James. He motioned with his hands, explaining James's height, hair, and complexion. The guy with the goatee nodded and pointed to the patio.

The dusty jeans guy slapped a hand over his mouth. There was another guy with a wad of chewing tobacco punching out his lower lip and a girl that appeared to be with him. They all showed signs of disappointment. If he had to guess, James was dead and was one of the bodies in the pile on the patio.

Three things happened in the next moment. The glass to the front lobby shattered. The girl turned, drawing her gun and taking the stance of a cowgirl ready to shoot. And Jed got a good look at her, which made him drop his French toast.

Ten

Somehow, all the dead in Lame Deer were trying to come through the door of the casino. Shay was ready. She had enough bullets to take out some of the dead. Nicholas was backing up to protect her. Clyburn was closing in on her right.

The door strained under the weight of the horde pushing against it.

"James is dead," Nicholas said over his shoulder. "We need to get out of here. Fast."

"Gotta go now," Clyburn said. "Those doors are going to shatter soon."

The three moved as one, backing toward the patio behind them.

Movement caught Shay's eye and she glanced to her left. A man stood in the doorway, dropping his food on the floor as their gazes met.

Shay's breath hitched. She'd seen plenty of men come through these parts but she'd never seen a man covered in strange tattoos or so tall or... striking. There was no other way to describe him. He tried to hide it with a low baseball cap and messy hair, but Shay saw him. She felt her face flush as she stumbled. Her father stepped on the toe of her boot. Clyburn grabbed her arm to stop her from falling.

Glass shattered and burst across the room. Red dripped into her eye.

"Damnit," Nicholas spat. "Run."

Gunfire erupted as security began taking out the dead filtering in through the front doors.

They ran. Clyburn shoved the patio door open. Shay and Nicholas ran through before turning to secure it.

"Don't trap them," Shay said, rubbing blood off her forehead and out of her eye.

Clyburn was pushing a heavy table in front of the door when it burst open. Metal slammed against metal and Clyburn skirted out of the way.

It was the guy with the tattoos.

Nicholas slapped Shay on the back and pointed to the area where they'd tied up the horses. It was a clear shot.

"Go," Clyburn said as he ran across the patio to clear the way.

Shay ran, focused on Nero in the distance. The horses stayed quiet and she was thankful for that. The noise brought the dead and Shay hoped they didn't lose their focus on the front doors of the casino.

Nicholas got to the horses first and untied their reins. Shay shoved her foot into the stirrup and launched herself onto the saddle with everything she had. Nicholas and Clyburn did the same.

"Around the foothills," Nicholas said, pointing. "There won't be any of the dead wandering through there for a while."

"Hee-yaw," Clyburn took off to scout the trail.

Nicholas held the reins of James's horse as they escaped the casino grounds.

Shay turned to get one last glance at the casino. Smoke rose from the front of the building. The guy with the tattoos was walking across the patio, digging a piece of paper out of his pocket. He saw her, indecision plastered across his face. He looked like a hitchhiker with his travel pack and worn boots.

"Here," Nicholas had a piece of cloth in his hand. "For the cut." He motioned to her forehead.

Shay took the cloth and pressed it to her skin. In the excitement, she hadn't felt the glass shards cut her face, but now she did. A sharp ache stretched from her hairline to just above her left ear. Momma was going to lose it when she saw the cut. Shay tried to get a good feel for the edges and the deepness of the wound. With all the blood, she was sure she'd need stitches.

Shay focused on Clyburn's back as he made sure the trail ahead was clear. Maybe the ranch hand would back off now that she was mutilated. Men rarely lowered their standards.

Shay gripped Nero's reins tighter and squeezed her legs together to gain some balance. It was hard galloping with one hand to her head. Shay could smell the acrid smoke from Lame Deer burning. She could smell the iron tang of blood running down her face. Her stomach lurched. Nero could tell something wasn't right and slowed his galloping.

"Come on," Nicholas said.

Clyburn turned when he heard Nicholas's voice. He turned his horse, galloping fast and rounding Shay. "Cowboy up," Clyburn urged. "Should've stayed home like your daddy said."

"Shut your hole." Shay's mouth felt dry, her tongue heavy.

"Did ya get bit?" Clyburn asked, suddenly worried.

Shay's mind raced. Had she been bit? They came across a few of the living dead but her father and Clyburn had cut off their heads. Shay didn't touch a soul. She kept her distance. The only thing was her cut face. Shay swallowed down the lump in her throat. What if the broken glass cut the dead before cutting her? What if their disease was a pathogenic type? They only knew it spread by being bit but what did anybody actually know for certain these days? It could spread by body fluids. If that was the case, Shay had little time left. She only hoped she'd be home in time to tell her momma goodbye.

Nero picked up his pace, the motion jerking Shay. Her head throbbed and blood began dripping into her eye again. She pressed the rag against her cut. Her vision blurred, she swallowed down the urge to vomit, and then, everything went black.

Eleven

Jed was sure he didn't want to get around Lame Deer by heading south, but he was on the heels of locals. They had to know better than him how to avoid the onslaught in the center of town. He picked up his pace, focusing on the cloud of rising dust ahead of him. He wasn't sure he'd be able to keep up with a horse's gallop. The crashing sounds coming from the casino prompted Jed to get moving. He took to following the horse tracks at a fast pace. Every few hundred yards, he'd take to the elevated foothills and hide his shadow among the pine and fir trees. He hadn't forgotten about that lone Angel who was searching for him near Chicago. Usually when one got near, they didn't stop tracking him.

The locals led him into the depths of the Montana wilderness. He remembered the pamphlets he'd looked at the night before and figured they were on the edge of the reservation grounds. He could still hear the screams and tire squeals from Lame Deer and the casino siege. Jed glanced behind himself every few hundred yards. The dead didn't hurry. At least he had that. They were easy to outrun. It was the quiet ones that showed up like a jump scare from behind a closed door or a run down car he worried about. Out here it shouldn't be a problem. He was far enough from town he'd only have to worry about a safe place to sleep or... the locals on horseback in front of him. If one of them went, the game plan would need to change.

Jed thought of the girl at the casino. He tried not to, but one glance had made him drop the precious French toast. Jed would like to meet her again, even if second encounters were dangerous. He relieved himself near a Douglas fir, wishing he'd grabbed a bottle of water before leaving the casino. There were spells to bring water if need be.

Jed walked along the ledge of the foothills. The pace of the group traveling slowed and he could no longer see their cloud of dust. He wondered if something had happened. The surrounding forest became thicker, the trees close together and harder to walk under. Jed descended the hill and walk along the hoofprints. He grabbed onto a skinny tree trunk, noticing an odd bend in it. Nearly a ninety-degree angle. He let go and ran down to the trail below. He walked for a bit, slowing when he felt a prickle on the back of his neck.

Shit.

Jed reached for his knife, but a quiet whoop distracted his attention. Suddenly, a man was standing in front of him. Tanned with hair black as pitch, the man didn't look happy.

"You're on the wrong land," the man said.

Jed's hand moved slowly to grip the knife in his pocket. "Sorry, man. Didn't know there was a difference in land here. Thought it was all God's land."

The man scowled. "You don't belong here. Your kind doesn't belong."

Jed was confused. This wasn't an Angel; he wasn't a Demon. The dark-haired man in front of him whistled. Eight more men moved out of the surrounding tree cover.

Jed began whispering the words of a spell, his fingertips tapped against each other lightly.

"No!" one man shouted, throwing a handful of dirt in Jed's face.

A mouthful of dirt was enough to impair his spell. He'd hoped to go invisible and escape, but as he coughed on the Montana dirt, he couldn't get the words out correctly. There was nowhere to run.

Jed looked up. If he had wings he could fly out of there, but he'd never been born with them and he'd only ever seen one Nephilim with some that were mutated and too small.

He didn't get to plan for an escape much longer, because someone smacked him in the back of the head and it was lights out.

———

JED WOKE to his arms and legs tied together. His back ached and felt raw, like they had dragged him. Panic set in as he realized his bag was missing and his pockets were empty. Jed rolled to sit up and took in his surroundings. Eyes bleary and gritty, it took him a minute or two to focus in the darkness. There was noise outside and the crackle of a roaring fire. Deep voices were arguing. Jed was in a room with one door, one window, a lamp with no shade and a slowly dying bulb. He noticed his gear on a table near the door. This was not how he wanted his travels to go. He needed to get the heck out of here. Jed struggled against the ropes on his wrists and ankles. He figured he must've upset the natives when he wandered onto the reservation. These people definitely had something against him. He'd never come across this problem before.

Jed whispered the words of a spell and flexed his fingers. The ropes at his wrists and ankles dropped away like falling paper. He flexed and stretched the stiffness out of his arms and legs. Now he needed an escape plan.

TWELVE

SHAY'S HEAD WAS POUNDING. THE STEADY HUMMING OF deep snoring made it worse. She recognized the sweet smell of chewing tobacco. Clyburn was nearby. Too close for comfort. She felt a knee pressing into the back of her thigh and inched away. She tumbled onto the floor. Catching herself on a hand and shoulder, Shay groaned.

How the Hell did he get into bed with her? Shay rubbed her face, stopping when she got to the bandage across her forehead and ear. Her skin ached and burned. She tried to scowl and felt the pulling of stitches. Shay moved to stand, weary on her feet. She tried to remember what had happened before getting here. The furniture was familiar. She'd been here before. They were on the Reservation. Probably at the family of James Crow. Damn. Shay didn't envy her father for having to break the news to the Crow family that James was dead.

If they were on the Reservation, then they had gone in the complete opposite direction of home.

Shay made her way to the door, eager to put distance between herself and Clyburn. Eager to let loose on her father about Clyburn invading her space much too often. Shay thought she'd made herself clear when she told Nicholas she didn't need a man like Clyburn to protect her. Fear settled in Shay's belly. If Clyburn was this close, was there something wrong with her father? Shay opened the door and strode down the long hallway that led to the center of the Crow family home.

She stopped in the kitchen, gripping the back of a chair at the breakfast nook to steady herself.

"You shouldn't be moving so fast," a familiar voice said. It was Grandmother Crow. "Sit now. I'll bring you something to drink."

Shay's head was spinning, and she didn't think she'd be able to stand much longer. She rounded the chair and sat.

The old woman set a steaming mug in front of her.

"Is my father okay?" Shay asked as she wrapped her hands around the mug and let it warm her fingertips.

"He's fine. Out with the men, working on a plan to get you home." The old woman fussed with the bandages on Shay's forehead. "I'll give you a salve so it doesn't scar too badly."

Shay flexed her forehead, feeling the pull of the stitches.

"Don't." The old woman smacked Shay's shoulder. "You'll stretch the skin and the scar will hold. Don't move your face until it's healed."

"I'm assuming that will take weeks." Shay brought the mug to her lips. "I can't move my face for weeks?"

"I did the stitches myself. Don't ruin my hard work." Grandmother Crow went back to her cooking.

The front door opened, letting in brisk morning air. Shay shivered. Summer was coming to an end quickly and being at the Reservation meant the ride home would take two nights by horseback. They could take Forks Rd to Highway 4 by truck, but that would lead them back to the center of Lame Deer.

Nicholas walked through the door with the other men of the Crow family.

"We should bury him on our lands," a tall man with a beaded tail of hair said.

68

"We can show you where we found him," Nicholas said. "Not sure how much of him will be left after the dead are done."

Crap. Shay didn't expect her daddy to sign up to go back to Lame Deer. If they hadn't run so fast, they could've brought back James's body. She didn't like the idea of going back to the casino.

"You're upright," Nicholas said, focusing on Shay. He walked closer, inspecting her face. "You gave us quite the scare with fainting and falling off Nero." He touched the side of her head. "Clyburn carried you all the way here."

Shay scowled at the thought of Clyburn touching her for more than a mere second. The tugging of skin and side eye from Grandmother Crow forced her face into a placid expression.

"Don't be like that, Shay-baby," her father said. "You were out for a while. Wasn't sure what to do before the Crow boys came along." Nicholas thumbed toward the crew of men getting comfortable in the living room.

Shay could remember four of their names: Elsu, Hosa, Iye, and Jacy. She always wondered how James got such a different name from the other men in his family. But he was the only one who left the reservation to find work. Maybe he had another name she never knew about.

Iye waved to Nicholas to join their meeting. He patted Shay's arm before leaving the kitchen nook where she sat.

Shay sipped at her tea and listened to the men. Her father told the others what they'd endured in Lame Deer. Elsu laid a map on the coffee table and the men discussed a path. The Crow men had a good idea of clusters of walking corpses in Lame Deer. They talked about traveling Forks Rd via trucks until the Pow Wow Memorial on Highway 4. There were some trails along the valleys of the foothills, but they'd have to approach the casino from the south.

"Might be able to sneak onto the property and get James without those walking dead noticing." Jacy rubbed his neck as his eyes studied the map.

"What about that Allegewi?" Elsu asked. "Our ancestors only

spoke stories of those creatures. Never come across one in a hundred years."

"The markings on his arms were worrisome." Jacy's focus went to the window and the small shed in the backyard.

"They were magic." Elsu said.

Shay sipped at her tea and leaned forward. The only person she knew of with markings on his arms was that man at the casino. The one who'd dropped his French toast when he saw her. He didn't seem dangerous. She thought of Clyburn. But attractive men rarely let their demons shine through at the first meeting.

Maybe he was dangerous. Shay thought of the look on his face when they made eye contact. Slack jawed and... surprised. The French toast looked good after a few long days on horseback. She was disappointed for him that he'd dropped it. She touched the bandage near her ear. Whatever he saw in her, she doubted the tattooed guy would ever see it again. The big ugly scar across her forehead would put a stop to that. She sighed. It would take her out of the picture for many. She didn't want to rely on a man but she got the feeling she might have to lower her standards if push came to shove.

"When you are in doubt, be still and wait," Grandmother Crow was watching Shay from the opposite side of the kitchen. She gave Shay a look that made her think the old woman was reading her thoughts. "My stitching is better than most. Take care of the scar and it will barely be noticed."

Shay nodded.

There was a noise in the hall behind Shay. It had to be Clyburn walking. Shay scooted to the side and tried to hide. Grandmother Crow watched and frowned as Clyburn entered the kitchen.

Elsu waved for Clyburn to join them in the planning.

Shay's stomach lurched at the smell of chewing tobacco as he walked by.

Nicholas and the Crow men were talking about what to do with the tattooed guy.

"Kill him," Hosa said with disgust on his tongue. "The ancients said his kind killed plenty of ours in the wars."

Nicholas frowned and stroked his beard. "Enough have died in this mess. Kick him off your lands. Drop him at the edge of the reservation and tell him to never come back."

Hosa made a noise in his throat. "What if he brings more of his kind? We are ill-equipped to handle the dead that walk and a war with giants."

"He's not that tall," Clyburn said as he sat in a club chair made of elk hide.

Hosa scowled. "His kin might be taller. Then what do we do?"

"What did he do to make you imprison him?" Nicholas asked.

"He set foot on our lands." Elsu crossed his arms and leaned back as though the charge was enough for prison.

"He didn't kill anyone?" Nicholas asked.

"Not yet." Hosa sounded convinced the guy was all sorts of dangerous.

"Let's focus on getting James a proper burial. Then we'll deal with the Allegewi." Iye seemed to be the only Crow brother with a level head.

Shay finished her tea and watched through the window. The shed didn't look like a prison but smoke rose from the center like a sweat lodge. Maybe they were trying to sweat the demons out of the guy.

THIRTEEN

The Crow men, Nicholas, and Clyburn left for Lame Deer at three in the morning. They were confident the reservation was safe from the walking dead. The families that lived there were in close contact and well-equipped.

Shay enjoyed the time with Grandmother Crow. She slept soundly knowing Clyburn was gone and she wouldn't have to deal with him.

Shay was standing at the living room window, watching the sweat lodge smoke.

"Is there something in that shack that interests you?" Grandmother Crow asked as she clanked mugs onto the counter and set a pot of water on the stove to boil.

"What?" Shay turned. She wasn't sure how to respond. She was interested in the man with tattoos. She didn't think he was dangerous, but what did she know?

Grandmother Crow tipped her chin. "An Allegewi is something to be feared."

"Why do you call him that?" Shay asked as she crossed the room to help with breakfast.

"It's the name of the giants."

"How giant are we talking?" Shay asked.

Grandmother Crow tipped her shoulder, then raised her flattened hand. "Over six foot. Maybe eight."

The woman's heavily wrinkled face broke into a smile and she laughed. "Men worry about giants. The giants of a hundred years ago weren't much taller than the Crow men of this time."

"Why do they think he's dangerous?"

Grandmother Crow clucked her tongue. "They sense magic." She pointed the knife that she was cutting onion with. "I watched them bring him in. There is something. A blue shine to his skin." Her eyes narrowed on the sweat lodge. "Didn't you see it?"

Shay opened the tin of tea and set bags in each mug. "I'm not a Cheyenne. I'm just a basic white cowgirl. I don't see the world like you do, Grandmother Crow."

The old woman made a noise and went on with her cooking.

Shay was always out of place. She felt it every moment of her life. When she was at school, when she was at the store, when she was on vacation. She wasn't comfortable around most and the unrelenting voice in her head made her second guess most interactions. When she was with her parents or Nero, those were the only times she felt like maybe she belonged. Shay knew she needed to get out more. She needed to see the world and meet more people. Then maybe she'd feel like she belonged somewhere. Her forehead ached and Shay pressed fingertips to her temple. No. That wasn't right. Her family would keep her safe. No matter what Shay wanted or thought, the truth was real. Her mother and father had gotten her this far. They'd taught her how to survive. They'd help her survive the walking dead until it was cleaned up and the world moved on like normal. Like it was before. Without her family and the ranch hands, Shay was nothing but a sitting duck in a screwed-up world.

"Don't rub it," Grandmother Crow said. "Try this." She sprinkled a black powder in Shay's mug.

Whatever Grandmother Crow sprinkled in Shay's tea helped

with the headache. It also sent her right back to bed until dinner time. When Shay woke up, she could smell dinner cooking but didn't hear the voices of her father and the Crow men.

"They're not back yet," Grandmother Crow said as she stirred a pot.

"I'm going to check on Nero." Shay borrowed a heavy flannel jacket from near the door and went to the horse barn.

Nero neighed, happy to see Shay. "I know it's been a few days, boy." She patted Nero's neck and took a scoop of treats out of the nearby bin. Nero sniffed her bandages, and the horse tipped his head to the side as though he were inspecting her injuries.

"I'm fine." Shay spoke to Nero as she inspected the barn. She found her father's horse a few stalls down, as well as Clyburn's horse and James's. She gave treats to all of them and refilled their water. Doing the chores without flexing her facial muscles became a challenge.

When she left the barn, she headed toward the house but the sweat lodge caught her eye. The guy was likely still in there. She focused on the smoke rising from the roof. Someone had to be refueling the fire. She walked to the nearby stack of firewood that was kept neatly under a covered section of the house. She picked up a log and headed toward the sweat lodge.

Shay pushed the door open slowly, using the end of the log. She wasn't sure what was going on in there. The Crow men had left and she hadn't noticed anyone visiting the backyard to check on the shed. The guy could be dead already or escaped.

The guy with tattoos all over his arms was there. He wasn't asleep and he wasn't tied up. He was just sitting by the roaring fire, reading from a small book, and chewing on dried meat.

"Hi," he said with a wave of a tattooed arm.

"Hi," Shay replied.

"I never thought I'd see you again." He closed the book and tucked it in his pocket.

"Same."

There was a pause as they studied each other. The air in the lodge became thick with questions and answers yet to be discussed. A need to know. An urge to explore. They stood that way for a long moment.

"Did the glass from the casino cut you?"

"What?" Shay asked.

He pointed to her head. "Your bandages."

Shay's hand flew to her head. "Oh. Yeah. The glass cut me and then later on, I fell off my horse."

"Are you okay?" he asked.

"I think so." Shay moved closer and dropped the log she was carrying near the fire. "You dropped your toast back there."

The guy smiled.

Something melted inside of Shay.

"It was good French toast." A pink tongue darted out to lick his lower lip. "Too bad I won't be eating any of that again."

"Sad life with no French toast." Shay tried to contain her smile because she felt like a teenager. "They said you're a giant." She judged his height.

The guy made a face. "I'm taller than average. Not really a giant."

"Why don't they like you?"

"Plenty don't like me."

"What's your name."

"Jed. What's yours?"

"Shay."

"I like that. Did you come to rescue me, Shay?"

"I don't think so. But maybe I should. They discussed killing you."

"Killing me, huh?" He scooted forward in his seat then stood. His movements were slow, steady. He gave her time to leave before walking closer. "If I'm going to die. I guess I should do one last good deed."

He was a few feet from Shay but she didn't feel threatened. Instead she had an urge to reach out and touch him and make sure he was real. She searched for the blue glow to his skin that Grandmother Crow mentioned, but her eyes only saw pale, sweaty skin, dark ink, and smooth muscle.

Jed held his hands out, reaching to both sides of her head. "May I?"

Shay nodded and Jed removed the bandages from her head. The gauze stuck to the stitches, and she winced.

"Does it hurt?" Jed asked. His movements were slow and gentle.

"I've had worse. Broke my leg as a kid."

"Let me fix it." His voice was low and deep, nearly a hum.

Shay heard his fingertips tapping together and she watched his lips as he whispered strange words that sounded like a good promise. It made her ears tingle. Her skin felt warm, electrified. The tiny stitches fell down her face and Shay no longer felt the pulling of her skin. The wound tingled more and more, until it finally just, stopped.

"There," Jed said. "Just like before." His expression was something between wonder and deeply pleased. No one had ever looked at Shay that way before, besides her father.

Shay touched her forehead and was amazed when there were no stitches, no wound, no pain. He'd healed her.

"Why did you do that?" Shay asked. "How did you do that?"

"You're too pretty of a cowgirl to spend the rest of your life with a scar like that."

Shay looked at the tattoos on his arms. "Ok. But how?"

Jed held up his palms and wiggled his fingers.

"Magic?" Shay asked. "The Crow men said you had magic. I've never seen magic in real life. Only books and movies." Shay rubbed her forehead again, harder this time. She didn't feel any pain, no scarring or ache from the wound he'd healed.

Jed smiled as he stepped away. "Yeah. It's magic." The reply was nonchalant, like magic actually existing wasn't a big deal.

"How?" Shay searched the room for anything that looked out of place, anything that could be an illusion and prompt her to wake up. This strangeness had to be a dream.

Jed bent and secured the clip on his bag. "How I did it is a long discussion. Probably one for another day."

The sound of truck engines and male voices ended their conversation. Jed began collecting items from where he'd sat near the fire and packed them into his bag. Before he could decide on which way to go, the front door of the shed blasted open. Along with it, came the brisk air of pending nightfall.

FOURTEEN

It was Elsu. Shay sighed a breath of relief. Of all the Crow men, Elsu was the calmest. His dark eyes landed on Shay, then Jed.

"You untied him?" Elsu asked.

Shay raised her hands in innocence. "I didn't touch him." She took a few steps back, closer to the door and Elsu. "I swear."

Jed held his hands up in defeat. "She didn't. I did it myself."

"How?" Elsu asked.

Jed wiggled his fingertips. "I'm flexible. Handcuffs would have been more of a challenge."

Elsu's eyes narrowed on Jed. "You should have left while we were gone. It would have been better for you."

"Leave?" Jed smirked. "It's warm here." He motioned to the fire then the meat drying on the far wall. "There's plenty of food." He pointed to the door at the back of the room. "You even left me an old-ass bed. Probably got some fleas from sleeping on that thing. Why would I leave with hospitality like this?"

Elsu didn't respond. Shay's eyes widened and she tried not to smile at Jed's sarcasm.

"It's safe here," Jed said. "I can feel it in my bones."

"You might not think that much longer." Elsu opened the front door all the way and they could see the rest of the men unloading.

Clyburn crossed the ground and shoved his way into the shed. He grabbed Shay's arm and pulled her outside.

"Stop it," Shay hit his hand.

"Hey!" Jed shouted from inside. "Get your hands off her."

"What are you doing?" Clyburn asked Shay, bending so they were face to face. It was intimidating and made Shay's stomach lurch.

"Nothing." Shay pulled her arm back.

"What's going on?" Nicholas asked, dropping a load of gear.

"Nothing." Shay moved away from Clyburn and straightened her jacket. She wasn't sure how she was going to continue with his overprotectiveness turned jealousy. On this trip Clyburn had lost all apprehension of Nicholas protecting his daughter. He went full steam ahead with the closeness, the touching, the *saving*. Shay was tired of it. Clyburn didn't make her feel safe. It was quite the opposite. He felt like a threat; bottled up and shaken, ready to explode. Shay could sense it and she didn't want to be around when it happened.

"Let's get rid of the Allegewi now," Hosa said. "We can burn two bodies at once."

An unease spread through the Crow family. It wasn't like the Cheyenne to demand death so confidently. Grandmother Crow had made her way to the back porch and looked over her sons as they argued.

Elsu had made his way out of the shed. Jed stood in the doorway threshold, free as a bird, eyes bright as he took in the family argument of his impending death.

Iye and Jacy argued right along with the other brothers.

"We've already lost James."

"He'll kill more."

"His kind will come for us. They always have."

"It's been over a hundred years since the Allegewi warred with Cheyenne."

"Doesn't mean they aren't willing to start again."

Grandmother Crow didn't offer her opinion.

"We'll take him off your lands," Nicholas offered. "No one deserves to die in these times. Enough have died already."

"What–" Clyburn started, but Nicholas cut him off with a raised hand.

"He's already tainted Shay." Hosa said with a sneer.

"Hey," Nicholas growled. "Off limits."

Hosa pointed to Shay's healed head wound.

All eyes were on Shay. She stood steady as they inspected her forehead.

"Did it hurt?" Nicholas asked.

"I didn't feel a thing." Shay glanced at Jed.

"That's not natural. There is something wrong with this world. Something broken." Nicholas said.

"Our medicine has healed great wounds." Grandmother Crow said as she stepped down off the porch. "I gave her the black powder. How do you know it wasn't me who healed her?" Grandmother Crow stared hard at each of her sons. "My medicine has been called magic before."

Jed tipped his head down in respect to the old woman. He was sure she knew much about healing plants and poultices that the modern world had forgotten.

Just as quickly as it began, the conversation of Shay's healed wound was forgotten. No one wanted to argue with Grandmother Crow.

"I'd like to stay for James's burial," Nicholas said. "He was like a brother to me." He looked at Grandmother Crow.

"White man cannot come to the burial," Hosa said.

There was a muffled moan. Everyone focused on the open door of the truck bed, and the cloth covering James moved.

FIFTEEN

"WE WAITED TOO LONG," CLYBURN SAID. "HE'S COME alive again."

Shay had never seen it happen in real time; a man being dead then coming back to life. She'd only seen the ones who'd walked too close to the ranch and the horde that had busted into the casino. She'd seen James's corpse devoid of life back there. But now, now he was moving again.

Guttural groans were muffled from the cloth covering his body. James rocked and rolled off the truck bed onto the ground with a thud.

Clyburn was closest. He grabbed the sheet covering James and pulled it off his face. Jaws snapped. Clyburn jumped back and held a hand over his nose.

"Black powder won't fix that," Grandmother Crow said as she ran to safety on the porch.

Jacy took three long strides, dropped to his knee, and slammed a hunting knife through James's skull. The corpse stopped moving.

"Better bury him quickly," Iye said, collecting firewood from the pile and loading it into the back of the truck.

Jacy and Elsu covered James's body and put him next to the firewood.

They took the body to the edge of the Crow family property. The men spoke and danced in ritual. Grandmother Crow chanted a prayer that Shay couldn't translate, even with her knowledge of some Cheyenne language.

Nicholas paid his last respects to his friend from a distance and the group decided they would head back to the ranch first thing in the morning.

Jed was left to the sweat lodge.

Shay slept soundly on a cot in Grandmother Crow's room.

They were used to waking up early and all were packed and ready to travel before the Montana sun rose.

They ate a quiet breakfast before heading to the barn to collect their horses.

Elsu brought Jed and Hosa was nowhere to be seen. It was better that way, Shay thought. Hosa would probably kill Jed with all of his anger bottled up.

Nero was happy to see Shay and pawed the ground with excitement at being saddled and released.

Nicholas and Clyburn collected their horses and secured their bags.

When they were ready to travel, Nicholas looked at Jed.

"I don't have a horse," Jed said with a shrug. "I can walk."

"You can ride with me," Shay offered. Nero was a big enough horse. He could carry them both. And Shay wanted to talk to him more.

"No," Clyburn said. "Shay can ride with me. He can take Nero."

"I'm riding Nero." Shay scowled.

"You will ride with me," Clyburn seethed. His grip tightened on Shay's arm.

Shay stopped struggling and raised her chin.

"Come on." Clyburn tugged her, hard.

Shay couldn't take the ranch hand for one more second. The

sweet smell of his chewing tobacco made her stomach churn. She had concluded that her family would keep her safe in all of this mess, but she couldn't stand one more second of Clyburn.

Shay swung her right arm as hard as she could and slapped Clyburn across the face.

The Crow men and Nicholas didn't stop their side conversations when Clyburn was man-handling Shay, but they did when they heard the clap of her open palm on his face.

"I am not your property," Shay said, bitterness on her tongue.

Something changed in Clyburn's eyes. It wasn't realization or remorse. It was anger.

Shay did something she never thought she'd have to do. She pulled the handgun from the holster at her hip, cocked it, and held the barrel under Clyburn's chin.

"Don't ever touch me again," Shay warned. She pressed the barrel harder. "Never again."

Clyburn raised his hands in defeat and backed up. "Good luck surviving this alone."

"I'm not alone. I have my daddy and momma. I definitely don't need you."

Clyburn's sleeve fell as he backed away and Shay saw a hint of reddened skin.

"Shay-baby." Nicholas tapped Shay on the shoulder. "Put it away."

"Why, daddy?" Shay asked. "You offered me up like a new pair of shit kickers."

Clyburn backed away, dropped his hands, and went to ready his horse.

"I told you I wasn't interested in no ranch hand." Shay holstered her gun and turned to her father.

"I'm sorry. I just wanted to make sure you are taken care of. I won't be around forever." He pressed his lips together, weary.

Shay noticed the dark circles under her father's eyes. The wrinkles on his face seemed deeper, his clothes hung a little looser. "Are you sick or something?" Shay asked.

"No." Nicholas wrapped an arm around her. "Just getting older every day."

"I'm not some property to trade, daddy." Shay never thought she'd have to have a conversation like this. "Don't ever try to sell me off again."

Elsu came forward, passing reins to Nicholas. "Here, take James's horse. He'd want you to keep him."

"That's very kind of you." Nicholas ran his hand over the horse's dappled coat. "Have you ridden before?" he asked Jed.

"A long time ago," Jed said. He secured his foot in the stirrup and hauled himself up. It took Jed a minute to get the horse under control, but he managed better than most new riders. The last time he'd ridden, it was with Declan, the last Nephilim he'd come across. Since then the world had changed. Travel by horseback was outdated and as Jed traveled the northeast, he'd never found the need to travel by horseback since.

Jed stroked the horse's mane. The smell of warm leather and the horse brought back a lot of memories. Out of habit, Jed searched the sky for Angels or Demons.

"Let's go." Nicholas led the way.

They took a path through the foothills, avoiding Lame Deer entirely. When the path became harder to follow, near the thicker trees, Jed asked, "How do you know where the trail goes through these parts?"

Nicholas pointed to a tree with its trunk bent at a ninety-degree angle. "Trail markers. Just look for them."

They crossed Spotted Elk Drive and Sweet Medicine Road without seeing another soul. This wasn't uncommon on a normal Montana day. It was just the walking corpses had them all on edge. They started smelling the Waste Treatment station while crossing Ghostdancer Drive.

Jed coughed at the stench.

"We'll be upwind soon," Shay said as she slowed Nero.

"Can't tell if it's rotting corpses or shit," Jed said.

"Probably shit," Nicholas said.

Clyburn had been eerily quiet as he rode behind everyone.

They reached US-212 by lunch.

"If we keep going, we can be home by nightfall," Nicholas said.

"I'm sure momma is worried," Shay said.

Nicholas nodded. "Clyde too."

They galloped across the road and took the familiar route from a few days prior.

Jed glanced down US-212. He needed to get to California; he'd already been delayed by a few days with the Casino and Crow men. He watched Shay and thought of the man named Clyburn who was a few yards behind them. Something wasn't right and Jed didn't want to leave Shay in danger. Usually, Jed was quick to move on, but he did something out of the ordinary when he'd healed Shay's wound and now he felt compelled to make sure she made it home safely.

There was some strange energy in the air and Jed was sure it came from Clyburn. He couldn't leave Shay right now. Jed decided he'd make sure she made it home then he'd carry on. He'd have two good deeds for the week and could move on without regrets.

———

SHAY DIDN'T HAVE what many would call a normal childhood. While she attended the local schools, she was frequently pulled out of class and missed days when a fresh load of cattle came in, or the gardens were ready for harvest and processing, or canning season was underway. She had a few friends when she was near ten, and they'd ride their bikes up and down the dusty roads searching for adventures. They drifted apart with time. After high school it became harder to keep in touch when the girls went to Texas and Florida for college and never returned to Colstrip, Montana. The calls and texts became less frequent until they stopped all together. Less than a year was all it took. Shay finally worked up the urge to apply to college and branch out.

One day she was packing her bags, ready to leave the nest. The next, reports of the dead walking and spreading their death was all over the news.

"You can't go," momma argued.

"I have to go. I have to do something with my life," Shay said.

"You can do it here," her daddy said.

"I don't want to do it here. I want my own life. I want more than a life on a ranch in the middle of nowhere Montana," Shay said. "Everyone has left. I have no one here."

"You have us," Momma said.

"It's not the same." Shay didn't want to stay. She'd worked hard to get into the Biological Sciences undergraduate program. She wasn't going to throw it all away.

As Shay argued with her parents, she could hear the pounding of hammers as the ranch hands built up the fence and gate to the property. Momma had been stocking up on food for her whole life. Daddy had been stocking up on guns and bullets, traps, and knives. They were probably the most prepared ranch in the state.

Shay ran off. She didn't make it far. She stopped at a dive bar outside of Lame Deer, something her parents told her never to do. It didn't take long for the cowboy with dark hair and charisma to buy her drinks. It didn't take long for him to invite her back to his truck.

"I'm just traveling through," he'd said.

Shay didn't care. Her life was ruined by the dead walking. As far as she was concerned, this was her last hurrah. She didn't say no when the drunk cowboy tugged at her clothes and hoisted her up against the side of his truck. She didn't correct him when he called her by every name that started with an S besides Shay. She wasn't sure she ever told him her name. She never asked for his. Not when she unbuckled his belt. Not even when he was holding back her hair as she puked in the parking lot.

After, Shay went home with a new understanding of the world.

Then three days later Clyburn showed up at the ranch looking for a work. Since another ranch hand vacated his post a few days prior, her parents were eager for help. And with his charming smile and muscular build, it didn't take her parents long to bring him onboard. They had an empty barracks and plenty of work for a healthy man.

Shay never told her parents she'd met the man that night at the bar. Neither did Clyburn. She ignored him and hoped he wouldn't remember. Shay hid in her room or the horse stalls. She avoided the farm hand at all costs. But that only lasted so long. The ranch was only so big and when their paths crossed, Clyburn recognized her and his relentless pursuit began.

Shay hated herself for running out that night. She wished she'd never met the ranch hand.

————

AFTER A FEW HOURS OF RIDING, they stopped to rest the horses at Castle Rock Lake. Jed asked Nicholas about the nearby strip mines and history. Nicholas seemed to like the conversation. It was the most Shay had heard her father talk in a long time. Jed had a real knack for chatting people up.

Clyburn moved closer to Shay, his movements so quiet she didn't hear him until he was right behind her.

"We should talk," Clyburn said.

"We have nothin' to talk about," Shay said.

"Look, I'm sorry I came on so strong." He sighed as he took off his hat. Dark hair fell over his eyes and he ran his hand through it. "I didn't mean to scare you."

"I've got nothin' to say to you." Shay took Nero's reins to feel secure in the moment. A horse was as good of a security blanket as anything. A baseball bat with nails might be better but she'd settle for a two-thousand pound stallion.

"We have something," Clyburn dropped to a knee.

Shay's stomach sank. No. No. No. No. "Don't you dare." She

backed away. "We are nothing. There is nothing between us." She was embarrassed, panicked, couldn't believe this was happening.

"I'll tell your daddy about that night. I bet he'd see his Shay-baby in a new light." He rocked back on his heels and acted like he wasn't just about to pop the question after Shay had held a gun to his chin and threatened to blow out his brains through the top of his skull a few hours earlier.

"You shut your mouth," Shay warned, hand resting on the handgun at her hip.

Nero tugged Shay away and she happily went. She followed the horse who seemed to know better for her than that man.

She made it past the cluster of trees and sand where Nicholas and Jed's conversation had stopped as they watched her. Shay's legs were wobbly, her hands tingling with anger and fear.

"You okay?" Nicholas asked.

"That one needs his head examined." Shay thumbed toward Clyburn in the distance. "Keep him away from me."

SIXTEEN

THEN

"JEDIDIAH JAMES PORTER." THE MAN IN THE CORDUROY coat and gold-rimmed glasses said his name like he was tasting wine.

"That's me," Jed replied. "In the flesh." Part of the name was fake, but he had forged papers.

"Hm."

Jed was hoping the man couldn't see the blue aura. Rarely anyone could, but some did. And when they could, it brought plenty of questions.

"Why do you want to work at the Peabody Library? We rarely see young men like you looking to mop floors at night."

"Well, any work is good work, sir." Jed nodded, hoping that was enough.

It wasn't.

Jed continued. "I like the books. I read. A lot. Um..." He was really losing traction here. Jed paused and cleared his throat. "I want to work. I don't mind mopping floors and cleaning. It's a starting point."

Papers shuffled. "Yes, we all need a starting point. Do you drink?"

"No."

"Get yourself into trouble?"

"No."

"Show up on time?"

"Always."

"Good. You're hired." The man stood and held out a hand to shake. "I'm John Vernon. I'll be your supervisor. Let's get you started."

"Thank you very much, sir."

Jed was hoping a new start was all he needed. He found trouble and sometimes it prevented him from showing up on time. Hell, the longest Jed held a job down was two years. It seemed like a lifetime ago. He'd done odd jobs on his travels to Maryland, hoping that warmer weather and salty air might help his predicament.

He knew it wouldn't, but it was a good lie to tell himself.

John walked Jed through the old library. There were signs for classes and meetings. The further into the building the quieter it got. They passed rooms with closed doors for private reading.

"Bathrooms are back here." John pointed to a metal sign hanging from the ceiling. "Each floor has them located in the same place. Made it easy on the plumbers when they built the place."

Jed nodded, his footsteps echoing in the expansive room turned large hallway.

"Locked section. You'll need a key to get in there at night."

Through the etched glass, Jed saw the shadow of a man walking with an enormous book in his hand. Maybe all the answers he needed in life were in there? Behind a glass wall and a metal lock. Jed's fingers twitched in his pocket. He had a certain luck with breaking into locks.

"Back here is where you'll find the offices and supplies." Keys jangled as John unlocked a door with a golden sign that said, *Employees Only*.

John led him down more halls; the walls turned to gray tile, the floors bare cement, the lights changed from decorative chandeliers to simple fixtures with a bare, single bulb. It was cold in this area of the library.

"There's the private collection room." John pointed to a steel door. "There's more storage down here. You wouldn't believe the things that show up at the library. Books from different countries, different eras, art, scrolls with claims that they're from the beginning of time." John chuckled. "Absurd."

The men finally stopped at a door with a wooden sign that read, *Janitor.*

John opened the door. "Declan, you in here?"

There was a rustling sound and footsteps. The room smelled like soap and brass polish. Jed had never experienced the two scents together, but he liked it. Strong enough to wipe out anything unpleasant but didn't burn the nose.

"Ahoy." A deep voice came from behind wooden shelves. "Excuse my–" The voice paused.

Jed knew why, instantly. The man named Declan had the same blue aura as Jed. They stared for just a moment before Declan looked at John.

"This is Jedediah Porter, our new janitor." John clapped Jed hard on the back. "He's replacing poor old Henry. Them boots will be hard to fill." John made his way to the door. "Show Jed around. He'll be starting on night shift tomorrow." John held onto the door and where his fingertips pressed, Jed saw a strange little mark carved into the wood. "Welcome aboard, Jedediah." He tipped his head and left.

When John's footsteps were far enough down the hall that they could barely be heard, Declan crossed the room and closed the door, locked it, then turned to Jed.

"What are you doing here?"

"I came for a job."

Declan's eyes drifted over Jed, nostrils flaring above a red mustache that had been waxed to points. "I know what you are. We shouldn't be here together. It's dangerous. I've spent a very long time getting comfortable here and you're not going to ruin it for me."

"I don't know what you're talking about." Jed pointed to Declan's shoulders. "I didn't know there were any more like me alive."

Declan's shoulders dropped. His expression changed from anger to recognition.

"How old are you?" Declan asked.

"Twenty, sir."

"How long have you been running?"

"Since I can remember." Jed kept his face still, he didn't want to reveal anything even if this was the first time in his life that he felt safe. There was something about the library and this room that set Jed at ease.

"My apologies. I didn't realize you were nothin' but a babe." Declan opened his arms and hugged Jed like an old friend, like close family.

Jed couldn't have hugged the man back even if he tried, because his arms locked straight against his ribs as Declan squeezed. "Thank you," Jed said.

"Which Archangel fathered ya?" Declan pulled out a wooden chair and motioned for Jed to sit.

"I don't know." Jed sat, noticing strange carvings under the lip of the table and chair seat.

"Your mother?" Declan sat opposite.

"Died when I was a child."

Declan nodded. "That's usually what happens. They run with the baby until they get caught." Declan pointed one finger at Jed. "But, she must've been running with you for a long time if you got old enough to take care of yourself."

"Yes, sir."

Memories came flooding back. Memories that Jed had buried deep down. Dark nights and hurried movements, his mother's hushed voice saying, "We have to go, baby." Horse hoofs running on soft dirt, the moon revealing shadowed beasts that no child should see. The smell of her as Jed buried his face in her clothing, arms tight around her middle.

His mother had learned to fight, taught herself how to wield a sword, then various knives that she could keep hidden in her skirts. She was good at finding food and safe places to sleep. She taught him how to run, how to recognize the change in the air when an Angel or Demon had broken through realms, the whisper of their wing beats, and the deception of an angelic face.

"Use your luck," she would say to get into hotel rooms or empty houses. Sometimes she would wash his face and trim his hair and set him on the street with a tin can. Everyone gave him money. "What a handsome boy," they'd say, dropping coins into his tin. But his looks and his luck only got them so far. He couldn't protect her. He couldn't save her that night.

"Do you know any tricks yet?" Declan asked.

"I can pick a lock."

"We can do better than that." Declan raised his hands, chanted strange words, and tapped his fingertips together. The saltshaker on the table rose in the air and floated across the room. Declan grinned, wide and satisfied.

"Can you show me how to do that?" Jed asked. He didn't want to sound desperate, but he was. Jed was desperate to survive as more than just a man on the run.

"Boy, I can show you so much more."

———

DECLAN TAUGHT Jed more than how to mop floors at the Peabody Library. Jed's nights were filled with learning Nephilim magic. He had more than just dumb luck and a pretty face. Declan made sure he learned it all.

"What are these markings?" Jed asked, his fingers rubbing the wooden doorframe where he'd just polished.

"You rubbed off the spell." Declan took a sliver of chalk out of his pocket and wrote strange markings on the threshold. The markings faded into the woodwork. "This is how we stay alive, boy."

Lessons on cleaning turned into lessons about spells and runes. "I keep track of them in this book." Declan showed Jed a small, leather-bound book he kept in his pocket.

Deep in the bowels of the library, there were hidden rooms that had been long forgotten. Declan helped Jed set up his own. He showed Jed how to carve runes of protection into the woodwork, what spells to write on the walls with chalk, that a line of coarse salt could protect or trap. Jed had never slept so soundly in all of his life.

Jed read every book, studied every ancient bible and text in the building.

"There, that one." Declan pointed to a page that Jed was reading. "That one is my father."

Remiel.

"He enjoyed the red-haired women of the Isle." Declan sat with a steaming cup of coffee he'd taken from the lobby. "That's how I survived. They don't like the boats." He took a sip from the mug. "Or at least they didn't."

"You don't sound Irish," Jed said.

"When you've been around for longer than you should, one learns to hide their native tongue."

———

"I've GOT some bad news for you, boys." John Vernon was standing in front of Jed and Declan. His face hallowed, skin pale, clothes threadbare. "Peabody Library is closing. We're all out. They're closing the doors until the Depression passes. Don't know how long it will be. You're both welcome to come back. Could be a few years, could be ten." John exhaled a haggard breath.

Dread filled Jed. He'd been safe for the first time in his life and now it was all being taken away. No more nights reading. No more lessons in magic casting. No more.

"We've got about a week to clean up and convert the rooms to storage. Then I'll need you both out of here."

"Sure thing." Declan's voice had too much hope in it.

Jed wanted to scream.

SEVENTEEN

THEN

PEOPLE DO STRANGE THINGS WHEN THEY THINK THE
world is ending. Some drink themselves into oblivion. Some loot and
riot and kill and fuck. When man is pushed to the edge, they can turn
into beastly things. Some might say God lived in Heaven because he
feared the beasts he'd created. Or maybe he feared the monsters with
wings and scales that liked to meddle on his Earthen plane and that
was why he didn't intervene the night Clyburn summoned a lesser
Demon at the crossroads in the middle if a starry sky Montana night.
What was one meddlesome Demon? Plenty had escaped to wreak
havoc.

Clyburn feared death more than anything and he made a deal
with a demon to come upon a homestead that was safe, secure, and
prepped for the apocalypse that was starting. He also asked for a
woman to live out the rest of his life with. What is a man without a
woman? Adam and Eve were first, Clyburn was going to make sure
he and Shay were the last.

"I want a deal," Clyburn said to the winged creature in front of him.

"A deal will cost you." The lesser demon's voice was smooth as whiskey. He scraped an X into the center of the crossroads with a taloned foot.

"Whatever you want." Clyburn would not die like the others. He was going to live, no matter what. He wasn't going to be bit, suffer, die, and be born again as a rotting corpse. No, he had more self-respect than that.

"Out of the eater will come something to eat. And out of the strong will come something sweet." The Demon smiled and held out a dusky hand with long necrotic fingernails and a golden ring on its middle finger.

"You want me to give you food?" Clyburn asked.

"You said anything. Something sweet. Something to eat. Shake on it."

The Demon's necrotic index finger scraped the soft inner skin of Clyburn's wrist as they shook on it. Etched in darkness, the deal was done.

EIGHTEEN

THERE WAS ONLY A SLIVER OF DAYLIGHT REMAINING IN the sky when the travelers reached the ranch outside of Colstrip.

The old ranch hand, Clyde, was using a dagger taped to a stick to clear the dead from pushing on the fence.

"Where'd they all come from?" Shay asked her father.

"Must've wandered this way. Won't be the first time. He cleared his throat headed for a crop of trees to tie up the horses. "We better clear them out before nightfall."

Clyburn, Jed, and Shay followed Nicholas. They moved quickly and quietly, chopping off the heads of the handful of zombies that had amassed. They dragged the bodies a good few hundred yards away from the ranch to a ditch Nicholas had dug months prior. They tossed the bodies in and lit them on fire.

Shay covered her nose with her shirt. The smell of burning human flesh was awful. She'd helped clear the fence before but there had never been so many at once. Black smoke rose and she hoped it wouldn't bring more of the dead.

"Let's go see momma," Nicholas said, bumping shoulders with Shay.

"I've missed her," Shay said. "She's probably worried."

They collected their horses and headed for the gate.

Clyde and Momma were waiting for them. Clyde swung open the gate then quickly closed it when they were through.

"I was so worried," Momma said as she kissed Shay's cheek. She looked Shay over for injuries, motioning to her dusty clothes before turning her attention to Nicholas. "Did you find James?"

"We found his body," Nicholas said. "Crow family put him to rest. Grandmother Crow says hello. She sent a few things for you."

Nicholas handed over a small bag filled with teas and herbal medicines.

"And who might you be?" Momma asked Jed as she looked him over, eyes stopping at the ink on his arms.

Jed introduced himself.

"He's just staying the night," Nicholas said. "Wanted to make sure we made it back safe and sound. He'll be moving on now that he's out of Cheyenne territory."

"Glad you're home," Momma said to Clyburn as he passed her, taking his horse to the barn.

Clyburn nodded and flashed a charming smile.

Momma focused on Jed again. "Dinner's ready, I'll go put out an extra plate. Why don't you all put the horses away and wash up?"

Momma headed for the house and Nicholas broke off in conversation with Clyde, updating him on what they'd seen in Lame Deer.

"Come on," Shay said to Jed. "I'll show you where the horses sleep."

She held Nero's reins loose as they walked to the barn. Shay thought it had been a long time since she hadn't run to the barn to hide from Clyburn.

"So this is where you live?" Jed asked.

"Yup." Shay's face pinched. "Boring, right?"

"Nah, it's nice." Jed pointed to the high fence surrounding the property. "Have you always had that, or did you all build it just for the dead?"

"It's always been there. Daddy was always planning for something like this to happen. Between the TV shows and movies, he got it in his head that something dire was coming. He and Momma built the ranch to withstand anything."

"Anything?" Jed's brows rose. "Like a nuclear bomb?"

Shay shrugged. "We have a small underground space." She pointed to a tiny shed in the distance. "You just have to get there in time."

"Damn." Jed rubbed his neck. "What about food?"

"Root cellars. Everything is canned. And we have the gardens and the animals." A rusty-colored hen waddled across their path. "Plenty of chickens and eggs."

"Seems Nicholas has it all figured out."

"Some things." Nero nudged Shay as they walked. "You want carrots?" she asked the horse.

Nero neighed and huffed. Clyburn was walking back to the house, giving them a wide berth as he passed.

Shay figured the horses were exhausted after their travels. She sure was. A few days on the road is tiring enough, let alone adding in danger and distress–Shay touched her forehead–and magic.

"Why did you come back to the ranch with us?" Shay asked.

"Well, your Crow friends were going to skin me alive. I figured they needed some time to cool off. And I wanted to make sure you got home safe." Jed turned and checked for Clyburn. "Seems you have some trouble with that ranch hand."

Shay huffed out a laugh. "You could say that again."

They entered the horse barn and Shay showed Jed where to hang the reins and saddles. They changed the water and gave the horses fresh oats and carrots.

Shay noticed Jed didn't let his bag out of sight while they worked. He kept it on his back or slung over one shoulder.

They washed up at the well pump that was near the house.

Shay could hear Nicholas's booming laughter as he told Momma about their travels.

Clyburn was wandering the wraparound porch.

Shay avoided him by taking the long way to the dinner table, through the back door and hallway. She led Jed along.

"Smells good," Jed said as the floorboards creaked under their feet.

"Momma's a superb cook. It smells like lasagna."

Dinner was lasagna, served with a side of uncomfortable shoulder rubbing when Clyburn took the seat next to Jed. Shay was relieved the ranch hand didn't sit next to her. She sat next to Momma and couldn't believe how much she'd missed the warmth of her mother's personality. Shay glanced at her parents as they talked through dinner and held conversation with everyone at the table. James was a topic of discussion for much of the meal. Then Clyde told them about the horde that had passed by the ranch.

"We tried to stay quiet, but those damn roosters," Momma said as she took a sip of wine. "We might have to make chicken soup out of them all." She shook her head. "They came for the roosters. What if the cow was mooing?"

"Rooster soup," Nicholas joked. He watched out the window. Shay knew that look; he was strategizing. "We'll have to do something about the roosters, I guess."

"There's a weak spot in the fence," Clyde said. He pointed with is fork. "Northwest corner. I reinforced it as well as I could, but it needs cement poured."

"We'll fix it in the morning," Nicholas said.

When they were done eating, everyone helped clean up. The table was cleared, and dishes done in thirty minutes.

Shay avoided Clyburn, even when her mother asked, "Why does he keep looking at you like that?"

"I threatened to kill him," Shay whispered back as she dried a plate then set it in the cupboard.

Momma laughed but stopped short when she saw the serious look on Shay's face. "Details. Later." Momma glanced to Jed who was sweeping under the dining table. "What about that guy?"

"I'm not sure yet." Shay hid her smile.

"He's very nice to look at."

"Momma, you're married."

"That doesn't mean I can't look." She watched Jed bend over to sweep debris into a dustpan.

Nineteen

The first few years outside of Peabody were the hardest. There were no jobs in the city. Jed and Declan went to the Maryland coast and traveled north. They stopped in Chesapeake City and found work fishing on the canal.

Darkness was everywhere during the Depression. Hell was an open hand waiting for anyone who would take it.

They used charcoal to etch the runes of protection into the seams of their clothing and the insides of their shoes. And so the progression of Declan and Jed's survival methods evolved.

"Hey," Declan threw a live crab at Jed. "Dare you to sell that to the woman at the bank."

Selling crabs was an ongoing gig between the two. Sometimes the coin was good, sometimes they gave them away for free to the hungry children.

Jed flicked the rim of his fedora and lit a cigarette. The tip burned brightly in the darkness.

"The woman at the bank?" Jed asked, picking up the crab. "With the red dress?"

"Wouldn't recommend anyone else for your cheekbones." Declan chucked and clapped the other fisherman.

"Ye can sell her this little fella." The other fisherman held up a giant Rockfish and wiggled it.

"I'll take my chances with the crab." Jed bent and picked it up. Pinschers snapped at his fingers. He picked up the crab by a leg and dangled it. "The bank lady could eat you in one bite."

"Could say the same for you boy," Declan slapped Jed on the back as the boat hit the dock.

The men collected the morning's fishing and headed for the pier. It was cold, but the walk in would warm their bones from the ocean chill.

They sold their fish and paid their dues to the boat owner. The men went home to a tiny, rented house on the bad side of town where the weeds were always taller than the flowers and the shrubbery looked anemic and ready to die. Jed grabbed the crab out of the sink and headed for the door.

"You're gonna do it?" Declan asked.

"Never backed down from a challenge."

Declan laughed and shouted vulgar encouragements as Jed left.

The woman in the red dress left the bank at the same time every day. Jed rarely ventured out alone, but he felt safe in their current routine. Not as safe as Peabody, but it would do. The nightmares of the day his mother died were fewer and further between. And while Jed knew better than to put down roots, the thought of a good woman on his arm was something he'd like to experience before he died.

Townspeople stared as he passed them. The women covered their mouths to whisper to each other. Jed knew it was his height and looks. He stopped at the bank and looked through the window. The woman in the red dress was at the counter. He went inside.

"Can I help you?" she asked.

Jed read her nametag. Eileen.

"Good afternoon, Eileen." He smiled. "I'd like to make a withdrawal."

"Sure. Do you have your account number?"

"No."

"Do you have an account here?"

"No but I have this crab." He set the creature on the counter.

"It looks sick."

"It knows death is coming." Jed stroked the crab with calloused fingers. "But that doesn't stop it from wanting a night with a beautiful lady."

The conversation morphed from simple greetings to a date. Eileen left for work in thirty minutes.

Jed gave the crab to a hungry stranger on the street then he went and reserved a table at the Italian restaurant down the street.

After dinner, Jed was charming enough to get a kiss and a promise of another date. He walked Eileen to her house and waited for her to lock the door.

Jed began walking home. He paused when he felt an abnormal chill in the air. The energy changed. He reached in his pocket for the knife he always carried.

"You shouldn't be here." A dark voice whispered.

"Neither should you." Jed flicked the knife, whispered a spell that would make him invisible.

The creature explored the street, looking for Jed before it focused on the light coming from the house. Spikes stuck out of its back, hunched like a hedgehog with legs thick as tree trunks. It was a creature he'd never seen before. With the smell of creosote, it could only have come from one place. Hell.

"Mmmm." The dark creature began walking across the road.

Jed thought about running and hiding like he'd done when he was a kid. He hadn't faced a creature like this in a very long time. He was out of practice with fighting.

The creature settled one foot onto Eileen's stairs leading to the porch. "I smell you here." It said, "Inside." The creature scrambled up the steps to Eileen's door.

Jed ran toward the house. The creature crashed through the front door. Searching. Sniffing. Roaring. "Come out!"

Eileen screamed. Glass broke.

Jed leapt up the front steps two at a time and ran into the house, following the trail left by creature. He didn't have much of a plan besides to try and kill it or lead it away from Eileen. He jumped over a broken vase, a busted table. Debris led him to the kitchen in the back of the house.

He was too late.

Eileen was crumpled on the floor. Her red dress was ripped to shreds; giant claw marks had torn apart her middle.

TWENTY

Jed followed Nicholas to the private rooms for ranch hands.

"You want to reconsider staying?" Nicholas asked. "We could use the help. Strong guy like you would be perfect."

"Nah, I'm behind schedule, got to get to California to meet a friend."

"In this mess?" Nicholas made a face. "Is your friend still alive?"

If Jed was correct and the darkness that the horde was following was Sparrow he'd be well and alive, more so than anyone.

"It's all I can hope," Jed said.

Nicholas opened a rough-hewn door and walked inside the room. "There's a private bath and clean sheets."

"Better than I've had most nights." Jed checked the window for locks.

"Welp, if you change your mind or want to swing by again in your travels, you're more than welcome. After healing Shay, we more than owe ya."

Jed nodded and moved to close the door as Nicholas walked out.

"I'll expect you for breakfast," Nicholas said.

"See you then."

Jed closed the door to the room and took a breath. His stomach had never felt so full and after the long ride to the ranch, he more was exhausted than ever.

Jed settled on the bed and kicked his boots off. He told himself he was only going to rest his eyes for a few minutes, then he'd get up and place some wards for safety. His last thought before falling asleep was that he should have warded Shay's room as well.

TWENTY-ONE

CLYBURN HAD THE ROOM NEXT DOOR TO JED AND WITH the thin, clapboard walls, he heard everything Nicholas was saying. Clyburn was getting anxious. He wanted more time to set things right, more time to get Shay on his side.

But time was running out. If Jed was leaving in the morning, he'd be back another time and it would be a surprise. Clyburn couldn't wait for surprises. He had to take matters into his own hands.

Clyburn left his room and walked down the hall of the guest area to the shared living room.

"Hey, man." Clyde tipped his beer and focused on the static television, searching for a channel that was broadcasting.

"Just stepping out for some fresh air," Clyburn said as he opened the door and closed it.

There was a chill on the Montana night. The moon was full and stars bright. Clyburn didn't need light for what he was about to do. He walked to the hen house, opened the door as silent as a fox and took out the fattest hen. He considered something bigger like the cow or a horse, but the hen would be easiest.

Clyburn went to the dirt path near the gate to the ranch. It was furthest from the house and hidden by three tall Ponderosa Pine trees. He scuffed an X into the dirt, took a knife from his pocket and sliced his hand, letting drops of blood fall into the middle of the X.

Then he waited.

Summoning a crossroads Demon wasn't common knowledge. It was a darkness no ranch hand knew how to call upon. He learned this dark magic from his grandfather. Clyburn's family was never rich or prosperous, but they survived. All it took was a little blood and a deal. It could pay bills, find the right job, pay off a lien, get a girl, kill a pesky neighbor. Clyburn's grandfather had used the crossroads Demon for all of the above in his lifetime. Unfortunately for Clyburn, not all deals were satisfied with death. Some were passed on to living relatives.

Clyburn waited and waited and waited for the Demon to rise from the X. He checked his watch. Thirty minutes. He exhaled a breath of frustration, but his eye caught movement in the upper window of the ranch house. Shay was walking through her bedroom getting ready for bed. Clyburn watched her. "Mine," rumbled out of his mouth.

"What's yours? Is it sweet?" the familiar voice of the crossroads Demon asked.

"Here." Clyburn held out the hen. "If you need something to eat, this is sweet enough."

The Demon showed sharp teeth as he took one step and inspected the surrounding ranch. The Demon dropped to all fours, like a panther scheming. He made a sound deep in his chest, something that sounded like a chant.

"Hey," Clyburn snapped, trying to refocus the Demon.

A long, bifurcate tongue tasted the Montana air. The X on the dirt opened up, earth crumbled and fell into the hole that appeared. Three hands reached up, grasped for purchase, and pulled themselves up.

"What are you doing?" Clyburn asked. Panic began flooding his veins. He knew better than to trust these things.

The crossroads Demon sniffed the air. "Out of the eater will come something to eat. And out of the strong will come something sweet."

"This is not our agreement." Clyburn reached for his gun.

The crossroads Demon hissed, kicked out a leg, its foot connecting with Clyburn's chest, sending him flying into a tree trunk. His head hit with a sickening thud. His body rolled into the hole where the X had opened up.

The Demons crouched close to the ground, scurrying like cockroaches, headed for the main house.

Twenty-Two

Jed woke in the darkness with an uneasy feeling. He cursed himself for sleeping for so long. He'd only planned to rest his eyes like the old folks would say. Now the moon was high and shining through his open window.

Open?

Jed didn't leave the window open. He'd checked the locks and had planned to set some wards but never did.

The floorboards creaked.

Jed knew that uneasy feeling he'd woken with. He wasn't alone in the dark room. He glanced to his bag at the foot of the bed. He needed the big knife with the runes etched into it. Just as he had the thought, his bag started slowly moving, being pulled off the foot of the bed.

It was now or never.

Jed clapped his hands and twisted his fingers into shapes like stacked pyramids. He spat words that sounded like the hiss of fire igniting. Light erupted from the foot of the bed and as it did, Jed launched himself forward to grab his bag and pull the knife out. The creature on the floor scurried to the wall and hissed back.

"You don't belong here," Jed said.

The creature jabbered in Hellspeak. It sounded pissed and hungry.

Jed secured his bag over his shoulder, gripped the knife and moved toward the lesser Demon as it crouched, trying to escape the ball of light.

"What are you doing here?" Jed asked the Demon, settling the tip of the knife at the base of the Demon's throat.

"Something sweet to eat," it garbled.

"You don't belong on this plane." Jed slid the knife down the creature's neck, but stopped when he heard a struggle in the living room. "How many of you are there?"

"More than me."

"How many?" Jed pressed the tip of the knife in. It required more pressure to pierce the Demon's thick hide.

"We are four of the crossroads."

The ball of light was starting to fade. The Demon watched it, muscles twitching, ready to fight when it went dark again.

Jed slammed his knife through the Demon's heart. "Not today, shithead."

The Demon's body slouched against the wall and inky blood pooled between its legs on the floor.

Jed looked at the open window, then the door. Old habits were hard to break. He climbed out the window. Whatever happened in the living room, he was sure the other Demon had won from the sounds. The chewing of human bone was a distinct sound, and Jed was sure whoever was out there wasn't chewing on the Demon's bones.

Jed glanced at the gate to the ranch. He could be gone quickly and save his own hide. He'd done it enough times throughout his lifetime. He glanced at the main house and the window on the second floor.

Shay.

Damn it.

Jed knew better than to get attached. But he knew Shay would die if he left now. At least he could try. He remembered the feel of her energy under his palms as he healed her forehead, the glimmer in her eyes as she joked about saving him. No, he couldn't leave Shay to die. Being eaten by a Demon was never a good way to go.

Jed inched along the guest house exterior. He watched the shadows for movement.

One Demon slunk out of the front door of the guest house. Another left the horse barn. A third moved from the kitchen window inside the house.

Jed moved. He ran to the house. The other two Demons made it to the front door before him. They blasted through and began wrecking the interior of the house, searching for blood.

Jed began climbing the railing. He jumped to grab the roof overhang of the front porch and pulled himself up. Arms aching, he was running on pure adrenaline. He climbed onto the roof and went to Shay's window. He tried to open it, but the frame didn't move. He tapped on the glass.

"Shay, wake up," he said just above a whisper.

Jed didn't want to make too much noise and draw attention, but he needed Shay to wake up or next he'd be breaking the window.

He tapped the glass harder. There was movement inside. On the bed, then the floor.

His stomach sank. He was too late.

But then footsteps moved closer. The window unlocked and opened.

"Jed?"

"Thank God you're okay." He moved back. "Get out here."

"Why?"

A large crash and the sound of Momma screaming broke through the night.

Shay ran back into the room. She rounded her bed and pulled a shotgun out from under the bed.

Without a chance of getting her out of the window, Jed climbed in.

"Shay," he warned. "There are creatures here."

"Oh no, the dead?" her face paled. "Are Momma and Daddy dead?"

"I don't know. But you're about to see something you've never seen before."

Jed was interrupted by the door blasting open. One demon charged into the room like a lion leaping to attack prey.

Shay shot it. Shotgun pellets left a blast hole in the creature's chest. She turned to Jed. "What the fuck was that?"

"A Demon." He moved closer to the corpse on the floor, used his knife to stab it through what was left of the heart, just to be sure. "Nice shot, by the way."

"Daddy didn't raise no sissy." Shay loaded the shotgun chamber, opened her nightstand drawer, pulled out a box of shells and tucked them into her pocket.

They heard the sounds of Nicholas fighting and shouting from the bedroom downstairs.

Shay ran out of the room without another word. Jed followed.

Momma was lying in a pool of blood. One of the Demons crouched near her shoulder, feeding from her neck like a vampire.

"Get out!" Nicholas shouted as he grappled with the other Demon. Blood was dripping down the side of his head. "Run."

Both Demons turned to Jed and Shay. The one near Momma rose. "Out of the strong will come something sweet." The Demon focused on Shay, body twitching, ready to pounce.

Jed tried his previous spell; it subdued the first one. He clapped his hands and twisted his fingers. He spat the words that sounded like the hiss of fire igniting. Light erupted in the center of the room. The Demons shrieked and scurried to the far wall. Jed leapt over to the bed to confront the Demons.

"Who summoned you here?" Jed had a knife in each hand, tips touching the leathery necks of the beasts.

"One who desires what he does not have." The Demon's eyes flicked to Shay.

"A name." Jed pressed harder with each knife.

"Clyburn," the Demon hissed.

Jed recognized nothing special about Clyburn, just that the guy had a serious hard-on for Shay and no boundaries.

"What is Clyburn?" Jed pressed the tips of each knife until dark blood dripped from the necks of the Demons.

"A foolish man with a plan."

"Just a man?" Jed asked.

"Nothing more than Earthen plane scum," the Demon on Jed's left said as it began moving, trying to escape. The creature had grabbed a lamp cord and swung it, the lamp colliding with Jed's back.

"Move right," Shay shouted.

Jed stooped and twisted, felt the force of buckshot scrape the air.

The Demon to his left slid down the wall, head tipped to the side and half of its face and neck dripping.

Jed's ears were ringing. He shook his head, hoping it would pass. His hand was steady on the knife holding the last Demon.

"A deal is a deal." The Demon focused on Shay. "The ranch and the girl."

"Focus, creature." Jed slapped the Demon on the side of the head. "You can't have her."

"Out of the eater will come something to eat. And out of the strong will come something sweet. A deal is a deal." The Demon knew he was outnumbered. There was nothing but death for him in this room, but he was driven by desire for something he could never have on the plane of Hell. A fresh human to eat. Nothing was sweeter or more filling. The crossroads Demon was going to get what he was promised. Taloned feet dug into the carpet as he readied himself.

The ball of light in the middle of the room faded.

The creature launched himself, twisting away from the tip of Jed's knife.

Jed twisted, grabbed the Demon by its ankle, slammed it to the ground.

Nicholas grabbed the Demon's shoulders and helped hold it down.

Jed stabbed it in the heart. As the Demon was dying, it howled like a wolf in the night and a wisp of a soul left its body, flying out the broken window and disappearing into the moonlight.

Jed looked the Demon over, making sure it was dead. He touched its hand with the golden ring and chain connected to a golden bracelet. He rarely came across Demons wearing anything like this. Jed cut the Demon's arm at the wrist, just above the golden bracelet.

"What are you doing?" Nicholas asked.

"Saving this for later." Jed stood and went to the kitchen. He searched the cabinets and drawers for a large Ziploc bag and put the Demon hand inside.

When Jed returned to the bedroom, Nicholas and Shay stooped over Momma's body. Jed hadn't seen a man like Nicholas cry in a long time and he felt uncomfortable watching.

Jed waited in the hall as they said their goodbyes. Nicholas and Shay closed the bedroom door as they walked toward him.

"We should check the rest of the ranch and make sure we got them all," Jed suggested.

"There's more?" Shay asked.

"I killed four." Jed headed to the back door on the far end of the kitchen.

A black shadow galloped by.

"That's Nero." Shay ran forward and out the door.

"Wait," Nicholas ran after her.

Jed couldn't imagine losing everything in one night. That was why he didn't connect with people like this. It never ended well.

Twenty-Three

Nero followed Shay as the survivors searched the ranch.

"So, you have magic," Nicholas said to Jed.

"I do." Jed was distant, his mind a million miles away. His first instinct was to run and save himself, but he couldn't this time. He watched Shay walk, one hand on Nero's flank. She seemed unfazed by what had occurred, while her father was nearly in shock. She fought by Jed's side and showed no fear of the Demons as they pursued her. Most of all, Jed's magic didn't scare her. Plenty of women wouldn't be able to compartmentalize what he was and what he could do. Shay hadn't seen most of it, but what little she'd experienced didn't scare her away. For the first time in his life, Jed wondered what life with a partner might be like.

"Didn't think that was real." Nicholas looked pale and the blood had dried on his face creating a crust. He didn't move to clean it off. "Those Crow boys weren't wrong."

"What in the actual fuck just happened?" Shay asked.

"Angels and Demons are real. The Demons are a bit uglier, sometimes." Jed said.

"Angels?" Shay turned to face him.

"Don't get all dreamy-eyed," Jed warned. "They aren't as wonderful as the movies make them out to be. They're just as deadly."

"Wonderful." Shay was looking at the front door to the ranch house. "First zombies, now Angels and Demons."

"We need to burn the bodies." Nicholas's eyes were focusing on the different parts of the ranch, calculating how to get everything done.

"Even the animal bodies?" Shay asked.

"Yes." Nicholas rubbed his face. "Better to be safe."

They all dreaded what the next few hours would bring.

———

THEY FOUND the bloodbath in the guest house: Clyde and the Demon from Jed's room. Jed, Shay, and Nicholas dragged the bodies to the dirt path near the gate to the ranch. Nicholas had moved his truck to bring the bodies to the ditch where they burned the other dead.

They piled on the dead chickens, goats, and the Demons from inside the main house. They had to tie up the corpse of the cow and drag it.

"Where's Clyburn's body?" Shay asked.

"I haven't seen him," Nicholas said. "We'll keep looking."

"Something could have taken him," Jed suggested, tossing a dead chicken into the back of the truck.

There were two dead walking across the prairie outside the fence of the ranch. The noise of the truck engine turning over gave them focus and they began meandering toward the ranch.

Nicholas and Shay rode in the truck cab. Jed walked and took care of the dead things on his way to burn the bodies. He dragged the corpses to be burned with the rest.

"You think more will come?" Shay asked.

"Yup." Nicholas replied with a grunt as he tossed the goat into the burn pit.

"Goodbye old friend," Nicholas said as Clyde's body was tossed last. He lit a match and threw it into the pile of bodies. "Now for the worst part."

Shay knew what the worst part was. Getting Momma. She hadn't cried over the loss of her mother. There wasn't time to process it all. The grief was coming off her father in waves as he drove them back to the ranch. Black smoke rose in the distance as the bodies burned.

Shay and Jed waited by the truck as Nicholas went inside to take care of the woman he'd spent most of his life with.

"What can I do to help?" Jed asked.

Shay was staring off in the distance. "I don't think there's anything else you can do. You fought those things." She rubbed her face, stopped, and looked at her filthy hands. There was dirt smeared down her cheeks.

"Should it be taking him this long?" Jed asked, watching the front door.

Glass broke.

Shay ran inside. Jed followed.

"Daddy?" Shay shouted as she ran toward her parent's bedroom.

There were thuds against the walls.

Shay shoved the door open. "No."

Momma had turned.

Nicholas was struggling with what to do. Shay could see that he didn't want to put a final end to Momma. Nicholas had tried to put a pillowcase over her head, but it was only halfway down her face.

"Let me," Jed said, pushing Shay aside and striding across the room, hunting knife in hand. He jabbed it through the side of Momma's skull and her resurrected body dropped to the carpet.

"Christ," Nicholas said as he bent, head in his hands.

"We got this, Daddy," Shay said. "Why don't you go get some fresh air?"

Nicholas left the room. Shay heard him open the liquor cabinet and drop a glass on the floor. He swore. Kicked something.

Shay stooped and pulled the pillowcase down over Momma's face. Jed tore the top blanket off the bed and laid it on the floor. They rolled Momma's body onto the blanket, then rolled her up in it.

Shay took the cords holding the curtains back and used them to tie up Momma.

"Why don't you get her feet?" Jed suggested as he tested the weight of her shoulders.

Shay hiccuped and it sounded like a half-stifled cry.

"You know what? Let me try something else." Jed took the small book out of his pocket and flipped through the pages. He read one page for a minute before putting it away. He sang words that sounded like the rocking of ocean waves, his fingers tapped in constant movement. Momma's body rose from the floor. Jed moved her with his magic, his hands guiding her out of the room, down the hall, and out the front door. He settled her in the back of the truck, his arms dropping in fatigue.

"Thank you," Shay said.

Jed nodded nonchalantly, before sitting on the porch steps.

TWENTY-FOUR

"I NEED SOMETHING TO DRINK," SHAY SAID, TOUCHING Jed's shoulder as she walked up the steps to the porch. "You want some lemonade or something?"

"Sure." Jed nodded.

The screen door creaked then slammed closed as Shay walked into the house.

Shay found a pitcher and filled it with cold water from the tap. She found lemonade mix in the cabinet and added it to the water, mixing with a wooden spoon. There was one lemon on the counter. She cut it into wedges and added it to the pitcher. Reaching for the glasses, she heard footsteps behind her.

"I would have brought it out to ya," Shay said, taking down a glass and filling it. "Do you want ice?"

A strange groan came from behind her. The floorboards creaked.

Shay turned and dropped the glass she was holding. Her father was directly behind her, skin gray and black-veined. She saw the bite mark on his arm.

"Daddy?"

Nicholas had turned. Momma must've bitten him earlier. He ran out of the room so fast she figured he just needed some time alone to process Momma's death. Shay didn't think about him getting bit.

Nicholas reached for Shay; his grasp uncannily strong as he gripped her shoulder. Shay struggled, tried her best to push him away but his hand wouldn't release her. She stumbled, reached back, and grabbed the knife off the counter that she'd used to cut lemons with.

"Don't make me do it," Shay said.

Nicholas's teeth were cracking like a snapping turtle. He leaned closer. She stabbed him in the neck. The wound didn't stop him. Shay's veins lit with panic. She had to fight. She couldn't die like this. Shay's heart was pounding. She wouldn't die like this. She stabbed her father over and over but nothing stopped him. He still pushed and grabbed and tried to bite her. Then Shay remembered the head. She positioned her knife and slammed it into the side of her father's skull.

———

JED WASN'T sure he could eat, but the sun had risen and they'd missed breakfast. He thought of coffee and decided against it. He held out a trembling hand. The caffeine would make him shake more. He needed steady hands.

Breaking glass echoed. Jed stood, weary on his feet, and walked through the kitchen door.

Shay jabbed a knife into the side of Nicholas's skull. The large man dropped to the ground like a sack of shit.

Shay was covered in blood. She tore at her clothes, wiping at her skin, grabbing a towel off the counter and rubbing her arms so she could see. Terrified and hyperventilating, she was looking for bite marks.

"Check my back," she yelled at Jed. "Am I bit?" She was in full panic mode. "I don't know what happened." Her hands flitted across her neck, she twisted her hair up and checked behind her ears.

"You're okay." Jed picked her up and took her to the bathroom.

"I'll look you over. It's going to be all right." Shay was a feather in his arms, warm and soft, and he wanted to hold her forever until she settled.

He released her legs and set her on her feet.

Jed turned on the shower and pushed Shay inside. From the entrance, he turned Shay, spraying her skin with the handheld piece of the shower. He checked beneath her clothes; her shoulders, wrists and arms, the soft skin of her neck. "You're good." He handed the shower head to her. "I'll be back in a few minutes. Don't leave this room until I come back."

Shay nodded.

Jed used the floating spell to get Nicholas and Momma to the burn pile. He didn't even leave the grounds of the ranch, couldn't imagine making one more trip there today. He sent sparks to the new bodies, ensuring they burned. Thick, black smoke rose into the sky. He was grateful the ranch was far enough away that the smell wasn't too strong.

Shay was still in the shower, crying–no-sobbing like he'd never heard before. That was wrong, she sobbed just as hard as Jed wished he could have the night his own mother died. They were bound by that trauma now.

He searched the kitchen drawers until he found a Sharpie. Then he went to work. Each doorway was etched with protection runes. He found a stock of salt in the cupboard and lined the doorways and windows. Then he went upstairs and did the same to Shay's room.

They needed to leave, but not tonight. First thing in the morning he'd convince her. Too much had happened here, and he was way behind on getting to California.

TWENTY-FIVE

SHAY SAT ON THE FLOOR OF THE SHOWER LONG AFTER THE water had turned cold. She sobbed, forehead resting on her knees, arms hanging at her sides. She felt empty. Alone. So much had happened in such a short time. So many people's lives had been affected; Shay told herself that there was no way she could avoid it all. The safety of the ranch was nothing more than a fairytale, a dream, a lie. It couldn't protect her. Her parents couldn't protect her.

Shay wondered if she'd never ran off to that dive bar and met Clyburn, maybe he'd never have found the ranch. This was all her fault. There were too many connecting points. She should have been a better daughter. She should have simply accepted that she wasn't going to college during the apocalypse instead of running off for one last night of freedom. It wasn't even worth what she'd gone through. Those few minutes with a handsome cowboy in a dive bar parking lot were definitely not worth losing everything.

Shay hated herself.

The water suddenly turned off.

"Come on." Jed's voice broke her concentration.

Shay looked up. Jed was holding open a towel. She wasn't one to walk around naked, but Shay suddenly didn't care anymore. There was no one; she was alone.

"It's gonna be okay." Jed tucked the towel under his chin, reached down, and pulled up Shay by her arms. He wrapped the towel around her shaking body and led her out of the shower. They walked down the hall, up the stairs, and stopped in Shay's room.

Her room smelled strange, like lavender and bergamot and thyme. There were candles lit with etchings. A bundle of sage was smoking in the corner. There were marks over her windows and doors, all over the moldings and floors.

"What happened in here?"

"Spells of protection." Jed rubbed her with the towel to dry her. His eyes searched her skin, closer this time.

"Do you see any teeth marks?"

"No." Jed's gaze stopped at her lips.

Shay was reminded of that feeling she had when she saw Jed for the first time in the Lame Deer casino. Something bloomed deep inside her stomach and tingled like a butterfly. She was experiencing it again.

Jed moved, just a quarter of an inch closer. His eyes searched her face. Shay knew she'd been through a lot today. She didn't want to think about all of that. She wanted to focus on the mood, the warmth of Jed's hands on her arms, the feeling of safety in this room. Shay reached up on her toes and kissed him.

Jed was gentle. His hands skimmed over her body, his lips brushed against hers. Shay wondered if he felt the same explosion as she did.

He pushed her backward, toward the bed. When her legs hit the mattress, he bent to pull the blankets back.

"Lay down." He was still so close. His breath moved her hair.

Shay sat and scooted back. Jed reached for the blankets again and pulled them over her. He tucked her in and kissed her forehead. "Sleep," he said.

Shay suddenly couldn't keep her eyes open. For an instant, she thought maybe she should panic or fear whatever he'd done to her and the room. But she couldn't. There was nothing left inside her to care if she lived or died. She had nothing. Her world had shifted so drastically that she welcomed the void of sleep and didn't care if she never woke.

Twenty-Six

Then

JED COULD BARELY KEEP UP WITH DECLAN. HOOVES
threw up dirt as the horses ran full gallop. Light from the full moon
reflected off the sandy beach. In the distance, there was a boat waiting
for them.

"Don't look back." Declan was out of breath. He'd been
chanting spells and throwing bolts of energy at the mass of beasts
that were hot on their tail.

Jed looked back, wishing instantly that he hadn't. A black cloud
was following them. Animalistic growls and claws made Jed's heart
tick faster. The thing was a demon like they'd never seen before.

"I said don't do that!" Declan shouted. Sweat poured down the
man's face. They'd barely made it out of the little house in Chesapeake City. The clapboard building they'd called home for two years
was currently burning to cinder. White smoke rose in the distance,
and both knew the fire had spread. By morning, half of Chesapeake
City would be ash because of them, because they were scorned men
in the right place at the right time. Jed wanted to leave after the beast

149

had killed Eileen, but Declan was adamant that their runes and spells of protection were solid.

————

THEY *WERE* SOLID. For a few weeks at least, until the simple push of a broom knocked over a chair, then a glass of water. The water washed away a perfectly placed line of salt, which melted away etchings of chalk and coal. The Demon found them before Declan could pull chalk out of his pocket and fix it. Jed had been wringing out a cloth to soak up the water before it could spread farther and cause more damage. The blast through the wall threw Jed into a table. Declan was crouched on the floor and shielded his head.

The roar was deafening.

Jed shoved clapboard off his body and scrambled to his feet. Dust and smoke filled the room.

"Run boy!" Declan shouted. "I'll take care of it."

Jed flashed back to a time when he was much younger, when he knew just enough, when his mother shoved him out of a moving train car near Boston. "Run!" her voice was hushed and anguished. Jed had rolled down an embankment. He stopped and looked up just in time to see her closing the train car door, trapping herself inside with the Angel who'd found them. He couldn't leave Declan. He was older now, stronger; he could do *something*.

Jed tapped his fingers together in spellcasting, he knew better than parlor tricks now. He spat words that sounded like potatoes frying, his fingers twisted like a ballerina's legs, and he shot bolts of electricity at the angry cloud. Striking a taloned foot, the creature roared and advanced.

"I told ye to go!" Declan's accent was starting to show through.

The men cast barriers, shocks, water, threw pieces of the table. Nothing worked. Jed noticed the creature strayed from the wood-stove. He changed direction, ripped open the door of the woodstove and used a spell to hurdle the burning coals at the monster. It howled as the coals left holes in its clouded body.

"Yes!" Declan copied Jed and they began hurdling the fire together. The coals dropped to the floor and within minutes the monster was as porous as Swiss cheese, but the wooden floor of the house was smoking. The clapboard house was the best tinder fire had ever met. The hot coals quickly took root against the floorboards and lit a flame that grew as tall as a man.

The fire kept the creature at bay while Declan and Jed grabbed a few necessities and ran.

They didn't get far before the creature was following them. Jed tried to cast invisibility glamour, but he hadn't perfected it and their images glitched and wavered like ghosts as they ran down Pig Alley and turned at Harry Jackson Street.

"The canal," Declan said. "We can lose it in the water."

Jed pointed to the two horses tethered at a shop. "Or outrun it. The boat is at Hack Point."

"I like your thinking, boy." Declan veered toward the horses and Jed followed.

The cloud had multiplied as they galloped over the bridge. Two taloned legs became four, then eight, then twelve. Jaws with rows of sharp teeth snapped and hissed. Jed didn't count how many. He told himself he wasn't going to look back again. He slapped the horse on its flank so it would gallop faster.

The boat was close.

"I'll cut the dock lines," Declan said. The blade of a hunting knife glinted moonlight. "You start the engine."

It sounded easy enough. Jed threw blasts of fire over his shoulder to distract the Demon that was coming for them. Sweat dripped into his eyes. Panic filled his chest. They were so close.

The horse slowed on the dock, unused to the wavering motion. "Ha," Jed slapped the horse, but it reared up. Jed slid off, glanced at Declan, and leapt onto the boat. He made a mad dash for the engine room, felt stupid when he looked for keys before using his luck to turn over the engine. He didn't even have to whisper the words of a spell, the magic came out of him naturally. The boat engine sputtered to life.

Declan wasn't on the deck.

Jed ran from the engine room, gripped the deck railing, and found him. Declan was warding off the beast with the hunting knife and a fistful of fire. Neither seemed to be working against the beast.

"Be gone with ya!" He shouted at the Demon.

The mass roared and snapped, its cloudlike body undulated and twisted like a tornado. Thunderclap reverberated and drowned out Declan's voice.

Jed raised both hands and threw fire. "Run!" He shouted to Declan.

Declan rounded the dock and ran for the boat. "Hit the gas!"

Jed walked backward, but to get to the gas he'd have to stop throwing the fire. He shook his hands, dashed toward the gears, and accelerated. He ran back to the deck.

The boat was moving away from the dock, Declan was running full bore. Jed held out a hand and steadied himself.

Declan leapt, stopping midair as wicked jaws clamped down on his leg with a sickening crunch.

"No!" Jed screamed into the night.

Jed would never forget the look on Declan's face. The man smiled as his body hit the wooden dock. "I knew it would come one day." Declan's fingers tapped together and made a strange motion before the black cloud of teeth and talons consumed him.

Jed felt a bulge in his pocket as Declan vanished. He reached for it and pulled out Declan's spell book.

Jed was filled with anguish and hate as he strode to the engine room, pushed the boat into high gear, and set toward Elk River then the Atlantic.

TWENTY-SEVEN

JED WATCHED THE SKY FROM THE BEDROOM WINDOW. There had been too much commotion. Four Demons escaping Hell would get around. The chatter between Heaven, Hell, and the Earthen plane would mention him. He didn't need more heat. Jed needed to get moving.

"We have to go," Jed said as Shay opened her eyes.

"I know."

She looked tired. She'd barely moved all night after he settled in the bed and curled around her, his arm wrapped tight across her stomach.

She smelled like leather and lavender. Jed didn't want to forget it as he buried his nose in her braid and breathed in.

Shay's fingers traced his.

Jed stopped. This was dangerous. He moved away, rolled, and stood on the opposite side of the bed. He began collecting the things he'd left around her room. The sage, a white feather, small pouches that held spells.

"Yesterday..." Shay started. "What happened?"

"Seems your buddy Clyburn made a deal with a crossroads

Demon and it came to collect." Jed opened Shay's closet and took out a backpack.

"What are you doing?" Shay asked.

"Helping you pack." Jed threw the pack into a nearby chair.

"I'm already packed."

Jed glanced around the room for another bag.

"It's downstairs. We have bugout bags ready to go. I don't need anything from in here." Shay moved to her feet, dragging the blanket to cover herself.

She was showing a lot of skin and Jed wanted to touch her, more than he had during the night. But that would take time, and they didn't have time for touching each other in a dark room.

Shay opened a dresser drawer and took out clothes. She dropped the blanket to dress and Jed turned around rather than watch like a creeper.

"We gotta go, Shay." Jed's voice was low. He wanted to stay here with her, alone and safe to play house. But *they* would come soon enough.

Shay nodded and headed for the door to her bedroom. Jed followed her downstairs and into the kitchen. Shay opened a closet and removed a large backpack.

"You want one?" she asked. "You could take Daddy's pack."

"Sure." Jed wasn't going to say no to supplies.

"We should just bring them all. Can't hurt." Shay pulled out two more bags. "We can get some food from the root cellar if you want." She removed the guns next and tucked a small, black handgun into her holster.

Jed stepped over the blood stain on the floor, grabbed two of the packs, and opened the door to the porch. "We should go now, before they find me next."

Shay followed. "We can take the Jeep." She grabbed keys hanging near the door and pressed a button on the key fob. "Why so urgent?" she asked, opening a drawer filled with ammo and emptying it into her bag.

"I'm being hunted. Every moment of my life. We can't stay here. Angels or Demons will come to find me." He threw the bags into the back of the Jeep Commander that was parked near the house.

"But why are they after you?" Shay asked.

"I'm forbidden; the product of an Archangel and a human woman. Most infants are killed at birth. I seem to have lasted a bit longer." A strange feeling warred inside Jed. He'd never told a human what he was, always skirted around the issue.

"I can't leave yet," Shay said as she began walking toward the horse barn.

Twenty-Eight

Nero was still alive, kicking and whinnying and not happy about being locked up while the ranch was overrun and destroyed.

"I know," Shay said as she unlatched the gate to his stall.

"We can't take him," Jed warned.

Shay nodded, emptiness in her heart. Nero was the last of her family. She opened the bin of food and got fresh water from the spigot. "I can't leave him trapped on the ranch."

"That wouldn't be humane." Jed stood near the door, watching the long path to the gates of the ranch.

Shay could tell he wanted to go. Now. She couldn't leave Nero to starve to death. She removed his blanket and brushed his back one last time. "We have to go, Nero. This man is going to keep me safe." She glanced up. "Or maybe I'm going to keep him safe. Seems we're both a bit of a mess right now. Either way, you can't come with us."

Nero neighed and shook his head as though he understood every word Shay said.

"You can't stay here either." Shay moved to the door. "Come on, boy."

The three walked past the gardens and empty chicken coop splashed with blood.

Shay passed Jed the keys and walked Nero to the gate.

Nero huffed, looking between the ranch and the open Montana prairie in front of them.

Shay stroked his neck. "Stay away from the roads. Stay away from those smelly walking corpses. Stick to the mountains." Nero nuzzled her. "You'll find the wild horses. I know you will." Shay's eyes were filled with tears as Jed pulled up next to her. "You'll forget me but I'll never forget you."

She got in the Jeep. Nero watched her with wide eyes, huffing and pawing at the ground.

Shay rolled down the window. "Go now, Nero." She waved him away and broke down.

Jed pulled away, leaving the horse alone at the open gate. Shay felt a warm hand on her leg, a squeeze. She cried harder. Jed accelerated and Shay watched the road in front of them with blurry vision. After a few minutes, there was a black blur in her periphery. She turned. Nero was running next to the Jeep, his black mane flowing in the wind. The Jeep accelerated. Nero tipped his head down, determined, and ran faster, keeping up with them.

"I can't do this," Shay cried, reaching a hand out the window. Nero was too far away, but he saw her and he ran faster, trying to keep up.

Jed squeezed her leg again before putting both hands on the steering wheel and accelerating to well over a hundred miles per hour. Nero couldn't keep up. Shay couldn't watch him give up on her.

TWENTY-NINE

JED KEPT HIS EYES ON THE ROAD. HE DIDN'T WANT TO HIT debris or an errant dead person walking across the road. Shay was wiping her face with her shirt and trying to put herself back together.

"I'm sorry," Jed said, swerving around an upside-down car.

"It's not your fault." She took a deep breath. "I've had Nero since I was a little girl. I never thought I'd have to let him go."

"We can't hold on to everything."

"I know." Shay's voice was quiet. She kept leaning forward to look at the side view mirror to see if the horse was following.

"Take thirty-nine to Rosebud Cut-off Road. That will avoid Lame Deer." Shay buckled her seatbelt and leaned back in the seat.

"Will it avoid the Cheyenne lands?" Jed asked.

"Until we get to route 212. Then Cheyenne lands border the south."

Jed nodded, his lips pressed together in thought. He didn't want to run in to the Crow men again. He had enough shit to deal with.

"I'm headed to California. There's someone there who can help me." Jed's voice was serious but hopeful.

"You sure this someone is still alive?"

"He can't really die."

Shay turned to stare at the side of Jed's face.

"I can bring you elsewhere. If that's what you want." He swallowed hard, gripped the steering wheel with both hands, and looked straight ahead. Sure he had magic and luck and his father's looks, but he still feared her rejection. She might have an aunt or an uncle in the next town over that she'd rather stay with.

"I've got no one else." Shay's voice was low. "Just you, Jed."

"It's gonna be dangerous." She might run away with what he was going to tell her next. "Things seem okay right now but they'll come for me. An Angel or a Demon. I think my friend in California can help."

"What's his name?"

"Sparrow."

"That's a bird not a man."

Jed shrugged. "He's kinda weird."

"Perfect. Zombies and Demons and Angels and weird men from California named after a little bird." Shay laughed. "The things I've learned since meeting you–" she glanced at her watch "–nearly 96 hours ago. You've changed my world in less than five business days."

"Sorry 'bout that."

Shay touched his arm and a feeling zipped straight to his chest. He didn't want her to go, he didn't want her to meet Sparrow. He wanted nothing more than to drive her to a secluded place and never leave. But that wasn't possible. He hoped she could accept a life on the run.

"Stay with me, Jed." Shay rubbed his arm.

"What do you mean?"

"You went somewhere just now. You looked lost."

"I have been lost for a long time. But I think it will get better now that you're here. Why don't you get some rest?" Jed suggested.

"I'll try." Shay shifted in her seat, removing her hand from his arm.

Jed felt cold at the loss of her touch. He turned off Route 39.

Glancing in the rear-view mirror he was almost certain he saw a black shadow in the woods.

———

Shay woke startled, the Jeep jerking to the right and accelerating.

"What's happening?" Her hand was on her holster as she sat up.

"Bumpy road," Jed was checking the windows and mirrors.

"Did you run over some corpses?"

"Avoided those." Jed chuckled.

The sun was setting over the mountains. There were craters in the road, like someone had thrown a stick of dynamite at a car or a body. Jed had to keep veering off the road so the Jeep wouldn't get stuck in one of the craters.

"That's ugly." Shay inspected the road.

"Do you want to stop up here and stretch your legs?" Jed asked. "We haven't passed a town in a while and the roadsigns said Big Sky is fifteen miles away.

"Big Sky is nice." Shay stretched and the hem of her shirt rode up, revealing skin. "I could eat. And we're going to need gas." Shay turned her attention to watching the pine trees that they passed.

"What's wrong?" Jed asked.

"I feel guilty." Shay touched her face. "It's all my fault."

"What happened at the ranch is not your fault."

Shay made a noise deep in her throat; it sounded like a strangled cry she was holding down. "I brought Clyburn. I ran away one night because I didn't want to stay at the ranch, I wanted to go to college with my friends." She took a deep breath in the middle of her confession. "I met Clyburn at a bar. Things happened. Then a few days later he showed up at the ranch."

"That explains his obsession with you." Jed was making a face like he'd sucked salt.

"What I'm trying to say is that if I'd never run off that night, he'd have never entered our lives. My parents are dead because of me. The ranch is gone because of me." Shay was crying again. Quietly. Tears streamed down her face.

Jed slowed the Jeep and pulled over. The roads were empty and he hadn't seen a soul in miles. He turned off the engine and got out, rounding the Jeep and opening the passenger door.

"What are you doing?" Shay asked as she wiped her face.

Jed moved her whole body so she was sitting sideways, facing him. He stood between her legs. "I can make it go away. If you don't want to remember."

"What do you mean?" Shay was shocked at the way he went to her side.

Jed touched her forehead. Calloused fingers causing her skin to tingle and heat. "Like I made this go away." His eyes searched hers. Shay saw pain there. Pain just as bad as hers and somehow he'd kept going all this time. "I can rid you of those memories."

Shay shook her head. "No. I hate myself for ever meeting Clyburn. But I can't forget. If I forget and I make that mistake again. I can't..." her gaze drifted away from his face until she was focused off in the distance.

Jed gripped her chin and forced her to look at him. "You will never make that mistake again." Jed leaned closer, his lips brushing hers. "Because I am here and no one else will be touching you ever again." His lips pressed against hers, harder.

Shay reached for him, her hands sliding over the hard planes of his stomach, his sides, around to his back. Jed leaned into her. Shay wanted to touch more of him. She gripped his shirt, wanting to feel the skin under his clothing. She wanted him to quell the ache in her center and was out of breath in a few minutes.

Jed pulled away. "We have to keep going." His face was pained; he tugged her hips closer and she didn't miss his hardness pressed against her center.

Shay hid her disappointment. "Yeah. We should go."

Jed swept a piece of hair off her cheek. "If you change your mind. Let me know." He was looking into her eyes intently.

"I won't change my mind." Shay moved in her seat as Jed closed the door and went to the driver's side of the Jeep.

———

THEY STOPPED at an abandoned gas station. Jed used his magic to make the gas pump work and topped off the Jeep. Shay had warned him that the road ahead was mountainous and few gas stations existed in the winding roadway. They had and extra tank, but it was better to be safe than sorry.

"See if the television works," Jed said to Shay as she went to investigate the shop.

"You watch T.V.?"

"Just the news, lately. There's a horde moving through California that I've been tracking." Jed's fingers twisted and tapped and the gas pump came to life.

He watched Shay as she went inside. They'd planned to make a few of the camp meals in the bugout bags but Shay didn't want to use up all the water. Just in case, she'd said.

He saw the blue light of the television turning on, static as she flipped the channels. The gas pump turned off when the tank was full. Jed secured it and went inside.

"Anything?" he asked.

"Not yet." She kept pressing the button on the television until a map displayed on the screen.

"Wait," Jed said. He moved closer. More of California was designated a red zone. There were no newscasters on this channel, just a display of the U.S. red zones and green zones. There were little army man clusters for where the National Guard was stationed.

"You want to go to California?" Shay asked. "Still? It looks like a bad idea."

Jed made a noise. "To some. But Sparrow is there. I'm sure of it. And he's going to keep us safe until this mess is over."

Jed turned, focused out the window. He was sure he saw a shadow out of his periphery. Shadows were never good. The veil between realms was thinning with whatever was going on with the dead walking. The four Demons at the ranch would have brought consequences and Angels, and he'd seen none yet. Whatever shadow he'd seen wouldn't be good, and it had been twice now. They needed to disappear.

"We should go," Jed said.

"Waters." Shay pointed to a package of bottled water on a shelf.

"Let's eat later," he suggested, feeling unease and something in the air.

Shay grabbed a few packs of jerky and tucked them under her arm. They each grabbed a pack of water and headed to the Jeep. Jed opened the cargo door.

"Why the rush?" Shay asked.

"I want to beat the California horde before it gets too far north." He didn't want to tell her about the shadow. He didn't want to scare her. It could simply be a bear or an elk or a passerby in the thinning veil between realms. Hell was simply a reflection of the Earthen plane after all.

THIRTY

THERE WAS A DARK SKY, THE MILKY WAY BRIGHT LIKE IT had never been before. Shay was leaned forward watching the stars out the front window.

"Look," she pointed at a falling star.

Something twisted in Jed's gut. Falling stars were interesting to those who didn't know what they could be. Sometimes it was more than a star; sometimes it was an Angel being cast out or dropping in to the Earthen plane to cause havoc.

"That's cool." Jed focused on the dark road in front of them as he descended the winding foothills. The route had become more cluttered with debris in the road; fallen trees and broken-down cars. It hadn't taken long for the roads to crumble into potholes as the veil between realms thinned and the Earthen plane darkened. There was an ochre cast to the sun and the moon, the shadows darker than they'd ever been before. Jed took in the changes on the Earthen plane and hoped finding Sparrow would set things back to the way they belonged.

"You want something to eat?" Shay was reaching behind the seat for one of the bugout bags.

"Nah." Jed leaned toward the window, relaxing. "I'll wait. If I start eating now I won't want to stop."

"You one of those people who eats every meal like it could be their last?" Shay was joking but a little serious.

The ground shook, vibrating the Jeep.

"What was that?" Shay asked.

A figure came into focus in the headlights.

"Fuck." Jed hit the brakes.

Shay gripped the door and braced herself for impact. "You're going to hit it."

"Probably not." Jed knew what it was and how fast it would move. He reached for his bag that was on the floor behind his seat. Fingers searching, he felt the worn fabric of it but couldn't get a good grip.

Jed slammed on the brakes. The Jeep came to a stop, inches from the figure. Jed finally grabbed the bag.

The figure sneered.

"Oh my God." Shay covered her mouth. "Is that?" She couldn't turn away from the giant winged man in the road. "Is that an Angel?"

"Nasty bastards." Jed pulled a knife from his bag. "He shouldn't have his wings out like that. Kinda uncouth."

"I don't see wings," Shay said, eyes wide.

"You can't?"

Shay shook her head. "Maybe just you can?"

The Angel jumped onto the hood of the Jeep and ripped the corner of the roof off, throwing it to the side. He looked at Shay and smiled darkly. Nothing good could come from a face so handsome and a smile so devilish.

"Not today." Jed's fingers danced with a spell. He spat words that sounded like hate laced with ice, and he shot an electric current at the Angel.

The Angel stumbled back two steps and redirected his focus to

Jed. He lurched forward and reached into the Jeep, grabbing Jed by the arms and dragging him out.

"Run!" Jed warned Shay just before the Angel took him to the sky. "Get out of here!"

"No!" Shay shouted.

Shay scrambled into the driver's seat, slammed the vehicle into drive and sped down the road after the two men.

She swerved around debris, trying to focus on the figures in the sky. When the road was clear, she grabbed the handgun from her holster and aimed.

The Angel and Jed were fighting in the sky. Shay couldn't shoot; they were moving too fast. She sped up, hoping to get a better aim.

As the Angel threw Jed, sparks and fire flitted from Jed's hands. Shay could hear their voices faintly as they fought.

Jed fell. He had to be a few stories up in the air. The Angel flung Jed by the arms and he dropped. Shay sped up, reaching out the top of the Jeep and aiming at the Angel. She fired off a few shots, glad that she'd missed as the Angel grabbed Jed just before he hit the ground. Jed swiped at the Angel with a knife.

Suddenly, the Jeep hit something. Shay focused on the road, weaving around large tree branches. She glanced between the figures fighting in the sky and the road which had become covered in branches. Not far ahead of her, there was a giant tree that had fallen across the road. End to end, there was no way around it. Shay cursed. She slowed as she got closer and tried to drive over it but the tires just tore apart the rotting bark. Shay got out. She took one look at the road and Jed in the distance and screamed in frustration. She was going to lose everyone and could do nothing about it. Defeat swelled in her chest. Shay didn't want it all to end like this. She wasn't about to run away like a coward but she didn't want to die at the hands of that Angel once it was done with Jed.

"Goddamn it!" Shay kicked the tree that was blocking the road.

Behind Shay, a familiar noise broke through the night; the sound of galloping hooves on rough pavement. Shay turned, barely believing the sight. Nero was running toward her at full gallop.

"Nero!" Shay scrambled and climbed up on to the hood of the Jeep. "Come here. Good boy." Shay jumped onto Nero's back as he passed. Landing hard, she gripped his mane and held on tight as the horse leapt over the fallen trees. "Keep going, boy. We gotta get to Jed."

Shay focused ahead. The men were still fighting, closer to the ground now. Shay saw a chance. She aimed and fired twice.

The Angel roared as a bullet hit its shoulder. Jed dropped and grabbed onto the Angel's leg.

Shay shot it in the wing as she urged Nero to move faster. The Angel dropped as one wing weakened its ability to fly.

Nero slowed. Shay saw her chance. The Angel was holding onto Jed with one arm, punching him. Shay shot the Angel in the arm. Blood and bone sprayed as her bullet hit bone. The Angel dropped Jed but they were closer to the ground. He fell hard, shouting as his legs buckled. He didn't get up.

Shay swung her leg and jumped off Nero. She shot the Angel again, running hard until she came upon Jed. The Angel fell to the ground. Shay stole the knife from Jed's hand, leapt over his body. In a few quick strides she was at the Angel's body. She paused, but knew she shouldn't have. She'd never gazed upon a man so beautiful before. Muscled and smooth skin, the man looked as though he had been chiseled from stone. The Angel's eyes flashed open. Shay slammed the knife into its chest. The Angel never took another breath; his body went limp, lifeless.

Shay stood slowly, weary, unbelieving.

Nero huffed, drawing Shay's attention. When she turned around, the horse was nuzzling Jed's still body.

A lump was rising in Shay's throat. She didn't see the whole fight, but what she did see was brutal.

Shay crouched near Jed noticing how pale his little bit of untattooed skin looked in the moonlight. Blood dripped out of his mouth. There were cuts all over his body. At least he was breathing faintly.

"Hey," she said as she shook his shoulder. She checked the pulse in his neck. It was weak but there. "What am I gonna do with you?" she muttered as she took in their surroundings.

Shay considered herself strong, but Jed was twice her size. They were sitting ducks in the road; there was no protection from the elements or the dead or an attack from an ethereal creature. Shay needed to get him back to the Jeep. She knew there was a tarp and rope in the cargo area. She glanced at the Jeep that was a few hundred yards away, then she glanced at Nero.

"You stay with him," she told Nero as she jogged to the Jeep.

Shay opened the cargo hatch. Everything was stored neatly and had been inventoried weekly at the ranch. Nicholas wanted everything ready to go in case they had to run. Emotion welled in Shay's chest. She never thought she'd be running without her parents at her side. She grabbed the heavy duty tarp and the paracord rope, then went back to where Jed was laying in the road.

Shay unfolded the tarp and set it out next to Jed. She lifted and shoved his body, pushing the tarp under one side of him, then pulling it out on the opposite side until he was centered. She used the paracord to fashion a harness of sorts around Nero's shoulders and back, then tied through the eyelets in the tarp.

"Let's do this, boy." Shay patted Nero, her arms burning from exertion, and led him toward the Jeep as he dragged Jed's body. They wove around the downed trees until they got to the giant one that was blocking the entire road.

"We have to go over it," Shay told Nero. She gripped the back of the tarp and lifted. "Slowly, boy."

Nero stepped over the tree trunk, dragging Jed over. Shay's arms ached as she lifted her side and did her best to make sure his head didn't hit the road.

Getting his body into the back of the Jeep was going to take a lot more effort. Shay put the seats down and laid out a wool blanket. She released Nero from the rope, wound it up and stored it. Shay tugged Jed closer and lifted him under his arms.

The man was dead weight. A lot of dead weight. Nero bit at Jed's shirt and tugged up to help.

"Thanks boy, but I think we're going to need more than that."

Shay got him into a sitting position and tried lifting Jed from under his arms. Her muscles ached and back ached. "Jesus christ," she muttered. "Why is he so big?"

Nero huffed and walked to the driver's side door, tapping it with his nose.

"You can't drive." She looked at the coil of rope, then the tarp and where Nero was standing. "You know, Nero, you're a genius."

Shay used the rope and tied a harness to Nero again, then she fed the rope through the driver's side window, through the Jeep and out the back cargo door. She tied the rope through the eyelets again.

"Okay, boy," Shay said as she picked up the end of the tarp and clucked her tongue. "Go."

Nero walked forward, tugging the ropes and the tarp. Shay lifted the opposite end and they got Jed into the cargo area without much damage. He maybe had a few extra bruises, but it was better than leaving him in the road.

Before leaving, Shay returned to the dead Angel only to find that his body had turned to ash. The knife was still there. Shay knew it was special because of the carvings in the handle. She collected the knife and brought it back to the Jeep.

Shay checked on Jed one last time before closing the hatch and getting behind the wheel. She kept the window down so she could talk to Nero.

"Gotta tuck away somewhere safe," she said as she reversed then turned around and drove from where they came.

Shay drove a good ten miles before she found a dead end road with a chain across a driveway. She let herself in and found an abandoned shack past a long driveway of thick trees. It looked like someone's hunting cabin and she figured it was safe enough. They were off the road and there was a stream nearby. Best of all, they weren't on Cheyenne land and she didn't have to worry about Hosa surprising them with the intention of skinning Jed.

Nero followed the Jeep, but eventually wandered off. Shay didn't try to stop him. She had a feeling he'd be nearby. She'd never been happier than the moment he broke through the darkness to help her.

Shay parked the Jeep under a large oak tree and turned off the engine before climbing in the back to check on Jed. She pressed her fingers to his neck. His pulse was good. She opened one of the bugout bags and got the first-aid kit.

Jed's clothes were torn, bloody, and dirty. She pushed the cloth away to inspect one of his wounds before deciding the clothes were going to have to go. She took the scissors out of the kit and began cutting his shirt away at the neck. Shay had never seen so many tattoos. They covered his chest and stomach. The more of his shirt that she cut, the more she saw. They weren't pictures but strange shapes and markings like what he'd carved into her bedroom doorframe.

A mosquito buzzed in her ear. Shay swatted at the bug and glanced at the ripped open roof of the Jeep. She needed to patch it or the mosquitoes would eat them alive in the night. Shay left Jed's side, took one of the rescue blankets and tucked it around the frame. It wouldn't last, but it would work for tonight.

Shay crawled to Jed's side again. She found a fresh cloth in the bag and used a bottle of water to clean his wounds. Some were shallow scrapes but a few were deep and still bleeding. Shay watched his face as she cleaned the worst of the cuts, a large slash over his abdomen. He didn't flinch or moan. She wasn't sure if that was a good thing or bad at the moment. She didn't need him howling in pain but she did need to know he had some life left in him.

Shay considered a pressure dressing, but when the wound kept oozing bright red blood, she decided suturing would be better. Thankfully momma and Shay had packed the med kit with everything they could need for wound care: Lidocaine spray, sutures, sterile gauze, and needles.

Shay set out her supplies and got to work. When she was finished stitching, the sun was fading fast. Shay made quick work of putting a sterile dressing over the fresh stitches before finding a camp light.

Her back and legs ached from being hunched over in the Jeep. She searched for the battery powered lantern, found it under the seat and clicked it on. Shay's gaze drifted over Jed's body. She still had to get his pants off. She reached for his belt, unbuckling the leather and pulling. She rolled it up and set it aside. Next she unsnapped his jeans, set the scissors just below the zipper, and began cutting. She tried not to stare at the corded muscles or trail of hair below his abdomen that tucked below the black band of his boxer-briefs. She assessed the cuts on his legs and bruising as she worked. After the jeans were cut and removed, she took his boots and socks off. She washed the dirt off his legs and used an ACE bandage to wrap his swollen right ankle. She'd seen his legs buckle when he fell and she was thankful it wasn't a break.

Shay still had to check his back. The tarp protected him from dragging wounds but she'd seen him fall and get tossed through the air like a ragdoll. As Shay moved closer, settling her knees against his side, she gripped his shoulder and hip. She rocked his limp body once, twice, and on the third time she rolled him. Nicholas had taught her how to move and carry the fainting goats or lifeless sheep in similar fashion. But Jed was much larger than a farm animal. She wasn't sure where she found the strength to move him. She pulled it from somewhere deep inside.

Shay tipped the lantern closer and inspected his back. There were fewer tattoos along his shoulder blades and spinal column, the rest was bare. Shay's fingers roamed over his skin, checking small cuts and palpating for bleeding. She'd read in one of the survival books that if the liver was injured there could be pain in the abdomen or shoulder. Jed didn't budge when she pressed her fingers into his muscle. She settled him back and tucked a spare blanket under his head to use as a pillow.

Shay found another blanket to cover Jed before she climbed into the driver's seat and turned on the headlights. She needed to stretch her legs and use the bathroom but didn't want any surprises. The night was quiet; she couldn't hear anything more than the rippling stream, the chirping of crickets and the echo of a barn owl. Across the stream Shay saw two eyes watching her. She recognized the form. It was Nero, settled down for the night. "Hey, boy," she whispered, happy that he was nearby.

Shay cleaned herself up, drank a bottle of water, and ate a protein bar before taking off her boots and climbing in the back of the Jeep again. She was bone tired. The fight with the Angel had amped up her adrenaline and now she was coming down off the high. Shay was thankful for all her parents had taught her on the ranch. If she hadn't spent her life riding horses and hunting and being pushed to survive, she wasn't sure how this day would have ended.

She settled near Jed, then decided to move closer when the chill in the air made her shiver. It was cold outside as a Montana winter was getting closer. The windows in the jeep fogged. Shay turned off the lantern and focused on the sound of Jed's shallow breathing. She hoped he'd wake up soon and infection wouldn't set in. She guessed he probably had some more broken ribs too but she couldn't tell with the tattoos that covered his body. They hid the bruises and scrapes. In better light she'd examine him further.

Shay closed her eyes, reached out and took Jed's hand, fingers threaded together in a prayer. She prayed she didn't dream of that Angel she'd killed. He was both beautiful and fearsome and somehow she'd found the strength to end his life. Her daddy would've been proud had he been alive to see it. Shay sighed and scooted closer until their shoulders touched and fell fast asleep.

THE WARM BODY next to Shay was both a comfort and a pleasure. She propped herself up on an elbow and watched Jed. Some color had returned to his face and his breathing wasn't as shallow. She checked the pulse in his wrist and concluded with the steady beat that he was better than last night. She pulled the blanket back and checked the dressing over his stitched abdomen. There was some oozing, but it wasn't bad. She'd seen worse living on a ranch; wounds that the ranch hands had hidden and let fester because they were too proud for medical care.

Shay pulled the blanket back further. Jed's skin prickled to goose-flesh with the chill. In the morning sun, Shay got an even better view of his body. There were deep bruises around his ribs and as she traced them with her finger, she felt the unmistakable bulge of a break. She tested it, pressing harder. Jed groaned, his face twisting. She moved on, tracing his other ribs and found a few healed notches. There were scars she came across as well, a deep scar with bad stitches under his bicep. Battlefield medicine. That's what it looked like. Jed had probably never seen a real doctor for any of his ailments.

She tipped his head to the side and noticed a small scar on his neck. Two holes. A bitemark from something. She stared at his relaxed face as the sun shone through the Jeep's windows. He was beyond handsome and Shay figured his kind were forbidden because they'd take all the human women. Shay wasn't sure she would ever find another man attractive after looking at Jed.

Shay took her bugout bag and Jed's torn clothing. She got out of the Jeep and made her way to the stream that was a few feet away. There was frost on the tall grass and the fresh scent of cold air. Nero was gone, probably off in the prairie looking for sweet grass.

Shay was thankful for the gently sloping watershed. She tore Jed's shirt into strips, then rinsed them out. She hung the strips on nearby tree branch to dry, saving one to wash herself. She took in the surrounding prairie to make sure she was alone and there were no wandering eyes or wandering dead in the vicinity. Then she stripped and stepped into the stream.

The water was ice-cold but the cloth smelled like Jed, sandalwood and musk and coffee. She scrubbed her skin until it was pink, removing the gore from the Angel battle and traces of Jed's blood.

Her hair was matted with dirt and sweat and blood. She laid down in the stream and let it rinse before scrubbing it with soap.

Air drying was more of a challenge in the Montana chill. She'd experienced colder while traveling with her father on a cattle drive. Although, there was much less fighting, blood, and death involved. She decided she could handle the chill if it was the worst inconvenience for the day.

THIRTY-ONE

HE SHOULD HAVE DIED. JED EXPELLED ALL THAT MAGIC fighting the Angel that he couldn't heal his own injuries. He could do nothing but sleep and heal slowly. Without Shay, he would've been a dead man. Jed owed Shay his life. He knew that the instant his eyes opened and he sensed her warmth near him.

He twisted to the side, sucking in a breath of pain. His entire body ached. His hand moved over his stomach and felt the rough edges of a bandage.

"Don't," Shay warned. "I can't heal your cuts like you did mine."

"The cuts are the least of my concern. I think a few ribs are broken." He righted himself, leaning on his elbow.

Jed touched Shay's cheek, his fingertips tracing her jaw, behind her ear, down her neck.

"Does it hurt?" she asked.

"Only because I can't do the things I want to do." His eyes were imploring, only focused on her.

"Don't pull your stitches." She warned. "I'm no Grandmother Crow but I did practice on the ranch pig once."

Jed chuckled then winced. He laid back and took deep breaths.

"Appropriate training." He touched her cheek with the back of his hand. "Your hair is wet."

"I took a bath."

He glanced at their surroundings. "There's a bathroom in here?" A smile tugged at the corner of his mouth. "Man this jeep is more spacious than I thought."

Shay pointed out the window and Jed saw the rippling stream. "Damn. I missed that?"

"The early bird gets the worm or the nudity." Shay moved. "I'll get some food. If you're up for eating something."

Jed grabbed the blanket that had pooled around his waist, prepared to throw it back, until he noticed he wasn't wearing much and it was quite cold without Shay next to him.

She was fully dressed.

"What happened to my clothes?" Jed rested his head on the makeshift pillow, feeling out of breath.

"I took them off you." Shay unzipped a bag and opened a bottle of water. "They're trashed." She pointed to the window to the strips of clothing drying in the tree.

"I'm not sure how I feel about being stripped naked while unconscious." Jed pulled the blanket up to his chest like a child hiding.

"Next time I'll do it while you're conscious." Shay smiled before returning to her task of preparing food. "There's a mark on your neck," Shay said, eyes watching him closely. "What is that from?"

Jed's hand flew to the small scars. "Ah..." He didn't want to tell her. "Something bit me once."

"Something?"

"Kind of like a vampire. But a person. Her name was Meg." Jed shook his head. "I'm not sure how to explain it to you but you'll understand when you meet Sparrow. He's different."

"Does Sparrow bite people in the neck also?" Shay handed him a water and a pack of protein chips.

"You could say that."

"Will he bite me in the neck? Should I be afraid?"

Possessiveness flooded Jed's body at the thought of Sparrow ever touching Shay. "If he touches you, I'll kill him." Jed didn't care if Sparrow was royalty from the Seven Kingdoms of Heaven, or Legion Commander of the Hellions. He'd send Sparrow's soul to another plane.

"Calm down, cowboy," Shay patted Jed's arm as she scooted closer to him with more food.

———

CLIMBING out of the Jeep was a challenge. Jed's ribs throbbed and the cut on his abdomen stretched against the stitches. Shay had given him a few hours of rest before she forced him to get outside. He felt relatively clean thanks to her scrubbing the grime off his body and tending to his wounds. He watched her now as he leaned against the Jeep, feeling weak and catching his breath. Shay was pulling a strip of cloth down from the tree branch for him. She found an empty bucket near the shed in the distance and set it in the water so he didn't have to stand or lay down in the stream.

"Let's go cowboy, the sun ain't waiting for you." Shay smiled and waved him over. She was strong and soft, barefoot in the creek, her jeans rolled up so they wouldn't get wet. Jed had a vision of children splashing in the water around them. He closed his eyes and remembered what he was. That was a future he could never have. It was dangerous enough bringing Shay along. He focused on her again as she was bent over, rinsing cloth in the water.

"It looks cold." Jed pushed against the Jeep until he was standing and cursed himself for missing the vision of her bathing naked in the sunrise. Need zipped down his spine and straight to his groin. Jed cursed and reminded himself he was wearing nothing but thin boxer-briefs and she'd definitely see what was on his mind if he didn't get his lust under control.

It was hard–not the walking, but the trying to ignore wanting her. After all, she had killed an Angel to save him, somehow gotten him to safety, and took care of him until he woke. She was strong, the strongest woman he'd ever met. Most would have left him there to die. But not Shay. Shay had determination in her bones and if he was the praying type, he'd thank God for her. But he never prayed, he learned that from Declan. Never pray to the God who forbade your existence and let all the planes relish in open season hunting your skin. Never.

Jed made it to the water, holding his breath when his bare feet met the cold stream. The chill felt good on his sore ankle but the rest of his body shivered.

"You can do it, big-boy," Shay joked as she held out her hand to steady him.

He moved past her and sat on the bucket. "You've dragged my hide through enough. Let me do it." Jed took a deep breath, flinching when his ribs flared with pain. It wasn't the first broken rib he endured, and he was sure it wouldn't be the last in his lifetime. He was certain a few more of his ribs were cracked and that's what made it so hard to breathe.

Shay passed Jed a wet cloth and the soap. "I'll get your back." She didn't give him a chance to reply. Instead she moved around him, pulled a cloth from the stream, and rinsed his back.

"Ah!" Jed's spine went straight as the cold water shocked his body.

Shay giggled as she rubbed the cloth with soap and went about scrubbing him with it. She was gentle around the bruises and cuts but scrubbed his neck with her bare hands. Jed leaned into her touch.

"Who did these tattoos on your back?" Shay asked.

"An old friend. Someone who was like me." The air changed and became uneasy; he wasn't ready to talk about Declan.

"Where is this friend?"

"Dead."

"I'm sorry about that."

Jed was thoughtful. Everyone he'd been close to had died. He worried about the same future for Shay. "Me too. He shouldn't have died."

She squeezed fresh water over his back to rinse. "Tip your head back," she said. She wet his hair that was crusted with blood and massaged the strands and scalp.

A deep moan escaped Jed's lips.

"Wash your front, boy." Shay squeezed his head in deep massage.

"I can't." He was far too distracted by her fingertips pressing into his scalp. No one had ever touched him like this before.

"I won't be doing it." She rinsed his hair until the shaggy, light brown strands were clean and dripping. "That's better."

Jed took her wrist and dragged her around to face him, pulling her onto his lap.

Shay wasn't a prude. She could feel the evidence of his desire pressing against her hip. It flooded her body with warmth.

"What did I do to deserve you?" Jed's eyes were half-lidded as he focused on her mouth and tugged her closer. He'd never wanted anyone like this before, never trusted anyone with his secrets. He was prepared for a lifetime alone. He was wrong. He never knew how much he truly needed someone. That someone was Shay.

THIRTY-TWO

NERO WAS BOUND TO SHAY FROM THE MOMENT SHE FOUND him bucking and kicking at a bee nest during a cattle drive. He'd only been born a few hours earlier, dropped in the prairie grass by a mare who wasn't sure raising a foal in the offseason was such a good thing. When the bees came out of the ground and swarmed on her, she ran. She left him to die, wet and cold. But the warm Montana sun dried the wetness from his coat and mane, and he rose up on knobby-kneed legs only to be stung over and over again.

Shay wasn't much more than a teenager when she pointed to the black foal in the distance. It didn't take much to convince Nicholas to take the foal home. Shay lifted him, draping the small horse over her lap as she rode back to the ranch.

She bottle-fed him and carried him around like a baby. Two long legs over her shoulders and his hindquarters nearly tripping her. She tended to the stings on his soft belly and backside. She kept him in her room those first months until he was too big, then slept in the barn next to him every night until he was settled. That was all it took for Nero to tether himself to Shay. They were inseparable.

That night the crossroads Demons came, one entered the barn. It took goats and sheep. It got Nicholas's horse but when the Demon came upon the giant black stallion, he got nothing more than a scratch on Nero's hide before the horse kicked him so hard the Demon decided it wasn't worth fighting for that meal. Nero's coat was so black and glossy it reflected the moonlight and devoured it at the same time. The Demon was frightened of the creature. But that sometimes happens when evil creatures come across someone who has walked the line of life or death. The dance to live is halfway known, the dance to death is easy. Nero could kill just as the Demon.

Nero was still scratched. Long black claws didn't kill him, but they did change him. He was no longer just a horse whose heart was broken when his human set him free and left with a faceful of tears. He was much more.

Nero was something wilder than ever before, his soul not restrained to the Earthen plane. With the thinning veil during this time of chaos, he could step through it into Hell and back to the Earthen plane. It did wonders for him hiding from Shay and Jed. He was a horse but he knew he wasn't supposed to be following them. Horses aren't dumb. And Nero was the smartest horse humanity had ever come across. Quite possibly, the most dangerous.

THIRTY-THREE

SHAY HAD NEVER BEEN KISSED LIKE THIS BEFORE. JED'S lips were firm, searching, his tongue demanding. Need grew in Shay's belly. Her fingers pressed into Jed's shoulders before sliding across smooth muscle exploring the dips and valleys of his body before delving up into his hair.

Jed's hands gripped her hips and pulled her down against him with a deep groan.

"We have to go," Shay said, out of breath, cheeks flushed and lips swollen.

"Where?" Jed buried his face in her chest, leaving wet marks from his dripping hair.

"California. We'll be two days behind if we stay another night here."

"Fuck California." Jed didn't care. In this moment, he only cared about the current situation; Shay on his lap, the cold stream keeping him grounded. Not a care in the world.

Tree branches snapped. Jed moved fast, standing to shield Shay with his body and holding out his free hand ready to cast.

Nero broke through the bramble and dipped his head to drink from the stream.

Shay started to laugh. "Nero! Where have you been all night?" She weaved around Jed and moved toward the horse, petting him and resting her head on his side.

Nero was a cock-blocking horse if Jed ever saw one. While Shay was distracted, he finished cleaning himself and got his body under control, cursing himself for letting his guard down. This time it was the horse, next time it could be anything.

THIRTY-FOUR

JED AND SHAY DECIDED TO PACK UP AND HEAD OUT IN THE evening. The land Shay had found wasn't far from the road where she'd killed the Angel and Jed was worried more Angels would come looking for them.

Shay said goodbye to Nero and warned him to stay away from the walking corpses. One large dark eye was watching Jed as Shay whispered at the horse. She didn't feel as alone this time, not as overwhelmed by death or her own mortality. All this time she'd thought her family would keep her safe, she'd figured Nicholas and Momma would help her make it through these times of the dead walking and demons wrecking the ranch. Shay was wrong. She was strong enough to stay alive, strong enough to keep others alive. She'd killed a murderous Angel and saved Jed. She took a deep breath and focused.

This time, the goodbye wasn't as devastating. Nero galloped off toward the prairie and didn't chase the Jeep like last time. It was easier for both of them, not a goodbye but a promise to see each other again.

Shay rolled down the window and let the night air fill the Jeep. The vehicle jerked to the side.

Jed made a noise and held his ribs.

"Sorry," Shay said as she looked at him, "just a pot hole."

"It's all good." Jed was eating one of the freeze dried camp meals. Cheeseburger macaroni and a pack of space ice cream.

"You gonna eat all our food in one night, big guy?" Shay asked.

"Sorry." He chewed and swallowed. "It's just the healing," he motioned to his body, "thing I've got going on. I burn a lot of calories."

Shay bit her lip, thinking of another way to burn calories.

Jed stilled. "Don't," he warned like he could read her mind.

"You said fuck California earlier." Shay tipped a shoulder.

"We have to go if we're going to make it out of this mess alive."

Shay gripped the steering wheel and focused straight ahead. She was the planning type and an adventure like this was sure to go sideways real quick without a strategy. "So we get to California and then what?"

Jed finished chewing a spoonful of cheeseburger mac. "We get to California and get ahead of the horde."

"A horde of the dead?"

"Yes."

"Won't they kill us?"

Jed waved the spoon. "Not necessarily. We come down from the North and find Sparrow first. Then we should be fine."

"*Should be.*" Shay wasn't sure she had enough bullets in her pack for *should be*.

Jed nodded. "The horde is following him. They won't get too close to him."

"How do you know?" Shay couldn't hide the concern in her voice. She'd done things these past few days that she never thought she'd do. She watched her family die. She'd killed an Angel. She was very much enjoying the man sitting next to her in the Jeep. She didn't want it all to end being torn apart by a horde of the walking dead.

"I know because I tattooed him with Meg's blood. Runes like mine to hide him from Angels and Demons."

"The same Meg who bit your neck?"

"Same one."

"Why did he need to be hidden?"

"He's been through some things. He was a prince of the Seven Kingdoms of Heaven. Then the Legion Commander of Hell. Meg's Legion Commander. But she stabbed him in the heart and released the last spec of his angel grace. He is darkness now, an enigma walking the Earthen plane. Darkness follows darkness."

"This sounds bad."

"It could be. But I don't think it will be. The horde is following something. It has to be him."

"So we find him and we have protection?" Shay asked.

"Until we get him back to Meg. They are supposed to be together. Or at least, that's what they're always saying to each other."

"Like a forbidden love kind of thing."

"Destiny. Maybe." Jed ate more, scraping the bag until every drop was gone.

"You believe in destiny?" Shay asked.

"I believed that I wasn't safe to be around. That anyone I loved would die if they were around me. I believed that I was meant for a solitary life. Then I met you." Jed was staring, he couldn't help it. "Something led us to meet. It had to be destiny."

"Maybe luck?"

"I do have considerable luck." Jed smiled as he tore open the pack of freeze-dried ice cream. "Chocolate?"

Shay nodded and he broke off a piece and held it to her mouth.

Shay's lips touched his fingertips.

Jed made a noise deep in his throat. "This is going to be a long ride."

THIRTY-FIVE

THE THING IS, WHEN YOU MAKE A DEAL WITH A crossroads Demon, you're rarely ever allowed to die and stay dead. Clyburn was dragged down into that hole the four Demons climbed out of at the ranch. He'd promised his soul to Hell and Hell was going to collect. Souls were important; they gave power to whomever sat on the throne. A deal became a transfer of souls upon death. When the crossroads Demon died by Jed's hand, Clyburn took its place. There had to be balance, after all.

Clyburn's corpse twitched and jerked and after his heart started beating again, he took a few breaths. His eyes flashed open. He was no longer on the Dunn ranch, he was near it. A thinning veil was the only obstacle. Clyburn's hand broke through the soil outside the gates of the ranch and he crawled out of the ground with purpose.

"Out of the eater will come something to eat. And out of the strong will come something sweet." Clyburn smiled and held out a dusky hand with long necrotic fingernails. One thing was missing: the golden ring and bracelet of the Crossroads Demon. "My precious," Clyburn said, anger and hunger in his black eyes.

Clyburn sniffed the air. There was no one alive at the ranch.

Everything was dead. Clyburn licked his lips as he turned toward the road. He sniffed again, smelled the trace of Shay that was fading fast.

Clyburn took to the road, dropping down to all fours like a bloodhound on the hunt, his elbows and knees bent awkwardly. He ran after Shay's trail.

-The End-

EMBRACE THE NIGHT

ONE

Shay wasn't one to believe in ghosts but she couldn't shake the feeling that someone was watching her.

Gooseflesh rose on her arms and the back of her neck, and it wasn't from the water she was washing in. Jed wasn't far away–he rarely was-but Shay took some time for privacy by the cold mountain stream. She didn't want to call out to him like a fearful child. From her periphery she momentarily saw a wavering figure in white, and then it was gone. She told herself it was nothing then turned and found Nero stepping onto the riverbank.

"Hey, boy," Shay wrapped herself in a blanket and walked toward the black stallion. "It's been a while." Shay stroked Nero's face.

They hadn't seen Nero since the last night they'd spent in Montana while Jed healed enough to travel. That had been several days ago. Jed and Shay had traveled through most of Idaho, sticking close to the National Forests where rest stops and stores were present but the population wasn't. They'd driven past Boise National Forest at midnight and avoided most of the dead wandering out of the towns and cities. Jed had been correct; the dead were headed west, toward California. They'd seen them moving in herds like a cattle drive without a cowboy. The largest of the zombie horde wasn't far from Fort Bragg. Jed had a plan to travel south to avoid them, intercepting Sparrow before it got too dangerous.

Jed and Shay were making their way through a portion of Oregon that was mostly uninhabited; there wasn't much to see besides foothills and the prairies and the mountains in the distance. It was scenic at least. The backdrop to their travels didn't force one to dwell on the fact that the dead were walking and biting.

Shay was surprised she didn't see Nero as they drove. She figured that he'd found some other route, maybe one with wild horses so he wasn't lonely. It's all Shay could hope for her beloved friend.

"I miss you," Shay said as she stroked Nero's flank and noticed how shiny his coat had become now that he was living free. She hoped he'd found happiness in the fresh air and open fields and had recovered from what they'd endured at the ranch in Montana.

Nero huffed and rubbed his head against her shoulder before drinking from the stream.

Shay dressed in clean clothes then gathered her belongings. She paused, finding a small ring with a blue stone tucked between the rocks at the bank of the stream. These days, money was no good most places but a ring could be a wager. Shay tucked it in her pocket, then went to find Jed.

"Don't be a stranger," she told Nero with the wave of her hand.

Two

Clyburn followed the fading scent of Shay across the Montana foothills. He didn't care to hide his hideous form of a man running on all fours, elbows and knees bent at awkward angles. His claws tapped on the crumbling asphalt of the road. He leapt over broken down cars, agile as a panther. Being a Crossroads Demon, Clyburn was nothing more than a shadow in the periphery to a human on the Earthen plane. One moment he was there, the next he was a figment of their imagination; an errant shadow of a bird flying overhead, the whisper of a heavy tree branch in the wind. Nothing, apparently. Clyburn moved swiftly with ease through the Earthen plane, undisturbed since the balance was off. The Veil separating the realms was thinner than ever now that a Hellion walked the Earthen plane.

Clyburn stopped in the road, sniffed the pile of ashes that were once a punishing Angel. There was a drop of Shay's blood. Clyburn licked it off the asphalt, tilted his nose to the sky and sniffed. She'd backtracked. Clyburn went off running and fueled by the drop of Shay's blood, he ran faster.

Stopping at a fork in the road, Clyburn smelled Shay in both directions. Humans were creatures of habit. And Shay-baby knew where she belonged: on the ranch. Clyburn figured she changed her mind, left that abomination Jed and went home.

He wanted her. He wanted the shiny dangle of the Crossroads Demon ring and bracelet. The old gold was ancient, powerful, his. He'd kill Jed for taking it. He'd kill Jed for taking Shay.

"Precious," Clyburn grumbled as he missed the feel of it on his wrist even though he'd never touched it before ascending. Jed had cut it off the previous Demon and ran off with it. It belonged on Clyburn's hand. It was *his*.

He leapt over fallen trees two at a time and veered into the forests of the foothills to hide his shadow from the sunlight that broke the cloud cover. He slid under the chain that crossed a hidden driveway and slowed his pace.

Clyburn prowled, hunted. He stuck to the shadows as he walked down the driveway. He wanted to surprise them, shock them; he wanted to consume them. The crossbreed abomination would be first. Clyburn licked his lips, imagining the taste of sweet meat, imagining the crunch of magic-filled bones. Yes, he would eat Jed first. But Shay, she would be a treat to be savored. She would display nicely at his hovel in Hell. He thought about the chains he could lock her in, the table he could strap her to. His filthy body hardened at thoughts of Shay at his mercy. He'd had thoughts of her like that since the moment he met her at that dive bar near Colstrip. She was easy, innocent, and followed his lead that night. Then she played hard to get. Clyburn knew better. He knew she craved his hard body just as he craved her softness. He'd make her see. He'd show her. Shay was his.

Clyburn stopped, dropped low to the ground, and watched the clearing ahead of him. There was a shack but nothing more. Fresh tire tracks in the dirt driveway led Clyburn to believe that they had been there. He walked closer, unafraid. Her scent was strong and it led him to a tree near a bubbling stream. Strips of cloth hung from a branch. Clyburn ripped them down and smelled them. Jed's scent was strong but Shay's was there. He examined the stream and tire tracks under the tree. They'd been there then left.

Clyburn cursed himself for assuming she'd gone home. He took the wrong path where the road bisected. She wasn't going home, she was still leaving.

Clyburn snarled and roared. He dug his claws into the dirt, using purchase in the soil as a launching pad and took off.

THREE

"Do you believe in ghosts?" Shay asked Jed as he drove a winding, empty road.

Jed gave her a hard look. "Ghosts are rarely ghosts." He bit the inside of his cheek, preparing himself for what she was about to say. He'd warned her to tell him when she saw something strange. She was new to his world. Things that'd seemed normal rarely were. They held a deeper meaning, sometimes a darker meaning or message that something was coming.

"What did you see?" he asked.

Shay thumbed behind them. "Back at that stream I thought I saw a white figure. But then Nero was there."

"Did it say anything?" Jed asked.

"Not that I heard."

"How long did you see it for?"

"Just a second. I think." Shay rubbed her arms, remembering the feeling of being watched as she bathed.

Jed tapped his fingers on the steering wheel and chose his next words carefully. He didn't want to scare Shay. She'd probably punch him in the throat if he ever appeared threatening. He still had thoughts of her stabbing that Angel in the chest and killing him. Jed never wanted her to turn that wrath on him. He took a cleansing breath and slowed the Jeep so he could look at her.

"One second is enough to bring death to us both." Jed touched her hand. "If it happens again, I need to know right then."

Shay nodded, feeling like an idiot. She reminded herself that the world was different now. Nothing would be the same. She didn't want to be making mistakes like that night with Clyburn. Shay swallowed hard. She'd never get over that guilt.

"It's okay."

"This is all new to me." Shay touched the tattoos on Jed's wrist with her free hand. "Childlike fears and weird feelings; I've learned to ignore them."

"That is the way of the Earthen plane." He rubbed her hand, soothing her. He knew he needed to stop because touching her too much brought thoughts of other things, other needs and desires that he would not burden Shay with right now. She needed time to heal and learn. She needed time to accept her new reality or change her mind. Jed didn't want to let her go, but a life with him would be dangerous and he'd warned her. She could change her mind at any time, Jed reminded himself daily.

"Tell me about Nero," Jed said as he accelerated the Jeep again. "I didn't see him while we were parked."

Shay smiled, and Jed didn't miss the way her eyes lit up at seeing her horse again. "He was just there, drinking from the stream. Completely surprised me. He must be learning stealth moves from those wild horses."

Jed read the road sign for California as they passed Silver Lake. He turned onto Route 97 and drove south.

Jed didn't pretend to be an expert on horses or how they snuck up on people, but he hoped Shay would see Nero again since it brought her happiness. After all that had happened, that was all he could wish for her.

"Oh look." Shay pointed to a sign. "There's a diner nearby." She patted her stomach. "I could really go for some greasy diner food. We could stop and see if they have French toast."

"No." Jed shook his head.

"Why not?"

"I'm never eating French toast again."

"Why?" Shay asked.

"I want nothing tethered to the memory of French toast besides that first moment I saw you."

"Well, ain't that the sweetest thing a guy has ever said to me?" Shay rested her chin on her hand and batted her eyes at him exaggeratedly. "To forever taint a man's desire for French toast. I never thought I had it in me."

Jed laughed.

Shay pointed toward the tree line. "There she is."

Jed looked. One second there was a woman in a white dress, staring. The next second she was gone.

"Is that what you saw by the river?" Jed asked.

"Yeah. That's her. Weird that it's twice now."

The sign for the diner came again.

Jed decided he could go for some greasy diner food as well. He really wanted a bottomless mug of hot coffee.

"Look," Shay pointed to the window, "they still have electricity and there's people here."

Jed turned in to the parking lot of the diner, parked the Jeep and turned off the ignition.

"Yes. I hope they have grilled cheese." Shay was tucking her bugout bag behind the passenger seat.

"If anything is sketchy, we are out," Jed warned. "I mean *anything*."

The diner was running like normal. The dead hadn't ruined this area, yet. Jed wondered if he should warn them that the horde was coming, probably by next week, and they should prepare to get out.

"Tell me if you see that woman in white again. I don't care if you're in the bathroom, Shay. It's more than a coincidence." Jed flipped through his spell book and racked his brain for anything he'd read in the Peabody Library all those years ago that might apply to the woman Shay had seen twice now.

"I'll tell ya," Shay promised as she got out of the Jeep and closed the door.

Jed held the diner door open for Shay and they were greeted by a smiling waitress snapping gum. "Just you all?" she asked.

"Two," Shay said.

"I got a window seat over here for you." The waitress led them to a window booth. Jed would have preferred the corner booth where he could get a better view of the room and not have people at his back, but he tried to tell himself to relax. This wasn't the Lame Deer Casino. He didn't smell death seeping from the walls. Jed took a laminated menu from the waitress.

"Can I get you both drinks?"

Jed motioned to Shay.

"I'll have a diet coke," Shay said.

"Coffee and a water, please." Jed touched the napkin that was wrapped around the silverware.

Shay noticed he was looking for something and leaned closer to him. "I think we're safe here. This doesn't look like a place that would house Angels or Demons."

"You'd be surprised," Jed said with a half-raise of the corner of his mouth.

The waitress brought their drinks and took their orders. Shay got the grilled cheese with fries. Jed ordered a cheeseburger with chips.

"If you want, we have a motel out back. Hot water and soft beds." The waitress looked at Shay. "The little things that help us feel human."

Shay turned to Jed. "A hot shower sounds nice."

The waitress snapped her gum. "Janice over there was a stylist before the dead started walking, if you're itching for a trim or scalp massage." She pointed at a woman with purple hair who was counting money on the countertop.

Shay touched her hair that was tied up in a messy bun. "New hair might be nice."

"I like your hair," Jed said.

"I look boring next to you." Shay ran a finger over his tattooed arm.

"No." Jed shook his head. "You're definitely not boring."

"Let's stay the night." Shay smiled wide. "We are almost to California. Just one last night with some normalcy."

Jed couldn't deny her, doubted he'd ever be able to. He wanted nothing more than a smile on her face. Shay had lost a lot these past few days. She'd fought for their lives and dragged Jed's lifeless body to safety. He'd give her the moon if he could. He looked down at his hands, tapped his fingertips together and sparks zipped between the pads.

"Maybe I could give you a haircut?" Jed suggested.

Shay laughed. "No thanks, cowboy. Leave that to the professionals."

When they finished eating, Shay went to speak to Janice about a haircut and Jed reserved the motel room. They met at the front door.

"Janice said she can do it now." Shay pulled the elastic holding her bun.

Jed leaned to the side and eyed the woman.

Shay smacked his arm. "Stop. Not everyone is a threat."

"Sure. Room twelve." Jed said with a dull tone and dangled the room key. "I'll go check out the room and meet you back here."

Shay kissed him on the cheek before turning around to follow Janice to the salon attached to the diner. It was a unique combination but Jed didn't dwell on it. Little towns like this typically had strip malls with random businesses. A diner and a salon didn't seem like such a bizarre combo after some things he'd seen on his travels. Tattoo shop and a comic shop. Massages and a dentist. It actually seemed a little normal here. Jed figured it was good for Shay to have a little normalcy.

Room twelve had two double beds and a tiny bathroom. Jed

checked it over for markings. He searched for satchels of bones, piles of sand or salt, anything out of the ordinary. There was nothing. He breathed a sigh of relief, pulled a Sharpie out of his pocket, and drew a rune of protection into the top center of the doorframe.

He added a rune over each window and the bathroom door before heading back to the diner for more coffee and to wait for Shay.

He asked for the corner booth this time since the lunch rush was over.

The same waitress snapped her gum, nodded, and brought him to the table. Jed grabbed a newspaper off the newsstand as he passed.

"You still hungry?" She had a smile that led him to believe she'd give him more than food if he asked. It wasn't new. It also wasn't desired. His mother had used his face to get plenty of money and help them survive when he was a kid. He knew what his face could get him, besides killed.

"Just coffee," Jed said with an empty smile and a nod as he opened the newspaper and began reading. He didn't want her to get any ideas that he might be interested. He wasn't.

The mug was chipped but the coffee fresh. Jed turned the pages of the newspaper, stopping when he saw an article about missing children. He continued reading.

"Sad story," the waitress tapped the paper as she refilled his mug. "That there is Jennifer Asheworth. Didn't live too far from here. Used to bring the kids in every Thursday for lunch."

"You knew them?" Jed asked.

"As much as a waitress can. Gave the kids free milk." She rested a hand on her hip and shook her head in despair. "Damn shame someone could kill a single mother like that and steal the kids. Especially in times like these."

Jed looked at the pictures in the paper. "They were kidnapped?"

"Some say poor Jennifer haunts these parts." The waitress popped a bubble. "You want some pie or something? All this coffee is going to give you the jitters."

The last bit was such a redirection of their conversation that Jed stared in disbelief for a moment before he said, "Sure."

"We got apple, pecan, or peach."

"Apple."

"Ice cream?"

"No thanks." Jed finished reading the article about the missing kids. He checked the date on the paper. It was a few weeks old. It did not surprise him it was old, news was scarce in all formats. Kinda hard to get the news out when everyone is too busy dying or defending themselves.

She brought him a slice of pie. It tasted sour. He slid the plate away and drank his coffee.

———

JED WAS ENGROSSED in the newspaper when Shay walked up to him. She stood at his elbow for a few seconds but all he did was hold out his coffee mug.

Shay took it out of his hand and set it aside. She ran her finger from his wrist up to the crook of his arm.

He was even more attractive like this; reading, drinking coffee, totally engrossed in something besides staying alive. So normal. Shay wondered if he'd ever really relaxed in his life.

When her fingertip made it to the sensitive skin of his inner elbow, Jed turned his head quickly and focused on her.

"Shay?" He was staring like he was seeing her for the first time.

"I might not have a blue aura like you, but now I have some blue. We match. A little." Shay touched her hair. Blowtorch blue was what Janice had called the color. "Do you like it?"

Jed scooted to the side and pulled her down next to him into the booth. "It suits you." He touched her hair. It was shorter than before, shoulder length but still manageable if she needed to put it up.

Shay smiled, warmth filling her center. She wasn't looking for acceptance. She'd change her hair if Jed liked it or not. But the way he was looking at her and the way his arm tightened around her back led her to believe she could dye her hair gray and he'd still be enamored with her.

"Hey, look at this." Jed directed her attention to the newspaper.

Shay read the article about Jennifer Asheworth and her kidnapped children.

"Is this the ghost woman?" Shay asked. "The lady in white?"

"Could be."

Suddenly, a yawn overtook Shay. She covered her mouth.

"You're tired." Jed motioned for her to get up. "Let's get some rest. Checkout is ten in the morning."

Jed was glad the diner and motel took money and hadn't switched to bartering. He didn't want to give up their supplies.

They stopped at the Jeep and got out their bags before heading to the room.

FOUR

JENNIFER ASHEWORTH WAS A SINGLE MOTHER DEALT A
life of hard work and sacrifice, devoted to her children and the
Roman Catholic Church. She'd survived most days on donations
and the good will of others. She'd raised her children modestly and
they found happiness in warm meals and clean beds. It was all
Jennifer could have ever asked for; a simple life in the mountains.

She hadn't planned to navigate life alone. It was simply the cards
she was dealt. She'd had love, but it had wilted and rotted like an
over-watered rosebush. It was a hard pill to swallow, the day Dan had
left her alone with the children. He'd left the state for opportunity
and promised he'd send money. It never came. But, he'd given her the
greatest gift, her children. Sarah and Jacob were enough for Jennifer
and she poured her whole life into raising them. Many days were
hard, but worthwhile.

When a handsome man started sitting near her in Sunday
church, she felt the way he gazed at her and smiled when she walked
by. It had been so long since someone had paid attention to her. It
had been years since Dan left. She didn't say no when the rugged
man named Alastor asked her to dinner, and even invited her chil-

dren. It was a whirlwind romance that ended in an unfortunate event near a valley stream.

That was the day Jennifer learned no woman was safe and her children even less so. Handsome men bring lies disguised as promised and unrequited danger.

Five men with red eyes came from the tree line. Fast. Dangerous. A dark energy seeped from them like nothing Jennifer had ever experienced.

"No!" Jennifer screamed as two of them grabbed hold of her little girl. Alastor gripped Jennifer and shook her, but a mother's strength is not to be reckoned with. She kicked Alastor in the crotch and ran for little Sarah, all the while screaming for Jacob to run away to safety.

There were too many of them. Sarah wasn't strong enough but she still fought, all the while wondering how her God could allow this to happen. Alastor grabbed Jennifer by the hair, kicked her feet out from under her, and held her under the cold water of the stream.

The last sound she heard were the screams of Sarah and Jacob as the men took them away.

Her soul never left the Earthen plane. She couldn't leave her children. She searched the forest, guided by their cries in the night. She followed the red-eyed men back to their camp and promised herself she'd destroy them, just as they'd destroyed her.

Jennifer tried to leave clues for the Sheriff. She followed the investigators assigned to her case and left bits of information. Nothing stuck. Everything was looked over and forgotten. Jennifer soon realized that nobody cared and justice would never be served. She'd spent plenty of time trying to be seen but no one saw her until that day Shay found her missing ring in the stream.

FIVE

Shay dreamed of Nero racing across the foothills of Montana, kicking up dirt as he ran faster and faster, blasting through wildflower clusters, petals flying everywhere. There were wild horses trailing him. Then there was snow. A whiteout. She couldn't see anything but snowflakes. She shivered and couldn't stop, it was so cold.

Shay woke up, the chill of the room seeping into her bones. She glanced at the other bed. Jed insisted on giving her space. If he were next to her, she wouldn't be cold right now. She thought of climbing into the other bed and snuggling up next to him. She wanted nothing more than to touch him. It was hard going throughout the day without touching him. She was drawn to him and Shay couldn't help but think there was more besides his good looks and height that drew her to him. He had a good heart. She knew that. Suddenly her mind was filled with thoughts of that night at the ranch when the Demons came and killed Momma, then when Daddy turned and she jammed a knife into his skull. Shay felt the tears welling in her eyes and swallowed hard. She hadn't cried about losing her family since they left the ranch that day. Now that it had come to the forefront of her mind, she couldn't stop thinking about it. Grief swelled in her heart and she wiped at her eyes.

She glanced at Jed sleeping. She should go to him. But then, something white caught her eye. She saw movement near the door. Jed had used his marker to ward the room and lined the window and door with salt. Still, something glowed outside and illuminated around the doorframe.

Unable to sleep or ignore the light, Shay slid out of bed. Drawn by more than curiosity, she stepped into her boots, turned the lock on the motel room door, and went outside.

Shay shivered as the winter chill met her skin. Wishing she'd grabbed a jacket, she looked down and saw the ring she'd found by the water on her finger.

I don't remember putting that on, she thought. She'd tucked the ring into her pocket near the water. She never put it on her finger and she wasn't sure how it had gotten there now.

"Whatcha doing out here in the dark, little lady?" There was once voice, but five men.

Fuck, Shay thought to herself. Bad odds. She'd left her gun inside on the nightstand.

"Je–" before she could get out a scream, a hand clamped over her mouth. Shay struggled. She kicked and wriggled her body, trying to get loose, but the man holding her had an unnatural strength.

They carried Shay to a black van parked at the road. She kicked and bit and scratched but couldn't get free. Panic flooded her as her arms were jerked behind her back and tied with rough rope. It tore her skin. She struggled as hands forced her to the floor of the van. One boot stomped on the small of her back. A blindfold was stretched tight across her eyes. This wasn't good. Panic started filling her chest. It reminded her of all those times Clyburn trapped her in the root cellar or the barn or the garden shed. This was worse. Much worse.

The last thing she thought was she didn't want to die like this. She'd barely gotten to experience life outside of the ranch and Colstrip.

———

JED JERKED AWAKE. Something was wrong.

"Shay," he called. Her bed was empty, her boots gone from near the door. "No."

Jed ran out of the motel room, barefoot and shirtless. "Shay!" he shouted. There was nothing outside, just the chill of winter that had arrived, the small snowflakes that were falling from the sky, and an eerie silence. The clouds broke and moonlight illuminated the disturbed snow in the parking lot. Jed followed the footprints to the road. She'd struggled and fought. Of course she did. This was Shay, the toughest cowgirl he'd ever met. He knew she'd give hell to whoever took her.

Jed's fingers twitched and tapped and bent like a row of pyramids. He whispered words that sounded like the darkest of promises. They sounded like *murder*. Slowly, an image appeared like a memory in the road. He saw a black van. The five men. And Shay, kicking one of them in the jaw.

That's my girl, Jed thought as he noticed there was something off about one man. He was tall, shadows danced along his face as though his skin was struggling to maintain its form. Jed saw the glint of sharp teeth, the flash of a red eye. Sickness tore at his gut. The van drove away.

There was a wavering figure against the snowscape across the road. It was the woman in white. She pointed down the road while staring at Jed. Jed nodded in understanding. Jennifer's ghost was going to help him.

Jed returned to the motel room to collect their belongings. He threw it all haphazardly in the back of the Jeep. He started the engine and took off, following the tire tracks in the snow until the snowfall became so heavy that the tracks disappeared.

Ahead, he saw the red glow of brake lights. He turned off the Jeep's headlights and trailed the van in darkness.

SIX

THEY TIED SHAY UP LIKE A DOG ON A STAKE. THERE WERE
three men testing the strength of the chain that was wrapped so
tightly around her waist that it pinched her skin. She should have
never left the motel room. She should have closed her eyes or crawled
into bed with Jed and gone back to sleep. That would have been a
much better scenario than the one she was in right now. Shay tried
not to let her thoughts run off. Despair would get her nowhere. She
needed a plan. She needed these men to know that she was a difficult
prey, maybe even make them regret they'd stolen her in the night.

A man with an unkempt beard and Carhart coat walked toward
her. Shay backed up, until the chain jerked taut. It was the ringleader.
She could tell by the sound of his voice. She'd heard him giving
orders in the van. There was something about him though, the way
the hollows of his cheeks seemed to change in the light. It made her
uneasy.

"Like what you see?" he asked with a leering smile.

"You're fucking disgusting," Shay spat at the bearded man.

"Just keeping humanity alive." He tossed a bottle of water within
her reach. "Someone has to, why not us?"

Shay looked to her left and saw smaller tents that appeared empty. The leaves and snow weren't disrupted. A sickening feeling filled her gut when she noticed a child's shoe near the base of a tree.

Something terrible happened here. Something terrible would continue to happen here. She could feel it—an uneasiness in her gut, a vibe that was menacing encompassed the camp.

The bearded man walked away and helped the others by adding logs to a fire and setting a large pot to the heat. He gave more orders and the other men went off and did what he commanded.

At least they could boil water. Shay wondered if they'd feed her. She hadn't eaten since the grilled cheese at the diner the day before. It had been a full day without food. Shay shifted and sat cross-legged. She grabbed the bottle of water, twisted off the cap, and drank it. She was thirsty and her throat ached from shouting at the men. At least she got a good kick out and probably broke the guy's jaw. She watched them cook, then watched them eat from the open door of her tent. They didn't share.

Night came. Shay was freezing. She shuddered and pulled her arms into her thin shirt. The awful sleeping bag they'd given her smelled like someone else's sweat. Shay wasn't too proud. She knew the cold could kill her. She'd crawled into the sleeping bag and put it over her head. She hated she couldn't zip the tent fully closed because of the chain secured around her waist. These men were idiots. They didn't have the slightest idea how to survive out here. Her daddy, Nicholas, would roll over in his shallow grave if he saw this mess.

Shay's body ached from the fighting and the shivering. Rocks underneath the tent didn't help. She could smell the fire in the center of camp and gave up on the cold tent. She opened the zipper, dragged the sleeping bag outside, and got as close to the fire as her chain would allow.

There was one man keeping watch. His beard was red and eyes dark. A shotgun was propped against his knee.

Shay didn't think he deserved a conversation, so she focused on the burning coals and was thankful for the little bit of heat that made it to her. Curiosity won, though. She wanted to know what she was up against. Nicholas had always told her humanity would turn to shit pretty quickly, and it appeared to have done just that.

"You have children here," Shay said.

"Had." The man closest to her made a face like he couldn't care less. "We'll have more. They're worth a lot." He eyed her up and down. "Worth more than you."

"What do you do with them?" Shay sipped her water.

"Sell them. If they make it."

"If?"

"Keeping kids alive is harder than you think. Haven't found a woman to help us." The man watched her. "But now we have you."

Shay shuddered. These sick fucks. She knew she'd been lucky her whole life. She had parents who loved her and made sure she was safe. Shay's stomach turned. She'd seen newspapers and missing persons' reports her entire life. Too frequently children went missing. She couldn't help but wonder if this group of men with their peculiar leader had been doing this for a long time.

SEVEN

JED DROVE FASTER. FEELING THE TIRES SLIPPING ON THE snow coated road, he let his foot off the gas in hope to gain traction.

Not tonight, he told himself as he eased the Jeep away from the shoulder.

He could barely see the vehicle's taillights. The snow was coming down faster and the van was nothing more than a shadow, the taillights a pinprick of red. Jed accelerated down a stretch of road that was straight. His heart started beating harder, adrenaline was coursing through his body as he got closer. Then, suddenly, it was gone.

No, Jed thought to himself. He went faster; the wheels sliding, unable to grip asphalt through the layer of slick snow. A sign came into view. There was a turn. Jed let off the gas. The tire tracks from the van had taken a sharp left. Jed turned. He could feel the Jeep sliding. This wasn't good.

The Jeep skidded. Traction control kicked on and the tires made a staccato motion trying to grip the road. It didn't work. The Jeep slid off the road, hit an embankment and rolled.

———

JED'S NECK and shoulders ached. His head felt full of fog. He blinked a few times, realizing he was hanging upside down by his seatbelt. Jed groaned, one arm searching for the buckle release. He hit it and braced for impact as he fell.

The windshield shattered. Cold air and snow blew into the Jeep. Jed was careful where he dragged his body, avoiding the glass shards. It was pitch black outside. He glanced at his watch. It was nearly four in the morning. He'd been out for at least two hours. Two hours was a long time for the van to get away. They could be in another state right now. Anger flooded Jed's body. He punched the passenger head-rest. This is why he didn't involve anyone. They weren't safe. Next time, he'd tie her up. He bit his cheek imagining Shay tied to the bed with that blue hair spread over the pillow like a crown. Damn. No. No. Next time he'd ward the door so it wouldn't open without him.

Jed crawled to the back of the Jeep and dug through the supplies. He found some wipes in the bugout bag and used them to clean the blood off his face. Jed could feel tiny scrapes on his skin. He needed a moment to think, to plan.

Jed lay on his back, hands gripping his hair. He needed to find Shay but knew it would be pointless in this weather and cold. He could only hope whoever took her was keeping her warm. He would find them.

Jed thought of the woman in white. There weren't many who believed in magic and supernatural lore, at least nobody he came across. Except for the Crow family. Jed considered them. The grandmother seemed to be the most knowledgeable of the bunch. She'd said that she had her own magic. He recalled passing a sign for Hoopa territory. Maybe the Crow family had connections. Jed hadn't asked a soul for help since Declan died. He didn't like the feeling of depending on others. Actually, he hated the feeling.

Jed rolled his shoulders, relaxed his body, and prepared for the astral projection. He had to be careful, too much magic would bring attention. It would ignite his aura and while most humans couldn't see any difference in him, others would. Angels would see the blue from the sky and dive-bomb him. Demons would see the glow through the thinning veil and climb out of the ground after him. Jed's magic was a blessing and a curse, but also a necessity.

His fingers tapped in spell casting. He spoke words that sounded like an echo through time, like a whale song from under the deepest depths of the ocean. He closed his eyes, felt his body lighten, and when he opened them again he was standing in the backyard of the Crow residence.

Jed wasn't his whole form; he was something lighter, transparent. A ghost to the unknowing.

Grandmother Crow was rocking on the back porch. The squeaking of old wood paused. "What do you want, Allegewi?"

Jed paused for a moment noticing the blue light illuminating her. Jed had heard her saying some called her healing magic and now he wondered if she was just like him. A zapping noise brought realization it was just a blue-bug zapper light hanging from the porch railing.

"You can see me?" he asked.

"Of course."

"Can the others?"

"Possibly."

Grandmother Crow had the usual suspicious curiosity but she was unshaken at his appearance. "Why are you here?" She stood and moved closer, inspecting him. "You're not whole."

"I am elsewhere," Jed said. "I need help. Someone has kidnapped Shay."

Grandmother Crow wasn't one for words. Her expression was murderous. "How did that happen?"

Jed explained only what he knew. There was the ghost of Jennifer Asheworth haunting Shay and the van he was chasing.

"You should have left her with us. She'd be safer here," Grandmother Crow said.

"She wanted to come with me," Jed said. "Did you know her family is dead?"

"Yes." Grandmother Crow crossed her arms and shivered as she looked off into the distance. Her lips pressed into a thin line before she focused on him again and spoke. "There is something dark running through these parts and it's not the dead walking."

"There were Demons," Jed warned her. "I killed them."

"I sense there are more."

"There always are."

"As for the ghost. You must burn the bones or personal items and the haunting will stop. Release their souls."

"And the men who took Shay?"

"There must be a connection. That would be why she chose Shay."

"Why would she choose Shay? Why not me?"

Grandmother Crow smiled. "You'd not help a ghost. You'd blast a cannon of salt through its center and move on."

Jed knew she was right. He wouldn't have helped. He would have kept moving and minded his own business. "I need help finding them."

Grandmother Crow's gaze bore into Jed's soul. "You need little help, Allegewi. Unless it is protection from my son Hosa who still speaks of leaving home to hunt you down."

Jed made a face. "He's not the first."

"Go, Allegewi," Grandmother Crow waved. "The ghost will help you. Go back to your body," she waved, "before something dire happens to it."

Jed whispered a spell that returned him to his body. He inhaled a deep, strangled breath. His eyes focused. He was not alone.

EIGHT

NERO RUBBED HIS FLANK AGAINST A TREE TRUNK. THE scratch from the Crossroads Demon had become inflamed and wept black fluid. He rubbed the area around the scratch, draining the fluid before walking into the nearby lake to soak. The water was icy and felt good on the wound. Nero drank from the clear water. He'd crossed the veil again. The moon was less ochre here. On the other side of the veil, Nero noticed everything was darker. The shadows, the creatures, the dirt. He didn't think he'd like it there, but both realms were beginning to feel alike. Darkness was spilling over.

Shay was on this side. He could feel her. Their bond was stronger. That other thing was on this side of the veil too. Nero knew Clyburn had turned into something evil. He'd seen the man change, he'd seen Clyburn searching for Shay where they'd rested at the stream. Nero had watched Clyburn, then followed him.

A scream tore through the night. Nero's ears flicked upright. The voice was far away but he knew who it was. He felt it in his bones.

Shay.

Nero walked out of the lake and shook. He felt the pull through their bond. She was far away, further than he'd wanted.

Nero took off at a full gallop toward the scream. He ran through the night, past empty roads and frozen foothills. He leapt over downed trees and crashed cars blocking his path. The sun rose, the sun set. His hooves left imprints in the snow melt and mud. He didn't eat or drink; he ran as fast as he could.

Suddenly, their connection flickered. Nero slowed and stomped his hooves. Eyes wide, he took in his surroundings. There was a snarl nearby, the smell of a creature that used to be a man. Nero focused across the prairie.

Clyburn was there.

If the stallion knew anything, it was that Clyburn was still hunting Shay as well.

Darkness consumed Nero as a desire to protect Shay became overwhelming. Something like a roar rose out of Nero as he galloped toward Clyburn, ready to kill.

There was another scream in the distance.

Shay!

Clyburn turned and ran toward Shay's voice. The movement was eerie and rapid.

Nero followed.

NINE

Jed's eyes finally opened and he took in a deep breath of cold air. There was something about his soul leaving his body that just felt wrong. The whole time, he had a feeling of detachment, emptiness, and an eagerness to return quickly. He'd only used the spell a handful of times but never to travel so far for so long. He didn't like it and desired to never do it again.

The sun was coming up. Jed was disappointed in himself that he'd taken so long to travel to Grandmother Crow. He stretched, cold and weary from draining his magic with the apparition spell. He was rusty with some of the magic that Declan had taught him.

Jed saw bone white feet and legs beyond the broken windshield. Jennifer's ghost was there. She was waiting patiently.

Grandmother Crow was right. He would have blasted the ghost with salt and moved on. But now he needed Jennifer. He needed her to get Shay back.

Jed listened for any noise, rolled to the side, grabbed his bag, and crawled toward the broken windshield. He wanted to take a bugout bag but it would slow him down. Jed had his spell book and everything he needed in his leather bag. He'd lasted this long with minimal supplies.

The snow was past his ankles. Jed wasn't prepared for winter and hoped the snow would stop for the next few weeks. Dealing with the chill in the air of pending winter differed from dealing with full-blown winter. Jed dusted off his jeans and shirt.

"You know where she is?" Jed asked Jennifer.

She turned, her pale form blending with the snow. She pointed the way.

He shouldered his bag and headed down the road. Jed was tired from the spell he'd used to visit the Crow residence. He wished he had time to rest, but every moment Shay was in the kidnapper's hands was one moment closer to her death. A bitterness boiled in his stomach. He knew this would happen. He had to make Shay see she was better off without him.

TEN

CLYBURN HAD ONLY STOPPED RUNNING ONCE TO FILL HIS gut on a nest of squirrels. After, he followed the faint trail left by Shay. He'd run across mountains, foothills, and the western plains. Clyburn couldn't move as fast as the Jeep Jed and Shay were driving, but he could almost catch up each time they stopped. He came across Shay's strongest scent at a stream close to the road. Clyburn paced and inhaled deeply, doing his best to soak up every molecule of her scent that remained.

"Precious," Clyburn murmured to himself as he stood up straight, looking more man and less animal as he inspected the land around the stream, looking for clues. He wanted Shay, and he wanted the golden ring and bracelet. It all belonged to him. They could've dropped it. They wouldn't know how important it was to him. He turned over rocks and dug frantically at the pebbled stream, pausing when he found nothing. Clyburn scratched his head. Or maybe they knew, and that's why they took it. It wasn't here.

Sharp claws dug into the soil. Clyburn had the desire to draw an X and invite up some friends to help. He remembered what happened at the ranch and what the abomination half-breed did. Clyburn wanted to end Jed. Taking Shay would be enough revenge.

Moonlight illuminated the prairie. Clyburn saw a dark glimmer in the distance. Darkness. It moved. Clyburn dropped to the ground once again, looking like a beast on all fours. Something was following him. He sniffed the crisp breeze and recognized the animal.

Eleven

THE SLAP ACROSS SHAY'S CHEEK STUNG. SHE PRODDED THE corner of her mouth with the tip of her tongue and tasted blood. Bastard.

Shay scrambled to her feet. She gripped the chain that hung from her waist and tested its weight. Her arms ached from fighting. Her body was cold and sore. She had too many bruises and scrapes to count. She'd gotten a few good hits in, but she was much smaller than the red bearded man. Brute was winning this fight, but Shay had one last trick up her sleeve.

He was close, shaking the sting out of his hand after hitting her. His back was to her ruined tent. The bastard had cut a hole in the side to surprise her. He wasn't expecting a fight, that's what she gave him. The scratch down the side of his face was bleeding. What Shay wouldn't do for her handgun or a heavy rope. Lord knows she'd rangled enough cows and horses. What was one stupid man to add to the mix? She was sure the cows and horses were smarter than Redbeard.

Shay swung the chain like a jump rope. Once, twice, three times before Redbeard noticed. Shay skipped to the side and swung, momentum looping the chain around his neck. Shay dropped to the ground and pulled tight. Redbeard fell, kicking at the frozen dirt and scratching at the chain around his neck.

"How do you like it, you fuck?" Shay spat out as she pulled the chain tighter. It jerked snugger around her waist as Redbeard struggled.

Redbeard yelled threats that were barely understandable as she crushed his windpipe. He rolled, twisting the chain and her arms. He grabbed her ankle and tugged, knocking her off balance. Shay rolled, her free ankle getting wrapped in the chain.

Redbeard still had a good grip on her other leg. His fingers were so tight she knew he'd leave bruises. Shay was cursing her shit luck as she rolled and scraped her tangled foot against Redbeard's knuckles.

The chain had loosened just enough for him to shout, "You bitch!"

That brought the cavalry. Suddenly, hands were on Shay, gripping her arms, throwing her back against the ground. A boot was at her neck, a large hand pulling her hair. The ringleader was wandering over, looking like he was annoyed.

Two men assisted Redbeard at getting untangled and to his feet. He rubbed his throat.

"What's going on here?" the ringleader asked.

Shay glared at Redbeard and struggled against the men holding her down. She was in a shit position on the ground like this and outnumbered. She was breathing heavy from the struggle and the boot on her throat.

The ringleader flicked his wrist and the men released her. "One girl did that to you?" he mocked Redbeard. "One little, pathetic girl. You're such a disappointment, Red. Get the fuck out of my face. All of you, move!"

Shay moved to her feet as the men left and scattered about the camp. Some went to the fire, others went to the cabins in the distance. Shay focused on the ripped tent. She'd prefer a cabin to sleeping on the cold ground. At least wooden walls would offer a little protection against these creeps.

"Sorry about that." The ringleader said as he inspected the ripped tent with the toe of his boot. "Wasn't supposed to happen."

Shay glared and tugged at the chain around her waist. She was calculating its length and judging if she could move fast enough to toss it around his neck. He wouldn't be too hard to strangle. The ringleader was a good bit taller than Redbeard, more muscular too. He'd probably put up a good fight. Shay didn't think too hard about it.

"Ah ah," the ringleader shook his finger at her. "Don't."

"Release me."

"Where would you go?" He walked closer. "It's dark. Cold. You're obviously frightened. If I released you into the night, who knows what could find you?" He flashed a smile and Shay was almost certain she saw sharp teeth. "A wolf, a bear maybe. Or something... darker."

Shay glared.

"I didn't properly introduce myself." He held out a hand. "Alastor."

"I'm not touching you." Shay seethed.

"That's your call." Alastor tucked his hands in his pockets, appearing nonchalant and unthreatening. Shay knew better. There was something not right about this man, from the shadows of his face to the sharp teeth she'd just seen. "I can help you with this transition."

"I'm not transitioning jack-shit."

Alastor chuckled. "You will." He took a deep breath and wandered the radius of where she'd been tied up. "If you want out of this set up, you'll transition. There's really no other option." He winked.

"To what?"

"One of us." Alastor said it so calmly, like Shay might know what the hell these men are.

"I refuse to kidnap children." Shay shook her head.

Alastor smiled. "You will help us. You have to."

"Nope."

Alastor moved quickly, just a few strides, and he was in Shay's space, his fingers gripping her chin and the chain near her hip. "I'd hate to see you turn into one of those walking corpses."

"I'm not afraid," Shay said, trying to move but she couldn't. Her body felt frozen in place. Fear prickled her spine and she couldn't look away from Alastor's black eyes.

"Your body tells me otherwise."

The chain snapped and fell away from Shay's hips. *Freedom!* Shay wanted to run but she couldn't. She felt frozen in place by some other force.

"Follow me," Alastor said as he released Shay's chin and began walking toward the cabin. "Since these men are so distracted by you, I'll have to keep you closer."

Shay followed him, against her will. Alastor walked her to the largest of the cabins and opened the door. Warmth greeted Shay. A roaring fire in a heating stove illuminated the corner of the cabin. There was furniture, a kitchenette, a separate bedroom, and a bathroom.

"Go," Alastor motioned to the fire as though it was the greatest gift ever given to her. "Get warm."

Shay moved past the man and dropped to her knees in front of the stove. She held her hands close to the heated glass. She didn't realize how cold she was after days of sleeping outside on the ground. Shay caught her reflection in the glass door of the stove. There was dirt on her face, her blue hair was disheveled, and leaves were tangled in the strands. She reached into her hair and began pulling out the leaves, crushing them in her free hand.

All she could think is she should have never left that motel room. Never. Tears stung her eyes. Shay hated the position she was in. Hated that it was her fault. There was something wrong with her to keep finding herself in these positions. She was stronger than this.

Smarter, too. She wiped tears off her face and smeared the dirt and blood down her cheeks.

"Don't be upset," Alastor said. "It will get better." He crossed the room and motioned to the bathroom. "When you're warm take a shower. There's clean clothing and towels on the counter."

Shay pressed her lips together and swallowed against her sore throat. She wondered how many women they'd done this to. How many families they'd ruined. Shay had thought the walking dead were bad. This ugliness was worse, and to think they'd been around since before the dead started rising. Alastor certainly wasn't all human, but the other men were, and they were participating in this willingly.

She glanced at Alastor, noticed the light from the flames made his face look less angled and devious. Shay closed her eyes, squeezed her handful of leaves, and focused on the crunch of them against her palm. She needed a plan now that she was free of the chain. Her stomach grumbled. She hadn't eaten in days. It was a distraction. Shay needed to focus and plan.

"I'll make you something to eat," Alastor said from the kitchenette. It sounded so normal, so nice and non-threatening. He was playing a game. "I bet you're hungry."

Shay could play too. Maybe if she could gain his trust, she could get free. Shay stood and walked toward the bathroom. "Thank you," she said as she closed the door.

The bathroom was small but at least there were walls between her and Alastor and the other men. She started the shower and let the crushed leaves from her hand fall into the nearby trash basket. Shay reached for the doorhandle to lock it, only to find there was no lock. Her stomach churned. She didn't like that. Anyone could walk in if they wanted.

Shay toyed with the ring on her finger, took it off and set it on the bathroom countertop. There was something about that ring.

Shay turned on the shower and waited. She watched the door handle intently, waiting for it to turn. She waited five minutes. Pans clattered from the kitchen on the other side of the thin wall.

"There's only about ten minutes of hot water," Alastor shouted. "Soon it will be cold as a mountain stream."

There was nothing worse than a cold shower–besides the situation Shay was currently in. She undressed and got in the shower.

The water swirling around her feet was brown with dirt. Shay had never been so filthy, not even after a week of cattle driving. She was quick to wash and wrap herself in a towel.

Shay glanced at her reflection. There were bruises on her neck and arms from the manhandling. Scratches lined her face. She tilted her chin, remembering the deep cut across her forehead that Jed had healed. These shouldn't scar but they'd leave marks on her pale skin for a few weeks once they healed.

There was a set of sweats on the countertop. Cheap and nondescript. Shay dried off and got dressed. The sweats were oversized but she was clean and warm and thankful to be out of that filthy tent.

She took a deep, calming breath and opened the door. This was nothing more than a game, a game that could save or end her life. Shay reminded herself that she'd done it before that night she ran off and met Clyburn at the bar. She'd seduced him and it was easy. She told herself that she could do this.

TWELVE

JED TRUDGED OVER CRUMBLING BLACKTOP AND THICK mud from the snow melt. He watched the sky and the shadows of the forest, waiting for something to surprise him. Nothing other than squirrels and birds came. He was thankful for that. Jed tapped his fingers together in exercise. He didn't want his fingers to freeze up from the cold. He wanted his joints nimble and ready.

Jed's mind wandered the further he walked. He worried about Shay and what was happening to her. Thoughts of his fuck ups brought memories and soon Jed relived his time with Declan all those years ago...

———

THEN

"Be gone with ya!" Declan shouted at the Demon.

The cloud roared and snapped, it undulated and twisted like a tornado. Thunderclap reverberated and drowned out Declan's voice.

Jed raised both hands and threw fire. "Run!" He shouted to Declan.

Declan rounded the dock and ran for the boat. "Hit the gas!"

Jed walked backward, but to get to the gas he'd have to stop throwing the fire. He shook his hands, dashed toward the gears, and accelerated. He ran back to the deck.

The boat was moving away from the dock, Declan was running full bore. Jed held out a hand and steadied himself.

Declan leapt, stopping midair as wicked jaws clamped down on his leg with a sickening crunch.

"No!" Jed screamed into the night.

Jed would never forget the look on Declan's face. The man smiled as his body hit the wooden dock. "I knew it would come one day." Declan's fingers tapped together and made a strange motion before the black cloud of teeth and talons consumed him.

Jed felt a bulge in his pocket as Declan vanished. He reached for it and pulled out Declan's spell book.

It filled Jed with anguish and hate as he strode to the engine room, pushed the boat into high gear and set toward Elk River, then the Atlantic.

There were plenty of places he could have stopped along his travels out of Chesapeake Bay. Little islands that only he could inhabit, plenty of rivers he could've followed until he found some small town to disappear in. He wanted to follow each idea that came to him. But, Jed remembered Declan had said, *"That's how I survived. They don't like the boats."* He took a sip from the mug. *"Or at least they didn't."*

Maybe taking to the water was Jed's best option at survival now? When the sun began to rise, Jed turned to see the smoke rising from Chesapeake City. He was sure most of the town had burned during the night. The Demon cloud probably tore it apart and ate its fill. He instantly wished to go back in time to the safety of Peabody Library. They should've stayed after its closing but Declan didn't want to break any rules or get caught.

Jed steered the boat around an oncoming fishing boat that was headed north. He waved to the crew and faked a smile as the fishermen onboard pointed to the dark smoke in the distance.

Jed couldn't look again, he could only focus on the sunrise and the open mouth of the Bay ahead of him. He'd coast out into the Atlantic and get lost amongst the waves and clouds. He could fish, he could find water, he needed nothing else.

It turns out, living on the ocean was incredibly lonely but Jed soon realized he didn't put others in harm's way. Demons didn't crawl out of the ocean to hunt him. Angels didn't drop out of the clouds onto the boat deck trying to send his tortured soul to the Astral plane. No, living on the sea was safe and it gave him time to practice the runes and the spells in the book Declan had sent him. Jed became quite good at it, practicing day after day, memorizing everything Declan had written down.

But, as life would have it, soon it became harder to open his eyes in the morning, fishing for breakfast and dinner became an unbearable chore, setting up the water containment during rain became an insufferable task–even as Jed's throat burned with thirst. When water rolled over the hull and the motion of the boat threw him from his bed, Jed simply rolled onto the floor and let the ocean that had invaded his boat cover him. He had been on the run for so long, that simply not running was too easy. There was no effort in it. This became a problem on its own. For darkness has a quicksand-like pull. It's slow, enveloping; the comfort of a firm embrace, the warmth of a mother's bosom pressed against her child's cheek. Jed had spent so long running from the darkness that surrounded him that he never took the time to explore it. Maybe the darkness was all that he needed, all that he desired, all that he wanted. Maybe the Demons and Angels were right to hunt and try to kill him. Water sloshed against his cheeks, and Jed tapped his fingertips against the book in his front pocket. It couldn't go with him. But, he'd spent so much time at sea it didn't matter anymore. There was nothing left for him in this life. Survival wasn't worth all that he'd thought. It had been years of only him and the salty air. He wasn't sure it was worth it any longer.

Jed closed his eyes as the water splashed over his eyes. He could see Declan again, he could see Eileen, he could see his mother. It was easy, simple, no effort. All Jed had to do was *let go*.

He felt himself slipping. Slipping and drifting and rocking into an abyss he'd never experienced before. It felt so... calming.

The water turned to ice. Jed sucked in a breath and sat up. The thin layer of ice crackled and broke, falling away from his body. He wasn't alone.

"Jedediah James Porter," a familiar voice whispered. "I never thought I'd see the day you gave up on life."

Jed focused on the corner of the room and saw the wavering spirit of his mother, Clara. Water sloshed over his knees as he rubbed his eyes.

"Have you not seen a spirit in all of these years?" Clara smiled as she moved closer to him, her dress disappearing under the water. "You saw them frequently as a child."

"I did?" he asked. He never remembered.

His mother nodded. "Most are harmless. I told you that once. Do you remember?"

"I don't."

"Son?" Clara's face was flexed in concern. "What exactly are you doing here?"

"I was sleeping." Jed cleared his throat.

"Sleeping under water?" She motioned to the open door. "In the middle of the ocean. Alone."

"It was peaceful."

"So is a summer breeze." She crouched, eye to eye with him. "I spent my life keeping you alive. Teaching you how to live. This is not living and you are far too young for death. I did not die for you to end up like this."

Jed's eyes burned. He was too dehydrated for tears. Salt crusted his face and hair. His clothing was frayed too thin.

Clara reached out a hand. "You must live. Even though you've lost."

He could feel her cold skin as she touched him. She had been warm when he was a child. Warm and soft. This feeling was too different.

"I may have died but I haven't been gone." Clara moved again. "I've been watching you when I can."

Jed blinked. He wasn't sure if he could believe his eyes or his mind. Plenty of illusions presented themselves on the ocean. Land, birds, fish. "You were young when you died," Jed said.

"I had lived. I had duty." Clara settled her hand on the helm. "You need to go back to the land. It's not right to be floating out here in the nothingness alone." Clara turned the boat.

"There's no gas." Jed ran a hand through disheveled hair and salt fell down his face as it came loose from the strands. "I burned through the last of it months ago." Jed stood and small chunks of ice fell off his body, melting in the water at his feet. "The sails."

Jed went to work setting the sails to catch the wind and bring him back to the mainland. His muscles ached, throat burned, and he was hungry but somehow he found the energy for the task.

Clara watched from the helm room.

After he set the sails, Jed went to work the manual bilge pump and get the water off the boat. He should have pumped the water off sooner. Now it had soaked in. He doubted he'd made it to the mainland before warping and mold destroyed the boat.

"You can fix it," Clara said, interrupting Jed's thoughts. She wiggled her fingers.

Jed looked down at his hands, calloused and rough. It had been a long time since he practiced magic. Somehow, survival had become more important. Jed searched his memories for the last time he'd tried a spell or felt the heat in his fingers as energy arced, eager to force change at his will.

"I'm not sure I can remember," Jed said.

"It's in your bones, son. You had it as a child before you ever knew a spell or the word magic. You've always had the *luck*."

It was true. He had the memories of opening locks and turning over engines and asking for coins in his cup. It always came and helped them survive life on the run together. But his luck had run out that night on the train when Clara sacrificed herself to a Demon and died. His luck ran out when that monster had tracked Jed's scent to Eileen's apartment and tore her apart. His luck ran out when the cloud Demon took Declan.

"If I go back to the mainland, I'll die," Jed said. "There's nothing for me there."

"You are many things, but a teller of the future you are not." Clara smiled. "There is plenty for you. Life, friendship, love." Her eyes twinkled with excitement. "You're so close, son." Clara's fingers drifted over the runes etched into the doorway and the helm. "Did you ever think that maybe you were meant to save someone?"

"Everyone has died."

"Not everyone, son. You haven't lived long enough to find out." She turned and focused on the sail as the wind blew. The boat picked up speed.

"Did you do that?" Jed asked.

"Never," Clara said. "As luck has it, you needed wind in your sail and someone gave it to you."

"Who?"

Clara shrugged.

"Who, mother?"

"If I knew who I could tell you, but I can only see so much from the Astral plane."

"You're not in Heaven?" Jed asked.

"Heaven is for some, just not me." Clara motioned to the ocean behind them. "You've read enough to know something isn't quite right with the record keeping."

Jed nodded. "There is no Heaven?"

"There's a Heaven, but a certain Archangel won't let me in."

Clara smiled gently. "It's okay though. It means I can keep an eye on you. I have autonomy in the Astral."

"My father." Jed took a step closer. "Which one is he?"

Clara pressed her lips together.

"I deserve to know who sends the Angels down to try and kill me. I deserve to know the one who hunts me from the heavens. Which one is my father?"

"If I say his name, I must go." She took in a breath she didn't need. "I'm not ready to go back yet. I want more time with you."

"You'll tell me before?" Jed asked.

Clara blinked and focused on the lapping ocean.

THIRTEEN

ALASTOR WASN'T MUCH OF A COOK, IT APPEARED. BUT he'd managed pasta with jarred sauce. Shay didn't complain that the tomatoes weren't homegrown like the sauce Mamma had made on the ranch. She realized she'd never have sauce like that again. It hurt her heart; every realization that life would never be the same, that she would always miss two people in her life. Three if she counted Nero.

"Are you going to eat?" Shay asked Alastor as he crossed the room.

"Nope. Got things to do." He shrugged on a jacket and reached for the door. "Keep the fire going. You can have the bed." He opened the door and the chill of the night air blew in. He glanced at her before leaving. "Don't try to run," he said, voice deep and gravelly. "I'll find you."

Shay swallowed hard as he closed the door. No way in hell would she be sleeping in his bed. She was glad to be off the frozen ground but not that glad.

Shay stirred the pasta and sauce, wary that it probably wasn't just an innocent meal. There could be poison or drugs mixed in. She wanted to devour the entire bowl and was so hungry she could probably eat an entire box of pasta. Shay had to keep it together. She couldn't be getting drugged–then she'd never make it out of here.

Shay pushed her chair back and searched the kitchen. There wasn't much there; a few pots and pans, some plates, bowls, and silverware. Everything was boxed or canned or jarred from the grocery store. Shay wasn't surprised. Out here in the mountains she was sure everything was scarce. She searched every cabinet, even under the sink. She didn't find any chemicals or poisons. Something didn't sit right with her. Shay rubbed her sore face as she glanced out the window. It was snowing again. She'd left her boots near the bathroom door and now had an urge to put them on and run for the hills. But, she remembered Alastor's promise. She was sure he'd find her. She needed a different plan.

Shay drank water from the tap and found a box of crackers in the back of the cabinet. She imagined the dry, salted crackers tasted like warm pasta. When she was done, she put on her boots and walked to the front door. She turned the handle and felt the icy wind seep in.

The fire where the men sat was a few hundred yards away; close enough to smell the creosote, far enough that she couldn't tell if it was Redbeard sitting by it. She could only see the large man's body turn to watch her, then the red glow in his eyes.

What the heck, Shay thought to herself as she slammed the door closed.

Shay rubbed her eyes and tried to make a connection between everything she'd seen. There was evil here, she could feel it. She thought about the red eyes of some men and the shifting shadows of Alastor's face. Shay would have thought she was crazy a year ago, but now she knew better. She'd seen things that made little sense. But now she knew. These weren't real men. They were Demons.

Shay scrambled, searching the drawers for a marker or something to write with. She finally gave up and took a knife off the counter. Shay went back to the door and began carving. Jed hadn't given her any lessons in the runes or what they meant. She'd only watched him make the shapes over every doorway. Shay tried her best to remember every angle and curve. She took a chair from the table where her bowl of food cooled, uneaten, and used the chair to reach and mark the top of the doorframe. She wasn't sure she could outrun these men, especially not knowing where she was.

When she was done, her arm ached from carving with the paring knife. Shay tried not to be too hard on herself, but the runes looked like shit. She doubted they'd do much. She went to put the knife away, stopped midway, and hid it in her boot.

Shay sat in front of the fire and waited. She watched the orange and blue flames. She had an urge to run, to plan, to do *something*. But she was frozen in indecision.

Shay picked at her nail. Daddy would be so disappointed.

Fourteen

Then

Jed made it to the mainland. The stolen boat was unrecognizable by anyone in port, the paint sanded off by the salty air from years at sea.

"You made it," Clara smiled. "I knew you would." Her image had become more and more transparent. She was nearly invisible now.

"You feelin' all right, buddy?" a man asked from the docks.

Jed stared. He couldn't find the words to say. It had been so long since he had to hold a conversation with another living person.

The man held out a hand. "Throw me your rope. Are you alone?"

Another man was there. "He looks to be in shock."

"He looks sick," the first man said.

"Goodbye, son," Clara's voice was an echo.

"Wait," Jed's heart was beating fast. He needed to know. "Who was he?"

"Michael." Clara was gone.

Jed fainted.

Thankfully, the men at the port didn't call the law, instead they took Jed to a tiny, rural hospital that didn't ask many questions.

"You're drier that the Sahara," an old nurse slapped his arm, searching for a vein to poke. Salt crusted off his arm when she rubbed it with an alcohol swab. "How long were you lost at sea?"

Jed blinked, unsure of what to say. He was sure she wouldn't believe him. Five years, two years, ten years, twenty, he wasn't sure. He'd stopped counting. In the time that he was gone, things had changed in America. Cars honked in the streets, computers filled the nurses' station. It seemed technology had blossomed while he was gone. There were no horses, no dirt-packed roads, no long skirts or bowler hats.

"Forgot your words, honey?" the nurse poked his arm. Jed felt the sharp needle pierce his skin. "Jeeze, I expected dust to flow back." The nurse leaned closer to his arm. "Your blood is thick as sludge." She connected a tube to his arm. "We'll get you hydrated and get you out of here." The nurse stood and pressed buttons on an IV pump. "Want a turkey sandwich?"

Jed nodded.

He drank seven ginger-ales, ate four sandwiches, and the nurse pumped four liters of fluid into his vein.

Afterwards, he felt better but still sad. Still lonely. Still worried about causing the death of others.

The curtain moved and his nurse popped in to ask, "Hey, hon, a lady from registration is here to get your insurance information. Did you bring that with you?"

"I don't have insurance," Jed said, his voice sounding unfamiliar.

"I thought so." She stepped into the room and closed the curtain. "I brought you some clean clothes since yours are nearly see-through. This lady from registration," the nurse seemed concerned, "she can help you with other things, connect you to social services and help you get food and living arrangements."

"I don't need help," Jed said as he accepted the clothes.

"Didn't think so." She paused at footsteps outside the curtain. "Let's get you to the shower. I'll have her come back later."

Jed was grateful for the hospital shower and soap. The nurse had given him a razor but his beard was too thick. He could use a pair of scissors. He did his best getting cleaned up and left the bathroom feeling refreshed and ready to resume the challenge of life.

"Well you clean up nice, honey." The nurse smiled widely and looked him up and down. "Very nice. Do you have someone coming to pick you up?"

"No." He watched her, fascinated with the way she looked at him and licked her lips.

It had been a long time since a woman devoured him with her eyes. Previously, he would have shied from it. Today he reveled in it. The attention was giving him energy and hope. It made him feel alive again. He smiled back at the nurse as he tucked the spell book into the pocket of his new pants. He didn't need magic to charm. That had always come naturally to him.

"I feel a lot better, thank you," Jed said.

Dinner turned into a new pair of boots and a haircut and shave at the local barbershop. By the time Jed was done using up his luck, he felt filthier than the moment he arrived back on the mainland. He didn't like using people this way.

Still, he needed time to prepare and plan and the kindhearted nurse offered her spare bedroom after she'd taken him to dinner. Jed agreed and paid off his debt in other ways before leaving on his own. He fixed a few broken cabinet doors, changed lightbulbs, hammered nails into the stairs until they stopped squeaking. When she took him to bed, he didn't say no. Payment with his body was easy and a simple tax, it was the least he could do for her compassion.

After all that; the battle, the ocean, his mother, he had a purpose now. He wasn't sure when he'd find the one he needed to save but at least he knew his time would come. And he knew which Archangel he'd kill. Michael.

Now

The winter wind was icy, and Jed was glad that no snow came with it. He'd been walking for days, searching for Shay. Jennifer's ghost had been pointing him in certain directions but he was wondering if she didn't know where the van had taken Shay. He'd walked so far into the forest that he hadn't seen a road in a long time. Jed thought to use a spell to help him, but he'd used so much magic visiting Grandmother Crow that he was depleted.

A stick broke. Jed turned his head and saw the familiar ninety-degree bend of a tree branch. His gut sank. He was on reservation land. More sticks broke. Jed held up his hands.

"You got me, although it was an accident." He heard a voice, sensed movement. "I'll just go back."

A man with pitch-black hair stepped out into the open. "No, Allegewi, you will not go back." It was Jacy.

"Wonderful." Jed sighed and wondered for a moment if he should just embrace death when Hosa made himself known.

"When I went to your mother for help, I wasn't requesting help in killing myself." Jed made a face.

Hosa scraped a finger across his neck in silent threat.

"We didn't come for you," Jacy said. "We came to help locate Shay."

"Good." Jed adjusted his pack. "I haven't been able to find where they took her."

"You can't track," Hosa sneered. "Worthless creature."

"Not on my skills list," Jed said.

Jacy was already kneeling and inspecting clusters of leaves and low branches. "That way." He pointed.

"It's just the two of you?" Jed asked.

"There's more, close to here." Jacy said. "If we need them."

"Perfect," Jed whispered to himself.

"This way," Jacy motioned and began walking silently through the forest.

Jed felt like a bull in an antique shop. He made so much noise compared to the other two men. He was tired and didn't want to draw on his magic to conceal himself like he'd usually do when danger was near.

"Mother said you'd been following a ghost," Jacy said.

"She told me to," Jed said.

A shadow blocked the dappled light from the tree canopy. Jacy held up his hand and hushed the others.

Jed recognized the feeling instantly. Something had broken through onto the Earthen plane. Something had fallen or flown in to hunt him.

"It's an Angel," Jed warned, taking a knife out of his belt and stretching his fingers.

"I told you he'd bring more. He'd bring war to us," Hosa seethed.

"It's not my friend." Anger was coming off Jed in waves. "It's here to kill me."

For the first time since he'd met Hosa, the man was speechless. He didn't spit hateful words about Jed being an Allegewi and the war he'd bring upon them.

"The war has always been against me," Jed said. "I'm going to use magic to hide us." Jed tapped his fingers and uttered words that sounded like crackling ice. He turned invisible. Jacy and Hosa soon followed.

The Angel dropped from the sky. Like chiseled marble, the man landed on a bent knee and steadied himself. The ground shook with his landing.

Jed stood still near a thick redwood. He'd seen Jacy and Hosa ready themselves on the other side of the Angel.

"I know you're here," the Angel said. "I saw the blue light. You were glowing like a torch." The Angel turned, crushing frozen leaves under his feet. "You should really put a damper on that."

The Angel was looking in Jed's direction. He had a blade ready in his hand. He walked closer to where Jed was hiding, his eyes searching. There was movement behind the Angel.

Jacy and Hosa were moving. Jed figured they were probably leaving him to deal with the Angel himself.

The Angel spun and started marching toward the movement.

"Leave them," Jed said as he ran behind another tree, trying to distract the Angel.

The Angel turned again. He scanned the trees, looking for where Jed's voice came from.

Jed crouched and grabbed a fallen pinecone. He tossed it, then sprinted away. His magic was weakening. He knew he was flickering, and his invisibility spell was running out. He focused all the energy on hiding Jacy and Hosa and showed himself.

"There you are." The Angel ran full-bore at Jed, blade drawn and ready to chop.

Jed braced himself, pulling the heavily runed knife from his cargo pocket.

Jed held his own in battle, chanting spells, and jabbing with his knife when opportunity arose. The two men watched, unbelieving.

In the heart of the wintry forest, the air crackled with anticipation as Jed faced off against the Angel. His wings shimmered like freshly fallen snow in the dim light filtering through the frost-laden trees.

Jed stood, waiting, his eyes ablaze with arcane power. Snowflakes began swirling around him as his incantations filled the frigid air. He summoned tendrils of mystical energy, weaving them into a shimmering barrier that encircled him protectively.

The Angel radiated an ethereal glow and hovered gracefully above the frozen ground. His eyes were pools of narrowed determination as his blade glowed with pure light, its edges gleaming with divine energy.

With the flick of his wrist, Jed unleashed a barrage of arcane bolts, streaking through the air toward the Angel. He deftly dodged, weaving between the trees with effortless grace, his wings leaving trails of glistening frost in his wake.

Undeterred, Jed tapped into the elements, commanding the very essence of the winter surrounding them. Using all of his power, he had to reveal Hosa and Jacy. Icy winds howled as he conjured shards of ice, sending them hurtling toward the Angel.

The Angel's movements looked like a dance, a symphony of grace and purpose. With a swift flourish, he swung his radiant blade, dispersing the oncoming ice shards with a shower of crystalline sparks.

The forest seemed to hold its breath; not a creature moved or made sound, not a leaf fell. There was silence as the battle raged on.

Jed and the Angel's powers intertwined and clashed. It was a spectacle of light and energy. Jed's incantations grew louder, his gestures and fingers tapping more fervently, channeling energies beyond mortal comprehension. Energy he hadn't called upon in many years.

The Angel remained steadfast, swooping down with a divine power none had ever seen. Before Jed could finish with his spell, the Angel grabbed Jed, intending on taking him to the air. Jed would be useless in the sky. He'd been there before. Gravity was a force he couldn't control.

He worked his spell louder, faster. He clawed and pushed at the Angel's hands then dropped to the ground, kicked out a leg, and kicked the Angel off his feet.

Suddenly, Hosa was there with a hunting knife, Jacy as well. Jacy jabbed a knife into the Angel's shoulder as Hosa began chopping at the Angel's wings, his face twisted in a rage like never before.

Jed moved to his feet. He searched the fallen leaves for his knife that he'd dropped.

The Angel fought and yelled. Jed's spell was working at keeping the creature grounded. He whispered words that sounded like liquid metal flowing. Roots came out of the ground and held the Angel in place.

The Angel roared as Hosa removed a wing.

"You aren't supposed to be displaying those on the Earthen plane," Jed said as he moved to stand over the Angel.

"I'll display whatever I want as I kill you." The Angel was full of vitriol.

Jed palmed his knife before slamming it into the Angel's heart.

Bright celestial light illuminated the Angel's body as it died.

Jed shielded his eyes.

Hosa stood, the severed wing weighing down his hand.

Jacy cleaned his hunting knife on the Angel's clothing. "You been running from monsters like this?"

"Since the day I was born," Jed said. "Some get a little too close for comfort." Jed shivered as adrenaline coursed through his body.

Hosa was listening intently.

The Angel's body turned to ash, including the severed wing in Hosa's hand. "Allegewi," Hosa looked up, dismayed, "I was wrong."

Jed said nothing. He didn't need the apology, he only needed to know if Hosa would stop threatening to kill him.

"You know, Allegewi, the old stories of our people always said that the half-bred Angels were the demons. But now I am wondering if it was the Angels all along." Hosa held his open palm up and ash blew away in the icy wind.

A woman's scream rang out. The three men turned in the direction where it was coming from.

"Shay!" Jed started running.

FIFTEEN

"THIS WAY," JACY MOTIONED FOR THE OTHERS TO FOLLOW as he veered around a thick cluster of trees and shrubbery.

The forest was dark, as daylight turned to night. Jed could see the light of a fire in the distance.

Hosa slowed and pointed to a trail marker. "We're off reservation land." He looked nervous.

"We get Shay out of there," Jacy said. "We owe it to Nicholas. We owe it to Shay."

They slowed and watched as they took Shay to a cabin. She was filthy, and Jed's body filled with rage when he saw the silhouette of tents in the distance.

"Calm yourself, Allegewi," Jacy warned. "Save that energy for the battle to come. We'll get her out of there."

Jed knew Jacy was right. He took a few deep breaths and closed his eyes, centered himself, and calmed. "How do you want to do this?" Jed asked.

Before them, a large fire roared in the center of the camp, casting dancing shadows that licked at the edges of the frozen trees. They waited patiently.

A man left the cabin where Shay was being held. Jed's heart pounded, the urgent need to rescue her echoing in the silence.

"We could just get her out through that window," Jacy said as he pointed. "Avoid those men."

"If they're men," Jed said. He'd learned to question everything and there was something about the glimmer in their eyes that told him those weren't true men.

Near the cabin, a silvery silhouette wavered. Jennifer was back.

"The ghost," Hosa warned.

"She's helping me." Jed repositioned himself, ready to move.

"Wait." Jacy grabbed Jed's arm. "Don't go running in there. That ghost only guided you in circles back there."

"How do you know?" Jed asked.

"We watched." Jacy made a face. "It needs to be sent away."

There was movement again. The door to the cabin opened. Shay was there, clean and dressed in fresh clothes. Whatever she saw made her quickly close the door.

"Create a diversion." Hosa pointed to the far end of the camp. "Get them away from the cabin, then run in and get her out."

"They'll follow," Jacy warned. He turned to Jed. "Have enough juice left in you for this?"

Jed was fatigued, but adrenaline kept him moving. He'd drain every molecule of magic out of his body if it meant getting Shay to safety. "I'm good," Jed replied.

With the twisting and tapping of his fingers, Jed summoned the bitter wind to howl through the trees, creating a cacophony that echoed through the camp. It sounded like hounds or a bear or some other dangerous creature. The Demons moved from where they rested, one by one, the noise drawing their attention away from the fire and the cabin.

Jed nodded to Jacy. "You go get her. I'll keep this up."

Jacy moved like a panther in the night, headed toward the cabin.

"This noise will bring the dead," Hosa warned.

Jed glanced to Hosa, wary. "There's a large horde of them close to here. Maybe twenty miles south, moving like a gathering storm and headed for this area."

Hosa's face turned grim. "Let's get this over with."

"Call the others," Jed warned.

"Not yet." Hosa shook his head. "We wait until the last moment."

Jed maneuvered around the trees, focusing his magic, drawing more men from their tents and cabins.

Jacy was crouched behind the cabin. He tried the window, but all the men realized now that Jacy was next to it. The window was far too small for anyone to escape through. Jacy moved to the corner of the cabin, watching for an opportunity to make it to the front door.

Jennifer's ghost was lingering, drawing attention from a large man near the fire.

"That ghost is going to give us away," Hosa warned.

"There's salt in my bag," Jed said, magic crackling in the frosty air as he unleashed bolts of icy energy, momentarily freezing a man who had appeared behind Jacy.

Hosa was digging in the bag until he finally pulled out a sealed bag of salt. "You carry this around for making soup?"

Jed smirked. "Take a handful and go throw it at the ghost."

Hosa ran across the camp and threw the salt like a pitcher in a baseball game. Jennifer's ghost disappeared, but the action caught the attention of someone else. Someone bigger and darker than anyone in the camp.

Jed took note. The man was a giant, the same one he'd seen take Shay to the cabin. But now he saw the man for what he really was. Shadows danced across his face, danced across his body as he transformed. His eyes glowed red. That was a pure-blooded Demon. Jed rethought their entire plan. This wasn't good. The other men were lesser Demons or possessed or a little bit of both, but this guy was massive. He pointed at Jed. A threat, a game plan. Jed instantly thought he'd rather take Hosa's murderous gaze any day over this guy's glare.

Jacy ran up to the cabin door and shoved it open. He ran inside.

Hosa was suddenly fighting with the man Jed had frozen.

The Demon took note before running toward the cabin door.

Jed's distraction at the far end of the camp wavered as he focused on the cabin. He ran out from under the cover of the trees.

The Demon threw open the cabin door but halted. He took a step to walk into the cabin but a force prevented him from going inside.

Pride flourished in Jed's chest. Shay must've learned some runes. She must've done something in there.

Jed cast a spell of protection on the cabin.

The giant Demon sensed the power then turned and smiled at Jed.

Jed paused.

The Demon raised his arm and pointed. Near the fire, the ground opened up. Dirt fell away and hands reached up. Bodies crawled out.

"Oh, shit," Jed said to himself as he watched a handful of lesser Demons crawl out of the ground. At least these were smaller, the size of cats and dogs. Fighting them would be like crushing ants. But they would keep coming in overwhelming numbers. The giant had to go down.

Jed reached for his belt, removing two knives and gripping one in each hand.

Sixteen

In the shroud of darkness, where the night held its breath and the stars were veiled, Jed stood facing the towering Demon. A colossus of malevolence, its form cloaked in shadows and eyes aflame with infernal fury.

"You don't belong here, half-breed," the Demon said.

"I could say the same about you." Jed gripped his knives, looking for a soft spot. "What's your name?" he tried distraction.

"Your little human woman will be screaming Alastor later." The Demon smiled, revealing sharp teeth.

Jed stood resolute, his silhouette outlined by a faint aura of crackling blue energy. His eyes glowed with an otherworldly light. The magic that pulsed in him grew with his anger. Grew with his pain as memories of everyone he loved dying by the hand of Angel or Demon pulsed into his mind.

Alastor bellowed a guttural challenge that reverberated through the bleak landscape. He appeared to grow. His immense form loomed over Jed, casting a chill that seeped into the very fabric of the night.

With the flick of his fingers, Jed summoned arcane sigils that danced round him like ethereal flames, forming a protective barrier against Alastor's encroaching malevolence. The air crackled with anticipation, the tension thick enough to slice through the darkness.

Alastor lunged forward, his hands turned to claws, and swiped through the air, aiming at Jed. With a swift sidestep, Jed narrowly skirting the attack, his movements were guided by a grace born of a lifetime evading creatures like the one that stood before him.

Jed released a torrent of mystical energy, hurling bolts of crackling power at the Demon.

Alastor lunged forward, raw power and primal rage clear. A massive claw struck Jed in the side, sending him flying across the camp. Dirt and debris tore up Jed's back as he slid.

"We are outnumbered," Hosa warned from where Jed had landed.

"Get in the cabin," Jed said. "It's safe."

Hosa ran, leaving Jed to face the Demons alone.

Jed uttered words that sounded like crashing waves. He wove intricate patterns in the air with practiced precision, spells he hadn't used since that time he spent in the ocean with no one to harm but himself. Arcane tendrils erupted from the ground, the dark tendrils wrapped around Alastor and squeezed.

Alastor roared, his claws scratching at the shadowed tendrils. Jed moved to his feet, his back aching. Blood trickled down his spine. Pain brought power. In a crescendo of unfathomable brilliance, Jed unleashed a surge of blinding light. The light engulfed Alastor, searing through his ethereal form with a cleansing fervor.

With a deafening roar that echoed through the night, the Demon dissipated, his form unraveling into fading wisps of darkness that dispersed into the ether.

Jed stood, panting, his fingertips zapping with blue energy, his form bathed in the fading glow of blue light.

The battle wasn't over. Jed had defeated Alastor, but there were more men, possibly possessed, and the lesser Demons crawling out of the hole in the ground. He took in his surroundings. The cabin pulsed with a protection spell, but that didn't stop the lesser Demons from running toward it like ants to sugar. They swarmed, defying the gravity of the Earthen plane, crawling up the walls and across the roof, searching for a way inside.

SEVENTEEN

ELSU AND IYE WAITED ON SACRED RESERVATION LAND where it was safe. They watched for the signal from Hosa or Jacy, knowing that it might never come. This was a simple rescue mission, one the Grandmother Crow didn't want to send all four of her sons on. But the men knew there was strength in numbers, and the Allegewi would bring about things they'd never seen before. All of them had seen the disaster at the Dunn ranch. From the dark blood to the burning bodies to the strange markings on the thresholds of the doors and windows. The Allegewi was trouble.

A scrambling and scratching sound echoed in the night. Both men focused on the direction of the sound. The shadowed figure of a four-legged creature crouched and running, joints angled strangely, ran across the nearby prairie.

The sliver of moonlight revealed another figure; the inky shine of a black horse chasing the creature.

It was like nothing they'd ever seen before.

"I don't have a good feeling about this," Elsu said. "That horse..."

"Looks like Shay's horse." Iye was squinting and pointed. "What's that other creature?"

"Looks like a man."

The moon came loose of the clouds and the creature ran across an open field.

"That's a man. Or it was once a man," Iye said.

"That's Clyburn." Elsu said. He looked at his brother with determination. "We go now."

Without words, the men knew something dire was coming. They'd heard the woman screaming and soon they'd hear the roaring of a Demon taking its last breath on the Earthen plane.

Iye and Elsu got on their horses and galloped after the dark duo. Everyone headed toward the scream that had invigorated the night.

EIGHTEEN

"Hosa!" Shay said as the door to the cabin burst open.

Hosa slammed the door closed and leaned his back against it as though something might try to blast through at any moment. He was out of breath and gore stained his arms.

"The Allegewi said this is the only safe place," Hosa surveyed the cabin, his eyes stopping at Shay. "Your hair is blue."

"That's all you have to say?" Shay asked.

Jacy was searching the drawers and cabinets for weapons or anything that could be used as a weapon. He had a collection of knives so far.

"What's going on out there?" Shay asked.

Hosa shook his head. "The Allegewi has it under control."

"Alone?" Shay's eyes were wide with worry.

"He can handle it." Hosa walked to the wood-burning stove and took a metal poker from where it was resting against the wall.

"He shouldn't be handling it alone." Shay took the knife from her boot, wishing she could remember the runes carved into Jed's knife. This would have to do. She didn't have time to carve the knife like she'd carved the doorframe.

A deafening roar echoed from outside the cabin. Everyone stilled.

"What was that?" Shay asked.

"My guess," Hosa said. "Is that big Demon guy."

"Alastor?" Shay asked.

"You best friends?" Jacy asked as he tucked the knives into his pockets before arming each fist with the last two, walking toward Shay.

"Never." Shay looked toward the door.

"You can't go out there," Jacy warned.

The cabin shook. The sound of a hundred footsteps echoed from every wall, then the roof. Scurrying and scratching threatened to break through the thin walls.

"What is that?" Shay whispered.

Jacy looked up. "They're on the roof."

Hosa touched the wall, feeling the vibrations. "They're on the walls."

"What are they?" Shay asked.

"Creatures that crawled out of a hole in the ground," Hosa said.

"Demons." Shay looked up at the ceiling as the cabin shuddered. They clustered together for safety. The cabin sounding like it would collapse at any moment.

Suddenly, a pale figure appeared at the door.

"The ghost," Hosa said. "I'll get the salt and make it go away."

"No," Shay stopped him. "She's saying something."

Jennifer's ghost was motioning to the fire in the nearby stove.

Shay shook her head. "We'll burn to death." She rubbed the ring on her finger.

"I will help you," Jennifer mouthed.

Somehow, with the connection to the ring, Shay understood her. "Set fire to the cabin?"

The ghost nodded.

"You'll protect us?"

The ghost nodded.

Jacy touched Shay's arm. "That ghost did not help Jed in the forest. She led him in circles."

Shay watched Jennifer. Communication ran through the ring in unspoken echo of memory. "That's because she didn't know where *here* was. She only knew where these men had brought her children nearby. She said she's never been good with directions."

Jacy made a noise. "Typical."

Shay focused on Jennifer. "She wants us to burn the cabin. It will kill the Demons."

Jacy and Hosa looked at each other. They had nothing to lose, they would die anyway.

The men worked fast, opening the wood burning stove and using the metal shovel leaning against the wall to scoop out the coals. They placed the red-hot embers around the perimeter of the cabin. The old, dry wood of the cabin didn't take long to ignite. Soon, they were surrounded by a ring of fire. Jennifer moved closer to them. She raised her arms and air blew toward the coals, stoking the fire to grow stronger. Flames licked the walls, engulfed the furniture, took over the cabin.

The Demons on the walls screamed as fire ignited them. Shay, Jacy, and Hosa watched as the fire burned holes in the walls of the cabin, then burned the smaller Demons as they swarmed, grasping for pieces of the structure that were intact. Burning bodies fell from the crumbling roof.

Jacy pulled Shay closer.

"That damn thing is going to get us killed," Hosa pointed to Jennifer.

"No," Shay said. "Watch this."

Jennifer opened her arms and her form grew like a lacy sheet. She no longer looked human, or ghostlike, just a swath of filigree that stretched over Shay, Jacy, and Hosa. The cabin burned around them, but they were protected.

The cabin fell away, charred. The bodies of the smaller Demons burned to soot, so devout in their command to get Shay, they didn't stop. Even as they burned, they reached and grasped and clawed until their life-force was gone.

When it was finally done, the three stood on a perch of unburned cabin flooring, and the lacy protective covering floated off them and turned into the form of Jennifer once again. She stared at the trio expectantly.

"What does she want?" Jacy asked.

"These men took her children, killed her and them. She wanted justice." Shay took the ring off her finger. "Alastor is dead. She got it."

"Burn it," Jacy urged.

"Yes." Shay tossed the ring into the hottest blue flames of the woodstove that was still standing. The metal of the ring sagged, then dripped over the coals as the heat destroyed the ring.

"Thank you," Jennifer mouthed as her ghostly form wavered and thinned and disappeared.

"She's gone to rest now," Jacy said.

NINETEEN

Jacy and Hosa took in the scene before them. Jed was battling men who appeared possessed. Shay ran toward him. Jacy and Hosa joined.

Shay noted Jed looked worse for wear. He was bleeding, his clothing was torn. There was a weariness on his face, but he kept going.

Jacy and Hosa weren't far behind Shay. They ran into battle, bodies dropping to the ground as hunting knives sunk into the remaining lesser Demons. Shay tried to get closer to Jed, but the Demons came in waves. Smaller than the others, she could kill them easily, but damn their sharp nails and teeth ripped her clothing and skin.

Jed noticed Shay and her presence gave him renewed energy. He used a spell that tore through the demonic creatures, some set to fire, some froze in place, some crackled and split in half like stone.

Hosa held up a man, his eyes an unnatural black, ready to send his soul to another realm.

"Wait," Jed warned. "He's just possessed. Let me release him."

Jed drew on arcane energy, blue electricity crackled from his fingertips. He chanted words that sounded like crumbling mountains. His fingers twisted into odd shapes.

"What are you doing?" Shay asked.

"Wiping his memories." Jed finally stopped, and the man sagged against Hosa. "He's still a man. He could have another chance."

Hosa shook him and slapped his face until the guy woke, startled and confused.

"Run for the hills, dude." Hosa warned.

The man took in his surroundings. There was no recognition in his eyes before he bolted.

Once the lesser Demons were killed, Jed wiped the memories of the remaining men.

When they returned to the fire, the hole in the ground was closed.

Jed turned to Shay. "Are you okay?" he asked.

"I'm fine." Shay was studying his face. "You came for me."

Jed touched the bruise on her cheek and the crack on her lip. "I'll kill anyone who touches you."

"Don't get too comfortable," Hosa warned as he redirected the others' attention. "We've got more problems."

That was when the dead ambled into the camp. It wasn't a large horde, but enough that the men backed against Shay to protect her.

Shay pushed at them. "I'm not a child." Jed made room for her to stand with him, knives ready.

"You said they were twenty miles away," Hosa shouted at Jed.

"I haven't watched the news in a few days." Jed's face twisted with forced humor.

"Stupid, Allegewi," Hosa muttered as he swung his hunting knife with focus and lopped off a head.

As the dead infiltrated the camp from the South, an eerie presence entered the North end of the camp. Jed felt it–the change in the air that his mother had taught him to recognize. The hair stood up on the back of his neck as he turned.

"What?" Shay asked as she braced herself for the invading dead.

"There's more," Jed warned. "More Demons are coming."

"Perfect," Jacy muttered before letting out a sharp whistle and a howl. "That was the signal. Iye and Elsu will be on their way."

TWENTY

THE CREATURE THAT WAS CLYBURN STOOD ON THE EDGE of the camp, focused on Shay. "Out of the eater will come something to eat. And out of the strong will come something sweet." Then Clyburn smiled and held out a dusky hand with long necrotic finger-nails and the golden ring missing from his middle finger. He focused on Jed's bag that had fallen on the ground in the center of the four. "My precious."

Jed turned, making eye contact with Clyburn. "You fuck," Jed said as he pointed the rune-covered knife in Clyburn's direction.

Clyburn's eyes snapped to Shay. "Mine."

"Run, Shay," Jed warned.

"No." Shay held her ground. "I am going to rid myself of this disgusting fuck."

Clyburn scraped a toenail into the ground, forming an X. He called his new friends to help.

"Christ, not again." Jed gripped his knife.

"Tell us what's happening," Jacy demanded.

"He's calling more Demons." Jed took a step forward. "This is going to get ugly."

Black smoke erupted from the X Clyburn had made. It twisted and moaned and went to the sky like a columnar cyclone.

Nothing less than chaos erupted. Just as Jacy and Hosa finished with the walking dead, Demons began crawling out of the ground. Clyburn stood to his full height, his arms and knees in the natural position of a man.

The sound of stomping horse's hooves broke through the chaos. Clyburn glanced behind himself before leaping away from the tree line. He ran full-bore toward Shay.

Jed summoned the last of his magic, the sparks from his fingertips sputtering like magic was burning out.

Clyburn was getting closer.

Jed was struggling with his magic.

Just then, three horses blasted out of the forest at the same time. Iye on horseback, bow and arrow drawn. Elsu on horseback, weapon drawn. And...

"Nero!" Shay shouted as the black horse reared up on his hind legs and neighed, sounding like a battle cry.

Clyburn took off, rounding the four near the fire.

The Crow brothers began fighting the Demons that came from the X in the ground.

Jed's fingertips threw sparks that did nothing more than make Clyburn pace in front of him and Shay. Jed noticed Clyburn's focus kept going to his backpack that was on the ground. He crouched, grabbed the bag, and shoved it at Shay. "Hold this and get ready to run."

Chaos was erupting around them. The Crow men shouted to each other as they fought. Clyburn's lesser Demons were drawing them away from where Shay and Jed stood.

Nero was galloping around the bodies, leaping over some, kicking those that tried to attack him from the back. Jed stepped in front of Shay as Clyburn lurched forward, swiping with his knife and cutting.

Clyburn hissed and stepped to the side. "Out of the strong will come something sweet," he taunted, showing sharp teeth.

Clyburn marked the ground beneath his feet with another X. He crouched, gaining traction on the soil before leaping like a panther. He kicked Jed, one long taloned foot cutting Jed across the chest. Jed went flying, landing hard on the ground. Clyburn grabbed Shay and began dragging her toward the new hole that had opened up.

Behind them, Demons scrambled toward Jed.

"Help!" Shay screamed as Clyburn's nails dug into her arm. She fought and struggled, her heart beating faster than ever as adrenaline surged. She stomped on his feet and kicked, but Clyburn had found a new strength as a Crossroads Demon.

The lesser Demons scampered over Jed as he fought. He heard Shay's scream. Adrenaline coursed through his body, bringing on a new strength. He spoke a spell that sounded like fractured glass as he flicked his fingers. Power blasted around him, sending the lesser Demons into the air, killing them instantly. Jed moved to his feet, energy arcing between his hands.

But he was too late. Clyburn was scrambling down into the hole in the ground, dragging Shay behind him. Jed ran toward the hole, dropped to his knees and slid forward with one hand out. Shay's hand was so close he could almost grab onto it before she disappeared into the ground and the hole closed up.

Jed dug at the ground. He blasted portal spells trying to reopen the hole. He dug harder, faster, his fingers giving off blue energy deeper and deeper into the soil.

Finally, he felt a hand on his shoulder.

"Allegewi," it was Hosa's voice, pained. "She's gone."

Jed turned to see the Crow men covered in gore; panting, sweat dripping down their faces even with the winter chill. Behind them, he saw the glint in Nero's black eye.

Nero stomped, let out a whinny that sounded like a howl, then took off into the dark forest.

Jed gaped at the hole he'd dug in the ground. After all the history he'd read at the Peabody Library and training he'd done with Declan, nothing had prepared him for this... emptiness.

"What do we do now?" Elsu asked.

Jed dropped his hands. Blood leaked from his chest. That familiar feeling returned to him, the one that reminded him not to get involved with humans; don't get involved with women because they all got hurt, they all died. That feeling came back full blast, and Jed hated himself for involving everyone in this mess. It would have been easier to travel alone and stay alone.

TWENTY-ONE

NERO KNEW WHERE CLYBURN WAS TAKING SHAY. HE could sense it now that he teetered on the fringes of the Veil. The mark on his hide burned as the need grew. Nero knew he needed to cross the Veil, no matter how uneasy it made him feel. If he didn't cross now and get to Shay, she'd die.

Memories coursed through Nero's mind. Memories of Shay collecting him in that field, of her tending to the hundreds of bee stings on his skin. She bathed him, tediously dabbed medicine on all the stings. She laboriously fed him from a bottle every few hours. Nero's mother might have left him to die that day, but Shay had saved him and now Nero was going to save Shay, even if it killed him.

Nero galloped in the night, focused on a feeling of darkness in his soul. He was close to a break in the Veil. He could see it ahead of him, an eerie glow resembling ochre candlelight. It was the dark glow of the moon in Hell. The color that the moon on the Earthen plane would soon shine if the thinning Veil wasn't fixed. But that wasn't Nero's problem to solve. He only needed to get to Shay. The rest would be a problem for another day.

———

Sometime between the dragging and the pulling and collapsing into the hole in the ground, Shay lost consciousness. Nothing prepared a human for the sickening feeling of traversing realms.

Shay woke to warmth and the smell of wood smoke. Something didn't feel right. Her body ached, her limbs felt heavy as lead and her eyes felt gritted with sand. She shook her head and tried to move but she couldn't. There was noise; an eerie voice and the sound of crackling fire.

"My precious," a familiar voice hummed.

Shay's eyes flew open. Clyburn had the hand that Jed cut off the Crossroads Demon at the ranch. He ripped open the Ziploc bag and removed the golden ring and bracelet. "My sweet, sweet pretty thing." Clyburn slid the ring on his finger and flexed his hand.

Shay couldn't hold back the squeak of fear that left her throat.

"Ah, you're finally awake." Clyburn moved closer.

Shay lifted her head. She was lying on a table, her arms and legs chained. Her sweatshirt and pants were gone.

Clyburn scraped one long fingernail up her naked side. "Out of the eater will come something to eat. And out of the strong will come something sweet."

"Get the fuck away from me," Shay spat, struggling against the chains.

A giant figure burst through the door. Wood flew across the room and hooves echoed on the stone floor. Shay could barely believe it was Nero.

"You," Clyburn hissed, grabbed a fire poker from nearby, and ran at the horse.

Nero kicked with his hind legs, hooves connecting with Clyburn's head and launching his body into the nearby fire. There was no life left in the creature.

"Oh my God, good boy!" Shay cried. "Come here. Help me get out."

316

Nero shivered. It looked like a wave passed over his body. Shay blinked a few times, not understanding what had just happened.

Just like Clyburn took the role of the Crossroads Demon after Jed had killed the original one, Nero now took the role as he had killed Clyburn.

The ring and bracelet materialized on Nero. The ring became an earring in his left ear, the chain dangled down to a loose, golden necklace around his neck.

Shay gasped as it appeared. "Get me out of here," she urged.

Nero moved closer. He gripped the chain around her wrist between his teeth and bit down. The metal shattered and fell to the ground. He repeated with her other arm and ankles until it freed Shay.

Shay sat up and rubbed her wrists. She moved slowly, her body sore and aching. "I need clothes." She wanted to get the heck out of this cave but she didn't want to go naked.

She found a pile of laundry on the floor and dug through it. Thankfully, Clyburn had clothes in his hovel. Shay found a shirt that hung down to her knees. The pants were all too big. She found a pair of rusted scissors and cut them into shorts. Shay rolled the waistband until they'd stay on her hips. She searched the lair until she found Jed's backpack. His notebook and satchels of powders and bones were littered about on the floor. Shay stooped down to collect everything and put it back in the bag. She searched more of the room to make sure she wasn't missing anything before she zipped up the backpack and put it on.

The body in the fire was smoking. The scent of burning flesh was getting stronger. Shay gagged.

Nero shook his head and nodded toward the doorway.

Shay was afraid. Wherever they were, it wasn't what she knew. Beyond that threshold was a land bathed in strange light, strange sounds, and an eerie feeling.

Nero nudged Shay's shoulder, eager to get out of the hovel and away from the burning body.

Shay finally walked, and Nero followed. She exited the threshold and let her eyes adjust. The sun was coming up in the distance, but the land that stretched out before her looked draped in smoke. She rubbed her eyes. "Where are we?" she asked, one hand moving to stroke Nero's inky mane.

———

NERO KNEW he was running out of time. He could feel the hole in the Veil shrinking as daybreak came. He huffed and nudged Shay but she didn't seem to understand. She was scared, mesmerized, frightened of this dark land. Something broke in Nero's chest. He was different now. More different than ever before. The scratch on his hide had healed with his transformation, but once the life force left Clyburn, it came to Nero. Now he belonged to this land. It was his.

Shay's small, warm hand comforted him and while Nero wanted to stand here forever with his human and feel her warmth and love, he knew she didn't belong here. Nero had to get Shay out.

Nero couldn't speak but he did his best to communicate. He stared at Shay, nudged her, stepped in front of her, offered his flank for her to jump on. He finally noticed she seemed much smaller than ever before and he felt much larger than ever before. Nero searched the ochre land before them until he found a downed tree. He walked to it and waited much like he would wait next to the stepstool on the ranch when Shay was a child. He waited patiently for her to climb up.

"What are you doing, boy?" Shay asked.

The hole in the Veil was closing.

Nero huffed and snorted. He pawed at the stump with his hoof.

"You want me to ride?"

Nero whinnied and showed his teeth.

"Okay." Shay sounded uncertain. She stood up on the stump, jumped and threw a leg over his side. "I don't remember that being so hard," she said, gripping the golden chain around his neck as she got her balance.

Nero began walking at a fast pace, hoping she'd get the message and hold on to his mane. He felt her knees tighten against his sides. His walk transitioned to a trot then a gallop. Shay leaned forward and gripped his mane tight.

He galloped faster. After the scratch he'd been lightning and blood rushed through his ears at a deafening pulse. Now, Nero was light; he was a cosmic ray; he was the expansion of the universe. He was a black hole hurdling through space. Nero felt the crack in the Veil. It was close, but shrinking. Shay made a noise as she gripped him tighter. Nero was worried she'd fall off... she couldn't. She had to hang on. He was running out of time.

There it was, a crack of white light between a boulder and a leafless tree. He couldn't simply walk through it like before. Nero put his head down and leapt through.

TWENTY-TWO

TIME IS A FICKLE THING WHEN REALMS ARE INVOLVED. IN the time it took Jed to turn desolate on his knees, mourning the loss of Shay and hating himself, Nero had saved Shay and made it back to the Earthen plane. But in the time it took for Nero to get Shay back to the camp where they'd last seen Jed, Jed and the Crow men were gone.

"Oh no," Shay whispered. "We have to find them."

A few men who'd had their memories wiped by Jed remained at the camp. They huddled around the fire, shotguns ready but eyes closed.

Nero didn't give Shay a chance to dismount. He trotted away from the camp, following a path of glowing blue light that was typically left behind by Jed.

Nero knew that this might be the last time he got to spend with Shay. The darkness was calling him; Nero could feel it tugging from his center. He'd have to go back to that place soon, and he wouldn't be able to come back like before. Another darkness had arrived on the Earthen plane, something with more force, something that Nero knew to fear. It was far away, but he could sense it moving closer—Dark creatures that didn't belong on the Earthen plane were here.

Nero took his time tracking Jed. He reveled in Shay's pats and strokes, wishing he could stay with her forever.

The trail wove away from the nearby road and onto sacred ground. Nero could smell the smoke from a fire. He'd passed two of the Crow men earlier in the night as he chased Clyburn. Now he assumed they were headed back to the camp to plan their next move.

TWENTY-THREE

JED WAS DRAGGING HIS FEET. NOT ONLY HAD HE LOST Shay to a Demon, but he'd also lost his pack with all of his worldly possessions. Everything he'd collected over the decades; fine grains of sand, sacred ash, tufts of hair, gemstones, holy water, and Declan's book. Jed was feeling lost. He'd need to make a new book and try to rewrite it all from memory.

"You'll be okay, Allegewi," Hosa said. The black-haired man reached out and slapped Jed on the back in an effort to comfort him. The force caused fresh blood to leak out of the claw marks on his chest. "Sorry about that."

"It's fine." Jed knew he could heal himself once he'd rested. He'd have to fix the runes that were tattooed across his chest as well.

"Where did Clyburn drag Shay to?" Jacy asked.

"Hell." Jed's head dropped. He'd never transversed realms. He wasn't even sure how to do it. He knew of portals in holy places but none were nearby. Sparrow could help him though; tell him how to get to Hell or even bring him there.

"We have to go get her," Iye said. The Crow brother looked utterly pale and held a hand to his bleeding stomach.

"Brother," Elsu watched Iye, skeptically. "You're hurt."

Iye shook his head. "I'm fine." Blood tinted his lips.

Jacy moved closer, touched Iye's shoulder, and moved his hand away. There was a gaping wound. Iye's intestines were falling out, blood began rushing down his legs. "How are you standing?" Jacy asked his brother.

Iye's face twisted in anguish. Jacy helped him to the ground. Elsu and Hosa moved closer. They scrambled to tend to the gaping wound. Elsu's hands packed his brother's intestines back into place, then he took off his shirt, tore it in half and pressed it to Iye's stomach.

Iye was shaking his head. His entire body began trembling. "You can't fix this." Tears dripped down the sides of his face. "Let me go."

"No," Jacy dropped to his knees and cradled his brother's head in his hands. "No. Don't, Iye," he begged.

"I'll turn soon." Iye held up his left hand that was already turning gray and green. "Don't let me..."

Hosa turned to Jed, "Allegewi, fix him! You have the magic, you healed Shay. Fix him now!"

Jed moved closer, his arms and hands shaking from all the magic he'd used. He knew his aura had to be glowing like the sun.

Iye shook his head. "It's too late." He coughed, turned his head and blood pooled around his lips.

"Do it!" Hosa demanded.

Jed twisted his fingers in and tapped them in mystical dance. He spoke words that sounded like a prayer from a child. Sweat beaded his forehead, his arms shook harder.

"No," Iye whispered. "It's not working."

Hosa grabbed Jed by the shirt and shook him. "Save him!" he demanded, pointing at his brother on the ground.

There was so much blood. Blood pooled around Iye's body and began soaking into the frozen ground.

"I'm trying," Jed shouted back. Jed knew it wouldn't work, but he owed it to the Crow men to try. He owed it to Grandmother

Crow for sending her sons to help find Shay. He tried every healing spell he'd ever memorized. Nothing was working.

Iye's body twitched as the living dead curse began taking over his body.

"Don't let me die like this," Iye begged, searching his brother's faces. "Please. Tell mother *neme'hot'tse*." I love you.

Jacy was the one who stopped it. He jabbed his hunting knife into Iye's skull, eyes full of anguish.

"*Neme'hot'tse*, brother," Jacy whispered as the light left Iye's eyes.

Uncomfortable silence followed until the Crow brothers started humming. It was a song deep and mournful, a song handed down from ancient tribes, a song that would guide Iye's soul onward.

Jed stood back and gave them space, his eyes watching the hole, wishing it would open again. It never did.

Jed was tired of watching the people around him die. It was safer when they didn't know him or when they couldn't remember him. He'd walked across the Earthen plane like a shadow. It was easier when he was the only one running for his life.

Jed kneeled next to an unconscious man, placed his hands on either side of his head, and chanted the spell to erase his memories. When he was done with one, he moved on to another. Only a handful of men were alive. The Demon possession had left their bodies during battle. Jed wiped everything after their possession. They'd wake up not remembering all the evil they'd taken part in. By the time he'd reached the last man, the spell fell from his lips like a kiss; easy, tranquil, final.

———

Iye's corpse was wrapped for burial on the Crow family lands. The brothers would take him home so Grandmother Crow could say goodbye.

Elsu asked Jed about a plan to find Shay as they walked.

"I know someone who can help." Jed scratched his neck. "He

should be nearby, closer to the coast. The horde of the dead is following him. I just need to see the news to try to get a better idea of exactly where he is."

"This sounds strange," Hosa said. "What kind of man knows how to get to Hell?"

"He was an Angel," Jed said. "But then he was a Legion commander, part of Hell's policing force. They're called Hellions."

"Why would he be here?" Jacy asked, eyes disbelieving.

"It's a long story." Jed gestured to the sky. "A very long, confusing, fucked up story."

"Seems we've got nothing but time," Elsu said, checking his watch. "Camp is a good thirty minutes away."

The sun was coming up and the air was warming. The figures of the five men cast long shadows in the dappled light that filtered through the canopy.

Jed inhaled a cleansing breath and told them the tale of Meg and Sparrow.

———

THE SUN DROOPED low in the sky, casting a pallor over the frozen landscape as the men trudged wearily back to their camp. None of the Crow men had much to say about the story of Meg and Sparrow, each ruminating on the details and Jed's plan.

Finally, a camp became visible from the trail. There was a squat building within a cluster of trees and shrubbery, barely noticeable to the untrained eye.

Jacy went to get the fire going.

As the embers flickered and the sun continued to rise, the day enveloped them. The camp was a haven, a sanctuary for the weary men who had seen wicked creatures for the first time. The Crow men had heard stories, but nothing had prepared them for the Demons, the dead, and the ghost. It was a culmination of supernatural events that each man needed time to digest. The Crow men busied themselves with chores and cleaning up. Jed sat by the fire, resting his weary bones and gathering his strength. The claw marks across his chest burned and ached. One brother handed him a bottle of water, another handed him a package of dried meat, then they all sat around the fire.

Despite the fatigue and scars that marked their bodies and souls, a sense of camaraderie and resilience pulsed through the group, a testament to their unyielding spirit in the face of darkness.

"Thanks for not killing me," Jed said to Hosa.

Hosa chuckled. "I never said it was completely out of the question."

Jed took off his torn shirt, using it to soak up the blood dripping down his chest. He whispered a healing spell and held his open palm over the oozing claw marks. Something pinched as the wound closed. Too tired to worry about it, Jed rushed to close his skin. Without his pack and tattoo gun, he'd have to wait to fix his tattoos. Without them, he felt exposed.

"We don't have a television here but we have a radio inside." Jacy said, staring at the flames of the fire. "You might get some information from that."

"Sure," Jed agreed. "Sounds good. Do you have any clothes? I need to go back to the Jeep wreckage and get something to wear later on."

"I'll look." Jacy left the men and went inside the cabin.

Jed drank his water and ate the dried meat. He had a plan. He'd get moving again soon so as not to waste any more time. He'd get to Shay, rescue her, and wipe her memories. He'd wipe everything. It would be hard to let her go, but Jed knew now that his initial thoughts were right. He's too dangerous. Too many people have died around him. Shay said no once already to wiping her memories but he'd convince her, he might even do it while she was sleeping. Either way, the next time he saw Shay, it would be his last. She deserved better. This was just turning into another Chesapeake City disaster.

"Here, Allegewi." Jacy dropped a shirt in Jed's lap before sitting next to him and turning on a handheld radio.

There was static as Jacy turned the dial, trying to find a station. After a few minutes, he sighed in defeat. "There's nothing," he said.

He passed the radio to Jed, his thumb hitting the dial. A voice rang through clear as day. "Southern and mid-California are complete red zones. Do not enter. The movement is headed north. Evacuation orders are in effect for Del Norte county. Get out. Get out now. The National Guard will not assist. They are headed East as numbers decline." There was a strange noise before static came from the speaker and the channel went dead.

Jed looked up.

Elsu moved to stand. "This is sacred land within Del Norte county. We must go."

The men stood and began packing up. In record time they smudged out the fire and buried the ash, and the cabin was secured for future travelers.

There were four horses for the Crow men. Two had returned from battle and another two were hidden in a roughly made pen behind the cabin.

"You ride with one of us," Hosa said to Jed. "Or you'll slow us down."

Before Jed could move, the sound of snapping twigs and rustling leaves came from the surrounding forest.

Jed turned, ready to battle once again.

A giant black horse stepped out of the shadows, carrying a woman with blowtorch-blue hair.

Twenty-Four

"Hey, guys," Shay exclaimed. She'd never been so happy to see familiar faces. She leaned forward and patted Nero's neck. "Look who saved me. My baby Nero came to my rescue."

"That's not Nero," Jed warned. His expression was one of pure horror. "That is not your horse."

"Of course it is." Shay continued to stroke Nero's neck.

"Get off him!" Jed shouted, fear in his eyes. "That's not him."

"It's him. Why are you acting so strange?"

"The creature teeters on the veil," Hosa said. "He is not what he was."

"We wouldn't lie to you, Shay," Jacy said. His eyes imploring.

Shay had known the Crow men her whole life. She knew she needed to trust them. Just what they were saying was so... bizarre.

Shay slid off Nero's back and inspected the horse. He seemed taller—she measured with her palm—by a few hands. She rubbed his coat. It was like polished onyx. She'd never seen it so dark, but figured it resulted from freedom.

"You're the same, right boy?" Shay looked into Nero's large black eyes.

Nero huffed and nodded his head. Shay only saw the abandoned foal she brought home from the prairie that day as a kid and nursed back to life. Nothing more. It was Nero through and through. It would always be just Nero to her because Shay could see nothing else. It was all a mother could ever see, her sweet innocent baby horse.

Shay touched the golden ring in his ear, her finger trailing along the chain and then the chain around his neck.

"That looks like the ring from the hand I cut off the Crossroads Demon," Jed said.

"Nero killed Clyburn. He had the ring on when it happened." Shay shook off the pack and tossed it to Jed. "Clyburn took it out of here."

Jed nodded. He didn't know everything about Demonology, but he knew a balance had to be maintained. He was putting the pieces together. "I'm sorry, Shay." Jed's voice was low. "He's changed."

Shay petted Nero's neck. "Yes. Yes he has."

Nero huffed and pawed at the ground, the tug of Hell becoming almost unbearable.

"Okay, boy." Shay stopped touching him. "It's not a goodbye. I love you."

Nero nodded and turned his head, one large black eye focusing on Shay before he turned and trotted off into the shadows of the forest.

Shay watched him go. She watched the shine of his coat as he ran through the forest. His image became a blur, and then... he was gone.

Something sank in Shay's heart as she put the pieces together. The speed at which he now moved, the difference in his body, the gold chain. He was more than a mustang released to the wild. Nero was something different.

Shay turned to face Jed and the Crow men. "It's over?" she asked.

"The camp has been rid of Demons," Elsu said.

Shay took note that there were only three of the Crow brothers present. "Where's Iye?"

"Dead," Hosa said. "We couldn't save him."

"What happened?" Tears stung Shay's eyes. A fleeting thought passed through her mind that it was best to die quickly in battle than rot as a walking corpse.

"The Demon battle," Hosa said.

Shay finally noticed the neatly wrapped corpse that was resting beside Hosa's bench seat.

"The horde is still coming this way," Hosa reminded the others.

Shay looked at Jed. She knew if the dead were close, then so was Sparrow.

Hosa and the others were packed and ready to go. "Come with us?"

"We are headed in the opposite direction," Jed said. "He's close."

Shay nodded, knowing. "I'm staying with him." She motioned to Jed.

"Are you sure?" Hosa asked. "There's much danger around the Allegewi."

"I know," Shay nodded as she stepped closer to Jed. "I can hold my own."

The Crow men said goodbye, each hugging Shay as Jed watched with a snarl on his face. He didn't want men touching her.

"Take care," Elsu said as he clucked his tongue and headed back toward Montana.

Twenty-Five

"Do you want to talk about it?" Jed asked as they walked through the dappled, day-lit forest.

"Not right now." Shay was doing her best to keep up with Jed's long stride.

"Did they hurt you in other ways?" Jed asked, glancing down at her body.

"They tried." Shay wished she had a coat. "I put up a hell of a fight. They didn't get anywhere."

Jed nodded, glad that she hadn't been damaged beyond repair by the men at the camp.

They came up on an overturned Jeep Commander on the side of the road. Jed crouched and looked inside.

"All of our gear is still here," Jed said.

"Did you wreck it?" Shay asked, crouching next to Jed. "Did you get hurt?"

"No more than usual," Jed laughed. "Our packs are in there if you want some real clothes."

Shay shivered. "I'd kill to get out of these rags."

Jed and Shay climbed through the broken window.

Shay found the tarp and laid it out, then set everything on it. She unzipped one of the bugout bags and found clean clothes and a jacket. She moved behind the Jeep and changed her clothes, leaving the dirty clothing from Clyburn's hovel in the muddy ditch.

Jed was drinking water and eating jerky when she stepped around the Jeep, ready to go.

They filled their packs with as much as they could carry, then started walking.

"Did you want to go back to Montana?" Jed asked.

"No."

"You're too confident in that answer. There's more danger on this trip," he warned.

"It's okay." Shay nodded, accepting.

Jed stopped in the road. He gripped Shay's shoulder and turned her to face him. He searched her eyes. "The offer still stands." He held up a hand near her head. "I can make the memories go away. I can make you forget all of this ever happened. You can go back to Montana, go live with Grandmother Crow, and be happy."

"I don't want to do that." Shay blinked, disbelief rising in her chest. She'd already told him no once before.

"You should," Jed said. "You'll be safe."

"I like where I am."

Jed's hand traveled up the side of her neck and he held her cheek. "You almost died."

"I feel quite alive." She leaned into his touch, wishing it would never end. She wanted to feel his hands forever touching her.

"I will never forgive myself if you die. If you'd died back there with Alastor."

Shay held her fingers up to Jed's lips. "I'm fine. I won't die."

"Just let me make you forget." There was something in Jed's voice, a deep longing for pain, regret, fear. It was all bubbling up inside of him. "Let me erase the memories."

Shay slapped Jed's hands and moved away from him. "I said no. That's what I meant. Stop asking." Shay was getting annoyed.

"Why?"

"I need to remember. It makes me who I am. Without those memories, I will be nothing. I will forget everything. I will forget my life. I will forget what makes me, me. I will forget... you." Shay's eyes were watery with tears. She took a deep breath and wiped at her face. "And if I happen to remember anything about you, it will never be like this." Her fingers were tingling with emotion and although Shay didn't hold magic in her bones, she worried that electricity just might shoot out of her fingertips and damn him for even recommending the idea.

"I'm going to do it," Jed promised. "One day you're going to see it my way. You're going to want out of this mess I've dragged you into. You're going to beg to be rid of me and everything I've exposed you to."

"I will break every single one of your magical fingers if you ever try," Shay promised.

TWENTY-SIX

THEY HAD WALKED FOR HOURS IN SILENCE. SHAY replayed Jed's threat repeatedly in her head. And she wondered if maybe the Crow family was correct in their assumptions about him. He was dangerous. He brought trouble. But he'd also saved her when he didn't have to. He could have left them back in Colstrip, he didn't need to follow them back to the ranch. He could have fled instead of protecting Shay.

She thought about the way he'd cared for her after Nicholas died. He checked her for bites, cleaned her, held her while she slept. Shay knew those weren't the actions of a man who didn't care.

There was a Jeep Wrangler on the side of the road up ahead. Jed pointed to it.

The vehicle was empty, the door ajar as though someone jumped out and took off running. Or maybe they were dragged out.

Shay looked under the hood. Everything appeared intact. She'd learned enough about engines on the ranch not to need a mechanic for most things.

Jed found a key in the ignition and tried to start it. The engine rumbled, then stopped. He tried a few more times.

"Let me try." Shay got in the driver's seat and turned the key. She got the same result. She checked all the knobs and dials before noticing the headlights had been left on. "It's probably the battery." Shay got out and looked around. "We can't jump it without electricity." She secured her pack.

Jed held up his hand. Blue sparks danced. "Lucky me."

Jed opened the hood of the Jeep. Shay turned over the engine as he zapped the battery. The Jeep roared to life.

"I need to use the bathroom." Shay set her bag on the backseat. "I'll be right back." She headed for the tree line, and privacy behind the forest shrubbery.

"There are more camps around here," Jed warned. "Be quick."

Shay nodded. She needed a few moments away from Jed to collect her thoughts. Her foot hit something hard, and she bent to find a solid baseball bat. She took it with her.

Movement caught her attention. Shay walked closer, not wanting a surprise. She'd had enough surprises these past few days.

———

"There was a man in the woods, just down there," Shay pointed to where the road split north.

Jed's shoulders dropped in frustration. "Can you stay out of trouble for one second?"

"He was watching a bird. There was something... dark and strange about him."

Jed stopped what he was doing and faced Shay. "Did he have tattoos?" He motioned to his arms. "Runes like these?"

"Yeah."

"Jesus Christ." Jed rubbed his face and ran his hands into his hair, tugging. "That was probably Sparrow."

Shay smiled. "Oh. I found him then." She pointed to the road. "He's headed that way."

They got in the Jeep and drove in the direction Shay had pointed. All signs led to Crescent City.

Twenty-Seven

THE SMALL CLAPBOARD HOUSE HAD BEEN EMPTY FOR LONG enough that a layer of dust had settled on every flat surface.

"This town was probably really charming before." Shay looked at the paintings on the wall. "Sad. I always liked coastal towns like this. They're always the setting for a romance movie." Shay shivered. "It's cold."

Jed had lit the stove and was boiling a pot of water. "Hot meal tonight."

"Turn on the oven and warm this place up," Shay suggested, walking closer to the heat, hoping to warm her numb fingertips.

"We should secure the doors." Jed picked up a chair and moved toward the back door they'd broken in through. "This will buy us some time," he said, propping the back of the chair underneath the handle.

Shay locked the front doors and pushed a heavy lounge chair across the hardwood floors. There was a noise from upstairs. The creaking of wood against wood.

Shay turned and ran into Jed, who was already on the move to investigate. The climb up the stairs was noisy. The old house creaked with every step. They took a left, avoiding the attic access, and searched the first two bedrooms, then the bathroom. The noise came again, like scratching on fabric. There was one last door that was cracked open. Jed pushed it with the toe of his boot and flicked on the light switch. An orange cat was stretching against the bedding, claws scratching at the comforter. It looked startled, then bored, before curling into a ball and falling asleep on the bed.

"It's just a cat," Jed said, relieved.

"Good. I can deal with cats." Shay began walking down the hallway.

"They're not innocent creatures," Jed warned.

"What do you mean?"

"They're half in, half out. Definitely touched by darkness. You can't tell?"

"Not on my radar." Shay began walking down the stairs.

Jed followed and by the time they got back to the kitchen, the water was boiling and the kitchen was toasty warm from the oven running.

Shay opened her bag. "What will it be tonight? Beef stroganoff, cheesy mac, or spaghetti in meat sauce?"

"Stroganoff." Jed made a face when he said it. They hadn't come across fresh food in a while. While the camp food filled his stomach, he preferred something more. Although there were plenty of days that he'd gone without a hot meal, Jed tried to be thankful for what they had amid the devastation.

"I'm taking the cheesy mac. I'd kill for some real macaroni and cheese." Shay tore open the packages and poured boiling water into them. "Real macaroni and cheese. My mom used to shred three cheeses and melt them together. I'd starve myself all day so I could gorge on it." Shay frowned, watching the camp food congeal as it cooked. "What I wouldn't give for a bowl of momma's mac and cheese."

"That sounds tasty." Jed opened the kitchen drawers until he found silverware.

Shay sat at the small dinette table, her foot kicked against a box. She leaned to the side and found a case of Diet Coke under the table. "Perfect." She dragged the case out and offered one to Jed. "They'd taste better cold."

Jed shrugged. "I've learned to lower my standards."

"Hopefully not too much." Shay stirred her meal.

Jed didn't reply. He simply ate and glanced out the window. "The dead should be here soon."

They'd been tracking the horde with the emergency radio in Shay's pack. News reports were inconsistent, but they'd gained enough information to expect the horde in Crescent City within the next forty-eight hours.

"You want to leave tonight?" Shay asked between bites.

"If Sparrow keeps up his current momentum, he'll be headed out of town by morning. My only worry is, he looked hungry and there's a bar down the street filled with people."

"Should we warn them?" Shay asked.

Jed shook his head. "We shouldn't go to places that will put you in danger. We can't save everyone."

Shay stopped eating, suddenly feeling empty inside. Every step of the way here, Jed brought up danger and keeping Shay safe. She was tired of hearing it. Shay wasn't as fragile as Jed kept mentioning. She'd killed an Angel and save his life. She battled the Demons at that camp. One of these days, she was going to have to remind him.

"I don't know how Sparrow is going to react to you. We can't get too close," Jed warned.

———

THE MASTER BEDROOM of the small house was equally small but had street-facing windows. Jed and Shay brought their belongings upstairs and prepared for the night.

"Keep the lights off," Jed said. "We don't want anyone from the street seeing us."

Shay sat near the window, the full moon illuminating the space. "What's the plan after we get close to him?" Shay asked.

"We have to get him to a portal and take him back to Hell." Jed pulled out a pot of paint and a paintbrush.

"What's that?" Shay asked, leaning against the bookcases at her back.

"You didn't want the tattoos, so I have another idea." He shook the pot. "It's paint."

"Oh," Shay glanced at his hands, then shifted in her seat. "You're going to paint me?"

"I'll paint the runes on you, try to protect you from Sparrow. I don't want him to see you as a threat or a meal." He rotated the pot. "This is like henna. It will stain your skin and last a few weeks."

"What if it doesn't work?" Shay asked.

"It should work." He twisted the lid, and it popped. He dipped the paintbrush into the pot and sat next to Shay. "Want me to do your back or your front first?"

Shay swallowed hard. She'd been with Jed for weeks now, but he hadn't made a move since kissing her on the side of the road after they'd left the ranch. Shay would have welcomed him to make a move. She craved his warmth, his touch, his attention. "Maybe start with my back," Shay suggested.

"Turn around," Jed said. "You'll have to take off your shirt."

Shay turned, her back facing him, and she pulled off her shirt, holding it close to her stomach.

He started at the nape of her neck. The paint was cold and tickled, but his brushstrokes were soothing. As he drew the runes to keep her safe, she closed her eyes and imagined in her mind what he drew. She knew some triangles and circles with lines. She wanted to know more because while she didn't have magic in her bones, she could draw and write.

Cool wetness tickled her shoulders, then ribs, then the small of her back.

"Okay, time for the front," Jed said.

There was something in his voice, but Shay tried not to focus on it. She turned and held the wadded-up shirt over her breasts.

Jed sucked in a breath and refused to meet her eyes. "You'll have to lean back a little."

Shay straddled the bench and leaned against the bookshelves behind her.

Jed moved the curtains to let in more light, then dipped his brush in the paint. He reached for the clothing that she was covering her breasts with. "Can you pull this up?"

Shay pulled the shirt away, dropping it on the floor, and used her arm to cover her nipples.

Jed cleared his throat and touched the paintbrush to the sensitive skin just under her breasts. Each stroke was cold and tickled and was highly sensual. Shay arched her back when the paintbrush touched the underside of her breast. She closed her eyes as Jed painted across her chest to the other side. He repeated the markings, the strokes, the... Shay bit her lip, holding in a moan. Never did she think being painted would ignite a fire deep in her belly.

The paint brush strokes moved down the center of her abdomen, around her bellybutton, then up her sides. Shay could feel the flush in her cheeks as he worked. She couldn't stop the heat that bloomed up her neck.

Finally, the paintbrush paused.

"I have to do between," Jed said, his voice sounding strange, pained almost.

Shay nodded, moved her arm away and covered her breasts with each hand.

Jed trailed the wet paintbrush up the sensitive skin, drawing the runes, then across her upper chest. Shay wished it was his mouth leaving wet marks on her skin, his tongue tasting her like no one else ever had. She wished... She wished. Shay lifted her chin. She was breathing fast, anticipating. She wanted more than some erotic body painting with Jed.

Jed painted her shoulders and upper arms. He collected her hair with his free hand, moving it away to expose the length of her neck, and painted a rune from her collarbone to just under the sensitive skin below her earlobe.

A soft moan escaped Shay's lips, released from her throat before she knew it was there.

"Are you okay?" Jed asked.

Shay finally opened her eyes and focused on the handsome man in front of her. The muscles of his arms and neck were tense. Jed's expression was pained, like he was holding in a dark spell or curse.

"What?" Shay asked.

Jed just stared, his eyes roving over her. "Have you seen yourself?" He finally whispered. "Are you sure you're just human?"

Shay supposed she looked a certain way in this position, back arched, breathing heavily. She felt her nipples pebble under the palms of her hands. It totally turned her on.

Suddenly, the paint and brush dropped to the floor as Jed moved forward. Both of his hands gripped Shay's head and delved into her hair as he pulled her forward, bringing her lips to meet his mouth.

Jed's fingers tugged, tilting her to his demanding mouth. He kissed her hard, tongue and lips dancing with Shay's.

It had been too long. Too many days of pent-up tension, too many days of adrenaline running on high with no release. Too many near-death experiences. Shay wanted to feel something more than the end of the world and a constant threat. She wanted to feel alive; she wanted to feel hope.

Shay's hands twisted in Jed's shirt, tugging and pulling until she could feel his warm skin beneath her fingertips. Her heart was beating a mile a minute and heat flushed her entire body. She felt like she was on fire, and Jed was the only person who could extinguish the burn. Her fingers slid over lean muscle and the outline of ribs, scars that she'd seen and wished she could heal. Jed tugged her closer. His hands roved down her back, under her thighs and lifted her onto his lap. Shay pressed her body to Jed's, her hands tangling in his shirt and tugging it up and over his head.

Jed groaned as she pressed her naked breasts to his chest. Skin on skin was like nothing else. Velvet and softness and warmth.

There was a noise in the street below.

Jed twisted to hide Shay and pulled the curtain until it was mostly closed, but they could see outside through a small partition. A man was walking down the middle of the street.

"That's him," Jed warned.

They watched from the window as Sparrow walked slowly down the middle of the road, headed for the bar on the corner.

"Do we stop him?" Shay asked, shivering against Jed's shoulder. There was something about Sparrow. He was becoming darker. Shadows slithered from under his feet. Ice crystals chilled the edges of the window.

"There is no way to stop him," Jed warned.

Twenty-Eight

The door to the bar was broken and a large, a bloody handprint stained the glossy wood. Jed and Shay sat in the Jeep Wrangler, an unease passing through the vehicle as they realized what had happened last night.

"Should we go inside and see if anyone survived?" Shay asked.

"No," Jed said.

There were vehicles on the streets; the last of the stragglers headed out of town.

"I've got a bad feeling," Shay said as she shifted the Jeep Wrangler into drive.

A vehicle lingered behind. Sparrow moved to the other lane and slowed. A Jeep Wrangler, with the top off, turned in front of him and stopped.

Sparrow grabbed his blade, holding it out at arm's length. He was met with the rounded end of a baseball bat. He looked past it and recognized the woman from the forest with blue hair.

"You going to slice me up with that?" she asked.

"If I need to," Sparrow replied. "You going to bludgeon me with that?" he nodded toward the bat.

"If I need to," she replied with a smirk. "You want a ride?"

Sparrow looked past her and recognized Jed from the diner in the passenger seat.

"I like to walk." Sparrow secured his blade.

"There's blood on you." She motioned to his hand and face.

Sparrow wiped at his mouth with an open palm. "Got in a fight."

Her eyes narrowed, and Jed whispered something. "I bet you won. Seem the type."

Sparrow smiled; it was arrogant and dark. "I always do."

Something fell out of the sky and landed at Sparrow's feet with a thud.

"What the heck?" the blue-haired woman made a face.

Sparrow bent and picked up the dead bird. "It's a raven." Sparrow stroked the feathers. His fingers petted the thick flight feathers at the base of its wings. He gripped two and tugged hard, pulling them out. He tucked them in his pocket before gently setting down the carcass off the side of the road. He dug a small hole in the dirt with his hands and buried the creature. The eerie sound of a dozen crows cawing from the power lines filled the night.

"I'd get a move on. The dead are following." The chick in the Jeep pressed down on the gas pedal and began driving away.

"They always do," Sparrow said as he stood and looked up. There were more dead ravens, more feathers went into his pockets–some he didn't have the urgency to bury.

An unkindness of ravens above him cawed louder.

SHAY DROVE SLOWLY down Redwood Highway so she could see Sparrow in the rearview mirror. Cars were passing her as the last residents fled Crescent City.

"He's not right," Jed warned.

"Clearly." Shay gripped the steering wheel.

"We just have to guide him to a portal."

"And where is the closest portal?" Shay asked.

Jed rubbed his face. "I'm not familiar with this area. I know of some back toward New York."

Shay gaped at Jed. "That's on the other side of the country."

"Yeah."

"We have to get him all the way over there. Him. That giant walking shadow who talks to birds?"

Jed leaned back in his seat. "It sounds impossible. But we've lived through worse."

TWENTY-NINE

SHAY WAITED AT THE EXIT TO ELK VALLEY CROSS ROAD. She turned off the Jeep to save gas and propped her feet up on the dashboard.

"He walks pretty fast," Jed said, digging in his backpack for something to eat.

"Then we shouldn't have to wait long." Shay shivered. She didn't like to be a sitting duck on the highway. The only solace was that Sparrow would be there soon, and he'd scare away anything threatening.

"Why didn't you just ask him to ride?" Shay asked Jed.

Jed chuckled. "Not so sure I want to be sitting in the same vehicle as him. Last time I was in the same room as Sparrow, his girlfriend nearly killed me. I have little trust for creatures of Heaven and Hell combined."

Shay nodded. "Understandable."

A few of the dead ambled by. Shay and Jed held their breath and sat still as stone until they passed.

"I haven't seen them move ahead of Sparrow before," Shay whispered.

Jed nodded in agreement. "There must be something going on up ahead drawing them."

It was just a few hours until Sparrow caught up with them. Shay rolled down the window as he headed toward the exit to Elk Valley Cross Road. "Where you headed, Sparrow?" Jed asked.

He didn't answer. Shay followed, her foot barely pressing the gas pedal.

They followed him past Sunset High School and turned right on Lake Earl Drive. They passed a pub and a T-shirt shop before Sparrow turned left onto Buzzini Road.

Shay and Jed saw what drew Sparrow. There was a giant house in front of them, set on a lake and surrounded by a stone wall. Music thumped from inside.

Shay and Jed made eye contact. They'd seen what he did to the bar in Crescent City.

"We have to shut this down," Shay said. "He's going to kill those people."

Jed shook his head and made a face. "We aren't the police. What those people are doing is a death sentence."

Shay kept driving, looking for a parking spot that was both hidden and close. "They're probably just stupid kids." She thumbed to the road behind them. "Did you see the high school we passed?"

Jed leaned forward to open his bag and take out weapons. "Just so you are aware, I am not a fan of this."

Shay found a spot under the canopy of a large tree and near the stone wall that surrounded the mansion. They could get in and out easily and avoid most of the zombies that were currently knocking on the gate.

Shay and Jed intercepted Sparrow as he was crossing the front yard and headed toward the door.

"Hey, Sparrow," Jed waved. "I don't think this is a good idea, man."

Sparrow's face was placid, like he couldn't care less. He leaned to the side to get a good look at the blue-haired girl standing behind Jed.

"Sparrow," Jed's voice was demanding. "Look. At. Me."

Sparrow focused on Jed. "I know you."

"Yes."

Sparrow made a noise that sounded like a growl. "Move."

Jed stepped aside. "Don't go in there. Please, Sparrow. We need to get you to a portal. We need to get you back where you belong."

"I'm going in here." His eyes flashed black. "I belong here."

"Don't." Jed motioned to the Jeep. "Come with us. We'll go for a ride. We'll bring you back to Hell. We'll bring you back to Meg."

"Who is Meg?" Sparrow asked, tipping his head to the side in a very birdlike mannerism.

"Meg is..." Jed was at a loss for words. He wasn't sure what Meg actually was right now or how to describe their relationship. "Meg is yours. Meg is your home."

Sparrow blinked, considering. "I have no home." He moved around Jed and headed toward the house.

The music pulsing wasn't much different from the pulsing of blood through veins.

Sparrow touched the doorhandle and let himself in.

Jed turned to Shay. "Do you like parties?"

Shay glanced to the living dead who were pushing against the gate at the end of the driveway. "Not really."

Jed took her hand and his fingers twitched with a protection spell. "Don't get bit," he warned.

———

JED LED Shay into the house and closed the door behind them. The music was loud and inebriated teenagers lingered in clusters.

No one cared they were there. No one greeted them, no one asked who they were. Jed assumed the party goers had given their last fuck some time ago and were now simply embracing the chaos that came with the apocalypse.

Shay pointed down a hallway. There was a room in the back

where people were dancing. Sparrow's tall form was easy to spot. They'd found him. Relief spread and Jed and Shay relaxed a bit, no longer carrying the tension of searching for Sparrow.

Jed followed, leading Shay behind him with his hand holding her wrist.

The music was loud; the song was something old with a great beat. Shay couldn't help herself. They could let their guard down for five minutes. Between the beat and the energy in the room, it was hypnotic. She danced as they walked. Jed paused as Shay raised her arms and began dancing with her arms in the air. She shook her head. Blue hair floated around her face as she spun.

A possessive force overtook Jed when he saw nearby guys looking at Shay. One dared to move closer to her, a smile on his face. A glare and a threatening gesture from Jed made the guy move on elsewhere.

Amidst the pulsating rhythm of music and flickering lights, Jed swayed together with Shay on the makeshift dance floor. Their movements were laden with unspoken tension–a mixture of longing and the unresolved tension from last night hung between them.

Shay's eyes were shimmering with uncertainty as she met Jed's gaze, tinged with a hint of sorrow. The music wrapped around them, its melody a haunting backdrop to the unspoken emotions that tangled their relationship. Shay moved closer, into Jed's arms. She tried to ignore the tangible ache in the air–she was left unsatisfied after the painting session last night as Jed made excuses to send her to bed alone while he kept watch. Shay had fallen asleep watching him gaze out the bedroom window, backlit by moonlight, the runes like dark shadows on his pale skin. She had wanted him to hold her like that last night at the ranch. His arm tucked tightly around her middle, his body curled around hers. That's what Shay wanted.

Their bodies moved effortlessly, following the rhythm, yet their hearts carried the weight of untold stories and unexpressed feelings.

Jed's fingers skimmed her arm, then her hip, sending shivers down her spine. Shay's breath hitched, a fleeting vulnerability betraying the façade she had crafted that morning. She searched Jed's eyes, hoping to find solace or perhaps a glimpse of the answers she sought. She found nothing within the depth of his gaze. So much had gone unspoken between them. He'd tried to wipe her memories, threatened that he would do it in the future. It broke Shay's heart that she was so easy to get rid of. She had nothing left.

Jed, his touch tender yet laden with the weight of unspoken apologies, tightened his embrace, drawing Shay closer as if trying to convey a thousand unspoken sentiments through their bodies moving.

Suddenly, Jed tugged her close so that the length of their bodies were touching. His breath tickled her ear as he said, "Something else is here." His hand pressed against her back. His posture curled toward her as he led her backward, toward where they came. "Whatever is here, it's not human. I have to hide you."

"I can handle myself," Shay said, her body going rigid. She tried to push back against Jed, her palms moving to his chest, but he simply wrapped his arm tighter across her back and lifted her off her feet. Sometimes she forgot how much bigger and stronger he was than her.

"Please, Shay," he begged. "Don't fight me." His eyes were pained as he searched her face. It truly looked like he was unnerved.

Shay didn't like it one bit. But before she could argue with him, a scream rang out and all hell broke loose.

The bodies on the dancefloor were fighting, biting, the kids were turning. It happened fast. A flood of bodies were forcing their way down the hallway that Jed and Shay were in.

"Upstairs," Jed said as he set Shay on her feet and shoved her.

Shay ran, grabbed the baluster, and went up the stairs two at a time. Jed was close behind her. The screaming and growling became louder.

THIRTY

JED AND SHAY LOCKED THEMSELVES IN THE FRONT bedroom. They watched the horror unfold in the side yard.

"Who is that?" Shay asked, pointing to a dark-haired woman with tattoos.

"That's Meg," Jed said.

"The same Meg who bit your neck?"

Jed's face turned to stone. "Yeah."

"And that one with the short blonde hair?"

Jed shook his head. "I don't know her, but she looks like an Angel."

"And that's Sparrow?"

"Yeah." Jed paced the room. "We need to get to them." He moved a dresser in front of the door, then returned to the window.

"Why didn't they come after you?" Shay asked.

"I'm assuming they had bigger fish to fry."

"Oh my god." Shay's hands flew to her mouth. "Jed... What the fuck is happening out there?"

The scene turned brutal. Meg cut off the blonde woman's arm. There was blood dripping down the stone wall they were perched on. Meg and the blonde woman were shouting at each other. But then, the dead started moving fast. Faster than they've ever moved before. No longer were they dragging their feet at the pace of a lame bovine.

"They're drinking her blood," Shay said. "Look."

The scene continued to unfold before their eyes. The dead scrambled to lick the fresh blood off the stone wall. They pushed and shoved each other out of the way.

"This is not good." Jed's voice was concerned.

And then, the three disappeared into thin air.

"Where'd they go?" Shay asked.

"Fuck." Jed slammed his fist into the wall. "Meg can travel almost anywhere like that. She took Sparrow somewhere."

"Where do you think she took him?"

"I have no clue." Jed wracked his brain for a logical answer, but the blood he saw dripping from Sparrow's boot before he *poofed* gave him a terrible feeling.

———

TERRIBLE SOUNDS WERE COMING from outside the bedroom door. The dresser slid an inch across the floor.

"Can you stop them?" Shay asked, her eyes wide as she reached for her pistol.

Jed held his hands out and chanted a spell to reinforce the door. "They aren't Angels or Demons; they're trapped souls. There's only so much I can do." He whispered a spell to block the noise in the room, hoping the dead would get bored and move on. He reinforced the wall parallel to the hallway with a second spell.

"This won't hold much." His eyes searched the room and fell on the closet. "I can make a smaller room more secure." Jed led Shay to the closet and began using spells to reinforce the walls and the door. "We'll just wait them out."

There was a sickening feeling in Shay's stomach: they were

trapped. They couldn't outrun the fast dead, and she doubted she had enough bullets to end them all.

There was movement outside the window.

Shay aimed and shot.

Bang!

Jed slammed the door closed. He shoved Shay behind him. Footsteps echoed on the other side.

"What did you shoot at?" Jed asked.

"A shadow."

The closet door slammed inward.

Meg was standing there. Covered in gore. "Jed, nice to see you again," Meg said as she motioned for them to follow her. "Would you like to get the fuck out of here?"

Shay nodded. She knew Meg would bring them to Sparrow, and Sparrow could help Jed. She wasn't going to follow the same fate as her parents. Shay picked up her bag.

Meg held out her hands. "Let's go."

Jed looked at Shay and nodded. They both took one of Meg's out turned hands.

Poof.

Shay's head was spinning when they appeared in a gothic style church.

Jed turned away and puked between the pews. Shay's face turned sour as she held down, bile rising in her throat. Traveling with Meg was fast and violent.

Everyone turned at a strange gurgling sound echoing through the church.

"Sparrow?" Meg asked.

Shay moved closer. Sparrow was hunched over the blonde Angel.

"Oh, my god!" Meg shouted. "Sparrow, no!"

Jed instantly regretted their situation.

"Kill her!" Shay would not die today. She would not take her last breath in this church. She grabbed the gun from the holster on her him. "Kill her before she turns!"

Everyone was so slow. Waiting.

"Who turns?" The blonde Angel asked as she rubbed her face. "What the...?" She finally saw the bite. "No."

"Kill her now." Shay was aiming at the Angel's forehead.

Meg had her hand in front of the barrel of the pistol. "Stop."

"Cut it off. Now, Meg. Cut it off now!" The Angel screamed.

"You'll have no hands," Meg shouted back.

"I don't care. Cut! Now!" The Angel screamed.

Shay watched as Meg gripped a wicked blade. It glowed faintly. With one quick movement, she cut off the Angel's other hand.

"Wrap it," the Angel told Meg.

Shay glanced at Jed, wishing they'd never come here. She would have rather stuck it out in that closet than deal with this shit show.

Sparrow was moving to his feet. He looked ghastly and unfocused, clumsy.

"Secure him," Meg demanded, tipping her chin at Jed as she bandaged the Angel's bleeding arms. "But don't kill him."

"What are you going to do with a dead man?" Jed asked.

"Whatever the fuck I want," Meg replied.

Shay had an idea. The walking dead were useless without their teeth. She grabbed a spare shirt from her pack and tore it. She jumped onto the pew and tossed a piece of rope from her bag at Jed.

Shay wrapped Sparrow's face as Jed wrestled with the giant man, forcing his arms behind him. It was a struggle. Sparrow still had a dark strength.

"You should have cut his leg off," the blonde Angel said. "You're going to need to help them. I'm going to pass out now."

Meg moved fast to assist Jed and Shay. She grabbed Sparrow's free arm and twisted it. Jed wrapped the rope around Sparrow's wrists.

"Where'd you get that?" Meg asked.

"Bugout bag," Shay said. "Never unprepared. My parents trained me for times like this." Shay wasn't sure why she added that last bit.

Meg didn't need to know anything about her, but she felt compelled to release the information.

Shay jumped down from the pew and Meg walked closer, looking her up and down.

Shay knew Meg was something else. She wasn't tall like the Angel or Sparrow or Jed. She looked human at first glance, but an intimidating darkness lingered across her gaze.

Shay could only stare, fighting the urge to turn tail and get the fuck out of there. "What are you?" she finally asked Meg.

Meg became distracted by Jed trying to wrangle Sparrow.

"Just let him go," Shay said. "He can't hurt anyone now. And he can't go far in this church." He was no different from the cattle. Penned.

Meg watched Sparrow wander.

"Hey," Shay was feeling bold. "What are you?" she asked again.

"He didn't tell you?" Meg pointed to Sparrow.

Shay didn't want to reveal that there had been little conversing with Sparrow.

Jed didn't interject, he just watched Meg the entire time, his fingers tense and ready to cast if she so as much threatened Shay.

Shay could see there was something more to Meg and she couldn't control what came out of her mouth next. "You are something." Shay gestured to the space around Meg. "Dark. It's very dark around you. I don't trust you."

Jed elbowed Shay.

Shay lost her focus for a moment. "What? You're just Meg? Nothing more than Meg?" Shay didn't believe it. Her stomach twisted in Meg's presence, similar to when Clyburn was nearby. No, Shay didn't trust Meg one spec.

"She's much more," Jed warned. The change in Meg had been drastic. The last time he'd seen her she was just coming into her power. Now she was chaos.

"Look." Meg raised her hands in defeat and the tension broke.

"Sparrow asked me to get his friends, so here we are. I didn't bring you both here for any other reason." Meg crossed her arms over her chest. "But now I have a busted ass healer Angel and a zombie for a boyfriend." Meg's stomach growled. Loud.

Jed's hand twitched.

"And I'm hungry," Meg said. "So, we need to get the fuck out of dodge before Heaven sends some shitheads down here to screw things up more."

"I knew that getting mixed up with you was going to send me on the run. I told you I can't trust anyone," Jed said. "Not even a girl who can flash between realms and slay the walking dead like she was born and bred to take on the apocalypse single handedly."

"You've said that before," Meg replied.

"I repeated it to remind myself." Jed ran his hands through his hair in frustration. He couldn't look at Shay, didn't want Meg to get the idea that Shay was important to him.

"We need to get out of here," Jed said. "There are too many forbidden creatures in one room."

"I went through a portal that dropped me here," Meg said. "Look for arches with inscription. I can't get everyone out of here at the same time."

Jed and Shay walked to the opposite end of the church.

"What the fuck kind of mess did we just get into?" Shay asked Jed. She felt sick as she did her best to hold down the terror and tried not to think about how she was the only human in the building. She was definitely out of her league.

"We just stepped in the hugest pile of shit." Jed was nothing but honest. He wanted to send Shay away, but he wasn't sure where exactly they were. He should have never let her leave Montana.

"How is Sparrow going to help you like that?" She glanced behind them at the wandering dead man.

"This has all gone very wrong."

"At least they're not attacking us," Shay said with a half-smile.

Jed rubbed his face. "Let's hope it stays that way. From what I can tell, Meg needs us to help her."

"And?"

"I think we should help her. Keep your enemies close."

Shay swallowed hard. "Okay." She had finally figured out the familiar feeling she had around Meg. It was the same feeling she had when Clyburn had dragged her down to Hell. It permeated off the woman. But there was an underlying sadness.

Jed and Shay searched, finding nothing that resembled a portal. "There's nothing here," he finally told Meg.

Meg made a face. "I have to check on Teari."

They followed.

Shay didn't think cutting off someone's hands outside of a hospital was a good idea, but it seemed to stop the spread of the walking dead.

Shay got one look at the Angel named Teari and took in her pale completion and rapid breathing. "I read about this in a survival first aid book. I think it's shock."

"Oh, yeah?" Meg asked. "Angels can go into shock?"

"Why not? They're just giant supernatural offshoots of humans."

"Ok." Meg touched Teari, brushing hair off her face. "What do we do?"

"Get the heck out of here," Jed said. "I'm sure there's a car here somewhere. The priest would have needed to get groceries and travel."

"But did this priest hit the road when the dead started walking?" Meg asked. "How do we get him in a car?" She motioned to Sparrow.

"Trunk," Shay said in a heartbeat. It was the only logical option. She wasn't sitting next to him.

Meg nodded. "Let's find it."

They searched behind the altar to the elaborate door that led to the priest's chambers. There's a large office. They search.

Shay rummages through drawers and cabinets until she finds a hook on the bookshelf. A set of keys. "Score. A Cadillac." Shay turned, holding up the keys.

"I hope it's got a big trunk space," Meg said.

Jed was familiar with churches, his mother brought him often enough in their travels. She always expected them to be a safe place, but they rarely were. They never got more than a meal and a blanket before their stay turned to shit. He headed toward the door at the back of the office. These places were all laid out the same. He turned down a few hallways until they came to another door that led to the garage.

"How far to the portal?" Jed asked.

"Almost a seven-hour drive," Meg said. "I'm not sure Teari is going to make it that far."

Jed starts the Cadillac. "There's a full tank."

Shay had never felt such joy. "Good, because there are no full gas cans here to top off the tank."

Meg walked to the front of the garage and reached for the garage door. She yanks it up. They are greeted by shuffling feed and groaning.

"Crap!" Shay shouted.

Meg used her blade to cut off a few heads.

Shay used more bullets than she wanted to part with. The car sped up behind them, rolling over the corpses.

"Meet me at the front steps," Jed said before speeding to the end of the street and taking a sharp turn around the block.

"Come on!" Shay slapped Meg's arm and ran inside.

They ran through the back hallways until they reached the altar. Both ran down the steps, headed for Teari.

"Help me lift her," Meg shouted to Shay.

Shay grabbed Teari's legs, and they maneuvered her out of the pew. She was dead weight, completely out of it.

Meg kicked open the front door to the church just as the Cadillac parked and Jed jumped out. "Come on. Hurry up." He opened the trunk.

"I hope you could fit groceries from a trip to Sam's Club in there. Sparrow's a big guy." Meg's tone was sarcastic.

"He'll fit," Jed said.

Meg climbed in the back seat, dragging Teari in with her. Shay closed the door with a quiet click.

Jed grabbed Shay's arm. "Let's get Sparrow and get out of here."

Shay didn't like the feeling of the church anymore. She wanted out and was grateful that Sparrow was lingering near the front door.

"Let's go, Sparrow," Jed said, as he guided Sparrow outside and down the steps.

"He's cooperating?" Shay asked, surprised.

Jed made eye contact with Shay. "He must still be in there somewhere." Hope swelled in Jed's chest. Maybe they could help him.

"You're going in the trunk, big guy." Jed backed Sparrow against the trunk then pressured him to sit and fall back. They tucked his legs in before slamming the trunk closed.

Jed and Shay got in the front. Jed was driving. He shifted the Cadillac into gear and slammed down the accelerator, eager to get as far away from the church as possible.

"This thing says we're going in the wrong direction," Meg said, holding up a cell phone from the back seat.

"Nah," Jed said. "We're going to avoid the busted down cars and roadblocks. I've been through these parts before. On my way to California."

"You drove to California?" Meg asked.

"There weren't planes flying when the dead started walking everywhere. They shut everything down."

"Sure weren't. Driving was safest and fastest," Shay said.

There was a long silence before Meg asked, "Where did you two meet?"

Jed and Shay glanced at each other. "Nebraska," Shay lied. Shay didn't want to reveal all her secrets.

"You don't have to tell me," Meg said.

JED TURNED RIGHT onto interstate 80. He passed two cars moving slowly. There were more broken down on the sides of the road. There were even some of the dead schlepping it down the highway. Jed weaved around them.

"Why'd you choose California?" Meg asked.

Jed cleared his throat. "You know I've been on the run my whole life. Months ago, the news stations were tracking the horde of dead. There were groupings of them all over the U.S. but the biggest one was in California." He cleared his throat again. "It moved strangely, stopping for days at a time before moving up the coast. I've been around long enough to know those things don't move in a coordinated pack like that. They're usually scattered."

"So, I had the thought that they must be following something... or, someone." Jed accelerated past three dead making their way across the highway. "I reached out to some of my contacts and they told me about the rumors of a tall, dark man walking his way up the coast. No one could tell what he was." Jed snapped his fingers and points into the rearview mirror at me. "But I knew. I knew because I never forgot the day you two showed up with Sparrow in that Canadian tuxedo."

"What's a Canadian tuxedo?" Shay asked.

Jed chuckled.

"Think jeans *and* a jean jacket," Meg said.

"Wow," Shay made a face, "impressive. Wish I'd seen it."

"Nothing like it," Jed said as he slowed to pass a family waving us down from their broken-down minivan. "Sorry," he muttered. "No room here."

"Keep going with the California story," Meg says.

Jed cleared his throat. "Once I started putting the pieces together, I headed that way."

"Why seek out Sparrow when you're trying to hide yourself?" Meg asked.

"Who better to hide with than a Hellion?" Jed asks. "I knew no one was finding him and the walking dead were keeping their distance. As far as I was concerned, being close to Sparrow was the safest option on the Earthen plane."

"It was," Shay said. "Most of the dead kept their distance when we got close to him."

"Why have you stuck with me?" Meg asked.

Jed pressed his lips together as he glanced in the rearview mirror again.

"Why?" Meg asked.

"Because you're different than you were last time I saw you, Meg. You're stronger, darker, quicker. You've lost your spark." He tipped his head. "What happened to you?"

Meg didn't say a word.

"Whatever happened to you," Jed said, "is going to keep me safe. You owe me."

"Shit," Shay blurted out and pointed. "Army men."

Jed pulsed the brakes to slow the Cadillac and moved into the right lane. A row of Humvees blocked the highway. Men in green fatigues loaded with ammo and weapons were stationed at the roadblock.

"What is this?" Meg asks.

"Some kind of checkpoint," Jed said, rolling down his window.

"Just speed through them," Meg said. "We can't stop."

"Nah," Jed said. "They'll shoot us dead." He rolled down all the windows and stopped the car. "A caddy won't win against a Humvee."

Men in fatigues, carrying lots of guns and ammo, surround the car. "Where are you headed?" The one at the driver's side window asked.

"Saratoga Springs," Jed replied.

"We've got injured," a man shouted from near the back window. "Unlock the door," he ordered. "Medic, medic, medic we need you at the on-ramp now," he hollered into his walkie-talkie.

"We have to get her home and get her help," Meg shouted. "Just let us go!"

The locks click. The rear door is opened.

"Weapons, they've got weapons!" a soldier shouted from the other side of the car.

"Everyone has weapons you imbeciles!" Shay shouted. The tension in the vehicle was sky high.

One of the soldiers dragged Meg out of the car by gripping her jacket and pulling her across the seat. Jed's hand snaked across the seat to Shay's and he gave the slightest shake of his head. The fingers of his left hand were raised and ready.

"Don't touch me!" Meg screamed like a cornered animal. "We have to get her home and get her help."

"Why would you wait that long?" the soldier asked.

A whole crew of people showed up and the soldiers slide Teari on to a stretcher.

"What happened to her?" someone asked.

"She was bit." Meg said. "She cut off one hand and then it happened again and she made me cut the other one off."

A medic checked Teari's pulse. "She's going to code soon," he shouts to the others. And then they ran her stretcher toward an ambulance.

"Wait!" Meg shouts. "Don't take her away."

"Let them do their work," one of the soldiers said.

One soldier motioned for Jed to get out of the car. He complied.

There's another soldier standing at the trunk. "What's in here?" he asked.

Jed said, "Weapons for killing the zombies."

"And a little bit of food," Shay added.

"You want to search it?" the soldier standing near the trunk asked the one in charge.

Shay felt a bead of sweat drip down her spine. This entire situation was deep shit.

The one in charge shook his head.

The soldier patted the trunk and pointed toward the ambulance. "You can go wait for your friend while they fix her up."

Jed, Shay, and Meg got inside and Jed drove away, pulling off the Scranton exit and following the signs to the hospital.

"That was close," Shay said.

"What are they going to do to Teari?" Meg asked.

Jed followed the signs for the emergency room and parked near the sidewalk.

"Go check on her," Jed said.

"And what about Sparrow?" Meg asked.

"We'll watch him," Jed said. "We'll be freezing our asses off in this weather while doing it."

Meg got out and ran toward the door.

When Meg didn't come back out, Shay turned to Jed. "What in the actual fuck?"

"I know." Jed's hands tore through his hair. He'd been doing that a lot lately. Shay hadn't seen him this frustrated, not even when they were fighting a horde of Demons. It made Shay nervous. She wasn't sure what to expect from these people, and she got the feeling Jed didn't know either.

———

A THIN LAYER of snow coated the sidewalk by the time Meg started walking back.

"How is she?" Shay asked. She didn't know these people, but she'd watched Teari get both her hands chopped off and live. It was brutal. She couldn't help but have sympathy for her.

Meg shrugged. "No one could tell me."

Thuds came from the trunk.

"They'll help her," Jed said.

"We need to go," Meg urged.

"And leave her here?" Shay asked.

"It's getting dark. We need to get to the portal. I have to get

Sparrow to Hell before we're found," Meg said. There was something about the worry in her voice.

Shay glanced at Jed, eager to avoid any more battles.

"So we are leaving her?" Jed asked.

"I'll come back for her," Meg said.

Shay wondered how Meg was at keeping promises. She had heard plenty of people make promises. She'd heard Jed promise to wipe her memories and their tone was the same.

———

JED DROVE AS FAST as he could toward Saratoga Springs. Meg watched out the window, disturbingly quiet. Jed turned onto I-84E, then I-87N. Dark cities surrounded the Newburg and Albany exits. But in the distance there were lights. It seemed some towns still had electricity. It gave Shay hope for recovery after all of this was over. Maybe her world could be saved.

In the early hours of the morning, Jed pulled into the stone driveway of the cemetery and parked the caddy against the wrought-iron fence. Everyone got out and moved to the trunk.

"I hope no one is watching," Shay muttered.

Jed popped the trunk open.

Sparrow stared at the three of them.

"Come on, big guy," Meg said, reaching for his legs.

Getting Sparrow out of the trunk was a challenge.

When he was on his feet, Jed took Shay aside, stopping under an overgrown oak that shaded a handful of tombstones. His hand gripped her wrist, and he stepped close.

"You can go back." He held a hand near her temple. He closed his eyes and sighed. "You can forget all of this and go back and live your life."

Something sank in Shay's chest. Then it burned. Shay slapped his hand away from her face. "No."

Jed's eyes were pleading. "Everyone dies around me." His grip on her wrist tightened. "*Everyone.*"

Shay motioned to Meg. "She lived."

"She is very different."

Shay touched the tiny scars on his neck. "You want me to go away because of her?"

"Never." His expression turned sour.

Shay searched his features. The sharp cheekbones, the days old stubble, and the blue eyes that made Shay wonder if they were the same color as his aura.

"You send me away and what?" Shay searched his face, her eyes falling on his lips. "You can't take all of my memories. The day my parents died... I can't go back not remembering that. And I'll remember that you were there." She jabbed a finger into his chest. "I'll hunt you down. If you ever thought the Angels and Demons were incessant, I'll be worse. I will be your biggest nightmare."

Jed smirked, fire in his eyes. "You think I'd fear you?"

Shay stepped closer until her chest touched his. "You have no idea."

Meg cleared her throat loudly. "Is she coming or are you going to annoy her to death?"

Shay let out a breath of a laugh.

Jed walked toward the arch, leading Shay by the hand.

"She's a big girl, Jed," Meg said. "Let her make her own choices."

Jed looked annoyed. He'd seen enough death in his long lifetime. He didn't want Shay to become another memory.

"To Heaven or Hell?" Jed asked.

"Hell," Meg replied.

He pointed to the words etched into the stone. "This can go to either."

"You can read that?" Meg asks.

He nodded. "You can't?"

"Tell me what they say." Meg pointed to the arch.

"Gradus ad Infernus," Jed said and the space between the arch wavered. "Step to hell. That's it. Easy peasy."

Meg grabbed Sparrow's jacket at the elbow. Shay grabbed his opposite arm, and they led him through. Jed took up the rear, to make sure nothing followed them through.

The travelers stepped into Hell.

THIRTY-ONE

SHAY RECOGNIZED THE FEELING OF HELL AS SOON AS SHE came through the portal into the open field on the other side. She recognized the ochre light, the dark shadows. Her eyes searched the tree line for Nero, hoping that he was here. He had to be here.

"Where do we go now?" Shay asked, eager to move and find cover.

Meg points in the distance. "You know it as Centralia, PA."

Shay's gut dropped. They had to backtrack. This was a mess. "Are you kidding me? We just came from Pennsylvania." Shay's hands tore through her hair in frustration.

"Seriously. Please tell me you have functioning vehicles down here." Jed looked around expectantly.

"We do," Meg said. "But I didn't leave any nearby."

"You didn't plan very well," Shay blurted out. She wasn't sure where the boldness was coming from. Maybe it was her trying to make up for being just human.

"Nope," Meg agreed. "Sure didn't. But no worries, someone will find us sooner or later."

Sparrow made a muffled noise from behind the cloth covering the lower half of his face.

Shay noticed Meg's face dropped. "Come on," she urged Sparrow to move.

The travelers walked down the road, their shoes echoing in the darkness. Shay moved closer to Jed, her hand on her pistol, ready.

"Weird," Jed said. "If I didn't know better, I'd say we already traveled these roads today."

"These are different," Meg said. "Do you feel any safer, now that you're in Hell?"

There was a pause. "All I can say is I've never been here before. But those Angels have their ways."

"Not here," Meg said with confidence.

The sound of shuffling feet echoed. Shay knew that sound. She'd heard it enough these past few months. The dead were here.

"Dead walking. They'll keep their distance down here," Meg assured Shay.

The sound intensified. Jed's back went ramrod straight. "Shit," he said, grabbing Shay's arm and tugging her away from the dead man who was currently running toward them.

Meg moved the fastest. Her blade was drawn and glowing as she moved to the middle of the road, walking confidently toward the fast-moving corpse. She raised her blade and chopped off its head. "Haven't had that happen in a long time," Meg said.

"Why are they so fast? Was it their blood?" Shay asked.

Jed stepped toward Meg. "What does that mean?"

"They usually keep their distance here. Maybe it's because there are so many of us." Meg looked at Shay then Sparrow. "Come on, let's keep going."

They walked quieter this time. Slower dead ambling in the forest kept their distance. Shay was relieved.

"Someone is waiting in the road up there," Shay whispered to Jed.

"Noah, where have you been?" Meg asked.

The guy in the road looked up to the night sky and said dreamily, "Birdwatching. You know how we used to do, watching those song-birds all day long. What happened to it all?"

Meg was thoughtfully quiet for a moment before she replied, "We'll get back to it." There was sadness in her voice that everyone could hear.

The guy named Noah took note of Jed and Shay. "Oh! You brought back friends and..." He leaned around Meg, noticing Sparrow. "What the fuck did you do to Sparrow?"

Meg grabbed Noah's arm. "Do not tell Nightingale. Actually, you are not to leave my presence until we figure this out."

Noah laughed. "No soup for you."

Meg's stomach growled. "I'll have to eat something else."

Shay glanced to Jed, not understanding. Jed motioned to the scars on his neck and Shay realized Meg and Noah were talking about Meg drinking Sparrow's blood.

"But, seriously," Noah said. "Night is going to be pissed. Beyond pissed, actually. You went back to fix things. This ain't fixing things."

"No shit, Sherlock," Meg pointed to Jed. "This is Jed. He's going to help us." She pointed to Shay. "And this is Shay."

"What's Shay going to do?" Noah asked, sizing her up.

"Something," Meg replied with a dull voice.

Something burned in Shay's chest. "Kick some ass," she said, eager to prove her worth to these creatures.

"I like her," Noah whispered to Meg but they could all hear him. "Why aren't we going to *poof* back to the castle? It would be faster than this method of travel."

Shay's stomach felt sick at the mere mentioning of traveling with Meg. She wasn't sure she could hold her stomach if it happened again.

"I can't take everyone at once. And I don't want to leave any of them waiting," Meg said. "Actually, go get the Hellions. Tell them where we are."

Noah's lips curled into a devious smile. "And leave your side?"

"Don't screw with me," Meg warned. "You've done enough of that. Go get the Hellions. They can fly us back."

Noah's eyebrows raised in jest. "Why don't you fly us back, Meg?"

"You little... shit." Meg lurched forward, reaching for Noah's throat but he disappeared into thin air.

Shay was staring, trying to process it all, trying to make it make sense.

"Let's keep walking," Meg said.

"What are Hellions?" Shay asked.

"Giant, scary Demon warriors," Jed replied.

"But you said Sparrow was a Hellion."

"He was. Or is. I'm not sure. Hey, Meg, what the heck is Sparrow these days?" Jed asked.

"Damned if I know," Meg muttered, refusing to look back at them as she walked further, one hand leading Sparrow.

Jed lingered further behind Meg so he and Shay could talk.

"Are you handling this okay?" he asked.

Shay shrugged. "This is all completely messed up. What the heck was Noah?"

"I think he's a ghost of some kind," Jed said. "These people, I don't know a lot about them. I only know Meg and Sparrow." He searched her eyes. "Are you wishing you'd gone home now?"

Shay pressed her lips together, ready to give him an earful but a shadow from the sky caught her eyes. She looked up to see giant winged Demons flying closer. They were dressed like black ops, carrying wicked blades and odd weapons. They had horns and wings like giant bats. They were massive, the size of Sparrow but thick with muscle. And they didn't look friendly.

"Oh my god," Shay shouted, grabbing on to Jed for safety. "What the heck! What are those?"

The biggest one landed near Meg. He had horns curled on each side of his head. His smile dropped as he walked closer to Meg. "You took too long. We were worried."

Meg threw her hands in the air. "How about, great job, Meg? Or, way to go, Meg? Or, look you found Sparrow, just what you needed to do?"

Three more Hellions landed, their boots echoing heavily on the pavement. They seemed relaxed. Shay was on edge. She'd battled Clyburn and Alastor and the small Demons at the camp, but these Hellions were so very different. She wasn't sure anyone could win against them.

Meg introduced Jed and Shay before asking, "Where's Noah?"

"He's at the castle," the Hellion closest to Meg answered. He motioned to the other Hellions. "Chel, you take Shay. Tukka and Klaus take Sparrow."

Shay backed against Jed as she looked at the one named Chel. He was mysterious, quiet, and when he walked toward Shay, it looked like he only moved in the shadows; a skip and a ripple of movement.

Jed's arm snaked around Shay's middle and tugged her closer. His free hand reached out, fingers twisted, tapping, ready to chant.

Chel paused in front of them. "I will not hurt her." He looked down at Shay. "She is nothing but human. But you," he looked to Jed, "you are something else. What are you?"

"Just another mixed-breed abomination." His arm tightened on Shay. "If you hurt her, I will end you."

Chel's face didn't flex with the threat to his life. He simply held out his arms. "A friend of Sparrow's is a friend of mine. Until proven otherwise. I will fly you to the castle, Shay. That is all."

Shay wanted to be strong. She didn't want to fear the Hellions, but anyone seeing them for the first time would be terrified. Shay's fingers tapped Jed's arm until he released her.

Shay took two steps closer to Chel. "Okay." She raised her chin and tightened the shoulder straps of her pack.

Chel lifted her into his arms. Shay glanced at Jed, thinking she should have hugged him or kissed him. Just in case. But he'd been cold in that aspect for a while now, since that night he painted the runes on her skin and kissed her like she'd never been kissed before. He kept his distance.

"Wrap your arms around my neck," Chel instructed as he flexed his wings wide.

Shay reached up, and the Hellion held her small body closer to his before launching them into the air.

Shay felt dizzy between the movement and the sound of Chel's powerful wings and the distance to the ground.

"Breathe," Chel suggested. "I prefer not to land with you unconscious. Your friend will be quite mad at me if I do."

Shay took a deep breath and closed her eyes for a moment. She tried to set her mind straight, tried to tell herself that she would not be dropped or maimed by the scary Hellion that was flying her. She was about to be in a castle, like a fairytale... or a nightmare.

"Your first time in Hell?" Chel asked.

"You could say that," Shay replied. "I had barely left home before this year. Never thought my travels would bring me here."

"You've been here before though." Chel looked down at her. "I can smell the brimstone in your hair. It's fading, but still there." His nares flared.

"Well, there was this Crossroads Demon who dragged me underground. I woke up and it felt strange. Too many shadows that moved. I wasn't sure where I was exactly."

"You were on the wrong side of the Veil. It's thinned and there are holes. Creatures have been passing through. Now that Sparrow has returned, it should go back to normal." Chel veered to the left and continued flying.

Shay wanted to look over his shoulder to see if Jed was following, but Chel was too massive to see over.

"Humans don't belong here," Chel warned.

"Are you going to send me away?"

"No," Chel said matter-of-factly. "This is Meg's realm. She will decide. The Hellions follow her lead."

Shay's eyes went wide as she made the connection. "Hell is Meg's realm?" Her mouth suddenly felt like cotton. "That means Meg is, like, Lucifer?"

"That was her grandfather. She killed him. We just call her Meg. It's what she prefers." Chel's motion changed. He shifted his body and his wings and they started descending. He landed in a U-shaped courtyard and set Shay on her feet.

Chel waited, arms crossed, watching her intently.

Shay stepped away from him and observed the courtyard. There was a leafless tree in the center, hard-packed dirt, a building that resembled a mountain. The design was menacing and macabre and absolutely beautiful. She'd seen nothing like it in her life.

"Your friend," Chel broke the silence. "What is he?"

"Half human and half Angel." After the words left her lips, she was unsure if she should have told him. She wasn't a spy or good at lying and didn't know what Jed wanted to reveal about himself.

"That explains it," Chel said. "Does he have the magic in his bones?"

Shay nodded.

Chel made a noise like a growl and his eyes narrowed. "Be cautious of him." He showed a hint of sharp teeth.

Three more Hellions landed; the two with Sparrow then the horned one with Jed.

As soon as Jed's feet were on the ground he made his way to Shay, his eyes searching her body for injury.

"I'm fine," Shay said.

———

JED AND SHAY got a crash course on the realm of Hell. Meg ruled. The Hellions followed her lead. Noah was a ghost and Meg's best friend, tethered to her. Clea was her mother–another ghost. Sparrow was her boyfriend. And Skeele was her Hellion Legion Commander. The Angels were not allowed in Hell–except for Meg's father, an Archangel named Gabriel. There were beings called Deacons who helped the newly dead ascend and kept the balance between realms. After a long conversation with Chel, he explained that when humans from the Earthen plane died, they all went to Hell, confused and unknowing. The Deacons would find the newly dead and bring them to their Safe Houses so the souls could repent and ascend to Heaven or stay in Hell. The power of Heaven and Hell was determined by how many souls a realm had. Currently, Meg had the most.

———

JED ASKED FOR SEPARATE ROOMS.

Shay's heart sank. She didn't want to be alone. Chel led them to a suite with two bedrooms. It was fully furnished with a kitchen and bathrooms and a living room, much like a small apartment. The furnishings were modest but nice. Leather furniture and dark patterned wallpaper gave the rooms a gothic feeling. Shay felt safe for the first time since before the dead started walking on the Earthen plane. Safe, but lonely and drained.

"Food will be brought to your room shortly," Chel said. "If you need anything, just ask. Stay out of the shadows and never go below the main floor," he warned. "Clea stocked the closets for you both. It's kind of her thing."

When the door closed, Jed set his pack down and rummaged through it. He pulled out a Sharpie and set to work warding the doors and windows.

"What should I do?" Shay asked, setting her bugout bag on the nearby chair. "I want to help."

"Why don't you go get cleaned up?" Jed suggested. "We've had a rough couple of days."

Shay checked both of the bedrooms and chose the one with an elegant four-poster bed and deep purple linens. She checked the closet and found women's clothing that would fit her, just like Chel said. Seems Meg's realm took good care of guests. Shay's mind wandered to Chel's warning and what could be kept below the main floor. She walked to the adjoining bathroom and tried to dispel the thoughts of torture and cages and scenes from horror movies.

Shay found fluffy towels in the linen closet. She ran the water and began filling the bathtub. Thoughts of bathing in ice-cold streams and dark Demon cabins flooded her mind. This was better. She dragged her hand through the bathwater and adjusted the temperature before standing and undressing.

The runes Jed had painted on her body were fading. She wasn't sure if they'd actually offered her any protection. Sparrow could see her and the other Hellions saw her clear as day. None tried to touch her though. Maybe the realms changed the spells? Shay wasn't sure. She released her pistol from the holster, then took off her belt and set it all on the bathroom counter. The Hellions didn't bat an eye at her carrying weapons, they didn't even check their bags. They must have no fear.

Thirty-Two

Shay toweled herself dry and checked the runes on her skin in the mirror. They were definitely faded after her bath. She turned to get a view of the ones on her back. They were the same. Shay shivered at the thought of Jed painting her again. The experience was nearly too much. She wasn't sure she could handle being that close with him and then being sent to bed like a child again. Shay dried her hair before wrapping the towel tighter around her body and walking to the bedroom closet.

She searched through the clothing and found a pair of dark denim jeans, a flannel shirt, and undergarments. She hadn't met Clea but she sure appreciated that the ghost could match her style and size. Shay dropped the towel and put on the undergarments. The jeans were form fitting but stretchy. She was buttoning the flannel shirt when she heard a noise behind her.

She turned to find Jed staring at her.

"What?" she asked.

Jed cleared his throat. "Dinner's here." He was staring at her exposed midriff.

Shay buttoned her shirt the rest of the way and followed him.

There were two plates waiting on the dinette table. Each had a large steak, a baked potato, and green beans with a large slab of butter. And... macaroni and cheese in a ramekin. There was a basket of bread and two cans of Coca-Cola dripping with condensation.

"Wow," Shay said as she sat. "I wasn't expecting his."

"I'm going to go wash up before eating," Jed said. "Go ahead and eat. I'll just be a few minutes."

Jed was covered in dust, his clothing stained with gore and fingers stained from the Sharpie.

"That's probably a good idea," Shay agreed. As she sat, he walked into the opposite bedroom.

Shay picked up a fork and knife and cut the steak. She sliced the potato then added butter, and salt and pepper.

It was the best food she'd eaten since living on the ranch. She reached for the ramekin of macaroni and cheese, dug her fork in and took a bite. Memories... of her mother and father, of her anger when they said she couldn't go to college and risk the walking dead, memories of running off to that dive-bar and seducing Clyburn. Her mind spiraled at that point. Everything hit her like a flash bang. The Crossroads Demon attack. The Demons killing her mother. Her father changing into one of the walking dead and attacking her. Leaving Nero.

Tears were streaming down Shay's face as she chewed. So much had changed in such a short period of time. She'd seen things that only existed in books and movies. She'd fought and killed an Angel. She'd survived being kidnapped by Demons. She was free of Clyburn thanks to Nero. Shay mourned all that she'd lost. She mourned her simple life on the ranch, the chance to go to college and be normal, the love of her parents. She mourned losing Nero to whatever darkness he was now. She wasn't sure she'd ever see him again. Jed's cold shoulder made it all worse. One moment he was protective, the next he was distant. It was all too much for her to take.

Shay stood up and paced the room. She wiped her face. The weight of grief pressed upon her like a suffocating blanket. Shay crumbled. Pappa and Momma's deaths were a loss that tore through her heart with merciless claws, leaving her shattered and adrift in a sea of overwhelming emotions.

Tears streamed down her face, sobs wracked her body. Memories of dinners and holidays and summers on the ranch intertwined with the stark reality of her current situation. She was no longer on the Earthen plane. She was in an unfamiliar place with dangerous creatures. She was more alone than she'd ever been in her entire life. She felt hollow and desolate, each memory a reminder of the laughter and love that she'd never experience again.

Jed's bedroom door creaked open, concern etched deeply into his furrowed brow as he took in the heartbreaking sight before him.

With a towel secured around his waist and water dripping down his body, Jed crossed the room. His steps were measured yet filled with urgency, afraid to exacerbate the fragile shell of emotions surrounding Shay.

Shay turned, her face tear-stained, her eyes mirroring a tumultuous sea of emotions; pain, loss, and desperate yearning for solace.

Jed enveloped her in a tender embrace, drops of water soaked into Shay's clothing but she didn't care. She rested her cheek against his bare chest, sobs echoing in the quiet room.

Jed was at a loss. He wanted to reassure Shay that she wasn't alone in navigating the unfathomable depths of their predicament. He was there, he just couldn't find the words. It seemed everything he'd said to her recently came out guarded.

Shay's cries softened into quiet sniffles as she listened to Jed's heartbeat. He held her close, warmth seeping into her bones.

"What's wrong?" he asked.

"It's all gone to shit. Everyone is dead and now we are in Hell." She felt his arms loosen and that was all she needed to fall off the deep end again.

"It's not all shit," Jed said. "We got hot showers and dinner."

Shay smiled but anguish threatened to overcome her once again when he slid his hands to her arms like he was going to move her away.

"You don't want me with you," Shay said, pushing at his bare chest.

"That's not true."

"It is." Shay pushed him away. "I lost everything. *Everything.* You are all that I have left in this world and you don't even want me."

Shay paced the room, hugging herself.

"You have more than me." Jed's expression was unreadable.

"Who? Who do I have?"

Jed's gaze searched her face. "You have to have more family on the Earthen plane. You have Grandmother Crow at least. The Crow brothers. Friends. You have others who won't put you in danger like I do."

"You're wrong." Shay walked closer to him. "Everyone is dead. And I do not want to spend the rest of my life on the reservation. I will always be an outsider there. You are all I have Jed. When are you going to realize that?"

Jed was afraid it would come to this. Shay knew what she wanted, she knew who she was and he'd been keeping her at arm's length since he kissed her in Crescent City. The truth was, he couldn't get the image of her painted with runes and half naked in the moonlight out of his head. He thought about it every moment.

Shay was pacing until she finally threw her hands up in the air in silent resignation and started walking toward her bedroom door.

"Wait," Jed reached for her but she kept going.

He caught up to her in a few long strides, grabbed her shirt and turned her to face him.

"You're not alone, Shay-baby." He backed her up against the wall. "You'll never be alone. I'm sorry if I made you felt that way. It's just... everyone close to me has died—"

"Same here, cowboy."

The corner of his mouth twitched. "I'm sorry."

"It's not your fault."

He was so close Shay rubbed the tip of her nose against his.

"It feels like my fault," he confessed. "It all feels like my fault. Ever since I met you at that casino it's been my fault."

"The world's problems are not because of you." She pressed a hand to his chest, feeling the dips and planes of his body as her hand moved up to his neck. "You didn't start the apocalypse. You didn't make the dead walk on the Earthen plane. You didn't kill my parents."

"Sometimes my world is very small. I've only had one focus and that was to stay alive." He leaned against her, pressing her to the wall with his whole body, caging her between his arms. "Now my only focus is to keep you alive."

"I can handle myself. I killed that Angel before it could kill you," she reminded him.

Jed nodded, remembering. "I wish I'd seen it."

"Maybe that's why you can't seem to remember because you were unconscious. I didn't die then." Shay licked her lips. "I'm stronger than you think. But..."

Jed searched her eyes.

"I cannot continue on like this," Shay confessed. "I need you to decide what we are together. I can't go on feeling alone. It's too much."

"You're not alone." Jed's hands touched the sides of her face and his fingers slid into her hair. "You'll never be alone."

"Stop trying to push me away," she begged.

Jed's lips pressed to Shay's. He kissed her, hungry and possessive. His fingers twisted in her hair, his thumbs pressed against the hollows under her jaw before sliding down her throat.

The floodgates opened again as he kissed her like a man starved, like she was oxygen and he needed her to breathe. Shay couldn't stop her tears from sliding along his fingers and down his arms.

"I'm sorry," Jed whispered against his lips. "If I made you think I didn't want you. I've always wanted you since the moment I saw you at Lame Deer Casino. I never stopped wanting you." His tongue speared into her mouth and he nibbled at her lips. He pulled his arms away from the wall and his fingers went to the buttons on her shirt. "I wanted you so badly the night I painted the runes on your skin."

Jed tugged at her shirt and the buttons went flying. He leaned back, tracing the fading runes on her abdomen with his fingertips.

Shay shivered at his touch. His hips were still pressing against her body, keeping her secured against the wall.

"This night was my favorite. I think about it every moment." Jed's eyes flashed to hers. "Did you know that?"

Shay was out of breath from his kisses. "You sent me to bed like a child."

"No." He kissed her hard, his hands gripping her waist. "I sent you to bed because I didn't trust myself for one more minute. Is this what you want?" His hands moved across her back, down to her hips and he pressed her against the bulge behind his towel. "Once we do this, I can't stop. You're mine. Forever."

"Yes." Shay gripped his biceps, afraid he'd change his mind the next instant. "Don't leave me alone. Don't make me be down here alone. I can't do it alone."

Jed moved away and Shay instantly felt cold. It lasted only a moment though before he lifted her and kicked open the bedroom door. He crossed the room and set Shay to her feet near the bed. He pushed the flannel shirt off her shoulders and let it drop to the floor. He traced the fading runes and bruises and scratches she'd endured on their journey. He whispered a healing spell over the scratches. Shay watched his lips as he murmured strange words that sounded like a good promise. It made her ears tingle. Her skin felt warm, electrified. When she looked at her arms again, all the scratches were healed.

"Thank you," Shay whispered, touching him. Her fingers glided over the rounded muscle of his shoulders as he kneeled, unbuttoned her jeans, and pulled them down to her ankles. She kicked them away. His fingers tested the elastic of her underwear before he slid a hand under the fabric at her hip and stood. She moved backward, falling on the bed. Jed pulled the scrap of fabric down her legs and tossed them aside.

"Lose the towel," Shay said.

Jed was sculpted like that Angel she'd killed but with a human softness she couldn't describe. He crawled toward her on the bed, supporting his weight with his arms. His mouth touched her thigh, leaving wet kisses that made her shiver as he worked his way up her body. His mouth touched the hollow of her hip, the softness of her stomach, the firm stretch of her bottom rib, the sensitive skin under her breast. Shay was trembling by the time he made it to her mouth, which he devoured. Shay's fingers stretched into Jed's hair as she kissed him back, desperate for his touch. He palmed her breast before his hand roved over her waist and hip to the apex between her thighs.

Shay gasped as he touched her, as his fingers worked her over and made her ready. When he finally slid into her, Shay was aching and burning.

He kissed her and she kissed him, pausing to take slow breaths with their foreheads pressed together as they moved unhurriedly together. Jed was slow. So slow that Shay thought she might burst into flames from the heat of it all.

———

SHAY WOKE to Jed leaning over her, his hands cradling her face, his lips whispering a spell she'd never heard him chant before. Her mind felt fuzzy, her brain hurt. She blinked a few times. There was a sharp pain in the center of her forehead.

Jed's face was intent as he chanted. His fingertips traced invisible shapes above her ears. He whispered words that sounded like the saddest bird song, mournful and low and heartbreaking.

Shay panicked.

He was doing it. He was wiping her memories. No!

THIRTY-THREE

Shay moved fast, whipping her fist up and cracking Jed on the side of the head. She shoved his upper body while he was stunned, knocked him on his back, and straddled his chest. She grabbed his hands, twisting his fingers until she could feel the resistance of bones and tendons.

"What the fuck do you think you're doing, Jed?" She screamed at him. "Erasing my memories? I told you no. I told you I didn't want that."

"I wasn't erasing them." He stared at her, hard and cold. "I was putting them behind a wall. So they weren't constantly making you sad." Jed bucked up and rolled so Shay was under him. "I was trying to help you."

Shay stilled and searched his eyes in the dim light. Her hand moved to his face and she traced her fingertips over his cheekbones.

"You could have asked." She searched his eyes. "You could have asked and made sure that was something *I* wanted."

Jed opened his mouth to speak but before he could say anything, a loud crash filled the room as the bedroom door was kicked in.

A giant Hellion ran into the room and tore Jed off Shay.

"Meg demands that no human will be harmed in her Kingdom."
Chel glared at Jed. "You're coming with me."

———

It had all happened so fast. One minute she was warm and falling
asleep on Jed's chest. Her body was deliciously sore. The next, he was
violating her trust then torn from the room.

Shay rubbed her eyes and held the sheet to cover herself.

"Chel?" She shouted as he slammed the door to the suite, dragging Jed along with him.

Shay scrambled out of bed and got dressed. She found her boots
and put them on before running out of the room.

She paused in the dark hallway. She didn't know which way they
had gone. It was too dark to see. There was a scratching sound from
the shadows.

"Chel?" she shouted. "Jed?"

Panic started rising in Shay's chest. She wasn't sure where to go
or where to look for them. One thing came to mind: the levels below
the main floor.

Yes, that had to be where Chel had taken Jed. Shay ran back into
the room, found her bag, and pulled out her pistol and knife. She left
the room again, backtracking from the direction Chel had brought
them earlier that evening.

Shay's boots made a hollow noise as she ran down the long hallway. She stopped at the winding, grand staircase and looked down
the center of it. It never ended and dark echoes came from below.

Shay ran down the steps, two at a time.

She stopped short when a white figure appeared at the landing
she was approaching. A woman appeared with dark hair and ruby red
lips. She was slightly transparent like Jennifer's ghost but became
more solid as Shay slowed.

"Where are you going, child?" the ghost asked.

Shay tried to dodge around the woman, but the ghost was quick and blocked her every move.

"Let me pass," Shay demanded.

"I do not like to ask the same question twice." The woman tipped her head down.

Shay realized she the ghost looked like Meg. It was Clea, her mother.

"I'm going to find Jed." Shay tried to pass again but Clea blocked her.

"You do not want to go down there, human child," Clea warned. "There are things not meant for your sight, things you can't comprehend, things that are ages old and not mean for human eyes."

"I've seen things." Shay backed up five steps. "I'm not afraid."

"Perhaps I am afraid for you," Clea warned.

"I need to get to Jed."

"What did he do to you?" Clea asked. "We all heard you screaming."

"He made me mad."

Clea smirked. "Are you going to save him?"

"Wouldn't be the first time." Shay glanced at the banister and considered leaping across to the other side. Her stomach clenched when she considered the possibility of falling.

As though Clea could read her mind, she stepped to the side. "I warned you." She disappeared up the stairs.

Shay shook her head in disbelief and ran down the stairs toward the dungeon.

THIRTY-FOUR

DURING THE REIGN OF LUCIFER, DEMON CHILDREN WERE not to be seen and not to be heard. Breaking either rule would result in severe punishment. It felt awful at the time but Chel would learn it was to prepare him for life under Lucifer's thumb. Chel learned early how to hide in the shadows. He learned how to avoid the light. Bred to be a Hellion and serve the throne, he spent his childhood years in training. It was the only thing that made his father proud. The only time he'd heard his father utter a whisper of delight was the day he'd completed his training. There had been no joy in the family household for years prior.

Chel would never forget that day because there should have been four people at the dinner table, but his sister's seat remained empty, as it had for nearly two years since she'd gone missing. It was the first moment in a long time that anyone uttered an emotion besides despair.

Demon women weren't known for their longevity. Many died in childbirth or defending their young from rage-filled fathers. It was a family dynamic like nothing else. Lucifer's reign kept his subjects in a constant state of dread. It trickled through day-to-day life like a dark tap left to drip and drip and drip.

Yelena was three years younger than Chel. She spent almost all of her time with their mother. Raised to be nothing more than a breed horse, she spent her time learning how to survive childbirth and motherhood. One day she was sent to the nearby stream to collect water for washing laundry and never returned. She was never found and it was assumed that she was murdered. A dark lull hung over Chel's family ever since. And Chel found he harbored an extreme dislike for any man who could harm a female.

———

"WHERE ARE YOU GOING?" Chel stopped Shay on the winding stairwell. His form was intimidating. The Hellion was huge, dressed in battle gear with a blade strapped to his hip.

"Where's Jed?" she demanded.

"Being punished."

"He didn't do anything."

Chel's eyes narrowed. "It sounded like he did plenty."

"You weren't there. You don't know." Shay swiped at a strand of hair and tucked in behind her ear. "It's a misunderstanding."

"What did he do to you?" Chel crossed his arms, waiting for her answer as though he had all the time in the world.

"I thought he broke a promise, but I misunderstood." Shay glanced away, not wanting Chel to see that what Jed did was still hurtful. She didn't want him using spells that would alter her memories.

"What did he do then?

"He tried to bury my memories so they wouldn't make me sad."

Chel's brow furrowed as he glared down at her. "Sounds like bullshit."

"It was."

"Meg gave orders you are not to be harmed by anyone in any manner." He shifted his feet. "You are well?"

"I'm fine."

"So you want me to release him?"

"Yes."

Chel's face shifted to a semi-growl, showing sharp teeth. He didn't believe her. He didn't trust the half-breed. "Go back to your room."

"I'm going with you to get him." Shay stood her ground.

"Go," Chel pointed up the stairs.

"I'll just get him myself." Shay weaved around Chel's enormous frame and began running down the stairwell again. It didn't take long for Chel to catch up to her. He gripped her by both shoulders with giant hands.

"There are things not meant for human eyes," he said.

"I've seen plenty already."

Chel sniffed the air and was reminded of the scent of brimstone that clung to her hair. "Fine," he said. "But I warned you."

They walked below the main level. The stairwell twisted and twisted. The lights became dimmer. The noises grew louder. Shay's heart beat heavy as she anticipated what she'd be exposed to in the castle's dungeon. Gothic décor turned to stone dripping with moss and stained water rivulets. Chel passed three floors before stopping their descent.

THIRTY-FIVE

Nero felt the moment Shay crossed the threshold into Hell. He'd been resting inside the Crossroads Demon hovel, deep asleep and recovering from rescuing Shay. The wound on his flank had opened again and throbbed. Black fluid leaked down his leg and Nero wished for a cold Montana stream to soak in. He was sure he could find a stream here but he didn't know what other creatures lingered below the surface. Maybe if he could find Shay she could help him.

Nero lifted his head and shook. The golden chain dangled and tugged at his ear. The gold was nothing more than a manacle that stole his freedom. Nero was a creature of Hell now. His soul was tethered to the realm just like he was tethered to Shay. It was worth taking on to see Clyburn turn to ash in the nearby hearth. Nero could not think of a better ending to that rotten man's life.

Nero moved to stand, his knees and joints aching from spending too much time on the Earthen plane with Shay. While he'd reveled in spending time with her before they'd found Jed and the Crow men, it took a toll. Nero couldn't spend long lengths of time where he didn't belong any longer.

407

He left the hovel and followed the tugging in his chest. Shay was in Hell but very far away from him. He headed away from the coast where the hovel was etched into a barren valley. He trotted then galloped, urgency drove him. Remember, Nero was fast. Nero was the fastest thing between the realms. He felt the tether thrum with danger. Shay yelled. It was nothing more than an echo in his ears. She was so far away. So, so far away. Nero tipped his head and ran faster. He was a blur, the darkest shadow, an errant breeze that left behind a cold chill. Nero didn't know who held the throne in Hell. He didn't know that she could travel in a *poof* of a second. He didn't know that he ran nearly as fast as she could travel. He took it as part of his being, embraced it, knew it was a gift that would keep on giving when it came to ensuring Shay's safety. It was all he could do for the human who'd saved him when he was a dying foal.

His hoof prints left an inky seepage from the wound on his flank.

THIRTY-SIX

IN THE DEPTHS OF THE ANCIENT DUNGEON, WHERE THE air hung heavy with the scent of damp stone and the echoes of distant drips reverberated through the labyrinthine corridors, Jed's cell had no light other than the dull bulb that hung in the hallway. Strange sounds and smells came from nearby. Jed touched the iron bars only to pull his hands back quickly, his fingertips red and singed.

He chanted a spell to release the lock but it didn't work. Sparks sputtered to nothingness on his fingertips. Jed paced the small space, cursing himself for going too far as he searched for runes or charms within the cell that could block his magic. He could still smell Shay's scent lingering on his skin, and it was driving him insane. Jed wanted to know where she was. He didn't trust Meg's Hellions or any creature in this realm. He'd worked too hard staying alive for it all to end like this. Jed was becoming more and more frustrated as the minutes ticked by.

———

SHAY FOLLOWED Chel through the dark hallways that twisted and turned. The doorways were spread far apart, most with iron bars, some with aged wood and small windows. The bare bulbs that were strung across the ceiling every few feet cast flickering shadows on the moss-covered walls, illuminating eerie passageways that seemed to stretch endlessly into darkness. Shay's heart hammered in her chest, driven by the urgency of finding Jed. The chilling atmosphere seemed to whisper tales of forgotten sorrows and lingering curses that haunted the ancient walls.

"Don't look into them," Chel warned, motioning down the hall. "There are creatures who will eat your soul with once glance."

"Why do you keep them here?" Shay asked. A distant humming sound from the hallway they passed was a desperate plea that resonated deep within Shay's soul. She quickened her pace to get away from the haunting echoes that would lead her deeper into the heart of the dungeon.

"They've been here for ages. We will not release them."

"Maybe relocate them," Shay suggested.

"Too risky." Chel made a noise in his throat as he neared a cell with a guard sitting outside of it.

The Hellions nodded. The one sitting in the chair didn't glance at Shay but kept his eyes elsewhere.

Shay knew she wasn't supposed to look in the cell, but Sparrow was standing right there, twitching and jerking as the death overtook his body. His skin had taken on an unnatural coloring of gray and green bruising.

Shay struggled with what she was witnessing as Meg kept Sparrow locked up. If there was a cure for whatever made the dead walk, she wished she'd known before her parents died. She would have rather cured her father than stabbed him in the head. Shay shivered as the memory replayed. She took in a stuttered deep breath and tried to clear her mind. She couldn't go back in time. She couldn't save them. She could only move on.

Chel led her down more hallways, sensing her grief.

"Why are you sad?" Chel asked.

"My parents died recently. A Demon killed my mother, and I killed my father after he turned into one of the walking dead."

Chel stopped walking and turned. "I am sorry for this." The Hellion searched her eyes, and he was silent for so long that Shay looked away. "My sister passed unexpectedly," Chel finally said.

"I'm sorry," Shay said, reaching out to touch his arm in comfort.

A clattering sound echoed in the hallways. Chel's focus snapped to a nearby door. "Keep walking."

The remainder of the walk was in silence.

———

"HERE," Chel stood in front of a closed cell door.

Shay looked past the bars to see Jed staring down at his hands, defeated.

"Jed!" Shay ran forward and touched the bars, only to have her hands scorch from the strange iron.

Chel pulled her back. "Don't touch," he warned before inserting a metal key into the wall. The bars of Jed's cell opened.

Shay ran forward, stumbling into Jed's arms.

"I'm sorry," Jed said. "I'm so sorry."

Chel motioned for them to get moving.

"Let's get out of here," Shay said.

———

CHEL WAS EERILY silent as they navigated the maze-like halls of the dungeon. He led them up the winding stairs and back to their suite. Before he closed the door, he focused on Jed. "If I ever hear her scream again, you're dead."

Jed stood his ground and crossed his arms, promising nothing.

The door closed.

Poof.

Meg appeared in the room; bloody, dripping in gore, her eyes wide with dread. She was carrying a baby wrapped in a blood-covered blanket.

"What the heck?" Shay said.

Meg ran across the room and thrust the bundle into Jed's arms. "No time to talk. Protect this kid with everything you've got."

Poof.

Meg was gone.

Shay moved toward Jed, a sickening feeling growing in her stomach. She leaned closer to the baby, taking in its dark hair and blue eyes. "Jed, whose baby is that?"

Jed touched the blood-stained blanket, pulling it away from the baby's face. The child was beautiful, like nothing he'd ever seen. Terror filled Jed.

"Hold this baby, Shay," he passed the child into Shay's arms. "Just... stay right there. Don't move until I'm finished." There was a concern in his voice that she'd never heard before.

Jed ran for his pack, brought it into the living room, and poured it out on the table. He grabbed chalk and sand. "I'm going to need you to stand there for a while." Jed drew a circle around Shay and the baby. He scrambled, drawing runes as fast as he could. He switched to coal eventually, accentuating the chalk, then poured a thick line of sand around the circle.

"What are you doing?" Shay asked. She'd never seen him so frantic. She'd never seen him set to work with the runes and protection spells so quickly. He lit a candle, then a bundle of sage, and left it to smudge in the corner. He etched runes into the doorway, then the wall. The floor became a tapestry of spells and protection charms.

"Do you think all of this is necessary?" Shay asked, her legs feeling tired. The baby was asleep in her arms. "Jed!" Panic was making her body ache.

He finally paused to look at her. "What?"

"What are you doing? Please tell me."

"That," he pointed at the baby, "is an Angel's baby and I have no idea why Meg has it, but we will not be murdered over whatever cluster fuck she's gotten us into."

THIRTY-SEVEN

JED SHOULD HAVE KNOWN THAT DEMONS NEVER DIE ONCE. But all the books on Demonology that he'd studied at the Peabody library never mentioned it. There was still much unknown between the realms. He'd learn, eventually. He'd learn enough to rewrite the books in the Peabody library so that future generations of half-breed humans might have a chance–if they lived long enough to learn how to read.

Alastor was a Demon of Lucifer's time, left to disrupt and damage as he saw fit. He supported his throne by collecting souls and selling them to the highest bidder. Children were worth the most, and he'd created a lucrative human trafficking scheme. Creatures depended on Alastor's dark deeds. Souls were delivered because of his work. Realms became more powerful.

The light engulfed Alastor, searing through his ethereal form with a cleansing fervor.
With a deafening roar that echoed through the night, the Demon

dissipated, his form unraveling into fading wisps of darkness that dispersed into the ether.

THOSE WISPS of darkness dispersed into the ether, only to collect in their rightful place. Hell. Alastor's threads of darkness collected in a tornado of dark vapors, whirring and spiraling as all the molecules and energy combined and reformed him. A Demon such as Alastor only died by fire.

-The End-

SHADOWS OF DESTINY

ONE

SHAY HAD READ ENOUGH BOOKS FROM HER PARENT'S library to know how to care for a baby. However, none of those books ever touched on the subject of caring for a baby Angel.

Jed was frantically drawing runes, casting protection charms, lining doorways with salt and ash. Sweat dripped down his face as he worked. He took off his shirt and wipe it away.

For the first time, Shay noticed the runes tattooed on Jed's skin glowed slightly as he worked.

The baby in her arms squirmed. Shay looked down at the dark haired child. Large blue eyes searched her face. Shay smiled. The baby simply stared as though it had seen something horrific.

There was blood on the blanket and small drops on the baby's head. Shay licked her finger and wiped them off. She folded the bloody parts of the blanket away from the baby's face and checked him over for injuries. She lifted the folds of baby fat around his neck and arms but found nothing concerning.

The baby yawned and made quiet mewling sounds before his eyes fluttered closed and he fell asleep. Shay rocked the baby and watched Jed as he laid a line of salt across the balcony doors.

There was a thud outside the room. Something pounded on the door.

Jed crossed the room carefully so as not to disturb his hard work.

The pounding became louder.

"Who is it?" Jed asked.

"Let me in," a familiar voice replied.

"Not until you tell me who you are."

Shay's eyes were wide as she looked between the sleeping baby in her arms and the door.

Jed was right to be wary of the shit fest Meg had dropped into their arms. Memories of the battles with Angels and Demons flooded Shay. She couldn't imagine fighting like that with a baby to protect.

TWO

NERO GALLOPED ACROSS THE WASTELAND OF MIDWESTERN Hell. Inky seepage dripped down his flank and leg, leaving a hoofprint in the hard packed dirt.

He hadn't felt a thing through the tether to Shay in days. She was here and quiet. Nero had slowed his pace, the wound on his flank throbbing and aching. He surveyed the land ahead, searching for a cool pond to soak in. The ochre sun of Hell wasn't terribly warm, but it still exhausted the stallion. Nero didn't have a good feeling about the wound on his backside. The Crossroads Demon had clawed him back at the ranch and while the wound had festered slowly, it never felt as bad as it did now.

Nero thought about lying down to rest, but he was afraid he wouldn't get up again. Creatures he'd never seen before slithered in the shadowed forests of Hell. The dead walked here as well. The creatures kept their distance. He assumed it was because of the injury or the golden ring in his ear and around his neck. He was more than simply a stallion on the loose in Hell. He had rank. Something he never experienced on the Earthen plane. While Shay cared for him like he was her child, he still lived behind gates and fences. Freedom was new and while Nero enjoyed experimenting with his newly found free will, he missed the days at the ranch with Shay.

He'd slowed to a snail's pace without realizing it. Nero hung his head, afraid he'd never make it to Shay in time.

There was a sudden tugging along the tether that joined him to Shay. Nero's eyes went wide as he realized she was afraid. Whatever was going on, she still wasn't safe.

Nero dug deep down. He whinnied and shook his head, gathering strength he didn't think he had, then picked up his pace to a gallop again.

THREE

"IT'S NOAH," THE VOICE ON THE OTHER SIDE OF THE DOOR sounded desperate.

"What do you want?" Jed asked, body tense and the short blade with runes gripped in his hand. He wasn't about to trust a soul.

"Did Meg bring you the baby?" Noah asked.

"Why?" Jed pressed his hand to the door and glanced back at Shay.

She shook her head, not wanting him to reveal anything. Not wanting him to open the door so they'd have to fight for their lives again. Shay's heart was beating faster than ever as she glanced around the room, looking for a way out or a plan.

"His name is Thrush," Noah says from the other side of the door. "He's my son."

Shay's gaze met Jed's.

"He's my son," Noah said again. "He used to have gray eyes like me. They're blue now. Sometimes that happens. Teari told us a baby's eye color can change."

Shay remembered that. She'd read about it in the medical survival books. A baby's eye color typically changed during the first year of life. The child resembled Noah in other ways.

Jed made a questioning motion.

Shay nodded.

Jed opened the door.

Noah stood in the hall. Blood and gore stained his clothing. He was disheveled, out of breath, and looked to be in despair. Noah didn't step into the room. He dropped to his knees in the hallway, buried his face in his hands and wept.

Neither Jed nor Shay knew what to do for him. After a few minutes, he wiped his face with his dirty shirt and stood again. He tried to walk into the suite, but an invisible force pushed him back.

"Let me in," Noah said, glaring at Jed.

"Maybe go get dressed and come back," Jed suggested. "He shouldn't see you like this."

"He's just a baby," Noah said.

"I know." Jed glanced at Shay as she rocked Thrush while he slept. "It's a memory that would stick, the day his father came to him distraught and filthy from battle, stinking of death."

"We'll wait here for you," Shay promised.

Noah disappeared, only to return in a few seconds, clean and refreshed. "Now will you let me in?" he asked.

Jed rubbed his boot across the line of salt at the door and motioned for Jed to enter.

"Fancy spells you've got here," Noah said, touching the runes marked on the doorframe.

"Don't," Jed warned. "We've been running for long enough. This predicament Meg put us in doesn't leave opportunity for the spells or wards to break. Especially with the baby here."

Noah pulled his hand away as though the doorframe were on fire. "You're right. What do you need?" Noah asked. "I'll do anything."

"We need supplies," Shay said. "A crib, bottles, formula, or milk."

"Nightingale was breastfeeding," Noah said.

"That could be problematic," Shay said. "Clothing, blankets."

"I can go find those things." Noah whispered, since he was leaning close to Thrush.

"Thanks," Shay said.

Jed continued warding the suite.

"I'll be back soon," Noah said.

———

"I FOUND a crib at an empty house in Buffalo," Noah said as he passed supplies across the threshold to the suite. "I have to go back and get it."

"There are no stores down here?" Shay asked. "Nothing new?"

"There are some new things, but the crib looks like the one Nightingale had for him. It's some rich person's house. I doubt I'd be able to find anything like it elsewhere." Noah disappeared.

Jed set the bags that Noah had handed him on the kitchenette table.

"You want me to look through that stuff?" Shay asked.

Jed met Shay with a few steps and took the baby from her arms. "I'm not sure what any of that is."

Shay searched through the bags. Noah had brought them just about everything they needed. It all seemed new. Shay took out the bottles and washed them, then searched for the baby formula he'd brought back. There were three different ones. Shay released a heavy breath.

"You okay?" Jed asked.

"I hope so." Shay opened one box of baby formula and made a bottle. She found diapers, baby wipes, a clean outfit, and a fresh blanket. She brought everything to the bathroom before getting Thrush from Jed.

"What are you doing?" he asked.

"Bathing him." Shay laid Thrush on a towel on the bathroom countertop and began removing his bloodied clothing. "Help me check him over," she said to Jed. "We have to make sure he wasn't bitten."

Jed's gut pinched. He hadn't thought about the baby being bitten.

"Meg went to the Seven Kingdoms of Heaven, remember?" Shay asked Jed. "She went to help them with the fast dead." Shay removed Thrush's diaper, checking every finger and toe for injury.

Thrush woke, but he didn't cry. He simply stared at the two strangers.

Shay began talking gently to the baby. Telling him what they were doing. "You're going to get a bath and clean clothes. Then a bottle. How does that sound?"

"I don't think he can talk?" Jed said.

"That doesn't mean we don't talk to him. He learns to talk by his parents talking to him." Shay turned on the sink water and when it was warm, she plugged the drain and held Thrush sitting in the shallow water.

"I know nothing about babies," Jed confessed.

"I wouldn't expect you to," Shay said as she rubbed soap over Thrush's skin and rinsed him. "He doesn't look injured." She scrubbed his dark hair, wishing she had lavender baby shampoo like momma used to use at the ranch.

A knock on the door echoed.

"I'll get it." Jed left the room.

Shay could hear the familiar voice of Noah. There was grunting and the sound of moving furniture. A final thud in the bedroom sounded just as Shay was drying off, Thrush in a fluffy towel. She diapered and dressed him in the clean clothes Noah had brought, threw the clean baby blanket over her shoulder, and carried Thrush out of the bathroom to find an elaborate crib. It was round with a lace canopy and white linens.

"Isn't that a bit much?" Shay asked.

"Never," Noah said, walking closer and holding his arms out.

Thrush finally smiled as Shay passed him into his father's arms.

Noah whispered to Thrush as Shay went to get the bottle she'd left in the kitchenette.

Four

Alastor searched his hovel for the carving knife that Lucifer had gifted him. He'd hidden it long ago when Hell came under new rule. He knew the knife would draw attention being carved of basilisk bone with a blade of sharpened onyx. Lucifer had blessed the knife with darkness. Alastor was going to use it to kill the half-breed Angel who'd banished him from the Earthen plane with blinding light. The dumb ass probably thought he'd killed Alastor. He hadn't. Simply sent him home.

Alastor found the knife tucked behind the dresser. He set it on the bed and began packing. Urgency thrummed through his body. He'd wasted enough time gathering his strength once he'd become whole again. Luckily, he'd collected a stockpile of potions that would help him regain strength.

He found clean leathers, a bag that he filled with dried meat, and a skin of water. He secured the bone blade in the harness on his thigh and set out.

Alastor followed an old path that led him to the traveling roads of Hell. Long abandoned, he was sure he wouldn't run into another soul for a long time. The hovel in the mountains was secluded for good reason. He didn't want others seeing that he dealt in the skin trades. Plenty of times he'd brought humans to his hovel to sell. Lucifer didn't care. The meddling Deacons would though. Luckily, he'd stayed under the radar. With new rule came new scrutiny, especially after the Fast-Zombie War. The Deacons were out in droves, looking for lost souls. While Alastor hadn't brought a live human home since Meg took the throne, he also hadn't come across any Deacons searching his property.

He simply needed to get back to a portal and back to the Earthen plane. Then he was going to find that Angel-spawn and kill him. After killing and bathing in the creature's blood, he was going to steal that woman with the blowtorch blue hair. She'd look nice in his hovel, cooking at the fire or tied up near the door to his room like a living statue. Alastor licked his lips, thinking about the ways he could torment her, the ways he could use and punish her. It was too easy stealing her that night at the motel. She'd run into the snow covered parking lot like a deer in headlights. He wasn't sure what she was doing there, but something distracted her enough for an easy capture.

Alastor had plans for her and she'd ruined them all. She'd ruined everything. His contacts wanted skin, and he had none. It would take months for him to find more Demons to replace the ones that had died. It would take even longer to successfully possess men from the Earthen plane and twist them to follow his plan. Alastor was going to make Shay and the half-breed pay.

Walking through the mountain forest path was calming. Alastor missed the quiet days in the hovel before he'd gotten the taste of power. Once he'd drank from that cup, he couldn't go back. He didn't want to. He'd spent eons roaming the forest like a predator on the hunt.

Alastor noticed black sludge footprint ahead. He knelt and inspected the hooved prints, touched his finger to the inky fluid, and sniffed it. He closed his eyes. There was something familiar. Something he'd smelled before. Alastor sniffed again. Some Demons were gifted when it came to scent. Like Alastor. That was what drew him to Shay. She smelled like sugar and sunshine; pure, unlike so many human women he'd come across. He could smell the hint of her in the fluid on his finger. Alastor studied the tracks. Horse hooves. He sniffed the air. It was a Crossroads Demon. Either the Crossroads Demon was on horseback, or the horse was the Crossroads Demon. Either way, they smelled like Shay.

Alastor smiled at his good luck. He didn't need to find a portal because it appeared Shay was in Hell. He followed the tracks.

FIVE

LITTLE JED WAS EXCITED to have nearly a cup full of coins that he didn't notice the plainclothes Angel watching him. When a hand circled his wrist, Jed looked up into the stone carved face of an Angel man.

"No!" Clara shouted as she exited the restaurant.

Everything happened so fast. The Angel jerked Jed to his feet, spilling the coins across the sidewalk.

Jed knew he was supposed to yell and scream and fight, but it was broad daylight people on the street would help him. He looked up at the Angel, malevolence etched in his face. Jed took a deep breath and let out the loudest scream he could manage.

No one stopped to help him. The Angel began dragging him down the street.

Clara was shouting and running toward them.

Two police officers were ahead, watching from the opposite side of the road.

Jed screamed again, his little heart racing. He didn't know what to do. After everything his mother had taught him, when it came down to an emergency, he panicked.

Suddenly Clara caught up with them. She hit the Angel and shoved at him. "Let go of my son!"

"Hey," one of the police officers shouted. "What's going on there?"

"This man is kidnapping my son!" Clara shouted, grabbing Jed's opposite hand.

The Angel was squeezing Jed's wrist so hard that it hurt. He felt the bones of his thin arm flexing under the Angel's grip.

"Let go!" Clara tore at the Angel's hand as the officers approached.

An old lady intervened. "Leave that boy alone." She hit the Angel with her purse.

Jed watched grown men walk by or avoid them and move to the other side of the street. The men who could help, ignored them. Everyone except for the old lady with her shiny black purse as she swung it at the Angel, hitting him over and over again and cursing at him.

The Angel shoved the old woman and she fell. His grip loosened on Jed's wrist just enough for Jed to get his arm free.

The officers were lifting the old lady up. Then one approached the Angel.

"Oh God, baby, are you okay?" Clara knelt and rubbed her hands over Jed's cheeks. "Did he hurt you?"

Jed held up a bruised wrist, too afraid to talk.

"What do you think you're doing?" the officer asked the Angel, squinting. There was something about the Angel, he looked like any other man just taller and more handsome. But humans weren't used to seeing Angels and couldn't tell them apart.

"The boy was begging on the corner." The Angel pointed at Jed.

"It's not a crime," the officer said.

"It should be." The Angel stepped closer to Jed, reaching for him.

The old lady swung her purse and deflected the Angel's hand. "Don't touch that boy. You are something wrong. You don't belong here. You are evil!" the old lady shouted.

Jed looked at the graying woman's face then his mother's. Clara smiled and moved Jed away from the ruckus. She knew the Angel couldn't risk being found out. He wouldn't risk his secret. If this commotion kept up, he'd have to prove his identity.

Clara moved away little by little as the officers and old lady argued with the Angel. There was an alley just a few feet away. Jed watched a shopkeeper picking up the coins on the sidewalk that he'd dropped. His heart sank. That was hours' worth of smiling and begging, now they had nothing. He'd collected more coins in this town than ever before. Jed started crying softly. He rubbed the tears away as his mother took a few more steps closer to the alley.

The old lady smiled as she argued with the Angel and the officers. When the men started to look for Clara and Jed, she started swinging her purse again.

Clara stepped into the alley and pulled Jed with her. They disappeared, walking fast, and turning onto a side street. They went back to the small woman's hotel where they had rented a room.

"Good afternoon," Clara said to the woman at the desk with a smile like they hadn't just avoided tragedy in the street. She tugged Jed along until they reached their room.

Once inside, Clara locked the door and sagged against it. She sighed heavily before crouching and looking into Jed's eyes.

"It's going to be okay." She started unbuttoning his coat. "Let's look at that arm. Does it hurt?"

Jed nodded, fresh tears sliding down his cheeks.

"It's okay, baby." Clara pulled him in for a hug and kissed his messy hair. "We'll get cleaned up and get out of here." She pulled his arm out of the coat and inspected it. "You have a big bruise." She rotated his wrist and asked him to move his fingers one by one. "You know, before I was your momma I was a nurse. I worked with important doctors in a big city."

"Really?" Jed asked. He already thought the world of his mother after watching her save them all of these years. He never thought about her life before him. Children rarely did.

"Really." She kissed his bruised arm. "And this arm is going to be right as rain in just a few days. We'll just take it easy. Okay?"

Jed nodded.

"Let's get cleaned up and get out of here."

Clara began collecting the few items they had and packed them in the single suitcase she carried. She got a washcloth from the bathroom and washed Jed's face and combed his hair. "There we go, all fresh. Like nothing ever happened." She glanced at the clock. "We're going to miss dinner tonight. We'll get a big breakfast when we get off the train in the morning. Okay?"

Jed nodded, his stomach grumbling. He was always hungry and meals were sporadic. He knew they had to leave town after an Angel had found them. They'd probably spent too much time here already.

They'd boarded a train the usual way, by sneaking behind it and entering through the caboose just before it left. Clara charmed the ticket master into believing they'd packed the tickets.

If Jed hadn't dropped the cup of coins, they'd have enough for tickets tonight.

"Come here, son," Clara said softly, candlelight flickering in the small train car.

Jed yawned, tired from the day. He crawled toward his mother and lay his head in her lap.

"You were so brave today," Clara said as her fingers combed through his hair sending chills down his back.

Jed watched the candle flame dance. He didn't feel brave. He felt weak and sad. He'd been begging on the street for coins while his mother bartered at a restaurant for a hot meal. Jed was good at collecting coins. He was good at unlocking doors and starting engines. He was good at a few things. Except knowing when to run.

He didn't want to leave his mother behind and his mistakes had cost them warm beds and hot meals before.

The train car jerked and the candle wax dripped to the side.

"Don't think about it, son," Clara said, scratching his head.

Jed couldn't stop thinking about it.

"Don't think about the coins." Clara combed through the other side of his hair with her fingers. "There's always more coins." She bent to kiss him on the forehead. "Always more coins but just one son of mine." Clara rocked him until he fell asleep.

It was that day Jed learned some humans were more of an Angel than the actual creature.

———

Now

THRUSH WOULDN'T TAKE the formula. After a few sucks on the bottle he gagged and puked. Then, after crying for hours, he fell asleep.

"Maybe he's teething?" Shay asked Noah.

"Nightingale never mentioned it." Noah's forehead creased in worry.

"Maybe something happened before Meg brought him to us?" Jed asked.

Noah shook his head. "I was there. He didn't get hurt."

"What about before you were there?" Shay asked.

"They were hiding in their bedroom." Noah paled and swallowed hard. "Everything that happened, it happened while we were standing in the same room with them."

"Shhhh." Shay soothed Thrush as she rocked him.

"I'll go find something else to feed him," Noah offered.

"Good idea." Shay moved across the room and set Thrush in the elaborate crib. When she turned around again, Noah was gone.

Jed collapsed in a chair across the room. Shay fell onto the bed and threw an arm over her eyes.

Not five minutes had passed before someone started pounding on the door to the suite.

Shay sat up. "Make it stop. It's going to wake him."

Jed had a knife ready as he approached the door. He opened the door just a crack and found the Hellion named Skeele standing in the hallway. He was covered in blood and pacing.

"Meg needs help," Skeele growled.

"What kind of help?" Jed asked, gripping the knife.

"The life or death kind." Skeele was staring.

"Sounds like Meg." Jed lacked surprise. Meg was always in some deep shit that involved life or death. Hence why he and Shay were here now babysitting the Angel-baby she'd kidnapped.

"Are you coming?" Skeele shouted as he threw his arms wide.

Jed motioned for him to wait a moment and slammed the door.

"What?" Shay asked.

Unease filled Jed's gut. He'd never seen someone so worked up. "I think something bad has happened. I have to go."

"You can't." Shay's eyes were wide as she stood, reaching for him. "Don't leave us."

Shay knew how to survive the apocalypse of the Earthen plane, but Hell? Hell was a different matter–for both of them. She'd never been here before. Jed had never been here before. But he had to go now. Because if something happened to Meg, they were shit out of luck.

"Tell Noah as soon as he gets back," Jed said. "Noah will know what to do."

Shay nodded, blue hair falling over her eyes.

"I'll come back as soon as I can," Jed promised, stepping closer and gripping her arm. "I'll be back." He promised, wanting to kiss her. He didn't want to leave her here, alone. But he knew Noah would be back soon and the runes of protection around the suite were working. He wouldn't be gone long.

Shay nodded but worry glazed her eyes.

Jed backed out the door, checking the runes along the floor and around the door lock to make sure they were intact. He locked the door and turned to find the Hellion.

Skeele was pacing, cracking his knuckles, and looking thoroughly on edge.

"What happened?" Jed asked.

Skeele didn't answer; instead he grabbed Jed by the collar of his jacket and ran for the stairwell. Skeele ran down four steps at a time dragging Jed along. Jed tripped and stumbled, slamming his knee against the wall as he caught his footing.

"Let go of me, you asshat," Jed shouted, arms flailing as Skeele dragged him through the air on the descent. "You're going to break my fucking neck."

Skeele let go. "We need to move fast." He kept running down the stairs, the sound of heavy boots echoing off stone.

Jed followed, shaking off nerves. He didn't know what he was about to walk into. But if Meg was in the room, that usually meant he'd be walking into a shit show.

Skeele led Jed to a Hellion-marked door on the first floor. He pushed the door open and dragged Jed by the arm of his jacket, slower this time.

The metallic scent of blood was thick in the air. It only took seconds for Jed to see where it was coming from. There was a body on the bar, and it looked pretty lifeless.

"Come on," Skeele urged as he crossed the room.

As Jed approached the bar, a hand flew to his mouth. Shit. This was not good. Meg was dead. That meant he'd probably be dead soon as well. Coming here was a bad idea; they should have stayed on the Earthen plane. Jed cursed their decision. Shay would be in more danger with Meg dead and with the portals down, they'd never get back. Jed's mind was playing through a hundred gameplans.

"We need your help," Skeele said, rounding the bar.

Jed threw his hands in the air. "How can I help you with this?" Hands went to his hair and tugged.

"Do *something*," the dark Hellion in the room begged, his eyes wide and black. "She's going to die soon."

Skeele was pacing and growling and muttering in Hellspeak.

"I can't bring dead people back to life," Jed said, he didn't deal in death magic. "That's a different type of–"

Skeele crossed the room and ripped Jed's backpack off. "You know magic." He pointed at the tattooed runes on Jed's arms. "You know spells. You must know something that can help."

"Are you sure she's dead?" Jed asked.

Tukka checked her pulse again. "It's faint. Very faint." The large Hellion touched Meg's hair, leaving bloody fingerprints on her forehead.

The Hellions were savage creatures and as far as Jed knew, they didn't care about much. But it appeared they cared very much for this lifeless person. If only Meg knew.

Jed took his bag from Skeele's hands and poured it out on the portion of the bar that wasn't covered in blood. There were vials, papers, bags of sand, bags of bones, and other strange little trinkets. Jed found his spell book. He flipped through the pages, searching for something. Anything that could help.

"Come on!" Skeele pounded his fists on the bar. Empty glasses clanged together; the pings of glass threatening to shatter added to the angst in the room.

"I'm looking." Jed's fingers danced over the stained pages, his eyes scanned in rapid movements. "Ok. Ok. I think I found something that might help."

Jed went to work. He marked the wooden bar around Meg's body with charcoal, sprinkled sand, and arranged small bones near her head and feet. Last, he chose a small jar of white liquid that luminated faintly.

"What's that?" Skeele asked with a growl.

"Do you know?" Jed asked, one brow raised. "Some call it grace.

Or at least, that's what I was told." He tilted the vial and the liquid inside luminated brighter.

"How'd you get that?" Skeele asked, eyes narrowed on the vial.

"I inherited it." Jed flipped the cap and stared at the two Hellions. There was a story behind the vial of Angel grace but he wasn't going to share it. "Now I need you both to shut up or join in."

Jed chanted ancient words from the book. He chanted words that sounded like ceramic crackling in a hot kiln, like ocean waves turned to ice, like the crack that declared the beginning of time.

The runes of sand glowed, the bones rattled like a rattlesnake tail. He tipped the vial onto his finger and pressed it to Meg's forehead. Chanting more, the words that originally sounded off and hard to wrap his tongue around became fluid and easier to annunciate the more he repeated them. The spec of grace on Meg's forehead pulsed. Jed was backlit in blue light as he motioned for Skeele and Tukka to join in.

The two Hellions made eye contact in apprehension but finally joined and repeated Jed's words.

Meg took a single breath. Her wounds oozed. Congealed blood dipped and formed circular crests. The spec of grace on her forehead glowed brighter.

Hope rose in Jed's chest. It was working. It was working!

Suddenly, Meg's wounds began gushing blood. Rivers flowed out of her. More blood than the Hellions had given her. Blood spilled onto the floor and the speck of grace turned from white to black. Meg's forehead smoked. Her body shuddered. The smell was putrid as the smoke billowed toward the ceiling.

"No," Skeele stopped chanting. "What did you do?" He grabbed a rag from the counter behind him and wiped the dot of grace off her forehead.

"What the hell," Jed shouted. "You broke the spell."

"You were killing her," Skeele growled. "And now I'm going to kill you!"

Six

"She was already dead," Jed shouted. "I didn't kill her, you all did!" He pointed at Skeele and Tukka. Whatever trouble Meg had gotten into had nothing to do with him. Jed wasn't taking the fall for Meg's death.

Skeele ran around the bar, headed for Jed. "I didn't kill her," he growled. "I'd never kill her."

"Who killed what?" Noah's voice pierced the room. He appeared in front of Jed. Protectively. "You won't kill my man, Jeddio."

Jed's fast beating heart finally slowed. He hoped Noah could help fix this.

Skeele paused as best he could. It was hard to stop the killing motion of a Hellion, but he managed. Then he pointed to the bar. "Meg," was all Skeele said.

If a ghost could pale, Noah did. "No. No no no no no." He ran toward Meg. "What happened?"

"She just poofed into the room at my feet all stabbed up," Skeele said. "We tried blood. Jed used some bullshit spell that burned her face."

"She took a breath!" Jed thrust his hands toward Meg's body. "You saw it! We all saw it. The spell was working."

"It was not working," Skeele shouted back.

Noah held up his hands. "Just shut up. Both of you." He touched Meg's face, brushing off the burnt skin. If she was dead or in between, she might be in the Astral. Noah placed both palms on each side of Meg's head and closed his eyes. His image wavered as he searched the Astral plane for Meg. If she were there, it might mean they could get her back into her body.

Noah searched. He searched and searched and searched. He looked between every shadow of the void of the Astral but found nothing. The Astral was infinite, but there were places that he and Nightingale had created. Places that a wandering Meg might find familiar. He searched for them; a red tree by a stream, a kaleidoscope of stars above a hilltop, a hot tub at the top of a snowy mountain. Each place he visited tore at his gut. The memories of Nightingale were strong, and even stronger was the knowledge that he'd never get to spend time with her here again. Noah tried to push thoughts of Nightingale out of his mind. But memories are a spiral of emotion. It was a battle Noah barely won.

He felt a coldness surround him. A familiar coldness. Clea was nearby. Noah scanned the Astral shouting for Meg one last time. There was nothing. He had to go back. He had to go face Clea and tell her that Meg was nowhere to be found.

———

"OH CHILD," Clea's voice was full of sorrow. Her ruby red lips pinched together. Everyone stared at her. "It seems this curse is familial. We lose children too often here."

Clea knew about loss. Lucifer had lost Clea then Clea had lost Meg to the Earthen plane in an attempt to save her. Meg had lost her own child before it had ever been born. Clea and Meg's reunion was bound to be ended soon enough. It was all a vicious circle in this bloodline. Clea could see some of the future, with visions and omens; nothing she'd seen ever ended well.

"We have to do something," Noah said, moving his hands away from Meg's head. He didn't know what to say. At least Meg was here. At least they didn't have to search for her bones like Gabriel searched for twenty-five years for Clea's. Noah knew the story. At least they had a tiny bit of closure, seeing her here, like this.

"Have you tried everything to save her?" Clea asked, her image wavering, nearly transparent.

"We tried blood," Skeele said.

"I had a spell and some Angel grace," Jed began collecting his items and placing them in his backpack.

"Angel grace?" Noah asked.

Jed nodded. "It didn't work." He pinched the vial between his fingers and held it up to the light before placing it in his bag.

Angel grace might not have worked, but they had an actual Angel in the castle.

"I'll be right back," Noah said, just before he disappeared. "Don't touch her," his voice echoed throughout the Hellion lair.

———

Noah and Teari burst through the door of the lair. Teari ran to Meg's side. It didn't look good. It didn't look good at all. The air dripped with a metallic odor. There was so much blood and the remnants of a spell. Teari brushed the sand away and destroyed the runes surrounding Meg's body.

Jed shouted in protest, but no one paid attention to what he was saying. All of his hard work was simply brushed aside. He hated that he'd come here. Hated that these creatures had demanded him do something about the mess they'd created.

Skeele filled Teari in on what they'd tried. "Can you do something?" he asked.

Teari rested her arm on Meg's chest. "I can't do what I used to." She bit her lip, wishing she had hands. After all her years of healing, she had never felt so useless. She couldn't do a thing without her healing magic.

"Have you tried giving her fresh blood?" Teari asked.

Skeele's back went straight. Teari would have to be blind to miss his reaction.

"Did she fix Sparrow?" Teari asked. "His blood would be the best option. They have a bond."

"Sparrow is gone," Skeele said. "He's out of the picture."

Teari frowned. "Gone?"

Skeele motioned to the sky. "I'm assuming he went home."

"Crap." Teari stepped away from the bar and paced for a moment. She looked at everyone, studying them. Jed wouldn't do. Even with his mixed heritage, Tukka was unhinged at the moment. Her eyes paused on Skeele, the only one in the room who was semi-calm, but Teari could tell under his skin he was ready to lose it. The worry on his face was different, deeper than the worry of a bystander.

"What are you?" she asked, looking at Skeele. She waved her nubbed arms in a flurry. "Who are you to her? There's a reason you're so upset that she's dying right now. There's something between you two?"

He cleared his throat and reset his demeanor. "Hellion First Command."

Teari knew the First Command was the closest to the leader of Hell. There was a bond. Duty and sacrifice demanded it. Even if Meg and Skeele never admitted it to each other. No matter how weak the bond might be, it would work the best. Without Sparrow, Meg was only tethered to Noah and being a spirit of the Astral, he didn't have blood.

"Your blood will do." Teari pointed at him with the nub of her right arm. "Give her your blood. Right now. Before she's gone forever."

It was a scene like Jed had never witnessed before as Skeele lifted Meg's lifeless body off the bar and walked out of the room.

Jed rubbed his neck, remembering Meg's bite.

SEVEN

SHAY PACED THE ROOM HOLDING BABY THRUSH. HER arms rocked him quicker than she was comfortable with. Shay thought babies were fragile things that should be handled gently, but Thrush was only calm when he was rocked at a rapid pace. It worried Shay, that she might give him brain damage or that he might develop some strange fondness for being shaken when he got older. Shay tried not to think too deeply about it. The kid had barely survived being eaten during the Fast-Zombie war. Whatever methods she used to soothe him had to be better than what he experienced during that ordeal.

It had been weeks since they left the child in Shay and Jed's care. Every night they still checked his skin from head to toe for bite marks or wounds. They'd found none, of course. Only soft baby skin and the occasional diaper rash.

Shay paced near the door, waiting for Jed to return. She tiptoed around the markings on the floor, careful not to disturb the charcoal marks or piles of salt. Jed had protected them all for this long, she wasn't about to put them at risk.

Shay paused when she heard shouting from another area of the castle. She had a strong urge to leave the room and find Jed. She looked at the dark haired baby boy in her arms and remembered her promise. She couldn't leave the room, she could only hope that Jed would come back in one piece. He had to. He'd promised.

Shay glanced at the bottles drying near the sink. Thrush didn't want anything to do with the formula Noah brought. They'd tried everything. Every milk: cow, goat, sheep, almond, and coconut. Thrush didn't want any of it and what he did take, he puked up not long afterward. Shay's clothes were perpetually stained. Jed entered the splash zone, but he usually had towels ready to soak up the baby vomit. Thrush's cheeks were slowly shrinking in size, dark blue circles had started under his eyes. The kid wasn't necessarily sick, but from everything Shay had read, Thrush was borderline malnourished. If this kept on, he'd be completely malnourished quickly.

Noah was anxious about Thrush not eating. He spent most of his time finding something for his son to eat. They'd tried jars of baby food and infant cereals. Thrush would eat it, but it wasn't enough. He needed the milk for a few more months at least. He wasn't ready to switch to solid foods yet.

Shay saw shadows under the door. Someone was outside the suite. There was whispering, tapping, and then the door handle turned. Shay moved to the far side of the room, reaching for the spell cast shotgun with runes carved into the metal barrel.

The door opened.

Shay let out a sigh of relief as Jed stepped in and latched the door behind him. He leaned his back against the solid wood door and took a deep breath.

"Is she dead?" Shay asked.

Jed nodded.

"Shit." Thrush stirred in Shay's arms. She rocked the baby again. "What do we do?"

Jed made a face as he skirted the markings on the floor to get closer to Shay.

"She might come back to life. Skeele is going to try something."

"I don't think I want to know."

"It's probably better you don't. These people are freaks."

Shay tipped her head to her shoulder, a motion that told him they might not be so freaky. Shay had seen worse in humanity. Unfortunately.

Thrush started crying. Jed made a bottle of the most recent formula Noah had brought them. He passed it to Shay. Thrush pushed the nipple out of his mouth and gagged on the baby formula. Shay set the bottle down and shifted Thrush in her arms.

Tears started streaming down her face. "This kid is going to starve to death." Shay wiped at her face. "One day we are going to wake up and he's going to be lifeless in his crib. I just want him to eat something."

Shay was crying. Thrush was crying.

Jed stood nearby feeling utterly useless. He couldn't save Meg and he was sucking at keeping this kid alive. And while Shay was alive she was miserable in their current situation.

Thrush started nuzzling Shay's chest, leaving wet marks on her shirt.

"There's one thing we haven't tried," Jed said, reaching for his notebook of spells and magic. He flipped the pages.

Shay looked down at the baby and realized what he was talking about. "I don't think so."

"Why not?" Jed asked. "It's natural."

"I'm not his mother."

"You don't need to be his mother. Wet nurses rarely are."

"I've never done this before." Apprehension filled Shay.

"It can't be that hard." Jed paused on a page and tapped his finger on the paper. "I think I found something that will work."

"Don't you need my consent or something."

"This isn't permanent." Jed paused. "You don't want to try?"

Thrush whimpered in frustration, his little arms and legs were limp.

Shay couldn't watch him fade before their eyes. They'd both promised to look after this baby. "Just do it."

Jed's fingers danced in rhythmic spell casting; he chanted ancient words from his book.

Shay's chest started to feel warm and full. She looked down to see wet marks where her bra was.

"Okay, I think it's done," Jed said as he closed his notebook and knelt near Shay. "Do you want help?"

"Have you done this before?" Shay asked, tears dripping down her cheeks. This felt strange and weird and she wasn't prepared to hand over so much of herself.

"No. But that doesn't mean I'm of no help." Jed brushed his shaggy blonde hair away from his eyes. He set a hand on her knee.

Shay lifted her shirt and pushed her bra aside. She'd never breastfed a baby before, but she'd learned about it in her parents' survival books. There were plenty of chapters on delivering babies and placentas and keeping children alive.

Thrush latched on and ate, and for the first time in weeks he didn't cry or vomit. He simply ate until the tears on his cheeks dried to salt and he fell asleep making faint snoring sounds.

"Was it bad?" Jed asked, moving pillows behind Shay's back so she could get comfortable.

"It wasn't terrible." Shay scooted down in the bed until Thrush was lying flat and she could release him. She looked at Jed. "This is way more than what I signed up for."

"But look at all the fun we're having. I told you there would never be a dull moment with Meg involved." Jed crossed his arms on the bed and leaned forward from his sitting position on the floor. He and Shay were almost nose to nose.

"You should have warned me in Montana that if I followed you, I'd be stepping into some mega shit." Shay pursed her lips.

Jed smiled. "What better have you got to do? Kill zombies and pick dumpsters for food?"

"I didn't get my food from dumpsters. I grew it and hunted for it."

"Okay. But had you stayed, you would have never experienced this shit show. You'd be so bored."

"I wouldn't be lactating to feed an Angel ghost baby hybrid." She smoothed Thrush's hair away from his eyes and smiled, relieved that the baby had finally eaten something and kept it down.

"True." He reached out and touched her hair. "I did warn you though. I offered to bring you back. I warned you that hanging out with me was a very bad idea."

Shay sighed, tired from the long day and the tears. She didn't want to argue with Jed. She wanted nothing more than to sleep a few uninterrupted hours, but they needed to talk. "Tell me what happened downstairs."

Jed made a face, but he told her about trying to bring Meg's lifeless corpse back to life.

"What are we going to do?" Shay asked.

"We can get out of here." Jed was looking toward the window. "The front door opens. We aren't locked in here." He ran his hands through his hair in frustration. "Noah will do anything to keep Thrush safe. He has to help us. We just have to get back to the Earthen plane."

"You don't think it's safer here in Hell?" Shay asked.

"I don't know," Jed replied. "I thought it would be safer with Sparrow. But that plan has gone completely to shit."

"So we go back home." Shay tilted her head. "We find a way back home and take this baby with us?"

Jed stared at the sleeping baby in Shay's arms, memories flooding him. Memories of a lifetime on the run, a childhood on the run, his mother fighting to save him every day. That day she pushed him out of the moving train car, he lost her forever.

Jed rubbed his face in defeat. He couldn't force Shay into a life like that. He looked away, thinking. He could still wipe her memories and bring her back to the ranch. He didn't want to be a liar but he'd much rather protect her from the life Clara had. Shay didn't deserve that.

When he looked toward Shay again, she was sleeping. He touched the soft fabric of the bedsheets, remembering the moments of ecstasy being inside her. The soft noises she'd made, the way she felt in his hands. The way she made him feel strong and loved and desired.

EIGHT

ALASTOR STOPPED AT A TAVERN THAT WAS PUSHED BACK into the forest. This was a place for Demonkind only, a place he'd frequented in the past. He was hungry and thirsty and wanted to get off his feet. He'd followed the horse tracks for the entire day. Judging from the distance between hoofprints, the horse had to be traveling at a decent gallop. Alastor would catch up eventually. The black substance was accumulating more and more with distance. The creature was bleeding and must have had some injury. Eventually it would slow, Alastor would bet on it.

Noise in the tavern ceased. Everyone set down their drinks.

"Did you feel that?" a deep voice asked.

"Something's happened," another voice said.

"She's dead. The Queen is dead." A Demon with four horns on the back of his skull stood.

"Fuck her." Another Demon with stubby legs shouted. "Now things can go back to the way it used to be."

A chair flew across the room and smashed across the back of the head of the Demon with the stubby legs.

In the corner of the tavern were three Hellion recruits, Alastor could tell from their clothing.

Something was happening. Alastor had felt the shift in energy. He looked out the window. The Veil between Hell and the Earthen plane was thinning again. If he needed to, he could find a hole and walk across. He drank his ale. He had a man and a woman to deal with. If the Veil stayed like this, it would make it easy for him to get back into business. No more sneaking across the portals in the night and bribing guards.

Alastor ate as the Demons in the tavern fought. Every so often, the tavern owner would throw a group of Demons outside to finish their fighting. Everyone had become considerably louder. The Hellion recruits took off, no doubt making their way back to the castle to check on their Queen. Alastor would have considered going to the castle to investigate but he had other things to do.

He paid his tab and left.

Alastor made his way back to the trail of horse prints that he'd been following.

There was another shift in the air.

Alastor looked around him. The Veil was solidifying again. The Queen did not die but something had happened.

He could see the Hellions flying and it took him a moment to realize that the hoof prints and the Hellions were going in the same direction.

If Queen Meg was keeping an Angel half-breed at the castle, something strange was going on.

With renewed energy, Alastor moved faster.

Nine

Meg flashed into the room.

"You're alive," Jed said with a full mouth as he chewed a bite of his turkey sandwich.

Shay stopped mid-bite and set her sandwich down.

Noah appeared next with inkpots and a handful of sterile needles. He dropped them in front of Jed.

"Let's go," Meg said to Jed. "Get your tattoo gun."

Jed turned to Shay, "I'll be right back."

"It's going to be a few hours," Noah warned, "at least. I'll stay with him."

Neither Jed nor Shay had left the room in days.

A lump formed in Shay's throat with the thought of being separated. She glanced at the door to the bedroom where Thrush was sleeping.

"It's fine," Meg said. "We just need some ink."

Jed crossed the room to grab his tools. "It's going to be fine," he breathed quietly to Shay.

Shay nodded and stood to check the wards and re-pour the line of salt across the threshold of the door.

Meg led Jed to the second floor.

There was an empty room near the stairwell with chairs and a table and good lighting. Meg opened the door and waited for Jed to enter.

It only took Jed a second to see Gabriel waiting in the corner.

"Oh no," Jed backpedaled toward the door. "Nope. Nope. Nope."

Meg grabbed his arm. Noah slammed the door.

Gabriel squinted at Jed. "Well, I'll be damned," he murmured.

"I have spent my life avoiding Archangels and you brought me to one." Jed was ready to lose it, his eyes wide with fear and anger. "Is this some sick joke?" He glared at Meg. "I knew I could never trust you, Meg. Never. The things I've done for you and now this?"

"Calm down, boy," Gabriel bellowed. "I'm not here for you." He frowned. "Damned surprised to see you upright and down in this realm," he raised his palms, "but the more days I live, the less this shit surprises me."

"He needs the runes," Meg said, holding out an arm. "He needs freedom from the other Archangels."

Jed tossed his equipment on the table. He glared at Meg. "This is not what I signed up for."

"We're in the same club," Meg moved closer to Jed. "Gabriel is my father. The other Archangel's are rallying against him, including Sparrow."

"Fucking Angels," Jed muttered, shaking his head. He pointed a finger at Meg. "You owe me big time for this." He set his equipment on the table and started prepping to tattoo Gabriel. "You owe me for the rest of your goddamned life."

"Done," Meg held out her hand, pinky extended. "Pinky promise. I am forever in your debt."

Jed jerked his hand forward, curling his pinky around Meg's and stared into her eyes. "I am a forbidden creature. They will always hunt me."

Meg nodded, understanding.

Jed picked up one of the inkpots that Noah brought. He set it aside and motioned for Gabriel to lay his left arm out on the table. "We'll do both," he said. "If you can handle it." Jed smirked.

Gabriel rested his arm on the table and Jed went to work with the buzzing of his machine.

"Would this prevent Sparrow from finding Thrush?" Noah asked.

"The runes?" Meg asked.

Noah nodded.

"I'd assume." Meg said. "But, wait. Are you suggesting tattooing a baby?"

Noah pressed his lips together and tipped his head in a maybe expression.

"I don't think that's a good idea," Meg said.

"Absofuckinglutly not," Jed said.

Ten

"Meg found us a place to live?" Shay asked Noah.

He kissed Thrush's cheek before replying, "Yeah. It's in a graveyard not far from here."

"A graveyard?" Jed stopped checking the wards and stared at Noah. "You want us to live in a graveyard."

Noah shrugged. "It's peaceful and safe. There's a chapel. It's like a cabin. I wouldn't let my son grow up in some awful hovel in the ground."

Jed and Shay glanced at each other.

"How safe?" Shay asked. "Meg has been on edge for a while now. I'll be happy to escape these four walls but I don't know anything about Hell."

"I'll stay close," Noah promised.

"And what about Meg?" Jed asked.

Noah nodded, understanding. "I'll tell her to stay away. She'll listen to me."

"Meg doesn't listen to anyone," Shay countered.

"I promise, she'll listen to me." Noah patted Thrush as he slept.

———

SHAY STEPPED OUTSIDE in to daylit Hellsky first. She looked up and took a deep breath. "I never thought it would feel so good to be outside again."

Jed touched the small of her back. "Even with this cold?"

Shay adjusted her backpack and rubbed her hands together before checking Thrush's snowsuit and hat to make sure the cold couldn't sneak in.

"Is Noah coming with us?" Shay asked.

"He's at the chapel, dealing with Meg." Jed began walking. He felt strange being allowed outside alone, but a shadow flying overhead reminded him they weren't completely alone. The Hellions were scanning from above.

"It's not too far of a walk is it?" Shay asked.

"Noah said maybe ten minutes." Jed shifted Thrush's weight as they turned down the empty road.

"Do you think we brought enough supplies?" Shay asked, making conversation. She'd spent hours in the kitchen collecting canned foods, fresh bread, and perishables. It seemed the kitchens of Hell weren't that different than the kitchens of the Earthen plane, just more rudimentary; no processed foods unless someone brought them back from their travels.

"If we need anything Noah will get it for us." Jed stepped over a large pothole. "Meg should get a road crew out here."

"She seems busy with a lot of shit," Shay said.

They walked, enjoying the icy chill of winter and the hollow noise their footsteps made. Jed and Shay had been locked up in their rooms for too long. The freedom was best enjoyed in silence.

"There it is," Shay pointed to a small building between the gravestones. "It doesn't look too bad."

"Like a chapel in a picture book," Jed said, his eyes landing on Meg in the distance. She was a few hundred yards away from the chapel, sitting with Noah. Noah's hand was on her shoulder. Meg looked utterly sad as she ate.

"You think he's telling her?" Shay asked.

"Yeah." Jed nodded. "She doesn't look very happy about being told she can't come near the baby."

"It must be hard for her after losing everything. Didn't you say she was from the Earthen plane?"

"She was. She didn't know what she was but the things she went through, no one should live through."

"Same for you." Shay touched Jed's elbow. "You've both had it pretty rough."

Jed smiled softly. "We've all had some trauma etched in our bones."

"So this is going to be our home forever?" Shay asked.

"For as long as Thrush needs us." Jed checked on Thrush who was facing outward in his arms. The boy had been quiet since they'd left the castle in the burning caves.

"He's fine," Shay said. "He hasn't had so many things to look at. Do you think he'll like living in a graveyard?"

"At least there's grass and trees," Jed said.

"There's fencing."

"To keep the dead from wandering too close." Jed's gaze went to the sky again. "The Hellions will be doing rounds to check the perimeter."

"Maybe we should get a guard dog or something," Shay suggested.

———

THE CHAPEL WAS COZY. Shay felt peaceful as she searched the rooms and acquainted herself with their new living quarters. There was a small kitchen, a bathroom, two bedrooms, a living room. She looked out the window to the expanse of grass out the back. There were no headstones obstructing the view, and for a moment Shay felt as though she were back on the ranch, washing dishes and gazing out the window as the Montana breeze blew the tall bluegrass into a swaying motion. Nostalgia tugged at her chest. She scraped her boot across the roughhewn wood floor as she moved to unpack her bag and put the food they'd brought away.

"Meg's gone home," Noah said as he appeared in the living room.

"Please don't do that," Jed said, holding the short hunting knife with runes carved into the handle. "I could have stabbed you." He gave an annoyed look before carving runes into the doorframe again.

"You don't need to deface the place," Noah said, watching Jed.

"If I trusted every person who attempted to give me a safe home, I wouldn't be here right now." Jed secured the knife in his belt and pulled out a Sharpie marker, marking the walls around the door-frame next.

Noah made a face that suggested perhaps Jed was correct in his statement. "Where's Thrush?"

Shay pointed toward the bedroom. "Sleeping. All that fresh air tired him out."

Noah moved toward the door.

"Don't you dare wake him up," Shay said, holding a glass jar of tomatoes. "That poor boy hasn't slept in weeks."

Noah stopped mid stride and turned. "Hey, he hasn't, so how is he sleeping now?"

"He just ate," Jed said, absentmindedly.

"Ate what?" Noah scratched his face. "Did he finally take the formula?"

"No." Shay set the jars in a cabinet. "Have you ever heard of a wet nurse?"

"Like from the movies back when women wore petticoats and bonnets and crap?" Noah asked.

"Yeah. Exactly that," Shay said. She turned, pointing to her chest. "Jed had a spell. And it worked."

Noah was staring at Shay's breasts stretching against her shirt.

"Hey." Jed grabbed a pillow out of the nearby chair and threw it across the room at Jed. "Don't stare at her boobs, you sick freak."

Noah scoffed. "I'm not the freak. She made me look. She pointed at them. What am I supposed to do? Ignore her?"

"Settle down, boys," Shay mocked as she continued unpacking her bag of food. "Are you going to be spending a lot of time here, Noah?" Shay asked. "Should we set up the other room for you?"

"Better not," Noah's shoulders dropped. "Meg needs me. I'll try to split my time with Nightingale gone. I'd like to spend as much time with Thrush as possible."

"Maybe stop working for Meg?" Jed suggested.

"I can't do that."

"Why won't she release you of your duties?" Shay asked.

"It's not that easy," Noah scrubbed at his hair. "Lucifer bound us. I'm tethered to her. Our souls are tethered. She calls, I show up."

"Always?" Shay asked.

"Every time." Noah sat on the couch and stretched his legs out.

"You could take Thrush to work with you," Jed suggested.

"With the type of crap Meg gets herself into? It's not for children. And if Nightingale knew, she'd kill me."

There was a long pause. Shay could sense something gloomy and brooding in Noah, similar to how she felt when her parents died.

"I'm sorry she died," Shay said. "I am, Noah. Life is hard enough."

"This is the afterlife for me." Noah looked at the ceiling.

"I guess the afterlife is hard enough." Shay put a container of milk in the fridge. "I never thought I'd ever say something like that."

Noah chuckled. "Me either."

Eleven

Life at the chapel was quaint and quiet. Jed and Shay brought Thrush outside for fresh air. The fencing obscured their views of the field behind the graveyard and the forest, but it was a minor discomfort. Thrush gained weight. He ate and slept and they'd fallen into a daily routine of breakfasts and lunches and long walks, Jed bringing Thrush with him to check the wards and runes around the house and property each day. Shay watched them from the kitchen window and thought how different and similar life was between Hell and the Montana ranch. She was glad she told Jed not to wipe her memories. She'd never get to experience these quiet moments. It was hard to think that she was in Hell after all.

Thrush was sleeping soundly in his crib as Jed switched off the nightstand light and collected Shay in his arms. He kissed her bare shoulder and his hands explored under her shirt.

"Again?" Shay whimpered when he touched her bare breast.

"It's been days." Jed leaned away and pulled Shay to face him in the darkness. "I like this. I don't ever want to lose it." He kissed her, slow and deep. "I want to touch you all day long but I can't. This is the only time we slow down."

The noise of footsteps interrupted them.

"Someone's here." Shay threw back the blankets. "Someone's in this room."

Jed rushed out of the bed as Shay turned on the light. A dark figure was leaning over the crib.

"No!" Shay shouted.

Jed ran toward the figure, blade in hand, lips ready to chant a spell.

Shay got a glimpse of the figure's face before it–*poof*–disappeared.

"That was Meg." Shay ran to the crib, tearing at the blankets as though Thrush might still be there. "Why would Meg take him?"

———

"The Nightjar stole Thrush," Meg said, her eyes wide and face pale. Her clothing was soaked and hair dripping wet.

"Tell me why I shouldn't trap you in the Astral for eternity," Noah was seething.

"You don't understa–" Meg tried to say.

"I told you to stay away from Thrush and you took him to another realm," Noah said.

"Why did you take him?" Shay asked.

"Yeah," Jed added. "Didn't you do enough damage already?" He'd watched Meg create more than enough problems.

"I had to get him baptized. He was going to turn into a Nightjar. I couldn't curse his entire life." Meg looked at Noah. "You knew. You knew what fate held for him without the baptism. I couldn't let him turn into something else. Something like Elise. Don't you want more than a jar of feathers to mourn? Don't you want more for your son?"

There was silence. Jed pulled Shay closer as Meg told them about the death of her unborn daughter. Sympathy flooded Jed. She could so easily have been his mother, Clara. That dead infant could have been him.

Twelve

Jed waited on the shoreline with Meg. Neither of them could fly like the others.

"This is ridiculous," Jed finally said. "Demore is playing with them." He watched Thrush hover over the water and Noah drift below him.

Jed crouched and emptied his bag onto the sand at the water's edge.

"What are you doing?" Meg asked.

"I have an idea." Jed laid out a red square of cloth. "I've been reading up on this. I think it's going to work."

"I'm not sure this is the time for experiments," Meg said.

"They're not experiments," Jed replied, annoyed. "They've kept me alive this long."

He arranged bones and small black feathers on the square of cloth followed by vials of strange liquid, and finally, a stick of cinnamon that he lit with a flame and set to smudge.

"What will this do?" Meg asked.

Jed pointed to the water. "You said that's a conduit?"

"Yeah." Meg nodded.

"Then watch this." Jed chanted strange words. His fingers danced in rhythmic and repetitive motions. The water in front of them bubbled softly. Steam rose into the sky. A white, wispy form began taking shape.

"What is that?" Meg asked.

Jed chanted louder, stronger, and his fingers danced faster. He spat words that sounded like a hissing snake, that sounded like a baby's first cry; it sounded like the gasses of the sun churning.

The wispy form coming from the bubbles solidified.

It was Nightingale.

"Night!" Meg started to move toward her.

"Don't," Jed warned. "She's not here for you. I didn't call her for *you.*"

Meg went still.

Jed had never met Nightingale but he was intrigued by the Angel Noah had fallen in love with. Nightingale wore a black crop top and tiny red gym shorts with white piping–straight out of the eighties. She had headphones resting on her neck and big, clunky roller skates. She turned, her dark hair flowing down her back. She glided across the pond, skating like she was at a disco. She twisted and turned so fast her image was a blur. She whistled a melodic trill.

Noah turned away from Thrush, recognizing Nightingale. Everything changed. There was electricity in the air. The light from the moon dampened to a dreamlike haze.

Nightingale glided toward Noah. She took him into the air as though there were an invisible elevator until Thrush floated between them. Thrush babbled as he recognized his mother. Nightingale whistled a gentle trill to Thrush before taking him into her arms and holding him close.

Plip-plop. Plip-plop. Plip-plop. Plip-plop. Demore came from over the treetops, fast. Her mournful melody getting louder and louder.

"Mine," she cried out. "My precious. My baby. My gift." The dark shadow of the Nightjar soared faster to meet Nightingale.

Nightingale held out a hand. She had a power that stopped

Demore in her path. Nightingale's sweet, high-pitched chirping trills turned into guttural chatter.

"What are they doing?" Meg asked Jed.

"They're gonna fight," Jed said.

Nightingale pushed Thrush into Noah's arms and then she illuminated, drawing all of the light from the moonlight until she was a giant, glowing orb. Demore's shadows grew and blacken, her tendrils draping the canopy of the forest.

Meg was waving her hands at Noah, trying to get him to move back. Whatever the women were doing, they were getting bigger and bigger and drawing energy from around them.

Gabriel swooped down, white wings spread wide in all their glory, and grabbed Noah and Thrush, bringing them to the opposite side of the pond.

Lightning crackled between the twisting balls of energy that Nightingale and Demore had become. They rose in the sky; swirling, crackling, screaming, and crying. Their forms shifted and blurred. They twisted and jabbed. The wind picked up, blowing leaves and sticks into the air.

Meg stepped into the pond and dunked her head. There was something strange about needing the water to see Demore.

Nightingale sent a blast of light and electricity to Demore. The dark ball of energy shrank and shuddered in defeat.

The fight was over. Demore's cabin was dark, her shadowed form roiling behind the windows.

Nightingale dropped from Hellsky like a ballerina, landing elegantly on one foot. She glided across the water on her roller skates, twisting and turning. She stopped in front of Noah and bent to talk to Thrush.

Meg turned to Jed. "That was the best idea you've ever had," Meg began walking toward the shore. "You saved Thrush." She was smiling. Happy. Elated.

Jed smiled and shrugged a little. "Nothing can defeat a mother's need to protect her child."

"It was per–"

Meg never finished what she was trying to say. She was jerked backward and fell. She scrambled, grabbing at the shoreline sand and rooted plants.

Jed ran forward to try and help her but it all happened so fast. One moment she was there, the next she disappeared under the water.

"Where did she go?" Skeele shouted.

Jed pointed to the pond.

"She went under the water and never came out."

Gabriel frowned. "It's a portal. We went through it before."

"A portal to where?" Skeele asked.

"Babylon." Gabriel was moving closer.

"No." Skeele shouted as he dove into the murky pond water.

Jed's back went stiff. A portal straight to the Seven Kingdoms of Heaven and he was standing directly next to it. No. He would not partake in this.

Noah approached Jed. "Come on, man. Let's get you out of here. The Hellions will take care of Meg."

Jed nodded. He wasn't a coward but he knew his limitations. He'd worked too hard bringing Nightingale back from the ether. Tremors shook his arms. Jed felt ill. Sweat dried to his back giving him chills.

"You okay, man?" Noah asked.

"I need to rest." Jed stumbled as he bent to collect his belongings. "Need to get away from this portal." He couldn't defend himself in this state if an Angel came through for him. He didn't know if his aura would shine through after all the magic he'd used to bring back Nightingale. He was sure he was glowing like a torch.

THIRTEEN

NIGHTINGALE WAS THANKING JED AND SHAY FOR TAKING care of Thrush. She kept her face half-turned in an attempt to hide the scars from the Fast-Zombie War. They didn't seem to impact Thrush's recognition of his mother. He couldn't stop looking at her and babbling, clapping his little chubby hands and drooling.

Noah kept touching Nightingale like he couldn't believe she was real again.

The handle on the fence turned halfway before someone shouted "Ah! What the heck?"

Jed was closest to the gate and recognized the voice. "Meg?" he asked. "Is that you?"

"Yes it's me."

Jed opened the gate. "Oh, thank God. We thought you were gone."

Meg entered the fenced chapel yard for the first time since she'd been banished by Noah. "You were supposed to be at the castle," she said.

"They were safe with me," Nightingale said. Thrush had fallen asleep in her arms.

"Where's Teari?" Meg asked.

Noah nodded toward the door to the chapel.

Meg headed there, passing Shay who'd taken up conversation with Chel about survival gear and weapons. "Welcome back," Shay said.

Meg entered the chapel.

A few minutes passed when Teari screamed, "Meg! What are you doing?"

Jed and Shay made eye contact before running toward the door with Chel.

Teari was sitting on the couch with her arms crossed; the prosthetics had fallen.

"I knew we couldn't trust you in here. What did you do?" Jed asked.

"Oh, just performing a miracle," Meg said. "But I'm hurt, really. Why must you always assume the worst of me?"

Jed had plenty reason to assume the worst. But, he also jumped to conclusions quickly when it involved her. It was a side effect of living on the run and always anticipating the worst.

Teari held up her arms and everyone in the room watched as her hands regrew.

"I always assume you're up to something," Jed said. "But this is better than I was anticipating." He jabbed Meg in the shoulder as a playful apology.

"Oh my God," Teari exclaimed as she stood. "This is the best." She moved toward Meg and threw her arms around Meg's neck. "Thank you, Meg."

Meg patted her back awkwardly. "It was nothing."

Teari grabbed Meg by her shoulders and held her away, wrinkling her nose in disgust. "You stink."

———

JED AND SHAY were walking shoulder to shoulder as the group made their way back to the castle.

Teari wanted to feel the fresh air on her hands. It was a strange thing to demand but since she'd spent the past few weeks with no arms below her elbows, no one argued about it.

Chel was there with Klaus, just in case. The forests of Hell weren't completely safe. The dead would come for this group without Meg with them.

Jed's arm itched to wrap around Shay but he didn't want the others to dwell on it. They'd done their best to skirt the details of their relationship. Jed didn't want word to spread, he didn't want a target on Shay's back.

The chatter of the group was interrupted by the heavy *clop-clop-clop* of hooves.

Shay turned and focused on the figure in the distance. It was coming toward them.

"What's that?" Teari asked. "Is that... is that a horse?"

"Stay here," Chel said. "I'll go check it out."

Chel moved to take flight, but Shay held out a hand to stop him.

"Wait. I think I know who that is." Shay walked away from the group, closer to the oncoming figure. She recognized the glint of his onyx coat, the sheen that soaked up every wavelength of visible light. He was fast–a blur at times–but then, his motion glitched and he stumbled.

"Nero?" Shay shouted. "Nero, is that you?"

"No," Jed warned. "Don't, Shay, he's not your horse anymore." Jed grabbed for Shay's arm to stop her from moving closer.

"That's ridiculous. He's fine. He's just bigger." Shay moved closer.

Klaus squinted at the horse moving toward them. "That's the biggest damn horse I've ever seen in my life." He looked at Shay. "That's your horse?"

Shay nodded. "His name is Nero. But, he's changed. He rescued me from a Crossroads Demon–"

"Oh, shit." Chel exclaimed as he moved protectively in front of Shay. "That's not just a horse."

Shay shoved at Chel. Jed tugged her backward. "Will you two leave me alone? It's just my horse!" Shay complained.

Nero slowed, his gallop becoming uneven. His head dipped lower and lower toward the road. He went down on one knee, hooves scraped against the asphalt, slipping. He collapsed before he could reach them, his sides heaving as he breathed heavily.

"Nero!" Shay shoved at Chel and Jed and ran toward the horse. She dropped to her knees and touched his face.

Nero's giant black eyes focused on her. He was in pain and exhausted. She wondered if something had been chasing him. Shay looked down the road but saw nothing in the distance.

"Are you hurt, boy?" Shay asked, petting Nero's cheek and the wide space between his ears. She inspected the gold ring in his ear and the gold chain that looped down to another chain around his neck.

"That's not just a horse, Shay," Klaus warned. "That there is a Crossroads Demon."

"He's my horse," Shay said, panic rising in her chest. "I've had him since he was a baby. Something is wrong with him."

Chel laughed. "He's a Demon, Shay. There's plenty wrong with him now. We got to get him out of here."

"No!" Tears were collecting in Shay's eyes. "He saved me more than once. Whatever is wrong with him, I have to help."

Teari was circling the giant horse, inspecting the side of him that was up. "He's injured." She pointed to the bright red wound on his flank that was oozing inky liquid.

"Oh no." Shay ran her hands over his face and neck, down his back and front legs looking for more injuries. "What happened to you?" she asked.

Nero didn't answer. Not that he could but Shay still felt the need to speak to him as though he could communicate in her language.

Teari was kneeling near the wound on Nero's flank, her hand hovering over it. Nero's muscles twitched and he whinnied weakly.

"I can't fix this," Teari said. "This is a Demon talon injury."

"What does that mean?" Shay asked.

"There's usually poison." Teari bit her lip as she thought for a moment. She held up a finger and pointed toward the castle. "A basilisk can fix this. And Meg just happens to have a tank full of them."

"What's a basilisk?" Shay asked.

"It looks like a snake but they have many uses and they're unique to Hell." Teari stood and looked at the two Hellions. "We need to get Nero back to Meg's stables."

Klaus laughed. "That beast must weigh four thousand pounds. I can't lift it."

Chel crossed his arms. "I don't approve of bringing a Crossroads Demon back to Meg's land. It's too dangerous."

"Nero is not dangerous," Shay argued.

Chel shook his head.

"It's not a good idea," Jed said, touching Shay's back.

Anger rose in Shay's chest. Her fingertips tingled as emotion flooded her body. "I'm not leaving him here in the road, half dead. He deserves better than that." Shay sat down in the road. "I'll just stay here with him until he's better."

There was a long silence as tears dripped down Shay's cheeks. She leaned against Nero and rubbed his neck like she used to do on the ranch when their lives were very different. She remembered the day she'd found him, covered in bee stings and half dead. She didn't carry him back to the ranch and nurse him back to life just to have him die in the road like this. No, it wouldn't do. Shay would stay with him and find another way, even if it was without everyone's help.

Klaus left. Shay watched his large figure shrink to the size of a pin head in the sky as he made his way to the castle.

Jed crouched next to Shay. "This is craziness, Shay-baby." His words were barely a whisper. "We can't save him."

"You could do something." Shay glared at Jed. "He crossed the Veil after Clyburn dragged me to Hell. *He* saved *me*." Shay pointed her finger, accusingly. "You could do something, anything right now."

Jed sighed, rose to his feet, and moved to inspect the wound. He glanced at Teari.

"You healed my stitched face," Shay reminded Jed.

"That was different. There was no Demon poison involved." Jed held his hand over Nero's wound and shook his head. "I can't, Shay. I can't make this worse. I haven't come across anything like this before." A hollowness filled his gut as he realized he couldn't do a thing to help Nero. It made him feel like dog shit. Jed would do anything for Shay. But he wouldn't risk fucking up healing Nero. If Nero died because of Jed, he knew Shay would never forgive him.

Teari touched Jed's arm. "The basilisk will fix it. We just have to get him there." She motioned to the castle.

"Maybe we should go get the basilisk and bring it here?" Jed asked.

"You guys can go," Shay said. "I'll wait here."

Jed glanced to Chel who was pacing near Shay. The Hellion was a bit too protective of her and it worried Jed. It made him wonder if he should lay some claim in Shay publicly so the Hellion would back the fuck off.

"Do you know what you are?" Teari asked Jed, her hand still on his arm.

Jed turned to face her. "Yeah. I know."

"The blue is very pretty." Teari was inspecting the aura around Jed. "Is it always glowing?"

"Usually," Jed said. He didn't want to talk about himself, especially toward a pure-blood Angel. "Are you going to try and kill me now?" he asked. "That's what your kind typically does next."

Teari shook her head. "No. No you brought back Nightingale and she's family. I could never kill you." Teari patted Jed's arm before moving away from him. She whispered, "You should do something about her," she motioned to Shay. "She's quite spectacular and I've noticed a few lingering gazes." Teari looked at Chel.

Jed rubbed his face. Wonderful, now he was going to have to fight a Hellion to lay claim to his girl. The fun was never ending on any realm.

The fading sunlight was blocked out and a large shadow covered the road. Everyone looked up.

"Oh good," Chel said. "She's here."

"What's that?" Shay asked, covering Nero with her upper body as though she could protect him from the giant shadow that was approaching.

Chel held out a hand to help her up. "It's Clea. She transforms into that giant bird. The argentavis." He tugged Shay away from Nero.

Jed and Teari moved away from Nero as well.

"Clea can carry him to the stables," Chel said.

Clea swooped down and gently grabbed Nero's lifeless body with her claws. She faltered under his weight, flapping her wings harder to get back in the air.

Breath caught in Shay's throat as she feared Clea would drop Nero. She didn't though. Her giant wings beat *one-two-three*, and she took off into the sky, headed toward the castle, veering from side to side every so often under the weight of the horse.

"Let's go," Jed moved closer to Shay and led her away from Chel. "We can meet Nero there if we walk fast enough."

"I can fly and carry her back," Chel offered. "It would be faster than walking."

"No," Jed said.

Shay's mouth was open, ready to say something but from the worry lines creasing Jed's forehead, she decided not to.

"It's fine, we can walk," Shay said as she glanced over her shoulder at the others. "You all can fly back if you want."

"We'll walk too," Chel said sternly. "Just in case there are any more surprises."

———

NERO DIDN'T WAKE when Noah brought in the basket with the basilisk.

Shay was kneeling next to Nero, petting him gently and whispering to him.

"I hate touching these things," Noah complained as he opened the basket. He reached in and after a few attempts grabbed the creature inside. Shay's eyes went wide as he pulled out the snake-like creature with sharp teeth.

"Are you sure?" Shay asked, looking to Teari.

"Yes." Teari nodded. "It's worked on other poison injuries. Meg had a cut on her arm that's been healing up nicely."

Noah lined up the basilisk with the wound on Nero's flank. The creature wiggled and struggled against Noah's hold. Thick slime dripped onto the hay where Nero was sleeping.

Nero didn't move when the basilisk latched onto the wound. Noah held it in place, crouching to get in a comfortable position.

"How long do I have to hold this thing?" Noah asked.

"Until it releases," Teari replied.

The basilisk stayed latched for a good ten minutes before releasing Nero's flank. The creature sagged in Noah's hands as though it were a sated infant. Noah tucked the basilisk in the basket and stood. "Well, my work here is done." He joked.

"We need to do this three times a day." Teari was inspecting the wound that was still red but weeping considerably less. "This thing has festered for a long time. It's probably gone to his bloodstream." Teari touched the sensitive skin around the wound. "At least he's not in as much pain now." Teari made her way out of the horse stall. "He needs rest."

"Come on," Jed helped Shay stand. "Let him rest. We'll come back later."

"You all should get cleaned up," Noah said as they left the barn. "We are having a party tonight in the ballroom. There's going to be music and dancing and pizza!"

FOURTEEN

THE CASTLE BALLROOM WAS EXQUISITE. DARK ETCHED
wood and forest green wallpaper stretched several floors up to a
cavernous ceiling. A wall of windows looked over Hell with an
expanse of balconies and open glass doors to let in the cool night air.
Dark curtains billowed in the breeze. Lightning was illuminating
dark Hellsky in the distance.

Noah was standing at a record player, twirling a record between
his palms. "I haven't heard this tune in ages." He set the record in
place and adjusted the needle arm, then turned up the volume. *Pump
up the Jam* started playing. Noah broke out in ridiculous exaggerated
dance, pumping his arms and hips in motion with the beat.

Nightingale stopped spinning with baby Thrush in her arms and
made a face. "This isn't music," she said as she skated over to Noah.
The music was too loud to hear what she was saying to him as she
thumbed through a stack of records. She pulled out a record and
tapped it.

With a face of disappointment, Noah changed the record and
Flashdance started playing.

"These people have something for the eighties," Shay whispered to Jed.

Jed was drinking cold beer for the first time in years. He'd never felt relaxed enough to let his guard down, but tonight seemed worthy. What could happen in a castle in Hell? There was plenty of protection.

"It was decent music," Jed said. His fingers were tapping on the table.

Shay watched his fingers. Jed had rolled up the sleeves of his dress shirt. The muscles of his lower arms flexed, strong and developed from decades of spell casting.

"You want something to eat?" Jed asked Shay, motioning to the table spread with pizza and snacks.

Shay shook her head. "I'm too worried about Nero to eat."

Jed leaned closer. "He's going to be okay. Teari is a healer."

The ballroom doors opened and handful of people walked in. Meg was wearing a tight, low cut black dress. Jed paused his table tapping and his hand flew to his neck, rubbing the scars from her bite.

Shay was watching him closely. Whatever had happened between Jed and Meg was before her time. But it had left a lasting impression on him. Still, it was easy to see he didn't trust Meg, he was easy to tell her when she'd gone too far, when she'd done something outrageous. Being the ruler of Hell, Meg never seemed to get upset with Jed, it was as though she allowed him to work out his frustrations with her as payment for what she'd done to him.

Shay wanted to rest her head on Jed's shoulder and watch the lightning display outside. She'd always loved watching the storms travel across the Montana flats. She turned away from Meg and Klaus dancing. Everyone was dancing. Nightingale twirled with Thrush in her arms, Noah grabbed her hand and spun them back to him. Thrush giggled and drooled. Everyone looked so normal, Shay could barely believe she was in Hell. She glanced at Jed, wishing he'd ask her to dance. She could sense his reserve. While they'd spent plenty of nights together wrapped up in each other, when the daylight came, he was distant.

Shay shuddered and rubbed her arms. She should have brought a jacket.

After Meg and Klaus finish dancing to *Time of My Life*, Meg made her way to the balcony.

Shay didn't trust her. Meg still seemed off, after everything that happened. Everyone else seemed to forgive her for stealing Thrush in the night and taking him to the Seven Kingdoms of Heaven for baptism. Shay realized that these people had history, one that she didn't quite understand or fit into. She rubbed her arm absently. She was the only human here in a realm she didn't belong in or know much about. She'd felt comfortable at the chapel in the graveyard for the weeks that they were there. Now everything was in upheaval. They'd been moved back to the suite in the castle. And while Jed had shared a bed with her at the chapel, he'd set his bags down in the opposite bedroom after they'd entered the suite.

Suddenly, Meg ran out of the room, holding a hand over her mouth like she was going to be sick.

Noah watched, a grim gaze on his face. Nightingale tugged at Noah's arm, redirecting him to dance more.

Teari calmly walked out of the room, following Meg.

"What do you think is wrong with her?" Shay asked Jed.

"She probably ate too much." Jed sipped at his beer.

Shay followed Jed's gaze; he was watching Chel on the other side of the room. Shay wondered why. The Hellion was nice and more than a few times had discussed survival gear and hunting knives with her. It was hard to come across people who could hold those discussions that weren't a little conspiratorial in nature.

Chel turned and looked at Shay quickly before looking away again and continuing his conversation with the Hellion named Tukka.

Jed's chair slid back and he stood abruptly.

"What's wrong?" Shay asked.

"I need some air. Stay here." Jed's pace was brisk as he walked to the balcony.

Shay was worried about Nero. It was dark outside and he was alone and injured in an unknown place. Shay didn't feel like sitting any longer, she stood and made her way out of the ballroom.

FIFTEEN

Shay went to the suite to grab her jacket. She found a thick flannel with lambswool on the inside. She decided to take her pistol as well, and a knife for good measure. She glanced at her empty bed then moved the pillows to make it appear a body was sleeping there. Whatever was up with Jed, she wasn't going to bother him. She was just going to let him assume she'd left the party and gone to sleep.

As she left the suite, she couldn't stop dwelling on Jed's strange actions tonight. He'd promised that she wouldn't be alone. He'd promised to be with her but tonight he seemed so distant. There was something going on with him and she was disappointed that he wouldn't tell her.

Shay made her way to the door of the castle, surprised with how easily it opened for her. The door was solid wood, marred from eons of use. She walked across the courtyard headed for the stables, thankful for the little bit of lighting along the walk way.

Near the forest, she could see Hellions on patrol. Since Meg had stolen Thrush in the night, Shay had noticed more Hellions than when they'd first arrived.

Shay made her way to the stables. She hadn't been completely alone since she'd arrived in Hell. There was always someone nearby, always someone watching her. There was freedom in being alone–an autonomy that she enjoyed. The night breeze was cold and Shay could see her breath. She hoped Nero wasn't cold.

———

NERO WAS SLEEPING in the same position they'd left him. Shay entered the stall and curled next to him, her hand on his side. She'd always felt comfortable hanging out with Nero on the ranch. Whenever there was a problem or she was upset, she could be found in his stall. Nero had comforted her plenty of times after one of Clyburn's incidents. Shay wished she could give Nero the same comfort.

Shay laid her head on Nero's shoulder and closed her eyes, listening to the strong beating of his heart.

The barn door opened and footsteps approached Nero's stall. The sounds of a man struggling with carrying something heavy echoed. The stall door opened and Noah was there with the basilisk in the basket.

"Oh," he smiled when he saw Shay. "I didn't realize you were here."

Shay was leaning against Nero, her hand resting on his neck. "I didn't like the idea of him being alone."

Nero's eyes flashed open and he whinnied softly.

"Glad to see he's awake," Noah said as he opened the basket and reached for the basilisk. The creature wiggled and slimed, its jaws opened in anticipation of Nero's wound.

"It's the first time," Shay said.

Nero noticed the basilisk and spooked. He struggled to get to his feet. He whinnied anxiously and got his front half up.

Shay tried to move away but the stall wall was against her back.

"Whoa. Whoa," Noah said as he maneuvered the basilisk. "Settle down, boy." He was quick to get the basilisk to latch onto the wound.

Nero lost it when he felt the basilisk on his wound. He stumbled, dragged his back end a few feet before falling again. Then he was still.

"Knocked yourself out did you?" Noah asked the horse.

It happened so fast. Shay was trying to soothe Nero but the giant horse didn't have his wits about him. Shay had been pressed against the side of the stall edging her way out but then Nero fell, his ribs pressed against her. She shoved at him as he slid, nearly crushing her. His belly hit her knee, dragging her down with him. He was too heavy to move, and Shay cried out when she felt the bone of her leg flex too far. There was a loud crack as Nero landed. *Snap.* Her femur broke in half.

"Ah!" Shay cried, her back pressed against the wall of the stall.

Noah's head jerked in Shay's direction. "Oh no!" Noah was looking between the basilisk and Shay. "Shit."

"Move." Shay pushed at Nero, biting her lip against the pain in her right leg.

Noah didn't want to lose the basilisk.

"Let it finish," Shay said, bracing herself against the hard floor. She wanted Nero to get better. Ten minutes wouldn't fix her broken leg. "Just, let it finish," Shay said the last word as an exhale, fighting the searing pain. She rubbed her hip and pressed her fingers between Nero and her trapped leg. When she pulled it back, it was covered in blood. "Oh god." Shay took a shuddered breath and wiped her hand on her jacket. "It's going to be fine. It's going to be fine." She chanted to herself.

Sixteen

Noah put the basilisk in the basket then moved around the side of Nero to get a good look at Shay's predicament.

"Damn," Noah rubbed his chin. "This is going to hurt like a bitch."

"You can move him?" Shay asked, panting in pain. She'd never felt anything so excruciating.

"A crushed leg and a broken bone." Noah rubbed his hands together. "I won't be gentle. We're moving this beast then I'm picking you up and running." He nodded. "It's going to hurt."

"Okay," Shay agreed, breathless. "Do what you have to do."

Noah called on his Astral magic. He moved Nero, lifting him and shoving him to the side.

"Don't hurt him!" Shay reached toward Nero.

She was free. Bone stuck through the rip in her pants and her leg was surrounded by blood.

"Time to go," Noah said, gathering her into his arms. "There's just one problem."

"What's that?"

"Hellions drink blood. I have to move faster than them." He gripped Shay tightly against his chest, then he ran.

Noah ran so fast it knocked the wind out of Shay. By the time they exited the barn, she was unconscious.

Noah was a blur as he moved. But, he could hear the Hellion new recruits sniffing out the fresh blood. They couldn't help it. At least three of them were running behind him, eager for a taste?. They hadn't learned control yet.

Noah made it to the front door and kicked it open. The slam echoed. Everyone in the castle had to have heard it.

The Hellion lair opened and Klaus ran out.

Noah didn't give him time to speak. "Get Teari to the infirmary right now!"

Noah kept running, down long dark hallways and up a set of winding stairs. He cursed whoever thought to put the infirmary at the farthest point from the front door.

Noah set Shay down on one of the cots. She was pale but still breathing.

Teari ran in with Klaus at her side.

"What happened?" Teari began inspecting Shay's leg.

"The Demon horse fell on her." Noah was cutting off her pants with a pair of medic scissors. "She was trapped for about ten minutes while the basilisk was on Nero's wound."

"Why didn't you stop the basilisk?" Teari asked, her hands hovering over Shay's leg.

"She told me not to." Noah threw the bloodied pieces of Shay's pants aside. "Damn girl cares more about that horse than most people." He turned to Klaus. "Three new recruits were following us. I'm sure there's a blood trail."

Klaus nodded, knowing. "I'll take care of it," he said as he ran out of the room. The new recruits couldn't get a taste for fresh blood, especially Shay's human blood–it would send them into a frenzy.

"She's going to need a transfusion," Nightingale said to Noah. "Can you get some from storage?"

Noah disappeared. There was a large storage refrigerator in the kitchen to stock the Hellion's with bagged blood. Noah never considered it could be of use for a time like this.

———

"WHAT HAPPENED?" Jed ran into the room, worry plastered on his face. His aura illuminated in Teari's presence.

"She broke her leg." Teari was connecting blood tubing to an I.V. in Shay's arm. "I healed the bone but her leg was crushed. She needed blood."

Jed pushed up his sleeves as he moved closer. He touched Shay's face. "Where was she found?"

"She was visiting Nero." Teari's hands glowed with a white light as she focused her healing energy over Shay's leg. "The horse fell on her."

"Fuck." Jed rubbed his hands together. "Let me help. I've healed her before." He pulled up his sleeves. "Never anything this extensive though."

Teari nodded, appreciating the assistance. "I'll help you if you need it," she said.

It had barely been a day since her arms grew back and she felt rusty. Healing humans was precarious, they died quicker than Angels and Demons. Teari didn't have a moment to waste and she'd already spent enough time starting the blood transfusion. There was internal bleeding and ruptured muscle to fix before it was too late and Shay never walked correctly again.

Jed whispered words that sounded like a good promise. Like a sunset over the lake. Like a humming prayer.

"You're good at this," Teari said, glancing up. "That aura though." She shook her head in concern. "How did you ever hide that on the Earthen plane?"

Jed nodded, knowing his aura was glowing strong. He was using every magical store in his bones to help heal Shay. He'd never forgive himself if he didn't give his all.

"The runes helped," Jed broke his chanting to reply. "But if I used too much, an Angel or Demon would show up ready to kill. It's nothing but a beacon."

Teari moved her hands toward Shay's knee, focusing on the damaged ligaments and bone cracks. "She's going to be out for a few days. This isn't an overnight healing. If she were on the Earthen plane right now, she'd lose her leg."

Jed nodded, knowing. "She's fragile."

Teari smiled, remembering. "I thought the same once. But humans are strong in many ways." She winked at Jed. "You'll find out eventually."

Jed focused on healing Shay. He knit together a leaking artery, torn ligaments in her hip, a crack in her pelvic bone. His hands moved over her pelvis and he strengthened that and her hip, sensing the torn tissue on the left side. It could be an old injury. A fall off a horse or something that happened during childhood.

"You care for her," Teari said.

Jed was about to reply but the door to the infirmary opened. He glanced over his shoulder as Chel entered the room.

Chel growled in Jed's direction as he stood at the end of the bed. "She lost a lot of blood."

"I know," Teari nodded. "It's being replaced."

"Noah said she broke her leg." Chel motioned to the red scar across her thigh. He turned to Jed. "Where were you?"

"I was here." Jed didn't want to argue with the Hellion, but the dude was overstepping and pissing him off.

"Answer me," Chel demanded.

Teari cleared her throat. "Maybe you two should take this discussion in the hallway. You're distracting."

Jed's aura dimmed as he glared at Chel and stomped toward the door.

SEVENTEEN

"I'm not sure what the fuck you think you're doing," Jed growled at Chel as soon as the door to the infirmary closed.

"I could say the same about you." Chel took a step closer.

"What the fuck are you doing here. She doesn't need you."

Chel laughed. "Really?"

"If you want a girlfriend, go find one of your own kind." Jed pointed down the hall. "She's not available."

"I don't want to date her," Chel scoffed. "She's human. A tiny, weak, defenseless human," Chel said with disgust.

"I don't believe you," Jed argued. "You are always near her. You just show up out of the blue."

"Look at me," he roared. "I'd crush her. I'd break her in half. I'm not that fucked in the head, you half-breed idiot." Chel jabbed a finger at Jed. "I don't trust *you* with her. She deserves better."

"What's so wrong with me?" Jed paused. Magic was swelling in his fingertips as anger overtook him. He was ready to blast this bastard with something like he'd given Alastor. He was sure that would get him kicked out of Meg's castle though. He did his best to control it.

"Fucking lay claim to her. She smells only faintly of you but you never touch her. You're too distant. She deserves better than that. There's a mistrust between you both. And you can't be living in a place like Hell with no faith in each other. This is too dangerous." Chel glared at Jed. "I've seen far too many females of my kind lost to the terrors of Hell. Shay doesn't deserve that. She is innocent." Chel poked a finger at Jed's head. "I know you're still considering it. Taking her memories and sending her back to the Earthen plane to die alone on that Montana ranch."

Jed blinked.

"The Hellions are still under orders to protect her. And you. Meg demanded it. But I don't trust you to protect her. I'm not completely convinced she doesn't need protection *from* you."

Jed was feeling like shit. Chel wasn't wrong. Jed had been struggling with Shay. He wanted her so badly but he wanted her to be safe. He'd made promises and broken them. He'd lied to her. That night she woke to him casting a spell on her memories, it was to wipe her mind of everything that had happened. And he'd hated himself for attempting, he hated that she'd woken up in the middle of it, he hated that he'd lied to her about what he was actually doing. Clara raised him better than that but somewhere along his lifetime, he'd disappointed her memory.

"You better figure yourself the fuck out," Chel said. "Or I'll get her a room in the Hellion barracks. I don't trust you sleeping next to her every night."

"We sleep in separate rooms." It was a half-truth. Jed rubbed his face, wishing he'd learn to shut the fuck up.

Chel laughed. It was a wicked sound. "See. That's your problem, you little fuck. She should be next to you every night. But you don't trust yourself." Chel paced in frustration. "It's you or me. I will not have her fall victim to the creatures of Hell or the new Hellion recruits we've been bringing in." He held up three large fingers. "And now three of them have gotten a taste of her blood. I can't guarantee that they won't come looking for more."

"She's mine." Jed's fingertips flashed with blue sparks.

"Oh, now you give a shit." Chel laughed. "Where the fuck were you when her leg was getting crushed under that giant Demon horse?"

"You piece of shit..." Sparks flew from Jed's fingers as he punched Chel in the jaw.

Chel didn't move. He barely flinched at Jed's assault. He shifted his stance, bracing himself for a fight. "Let's do it, shithead half-breed." Chel grabbed his blade and threw it aside. "I'll just use my fists." He cracked his knuckles. "Promise."

Jed had never fought a Hellion before, but he'd fought other giant Demons in his time. They were all the same. Brute strength and stupid.

Chel's fists were twice the size of Jed's, but that didn't stop him from throwing the first punch. Jed's wrist made a terrible sound as it bounced off Chel's jaw.

Chel didn't move, only smirked. Tension crackled between them. Chel squared his shoulders, his uniform stretching against muscle and the glint of resolve in his eyes. "That's all you got?"

Jed made a swift gesture with his hands, conjuring swirling tendrils of iridescent energy that crackled in the air.

Chel held up his open hands. "I got rid of my weapon. Leave yours." His muscles tensed, preparing for Jed's assault.

"No." Jed's arcane energies swirled into a vortex, aiming to disorient and immobilize Chel. He chose violence.

Chel dodged the tendrils of energy, narrowly evading the attack. He dropped to the ground, rolled with surprising agility, and grabbed the blade he'd tossed aside. The blade sliced through the magical energy, dispersing the tendrils like mist.

Chel lunged forward, his blade gleaming in the dim light.

Jed's fingers twitched, casting battle spells. The air crackled with the clash of steel and the ethereal.

Their fighting echoed through the halls of the castle. A battle was nothing more than Jed's power versus Chel's unwavering determination.

Suddenly a voice shouted down the hallway. "Stop!"

Jed and Chel froze, their eyes meeting in silent understanding. Chel sheathed his blade. Jed shook the energy away from his fingertips.

Skeele approached. "Take this fight outdoors," he growled at the two as though they were boys playing. "You're too loud."

Skeele entered the infirmary without another word.

"I'll refrain from killing you on one condition." Chel smiled, showing sharp teeth.

"What's that?"

"You shut your mouth and let me train her to defend herself."

"She's killed Angels before. She can fight."

"She can fight better," Chel said.

Jed rubbed the overgrown stubble on his face, contemplating. He knew Shay needed training. She could hunt and kill but they were in Hell now. Demons were different creatures. They'd survived the camp in California because there was help and Jed had nearly drained his magic stores fighting. Shay didn't have magic and he knew if she came across a Demon like Alastor again, she'd be dead.

"I'll train her as though I'd train my sister if she were still alive," Chel promised.

"Fine," Jed agreed. "But if I get wind of anything more. I'll kill you."

"I *dare* you." Chel leaned toward Jed, his smile jeering.

Eighteen

The dead were wandering about quietly in the forest behind Jed and Shay. Sticks snapped, leaves rustled, groans interrupted Jed's teaching.

Shay rubbed her sore leg. She'd ventured out against Teari's wishes. She'd been cooped up inside for days. The castle was starting to feel like a prison and Jed's thoughts seemed so far away.

"Let's start with a warm-up exercise," Jed said, showing Shay how to stretch, twist, and tap her fingers into nimbleness.

Shay mimicked Jed's motions, her fingers moving faster and faster to keep up with him.

Jed watched her hands intensely. "That's good." His fingers moved in a rhythm only he seemed to know. He clucked his tongue lightly like a conductor so Shay could follow along to the beat. After three rounds he started with the first spell. Jed backed up in a circle, looking for the nearest walking corpse to practice on.

"That one," he jerked his chin to a dead man dragging his foot. "Like this." Jed's fingers danced as he cast a spell to freeze the zombie in place.

Shay's fingers followed along in the same dance, the same nimble spellcast. But no energy moved from her hands like it did Jed's.

Shay dropped her shoulders, defeated. "It didn't work." She flexed her fingers.

"Try again."

"I'm too human." Her voice was thick with disappointment.

Jed touched her shoulder. "I won't think less of you," he joked, the corner of his lips tipping up.

Shay swung at him. "You shit." Her fist landed on his bicep, and she moved to smack him again.

"I think you can do it," Jed said as he sprung away from Shay's fist. "You just need more time."

"It's been a long time. It's been forever," Shay exaggerated. She wanted to do something special. Everyone around her had power or wings or super strength. She had nothing.

Jed's eyes went wide and he held a finger to his lips. "Shhh. The dead will hear and come."

Shay paused and looked around. It wasn't long before the shuffling of feet started getting closer. "Shit."

"Let's go." Jed grabbed Shay's arm and tugged her in his direction.

The old Shay would have been pissed for not being asked which direction to run in, but she'd spent enough time with Jed to know that he had a knack for finding a way out. He'd never led her wrong.

Jed and Shay ran through the forest in a roundabout path toward the burning caves.

"Should we go to the cemetery?" Shay asked. "To lose them?"

"We can't risk bringing a horde to Thrush." He ducked under a low branch then held it up for Shay. "If we go back to the burning caves, they'll just wander away. They won't get close. Meg's there. They won't go near her."

"Not like the fast ones did?" Shay asked.

"The fast ones didn't follow the rules of Hell." Jed slowed to check their surroundings. "These slow ones will just move on." He motioned for her to move faster.

Jed and Shay moved quickly through the forest. Once they found the road, they ran parallel to stay hidden. Soon the moans of the walking dead got further and further away. Jed and Shay slowed, only to hear voices not far away. They both came to a stop and listened.

Shay ducked near a fallen tree and focused in the distance. She pointed. Jed crouched near a thick tree trunk coated in lichen and followed her line of sight.

There were three men dressed in black with white collars. Deacons.

Shay tapped her ear. Jed shook his head. Neither could hear what the Deacons were discussing. The dragging footsteps of the dead were getting closer. Jed and Shay were stuck in the middle.

Shay's heart thumped in her chest as they waited. She didn't like the feeling of being trapped. She'd spend too much of her life stuck between safety and the bliss of freedom. She turned to see the decaying forms of the dead as they meandered toward them and estimated how much time they had. At the rate they crept and how easily they were distracted, Shay figured it was less than six minutes before they needed to move again. She focused on the meeting of the Deacons in the road. Hopefully the men in black would be done by then.

———

JED AND SHAY broke through the forest line and right into the Hellion training grounds. Both were running and panting.

The Hellions secured their weapons and let their guests enter the training fields. Skeele and Chel stopped training.

Jed bent over, hands on his knees. "Damn, I need to run more." He wiped perspiration off his brow. "Been a long time. Too long." He patted his stomach. "Getting comfortable is never a good thing."

Shay coughed. "I was kind of enjoying not running for my life on a daily basis." Shay rubbed her right leg. It was sore and while Teari and Jed had healed her, there were still strange aches that she got when she pushed herself too hard.

"Why were you running?" Skeele asked as he sheathed his blade before crossing his arms and looking down at the human and Nephilim.

"We were training in the forest, past the cemetery and a horde came," Jed said.

"They don't move that fast," Chel said.

Jed held up his hand as he said, "As we were leaving, we found three Deacons in the road not far from here. We had to wait for them to leave. The dead caught up."

"Deacons?" Chel's brows rose in attention.

"Did you hear what the Deacons were saying?" Skeele asked.

"No," Jed shook his head. "We can show you where they were."

Skeele nodded and motioned for Chel to follow.

They hadn't left a single thing behind, not even a footprint. But the Hellions did a thorough job of surveying the area and back to the crossroads.

"Did they have a vehicle?" Skeele asked Jed.

"Not that we saw." Jed did his best to help but he wasn't trained in tracking, only running and hiding.

"You have a spell or something that could help us gain some insight?" Tukka asked.

Jed thought for a moment before reaching into his pocket to pull out the ages old notebook he carried with him. "I might have something. Let me look."

Shay stood close, watching Skeele as he searched. The Hellion Commander had always been hulking and intimidating, but today he seemed gaunt and bony.

Skeele caught her eye more than a handful of times before he finally walked over to her and asked, "What?"

"You seem different," Shay said.

"Nothing's changed." Skeele ran a hand over his head and horns as one runs their hands through their hair in frustration.

"Sure." Shay stepped closer to Jed.

"Why do you ask?" Skeele said.

"You seem tired or sick, and you've lost a lot of weight. You're the Commander of the Hellions." Shay lowered her voice. "Maybe you should see that healer, Teari."

"Not necessary." Skeele walked away from the human and continued on his searching until Jed cleared his throat.

"I found something." He motioned to Skeele and Tukka. "It's a spell that can rewind time but only for a few moments."

Chel watched from a distance.

Jed's fingers tapped and twisted as he chanted the spell, motioning in the area of the road where they'd seen the Deacons.

Transparent leaves rolled across the road before the images of the three Deacons appeared. They were see-through and faded, like Clea's wavering image. Ghosts of the past. Skeele moved closer and watched their lips as they spoke.

"Dead Newcomers."

"Her condition."

"Unlawful."

"What did they say?" Tukka asked.

"What kind of a mess did Meg get herself into now?" Jed asked.

Nineteen

Meg had been missing for weeks. No one had told Jed or Shay until a few days ago. Now everyone had collected at the chapel in the graveyard to discuss a plan. Without Meg present, there was risk that Hell would digress into chaos.

"He's found her," Nightingale told the others at the table. "I didn't approach her in the dream. She hasn't slept in a long time."

"Let her sleep," Noah said, shifting a sleeping Thrush in his arms. There was a wet drool mark on his shoulder.

"How long will it take Skeele to bring her back?" Shay asked.

Jed was in the middle of updating the runes on her arms, with real ink this time since the paint didn't last. Shay's blowtorch blue hair contrasted against her pale skin and dark clothing in a newly shortened haircut to her chin. Shay sucked in a breath as Jed tattooed deep over bone.

"Sorry," he said as his thumb rubbed her skin to soothe.

Rumors were starting. Someone had destroyed portals on the Earthen plane. The Deacons had already come knocking on the doors of the burning caves. Clea distracted them and sent them away. But it wasn't enough. The new Hellions had mouths that spoke freely at whatever post they were stationed. They were instructed to bring the rumors back to Klaus and Chel, but some had loose lips and spread their own rumors. The demons of Hell knew the throne was unseated. Meg wasn't as visible as she had been.

There was a knock on the door.

Nightingale moved to answer it. Chel, Klaus, and Tukka entered the room. Suddenly the chapel in the cemetery felt very small.

Klaus was carrying a bag. "This should be everything."

Nightingale took the bag as Jed stopped his tattooing, wiped Shay's skin, and rubbed a layer of healing balm over the fresh ink.

"Are you ready?" Jed asked Shay.

Shay nodded and stood. Her stomach felt queasy. She felt extremely out of place in this realm and she was about to do something crazy.

Tukka grunted in disapproval. "They are nothing alike. This will not work."

Nightingale pulled clothing from the bag and held them up to Shay. "The clothes will fit."

"Her hair is blue," Tukka motioned to Shay's hair. "Meg's is black. Everyone will know it's not her. She doesn't even have Meg's tattoos."

"Or her attitude," Klaus said with a smile, trying to lighten the mood.

"Hush, all of you." Noah patted Thrush's back, soothing him to sleep again. "She has a few of the tattoos. Jed still has time to add more."

"Or we could try the paint again?" Jed suggested, knowing that Shay was hesitant to ink her skin.

"They didn't last." Shay shook her head. "It won't work."

"Here," Nightingale thrust the clothing into Shay's hands. "Go change."

"Come with me." Shay tugged at Jed's shirt as she headed to the bedroom.

Shay closed the door behind Jed and listened to the chatter in the living room.

"They don't want me to do this." Shay tossed the clothing onto the bed and kicked off her boots.

"It doesn't matter." Jed turned his back like a gentleman. "We have to do something until we can get Meg back where she belongs."

"What if she never comes back?" Shay asked. "I'm a human. I am not whatever magical creatures you all are. I don't have wings or magic or battle training."

"Meg doesn't have any of those either." Jed pressed his ear to the wooden door to hear the others speaking.

"She has something that keeps you all in check." Shay pulled on a pair of jeans that were a little too tight on the butt. She changed her shirt to the wide-necked blue T-shirt of Meg's. "Okay. Turn around. Tell me how bad this is."

Jed turned and walked a circle around Shay. "I think this could work." He stopped in front of Shay and frowned.

"It's the blue hair, isn't it?"

Jed shook his head in defeat. "Everyone knows you have the blue hair. We have to hide it."

"It took a really long time to get this shade just right." Shay was annoyed. "If you fuck it up..."

Jed's lip tipped to form a half smile. "Say it like Meg would."

Shay closed her eyes and took a deep breath, collecting every speck of attitude and edge in her person. "If you fuck it up, I will drain you dry." Shay opened her eyes.

Jed was nodding in approval. "That was pretty good." He held out his hands and his fingers danced in rhythmic spellcasting. "Let's just add a little glamour so as not to fuck up your blue."

When Shay left the bedroom, the visitors in the living room were silent, judging, and one of them eating crow, figuratively.

"Fine," Tukka said, his tone dull. "But don't let anyone get too close to her. Meg has blue eyes."

"We will make sure," Klaus said, reaching for the door handle so they could leave.

Chel motioned for Shay to follow them. "After you, Queen of Hell."

Twenty

Shay stood in the middle of Meg's room feeling uneasy. "This seems so wrong," she said.

Jed was brushing crushed bird seed off the balcony railing.

"What's this?" Shay picked up the jar of mottled feathers from Meg's bedside table.

"I'm not sure," Jed said as he walked into the room. "But judging from the scarce decorations in this room, if it's here then it's important to her."

Shay set the jar down and wandered around the room, then the closet, then the bathroom. "Do I have to stay in here?" she asked. "It really feels like a violation of her privacy."

Jed followed Shay. "Look, we are doing her a favor."

"No one will know." Shay made her way to the balcony for some fresh air.

Jed stood next to her, scanning the tree line. He saw movement and pointed it out to Shay. "That creature would know if this room were empty."

Shay leaned forward and squinted. "What is it?"

"Probably a demon."

531

"You don't think it's Demore?" Shay asked.

Jed shook his head. "It's too early in the night for Demore." He took a piece of sharp charcoal from his jacket pocket and began sketching runes of protection on the balcony railing. "It could be another Deacon."

"Meg drinks blood," Shay said. "Are they going to want me to drink blood?"

"You don't have to drink blood. You're human."

There was a cry off in the forest. It sounded like an animal or a bird. But Jed and Shay knew it could be something else.

Shay's breasts felt warm as milk letdown. Her body thought the sounds was a baby.

"Ugh." Shay touched her chest and felt wetness. "Is this ever going to stop?" She knew it could go on for weeks while her milk dried up. Now that Nightingale was back, Thrush didn't need a wet nurse.

Jed touched her arm. "Come inside, I'll help you with that."

"Are you going to try the reverse spell again?" Shay asked, wincing. "It kinda hurt."

Jed closed the balcony doors and brought her to the bathroom. He closed and locked the door.

"Can you do something so it doesn't hurt this time?" Shay asked, nervous. She was glad she could help Thrush but she didn't think she'd ever put herself through that experience again.

Jed turned to Shay, moving close. He wrapped his arms around her, rubbed her back before his hands traveled down to her thighs and he lifted her onto the counter.

Jed reached for the hem of her shirt, pulling it up.

"What are you doing?" Shay asked, warmth curling in her abdomen.

"I think I know what went wrong last time." He pulled her shirt off then reached for her bra, unclipping it.

"What went wrong?"

"The milk was stuck." He kissed her neck.

"In my boobs?" Shay giggled.

"Um hm." Jed's mouth trailed across her collarbone and down the front of her chest.

"Oh my gosh, you're not going to—"

Jed's mouth covered her nipple and she felt the sensation of a gentle tug. He drained her then whispered a spell that sounded like the gentlest lapping of the ocean.

"Did it hurt this time?" he asked.

Shay shook her head, the warmth that had pooled in her abdomen had turned to fire. She reached for his jeans and tugged him closer. "You're going to have to finish what you started."

"Anything for my queen," Jed said with the quirk of his lips.

It had been days and days since they'd last been together. Jed was hesitant to touch her after she'd nearly been crushed in the stables. Her leg had healed but Jed's emotions remained buoyant after Chel's demands to lay claim to Shay. And now she was a body double for Meg. Things had gone from bad to worse. Jed couldn't get caught being handsy with the Queen of Hell. That was Skeele's job. Anger seethed under Jed's skin as he thought of Skeele touching Shay.

"What's wrong?" Shay asked, her fingers tracing the planes of his abdomen.

"I was just thinking." Jed ran a hand through his hair.

"Stop thinking." Shay leaned forward to kiss him, wanting more after he lit the flame inside her with his mouth a few moments ago. "Please stop thinking."

He leaned into her kiss, devouring her mouth. Nimble fingers made quick work of removing her jeans. Jed rubbed her thighs, his fingers touching the scars on her right leg.

Shay flinched. The scar was tender, but the memories it brought back were worse. Nero was still comatose, even after all of the basilisk treatments.

Jed's fingers moved to her core, rubbing against the thin fabric.

Shay made small noises as he stroked her.

The scar on his neck pinched. He opened his eyes and saw Meg on the countertop. Jed froze, pulling away. "I'm sorry." He cleared his throat and adjusted Shay's shirt.

"What's wrong?"

It was too much. Jed didn't want to hurt her. He was at a loss. Chel's threats were echoing between his ears. He saw her scar, the fear in her eyes. He'd done this to her. If he'd just left her alone and never followed her to that ranch she'd be home and safe. She wouldn't be in the middle of this shit show with him.

"Jed?" Shay searched his face.

He didn't answer because they were soon interrupted by two Hellions looking to escort Shay/Meg to watch the new recruits get their uniforms at the training barracks.

TWENTY-ONE

NOAH VISITED JED AND SHAY, INTERRUPTING A PERFECTLY serene breakfast on the balcony. Noah sat between them, crossed his hands over his stomach and leaned his head back. "Ah, it's so quiet here. I forgot what silence was like. No baby babble. No Nightingale asking me to go find diapers. No Meg demanding waffles." Noah took in an exaggerated deep breath. "I could sit here all day and enjoy the silence."

Jed's fork clattered against the plate as it dropped. "Except you can't."

"What?" Noah laughed. "You don't want me hanging around as a third wheel?" Noah looked back and forth at Jed and Shay. "Bullies."

"We really love having you around, Noah," Shay said, patting Noah's hand. "It's just..."

"You'd rather walk around naked and screw like rabbits all day?" Noah dead panned.

"Dude," Jed leaned forward.

"Men are such pigs." Shay took a sip of her coffee and shook her head, wishing it were true.

"Don't talk like that around her," Jed said.

"I grew up on a ranch, I've heard worse," Shay said.

"You shouldn't have to." Jed took a bite of bacon.

"Welp, seems I've outlived my welcome this morning." Noah stood. "I just stopped by to tell you that we've found Meg. She's in a Safe House. I need you two to go visit her. We're trying to keep her spirits up until we can figure out what the Deacons want." Noah's hand lingered on the balcony railing. "You know, there's lots of birds here. If you put a little seed on the railing they'll visit."

"Maybe you could bring us some," Shay suggested.

"My time here is done." Noah smirked before disappearing.

Shay looked at Jed. "I guess he doesn't want to be bothered with running errands for me."

"What do you need?" Jed asked. "I can get it for you."

Shay shook her head and wiped her mouth with a napkin. She was thinking of their moment alone in the bathroom the other day. She wanted him to finish what he'd started but she had been pulled away. She studied him, unsure if he'd live up to the promise he'd made her. It was disappointing. She tried to see everything from his point of view, but it was difficult. Things hadn't been easy for her these past few months. Her life had been turned upside down and she'd followed Jed hoping he'd be something more than a travel companion. There were too many intimate moments.

Shay closed her eyes and remembered the night he'd painted her. The look in his eyes. The feeling of the cool paint spreading across her sensitive skin. She felt her cheeks flush.

"What are you thinking about?" Jed asked. His gaze was intense.

Shay reached across the table to touch him but he pulled his hand away.

"Someone could be watching," Jed said. "Be careful, Shay, Meg and me, we're not a thing."

That hurt, like stones falling into her stomach. She tried not to take it personal. They were playing a part. Shay stood and looked over the landscape. Meg had a great view from her balcony. She could see the Hellion training grounds, the stables, and the forests in the distance.

"I want to go see Nero," Shay said as she turned and headed for the door.

"I can't be caught hanging around you outside the castle. They'll get suspicious."

"Sure." Shay forced a smile to hide her disappointment. "You stay here."

———

SHAY MADE her way down the winding stairs to the first level. Jed trailed behind her, trying to look like he wasn't following her.

The door to the Hellion's lair opened as Shay walked by and Chel stepped out with Klaus close behind.

"Going somewhere?" Chel asked.

"To the stables," Shay said.

"Is this glamour going to last?" Chel asked Jed.

"Of course," Jed replied.

"Remember, you can't go alone," Klaus said.

"Doesn't Meg go places alone?" Shay asked.

"Meg is a bit different. She can hold her own, most of the time," Chel said, motioning for Shay to follow him.

Jed stood in the doorway and watched as the Hellions escorted Shay to the stables.

———

THREE NEW RECRUIT Hellions stood guard at the edge of the courtyard. Osiris, Doyle, and Erebos paced and surveyed the land beyond the castle in the burning caves, standing to attention when the Queen walked by with two senior Hellion guards.

The new recruits stood at attention as she passed.

"Did you smell that?" one asked.

"Yeah. She smelled very familiar."

"That wasn't Meg."

"No, that was someone else."

The new recruits recognized the smell of Shay because they had found her blood trail the night the giant horse-beast broke her leg. They'd found her blood and tasted it and they wanted more.

The younger Hellions moved away, back to their assigned posts so no one would catch them gossiping.

"I want to eat her," one said.

"Slice her arteries and let the blood flow down my throat," another dreamed.

"Fuck." The third one made a fist as his shoulders went rigid. "All this time we searched and she was right under our noses."

Twenty-Two

"Hey." Shay leaned forward and moved her hand to cover Meg's in soothing greeting. Shay knew Meg didn't like to be touched so she let Meg make the final move.

"It's okay." Meg lifted her fist to touch hands. "I'm glad to see you. Are you both doing okay?"

"No complaints from this department," Jed said, inspecting Meg, his fingers tapping on the wooden table in a rapid beat.

"Are you nervous?" Meg asked.

Jed tipped his head toward the Deacon. "You think they know what I am?" He'd never been in the presence of a Deacon before and they were making him feel uneasy.

"I'm sure. They tend to know everything. Or at least they think they do." Meg poured a handful of dirt and rocks under the table.

A few moments later, Skeele walked in the room. Jed stood and clapped him on the shoulder. "Hey man, you alright in there?"

Skeele said, "As well as I can be."

There was a moment of awkwardness.

"I already know," Meg said. "I know he glamoured himself and followed me."

"Hey, man, it worked." Jed smiled and slapped Skeele on the shoulder again. "You brought her back."

Skeele winced and held up a hand. "Easy." He rolled his shoulders. "My assigned method of contrition has been physical."

"They couldn't give you some prayers to say?" Jed asked, lifting his hand, and inspecting Skeele's back. "Dicks."

"I go back next week and they tell me if I'm forgiven." Skeele rubbed his hands together and refused to look in Meg's direction. "My father was a Hellion. I've had worse."

"We have got to get you all out of there," Shay said, patting Meg's hand.

"I have a plan–" Meg started to say.

"It will not work," Skeele argued.

"I've dug a hole. It's almost completed." Meg lowered her voice. "I should be done by next week."

"Good," Skeele said. "At least you can get out of here."

"Wait, wait." Jed held up his hands. "We can't leave Skeele in here." He pressed fingertips to his head for a moment. "Tell me more."

"The hole is small," Meg said. "I can get out. He won't fit." She motioned to Skeele.

Shay turned to face Jed. "She can get out. I can go in. Then you all can storm the place and get Skeele out. Can you still poof from place to place?"

"Not since I was struck by lightning." Meg shook her head.

"Jed could do a glamour. We've been practicing." Shay touched Jed's arm. "Show her. She should know."

Jed's fingers danced in rhythmic spellcasting and Shay turned into a mirror image of Meg.

"Holy shit." Meg leaned forward and touched Shay's hair. "That's amazing."

"Jed's been practicing new spells from his book," Shay said.

"Have you been pretending to be me?" Meg asked.

"We had to," Jed said. "The Deacons showed up and the new

Hellions were spreading rumors. She didn't do anything you wouldn't do." A mischievous smile lifted the corners of his mouth. "So next week. You get out. Shay can get in. Skeele, create a distraction. Maybe start a fight. Then we raid. Watch this." Jed's fingers moved again, and he disappeared then reappeared a few minutes later. "We can get in, get the keys, get Skeele and Shay and get out. You know the layout. You can lead us while we are cloaked."

"Is there a backup plan?" Meg asked.

"We just thought of this like two minutes ago. I haven't thought of a backup plan," Jed said.

Meg nodded. "Let's do it."

———

JED AND SHAY waited at the tree line with Klaus and a handful of Hellions. Meg crawled out of a hole in the ground and ran across the empty field. Klaus grabbed her and pulled her in for a tight hug.

"Ready?" Meg asked Shay.

Shay nodded and began walking toward the hole Meg had crawled out of.

Meg grabbed her arm to stop her. "Just wait for us. We'll get you out."

Shay patted Meg's hand. "I know, Meg. I know you'll get me out."

The little owls hopped around the entrance to the tunnel as Shay climbed inside. The hole was tight and dark. In the distance Shay could see dim light. She focused on the light, crawling as fast as she could.

———

"HOW LONG SHOULD WE GIVE HER?" Jed asked.

"A few minutes, then we follow the next Deacon inside," Meg said.

Jed cast his spells turning everyone invisible, then the crew made their way to the front door of the Safe House.

———

"SKEELE," the man on the left said. "You ate a family of Newcomers. This is forbidden."

"I was hungry." Skeele replied.

"An entire family, before they had time to reach us." The man at the desk was disgusted. "There are few rules in Hell. Surely you can follow the simplest one."

"It was an emergency." Skeele rolled his shoulders.

"What kind of an emergency?"

"Meg was dying," Skeele said.

"You killed to save the ruler of Hell?"

"Yes." Skeele cleared his throat. "And I'd do it again. I was born and bred to serve the throne."

One man tapped his fingers together. "You are like your father, so faithful to Hell."

"There is no other way to be." Skeele lifted his chin, proud. He was a Hellion.

There is a long pause before the men turned their attention on Shay/Meg.

"We need to discuss your situation," the man to the left said.

Shay pressed her lips together. She glanced at Skeele but couldn't gain a thing from his expression. Shay wished she had notes for this. She had no idea what Meg did on a daily basis besides lose her cool and scare the shit out of everyone. Shay couldn't blame her. The chick was under a lot of pressure.

"The Queen of Hell should not be trying to abort her fetus or be acting recklessly. You were doing drugs to harm your unborn child. God cast you out of the Earthen plane with force. What do you have to say?" the man said.

Shay couldn't say a thing. She couldn't even think of anything to say. She just stood there with her mouth slightly open trying to find words but the only thing going through Shay's mind was what a terrible mess she'd gotten herself into; taking the fall for Meg. Judging from the look on the man's face, this wasn't going to be good. Shay felt like puking. She wished she could rub Meg's face off her own but the glamour wasn't makeup, it didn't work that way. Shay trembled as she stood. She wasn't ready to spend the rest of her life being punished for this. Maybe Jed was right. Maybe she should have gone back to the ranch.

Suddenly a familiar voice broke through the silence, "Break the glamour. This is not her sin to answer for."

Twenty-Three

NERO'S EYES FLASHED OPEN AS PURE TERROR SPED DOWN the tether he shared with Shay. Something was happening.

Nero was still healing from the Demon wound on his flank and couldn't move. He tried but he could barely lift his head. He could only wiggle his legs. He couldn't even get up on his knees.

Nero had half a mind to kick Jed in the head the next time he saw him. The half-breed man should have protected her. He'd done a good job at in on the Earthen plane, but something was off with the man now that they'd crossed the Veil. Nero could sense it, even from a distance. Jed was uncertain and Nero didn't like it one bit. Someone needed to protect Shay at all times. She couldn't be left to the wild things on this plane.

He hoped Shay would visit soon so he could see her. He hoped she was okay. Nero hated himself for being injured this badly and unable to roam freely.

The door to the pen opened and a Hellion with curled horns walked in carrying a basket. Nero knew it was time for the basilisk to drain his wound. Usually Shay came during the treatment but she'd been gone for most of the day.

Nero reached across the tether and sensed that the fear had passed. She was now feeling relief and concern. Nero settled his head on the floor of the pen and let the Hellion do his work.

The creature spoke to him like they were brethren. Nero could only think that this Hellion must be too young to realize that horses didn't turn into Crossroads Demons under normal circumstances.

The basilisk treatment didn't hurt. Nero was no longer afraid of the snakelike creature. It was helping him get better. Gone were the days of Nicholas calling the veterinarian to visit Nero on the ranch with antibiotics and steroids. This type of medicine was bizarre, but it worked. Nero sighed, the air blowing out his nose disturbing the hay he was resting on.

Nero saw dried blood on the concrete underneath and remembered injuring Shay. It was an accident. He couldn't remember exactly what happened just that he'd tried to stand and fell onto Shay.

She'd visited since then with a mild limp. Nero didn't know how to apologize. He'd nuzzled her leg and licked her hand and face. He told himself he had to be careful now. He'd changed. He was no longer just a stallion. The ring in his ear itched.

The Hellion removed the basilisk and patted Nero on the flank.

"All done for tonight, chum." The Hellion stood, glancing down at Nero, indifferent. "I hope it's alright that I called you chum."

Nero nodded. He could sense the Hellion feared him. Nero feared himself. He wasn't sure what kind of power he had now, but he could feel it swirling inside of him. There was something dark that hadn't been there before.

He needed to get well so he could help protect Shay. And, before long someone would summon a Crossroads Demon and Nero needed to be ready to step into his new role.

Twenty-Four

The scenery changed quickly for Shay. Thankfully Jed had broken the glamour. Everyone was there and Shay looked like herself again. She moved away from Skeele as Meg took her place, stopping next to Chel as they were all informed that they would be present for Meg's trial. Shay looked to Jed, unsure of what this meant. She didn't want to spend any longer in the Safe House than she had too. It felt wrong and one of the Deacons was staring at her. Sooner or later they were going to find out that she hadn't died and gone to her rightful place. She wasn't a creature of Hell. She was a full blown, pure blood, undead human. And she was quite sure someone in this forsaken building was going to figure that out.

———

"How do you know Meg?" the Deacon asked Jed.

"I first met her in my shop. She came to me for a tattoo." He held up his arms, showing off his ink.

"Did she know what you were?"

"She didn't know. I had to explain myself."

"You were comfortable explaining yourself to her? You've been in hiding for so long."

"She was in hiding at the time too. We were kindred. Plus, she needed a tattoo, and she could see my blue light." Jed said.

"Any problems after meeting Meg?"

Jed rubbed his neck. "She did bite me once." He laughed lightly. "It didn't hurt. It was kinda nice, kinda sexy." He cleared his throat and sat up straight. "But then she ran off with Sparrow. Our paths crossed again when the zombies started taking over on the Earthen plane."

"And she brought you to Hell against your will?"

"Nope." Jed shook his head with certainty. "Never against my will. She's never forced me to do anything." He paused. "Well, besides tattooing Gabriel but that situation wasn't terrible."

———

SHAY TOOK the stand next and the Deacon began his questioning.

"Was that the first time you met Meg?"

"Yes, she rescued us from a house that was under siege with the dead. Jed and I were going to die. Then she showed up at the window and did that *poof* thing. And got us out of there."

"You're full human?" Deacon asked.

"Yes." Shay paused, waiting for something terrible to happen, expecting them to thrust her across the Veil on her ass.

"How do you feel about being in Hell? You don't necessarily belong here."

"I hope to stay here." Shay tilted her head like no one was going to tell her what to do with her life. She didn't want them to know she was scared shitless of these unknown beings. "I spent plenty of time on the Earthen plane and Hell has been much nicer to me. I have freedom and safety here. I have people like I've never had before."

"Does Meg ever scare you?"

"Of course. I can tell she's struggling, but most of us are. I can't imagine the things she feels responsible for. But I can tell you when Nightingale and Sparrow were injured, she did *everything* in her power to get them to safety. And when Thrush was stolen by Demore, she never slept until he was home. Most humans care less about their own children than Meg cared for Thrush. Do you know how many missing children there are on the Earthen plane? How many kids are abused, stolen, left to raise themselves and given nothing?" Shay was shaking. She tucked a piece of blue hair behind her ear. "Meg isn't perfect. Neither am I. But Meg tries, even if she doesn't realize it."

TWENTY-FIVE

THE DEACONS RELEASED MEG AFTER HER HEART WAS weighed against the feather of truth. Shay recognized the jar of feathers that Meg had brought back. It was the same jar that sat by her bedside. She recalled being told how Meg lost her first child while she was pregnant. She had been attacked by Hellions. That was before everything. Shay felt for Meg. It was a tragedy no one should have to go through.

Shay was relieved when the scale tipped up, revealing Meg's heart was true. She wasn't evil or bad, just dealing with a boatload of bullshit on a daily basis and trauma that she needed to work through. Then there was the pregnancy. Shay was on edge watching the story unfold in the courtroom. The look on Skeele's face when he realized the child was his, the shame Meg tried to hide, what she'd done to try and get rid of the baby. Shay couldn't judge. The world was a scary place for a pregnant woman. Just look at what happened to Jennifer Asheworth and her two children. Shay glanced at Skeele. He would protect them, she could tell.

Chel flew Shay back to the castle in the burning caves after the trial was over.

Tukka flew Jed.

Jed kept his distance as they got ready for dinner in the ballroom. Nightingale had demanded it.

Jed dressed in his room.

Shay dressed in hers.

Jed was wearing a black silk shirt, black slacks, and cream colored oxfords. He'd tied his hair back in an effort to not look disheveled. He needed a haircut. His hand rested on the door handle of his room. He felt like a dick. He should have been getting ready in the other room with Shay. When they were forced together, he didn't have an issue dropping his guard. Now that there was a second room, he'd gone cold and wasn't sure why. He promised he wouldn't do this. He'd pressed her against the wall that night and promised he'd never do it again. He was going to have to fix this and get his head straight. This was the last night he could live like this. He couldn't live in fear his entire life.

Jed stepped into the living room of the suite and waited for Shay. He was trying to think of what to say to her, but then she stepped out of the bedroom.

Her blowtorch blue hair was arranged in a half updo with curls hanging against her neck. She was wearing a gauzy blue dress that accentuated every curve. She looked like a goddess.

Suddenly, Jed couldn't form words. She had so much skin showing. He swallowed hard.

"Ready?" Shay asked with the rise of her brows.

"Yeah." He followed her. He stumbled to get to the door before she did and held it open.

"You look nice," Shay said. "Did you find that or did it just appear in the closet?"

"It was there." Jed's mouth felt full of cotton as he struggled to find words. He was too busy looking at her.

"This too," Shay said as she smoothed a hand over her dress. She didn't tell Jed that the heels made her leg ache and she did her best not to limp.

Chel and Klaus were in the hallway, lingering. Both were dressed nicely in black slacks and silky button-downs.

"Come on, clowns," Klaus prodded. "We are going to be late."

———

CHEL LINGERED TOO close to Shay. He smiled a lot and told Shay jokes that she didn't quite understand because she hadn't lived in Hell her whole life. Chel had to explain most of them, but Shay laughed and her gaze met Jed's as he stood near the window and sipped from a glass of wine.

Jed was annoyed; Chel was fucking with him and would continue to do so. He knew it.

Meg and Skeele were on the balcony, then the air. Everyone saw her drop from the sky and ran to watch.

Shay gripped the stone balcony railing and leaned forward. Chel pulled her back. Jed glared, ready to push Chel off.

Suddenly, Shay turned, smiling. "Did you see it?" she asked, moving closer to Jed. She looked so pretty in the blue dress. Jed wished they were elsewhere, alone.

He shook his head. "I didn't see."

"Meg got her wings. They are beautiful. Kinda gray. Is that because she's half Angel and half Demon?"

"Probably," Jed replied, taking another sip of his wine, trying to drink off the edginess that was growing with each minute.

"Will you get wings?" Shay asked, touching his shoulder.

"Nope." Jed shook his head. "My kind doesn't have wings." He paused. "Well, some are born with them but they're usually too small and then they all die anyway. So..."

"Jeeze," Shay said. "That's freaking depressing."

"I know." It was a shit set up. With wings and magic, he could have stood a better chance with all the creatures he'd battled on the Earthen plane. He could have saved his mother that night on the train.

The song changed and Shay turned to see Noah at the record player, turning up the volume. *Billie Jean* played and nearly everyone began dancing to the beat.

"Want to dance?" Shay asked as she moved toward the dance floor.

Jed downed the last of his wine and turned to set the glass down. When he turned again, Chel was dancing with Shay. She laughed, touching his shoulder. Chel's hand was on her hip, his large frame bent over her, whispering in her ear.

It was Jed's fault and he knew it. He had gone hot then cold. He shouldn't have. His worst fear was seeing Shay hurt or worse, dead. He couldn't keep her at arm's length. Living in peace was all he'd ever wanted, and that's finally what they had here. Until Chel came along.

Rage flooded Jed. Absolute, unadulterated rage like never before in his life. He was going to kill the Hellion in front of everyone. Right. Now.

Jed marched across the ballroom to where everyone was dancing, his fingertips tingling with magic. Sparks flew from him only to sizzle on the tile floor. He cracked his knuckles as he got closer, ready to send Chel to another plane. Preferably the Ether from where he'd never return.

Just as Michael Jackson hit the high note in *Billie Jean*, Jed flung a shot of electricity with the flip of his wrist. It was barely battle magic but it was enough to send Chel flying across the room on his ass.

Shay's eyes were big as she turned to face Jed.

Jed stepped closer, grabbed her hand and twirled her until she slammed against his chest.

The music came to a static and abrupt stop. Noah was changing songs. *Pretty Young Thing* blasted through the speakers.

Jed shot a glance of thanks to Noah. He wasn't a skilled dancer but he could keep up with Michael Jackson's beat in this song.

Jed turned them both so his back was to the crowd, he pressed his mouth against Shay's ear. "Mine," he growled before turning her quickly, holding her at arm's length just for a second before tugging her back to his chest. He fit his leg between her thighs and took her hand, guiding it up his chest and around his neck.

His large hand stretched across her back and pulled her tight against him so every part of their bodies that could touch, did.

Jed knew the Hellions were nothing but animals half the time. Their sense of smell was strong and he couldn't forget that had Chel shamed him for not making Shay smell like him. He'd rub himself all over her to keep them away starting right now. Jed guided her, grinding together with the beat of the song. He wished there was no clothing between them.

Shay's lips were open, her tongue darted out to wet her lips as she watched him with half-lidded eyes.

Jed's free hand cupped her cheek, slid into her hair, and tilted her head back. He searched her eyes for fear. She wasn't afraid. She rarely ever was. She was human but she was strong. He knew it. He wished he'd been conscious that night she killed the Angel on the Earthen plane. He was sure she looked spectacular, just like she did tonight.

Jed's mouth closed over Shay's. He kissed her deeply, for all to see.

The room erupted in clapping.

"It's about fuckin' time!" Noah shouted.

TWENTY-SIX

ALASTOR FOLLOWED THE BLACK SLUDGE FOOTPRINTS AND they led him straight to Lucifer's castle. He knelt near a cluster of trees. In the ochre cast of Hellsky night, he noticed a dried puddle of blackness. Alastor moved to the middle of the crumbling road and touched his finger to the dried inky fluid and sniffed it. He closed his eyes. There it was. Sugar and sunshine, pure. He could smell the hint of her in the fluid on his finger. He sniffed the air. The Crossroads Demon was here. And so was Shay.

It had been decades since Alastor was last at the castle. He didn't see any Hellion patrols as he moved closer. He could hear music and laughter.

Wingbeats overhead startled him. Alastor shifted back into the shadows and sank to the ground, watching the shadows that passed overhead.

It was a Hellion and... the Queen. Last he'd heard she couldn't fly. It appeared things had changed. Alastor cursed this transformation. He'd hoped someone would battle Meg for the throne and things could go back to the way they were when Lucifer ruled. He doubted Meg would let him continue with the skin trades if she ever found out. She'd shut it down. She'd brought too much light to Hell.

He waited, crouched and planning while the two flew overhead, letting out a breath of irritation when they finally returned to the castle. He studied the grounds, the patrols, he'd wait here for as long as he needed to and find his way in.

Twenty-Seven

Shay woke with a startle. She was dripping in sweat and naked. Jed stirred and Shay watched the sheet slip down revealing the sharp curve of his back.

A twinge in her chest forced her to look out the window. Shay grabbed Jed's silk button-down and put it on as she walked to the balcony. The twinge tightened and Shay rubbed her sternum. In the distance, she could see lights on in the stables. Then, the unmistakable panicked neighing of Nero.

"Nero!" Shay whispered.

Shay ran into the room and found her jeans and boots. She buttoned Jed's shirt as she grabbed her gun from the closet and her hunting knife. Then she ran out of the bedroom.

She ran down the stairwell two at a time, ran down the hallway and shoved the door to the courtyard open with her shoulder and a grunt.

"Nero!" Shay shouted as she ran across pebbled walkways. It was dark, nearly pitch black. Shay's eyes were adjusting to the night. The only light came from the barn in the distance.

Nero whinnied again.

Shay ran faster, tripping over rocks and uneven terrain. She had made it off the walkway and was making a beeline toward the stables.

She made it to the barn and shoved open the door. The lights blinded her and Shay held a hand up to shield her eyes.

"Told you she'd come," Osiris said.

"Like a fly to honey." Doyle gripped his blade.

"What's with her and this horse?" Erebos jerked hard on the harness tied to Nero.

Nero reared up, or at least tried to. He was still weak from the healing wound on his flank. He limped twice then slid to the ground.

"I'm going to kill it," Doyle said as he moved closer to Nero, blade gleaming.

"No!" Shay said. She was aiming her gun in Doyle's direction. "Don't you dare touch that horse."

The three Hellions laughed. Shay had never seen them before. Unease filled her gut. This was not good but she'd be damned if she wasn't going to stand her ground and protect her best friend since childhood. She wasn't a coward even though the tiny voice in her head was screaming at her to run.

Erebos moved faster than Shay had ever seen anyone move. He punched her wrist and the handgun went flying.

Shay scanned the dimly lit stable as she dropped to the ground and rolled away from Erebos's grip. Her wrist and leg ached as she scrambled to her feet toward the dropped gun. Doyle kicked the gun to a dark corner, straddled her back and grabbed a fistful of blue hair.

Shay winced as he pulled her up to her knees.

Doyle sniffed her neck. "Oh yes. We've tasted your blood before." His long tongue licked her skin.

Shay struggled and gained just enough distance to draw back her arm and punch Doyle in the knee. He let go of her hair. Shay dropped to the ground, rolled to her back, and faced the Hellion straddling her. Her wrist ached but she had one shot to get away from this bastard. With everything she had, she punched him right in the balls.

Doyle roared in pain and dropped to the ground.

Erebos and Osiris roared in laughter.

"You let that tiny human touch your balls," Erebos said, smiling, revealing sharp teeth. "She'll be touching mine next."

"I'm not touching any of you." Shay lunged for her gun in the dark corner, landing on her stomach and sliding across the hay. She clambered, her fingers feeling the slick metal of the gun. She grabbed it.

Osiris grabbed onto both of Shay's ankles and dragged her back.

Shay rolled, aimed, and shot him in the shoulder.

"Bitch," Osiris sneered as blood leaked from his shoulder and soaked his uniform.

Shay shot him again and he let go of her ankles.

A dark shadow was coming for her. Fearing another fist to the wrist, she rolled, twisted, and braced her back against the wall of the stables.

Erebos was coming at her. She shot him twice, hitting him in the gut and grazing his neck. He came at her faster, grabbing her by the neck and shoulder and dragging her up the wall.

Shay's feet scraped the floor to support her body so her neck didn't snap. He pressed his arm to her neck, securing her with one arm. He tore at the loose shirt, ripping the buttons to reveal her shoulder.

Erebos made a nauseating sound as he licked his lips and leaned in, eager to consume her.

Shay used her last bullet to shoot Erebos in the foot. It bounced off his boot and clanked against the concrete floor. She rotated the gun in her hand, holding the scalding hot barrel, ready to hit him in the head with the heavy handle.

"No," Erebos said as he pressed his arm against her neck until she couldn't breathe.

Shay's head swam. Her vision blurred. She didn't want to die like this.

She barely heard the groan of breaking wood as Chel ripped the stable door off its hinges and tossed it aside. Skeele and Tukka were close behind.

Lightning crackled and arcane wisps of smoke slithered along the floor as Jed entered the barn.

Erebos was holding Shay up against the stall wall with an arm pressed across her neck. He'd bitten her shoulder and blood coated his lips. Doyle and Osiris were close, anticipating their turn.

"Make her stop bleeding," Skeele demanded of Jed.

Osiris was licking a cut on Shay's arm. Doyle was feeding from a wound on her leg.

The small space erupted in chaos.

The commanding Hellions knew this would be a challenge. With fresh blood in their systems, the new recruits would be just as feral as a Demon from the forests.

Nero got up but was struggling to stay on his feet.

Jed's finger's twitched as he drew on power from deep in his bones. Ropes of shadows wrapped around Erebos and tore him away from Shay.

The younger Hellion hissed. He reached out at the last second and grabbed Shay by her shirt, dragging her along as Jed flung Erebos across the room.

Nero was watching and judging the right time to kick Erebos in the head. He didn't anticipate Erebos dragging Shay and when Nero kicked, his hoof glanced off Shay's right thigh, hitting Erebos in the stomach with the sharp hoof tearing skin open.

Erebos dropped Shay and gripped his stomach wound.

Jed sent a string of power toward Erebos, closing the distance between them. He slammed Erebos through the wall of the stables, leaving a gaping hole to the outdoors. He collected Osiris and Doyle with black wisps of smoke wrapped around their necks until they went unconscious. He laid the three Hellions in the grass outside the stables.

They were in direct sight of the Hellion new recruit barracks. Recruits were gathered around the windows and doors, watching.

"Should we take them to the dungeon?" Tukka suggested.

"No." Skeele was pacing beside the unconscious recruits. "The others need to see this."

Skeele gripped their heads, one by one, and twisted with quick movement, effectively snapping their necks.

———

JED TURNED, searching for Shay. Chel had her in his arms, bleeding, bone sticking through the skin on her right leg. Again.

Chel set Shay on the ground in front of Jed. "Fix her. Now. We must get her to safety."

Jed dropped to his knees. He splayed his hands. Whispered words that sounded like a good promise. Like a sunset over the lake. Like a humming prayer. He'd whispered them not too long ago as Shay lay in the infirmary. He didn't have Teari this time but Jed knew what to do. White light streamed from his hands and mended blood vessels to stop the bleeding. He paused over the exposed bone. Teari had healed that last time, and Shay had been unconscious. He barely tapped the bone with a tendril of light.

Shay screamed in agony.

Chel dropped to his knees opposite Jed. He pulled off his belt and wound the ends in his fists. "Open your mouth," he said to Shay. "Bite down."

Shay bit the leather between her teeth. Chel leaned close to her face, did his best to ignore the smell of fresh blood. He had more control than most and he remained in control as memories of Yelena played in his mind. He wouldn't allow Shay to suffer the same fate of premature death.

"This is gonna hurt like a sonofabitch," Chel warned Shay. "But you can do it."

Shay nodded, blue hair matted to her face by blood and tears and sweat.

Chel turned to Jed and nodded. "Do it."

571

Jed's expression was tortured as he met Shay's eyes. "I'm sorry," he said before turning back to her broken leg. He whispered words that sounded like a good promise. Like a sunset over the lake. Like a humming prayer. Again. And again. And again. White tendrils dove into her leg and reset the bone. Her femur settled back into place. Jed did his best to ignore the sounds of Shay screaming against the belt between her teeth.

Skeele was watching the lights go out in the new recruit barracks with Klaus. Their large bodies shielded Shay and Jed from any onlookers.

Jed chanted. He mended the bone, the ligaments, the torn muscle. He worried that she'd need a blood transfusion but decided against it since she was still awake and there was significantly less blood than before. He continued his work fixing her leg, then the soft skin of her shoulder. He made sure the bite mark was completely healed. She would carry no scarring of a Hellion's teeth on her neck. He could at least give her that. The scar on her leg would be another issue.

Jed was glowing like a torch with the amount of magic he was using. There was no way the Hellions could shield it. He was sure the Seven Kingdoms of Heaven could see him all the way down in Hell right now. His light blasting between planes.

When he finally stopped, Shay's eyes were closed.

"Done?" Chel asked.

Jed nodded, his voice hoarse, throat dry and burning. His glowing aura dimmed as his shoulders sagged.

Shay's eyes fluttered open groggily.

Chel removed his belt from between her teeth and began putting it on again.

"He has to go," Chel warned. "Twice now he's broken your leg." Chel was shaking his head. "We can't keep him here."

"No!" Shay cried. "Don't send him away. It wasn't his fault." She'd lost everything and she so desperately wanted to hold onto Nero.

"We have to go back. Now." Skeele was checking on Nero. The giant horse was unconscious again.

Jed was lifting Shay off the ground as she reached toward the barn. "The wall is missing," she said.

"He's not going anywhere," Chel said. "For now."

Skeele motioned for them to move. Jed held Shay close.

"I can walk," Shay said.

"Barely." Jed refused to look at her as he kept pace with the Hellions, headed toward the courtyard and door to the castle.

Rocks crunched under Jed's boots as he stepped up.

"What was that?" Chel asked.

The group paused and turned, everyone watched the darkness.

Skeele turned slowly. A gentle wind blew across the courtyard. He held up a hand. Chel and Tukka turned to stone, awaiting orders.

"Something else is here," Skeele said.

The Hellions lurked, pantherlike in their movements as they surveyed the courtyard but didn't stray far from Shay and Jed.

"Get inside," Skeele commanded. Skeele took to the sky, blade in hand.

Chel hurried Jed to move faster until they were behind the door to the castle.

"Get to your rooms, half-breed," Chel demanded. "Now."

Twenty-Eight

Jed kicked the door to their suite closed. "Fucking Christ," he muttered as he checked the wards. "This was a bad idea." He pulled a piece of charcoal from his pocket and drew a large rune on the back of the door, whispered a spell that sounded like fate and death dancing. Then he took the etched blade and cut two of his fingertips, drawing on the door in his own blood.

"What's going on?" Shay winced and held onto a nearby chair for support. She'd never seen him use blood in his runes and the gravity of the situation worried her.

Jed approached her, livid, magic burning in his fingertips. "Don't you ever leave while I'm sleeping again. I'll ward every room so you can't. I want you to have your freedom but you have to have some sense of danger here. We are in Hell. There are Demons everywhere. You are human. It was past midnight and black as pitch outside."

"Nero was in trouble!" Shay argued.

"Nero is a Demon now. He can take care of himself. He's no longer a foal on the prairie."

Shay was shaking her head. "No. He's mine. He's my horse. He's not a Demon, he's good and gentle–"

"He broke your leg. Twice."

"He didn't mean it. Those Hellions are at fault. Not him. Not Nero." Tears burned Shay's eyes. "Accidents happen."

"Accidents like you slipping out in the night and getting into trouble? Life or death kind of trouble?" Jed's hands wrapped around her wrists and tugged her close. "I'm tempted to lock you in this room forever." He searched her face for understanding. "I'll hold you down and tattoo runes all over your body, every inch of you. You cannot ever do this again. I will not lose you." He kissed her, hard and punishing. Everything he'd feared had almost come true tonight. The moment he let his guard down and opened his heart, he nearly lost everything he cared about. Her.

Shay winced.

"Show me where it hurts," Jed demanded.

"I'm fine."

"You're not." Jed took her arm, extending it and searching her skin for injuries.

"You've used enough magic on me tonight."

"Tell me."

She pointed to a bruise on her jaw. Warmth flowed from his fingertips as he found every scratch and bruise on Shay's skin. He healed them, then pressed open-mouthed kisses to her heated skin, peeling her clothes away as he worked. He stopped at the scar on her thigh, worried that her femur would never be completely the same if she broke it again. He had noticed when she tried to hide her limp. He pressed his fingertips against the scar and whispered words that sounded like a cracking fire on a cold night. The scar remained. He pressed his lips against her thigh and hoped it would heal completely. He wouldn't pray. He knew better than to do that.

Jed's hands slid up her body possessively. "Now, I'm gonna check you for zombie bites." He kissed her shoulder, exposed by his torn and too big shirt she was wearing.

Shay sucked in a breath. "I didn't get bit."

"How can you be so sure?" Jed asked with a wicked smile. "I'm just going to double check."

"What about the others?" Shay asked as Jed lifted her and carried her to the bedroom.

"They definitely aren't invited."

"Skeele said *something* was here," Shay clarified, worry in her voice.

"Sounds like a *them* problem."

Jed kicked the bedroom door closed.

TWENTY-NINE

NERO'S EYES FLASHED OPEN. HE SMELLED BLOOD AND IT wasn't his. Self-loathing flooded his body as he took in the scene before him. He lifted his head. The stable was destroyed. Blood was everywhere. It wasn't just Shay's.

Nero heard a noise and looked toward the gaping hole in the wall. Noah was standing there with the basket.

"What a shit show," Noah said as he walked past the dead bodies.

Nero whinnied in agreement.

"Best you just stay down, beast." Noah kneeled and pulled the basilisk out of the basket. He glared at Nero. "I'm not sure if you remember what happened here."

Nero stared.

"Seems there was a fight. From what I was told you managed to kick Shay's leg and break it. Again."

Nero neighed sadly. He wasn't aiming for her but his reactions were slow with the poison that was running through his system.

Noah held the basilisk as it attached to the wound on Nero's flank.

"I don't think they're going to let you stay here." Noah shook his head.

Nero looked away.

"We'll leave this on for longer. Just in case they make you leave in the morning."

Nero nodded, wishing he could speak in plain language. He sensed there was something different about Noah. He was also tethered to someone. Surely the ghost would understand if he could tell him that Shay and he were tethered also. Nero could never stay away for long. He had to see her. Had to be there for her. It was his duty. He could never repay Shay for saving his life.

Nero's side twitched as the basilisk drew deeply from the wound. Nero felt the poison within his body being drawn out.

"Is it getting better?" Noah asked.

Nero nodded.

"Guess Teari's timing was off. I'll tell her ten minutes isn't enough for Demon poison." Noah shifted and glanced at the mess surrounding them.

Silence stretched between them. Nero felt his body growing stronger. The weakness and ache that had rampaged his body was lifting. He held still and waited for the basilisk to continue.

Nero's legs ached from days of unuse. That familiar itch to run was intensifying in his body. Nero hadn't realized how much this illness had taken from him. He hadn't run in the mountains in ages. Something wild was slithering under his skin, waiting to be released.

Noah packed up the basilisk and stood. He filled the water basin for Nero.

"Well, giant horse," Noah said. "That boo boo looks like nothing but a scratch now. It's been a pleasure to serve you. All this ranks up there on the list of crazy shit I've experienced since arriving in Hell. Never gets old. Does it?"

Nero whinnied and lowered his head, nudging Noah's hand.

"I guess this is a thank you?" Noah took the hint and stroked

Nero's nose. "You don't seem that bad. It's no surprise Shay loves you so much."

Noah returned to the castle and left Nero amid the destroyed barn. Nero felt better than he had in ages. His leg no longer ached and the burning pain was gone from his flank. He was suddenly starving. Nero walked to the grain bin and helped himself.

The angst slithering under his skin grew stronger. Nero shivered and stretched his neck. He drank nearly all the water Noah had filled the basin with. It didn't quench his thirst.

Nero snapped his teeth together in gnarled chatter. Something strange was happening to his body. He left the stables through the giant hole in the wall and noticed the three bodies on the ground. Their necks had been snapped. Nero recognized them as the Hellions that had attacked Shay.

Nero didn't know much about Hell and the creature he had become. There was no warning. No book. No horse educational video. He didn't know that the Demon poison had prevented him from changing into his new form. He was more than night lightning or a black hole, he was more than a friend of a human girl, he was more than just a Crossroads Demon. He'd survived the poison, he'd jumped through the Veil. He had goodness in his heart no matter how black the blood pumping through his veins had turned. That didn't stop him from turning into a monster.

Nero changed forms. It only happened for a split second, under the ochre glow of Hellsky moon. He shivered, gnashed his teeth together, tensed his body, and *changed*. Nero was already huge but in that second he doubled in size, his long black tail and mane became stiff as needles and sharp as razorblades. His veins became giant ropes of obsidian, twining and swirling under his skin like protective armor. The hunger was the worst part. The oats did nothing to fill his stomach.

The three bodies of the dead Hellions were right there. And Nero ate them.

M. R. PRITCHARD

-The End-

MIDNIGHT SERENADE

ONE

ALASTOR HEARD AN ECHO THAT SOUNDED MORE LIKE THE crunching of bones than the breaking of sticks underfoot. He shifted on his haunches and watched the Hellions survey the perimeter of the castle grounds.

Alastor gripped the basilisk tooth knife in his fist and turned only to find... nothing. There was nothing there, but the hairs rising on the back of his neck told him otherwise. Alastor felt something wasn't right as he began backing away. He needed a better plan than barreling in, especially because he heard someone walking nearby. Alastor shifted to get a good look at them; a Hellion. He was clearly young and must have pushed through the ranks to make guard duty. Alastor would use this weakness; the Queen's Commander unknowingly gifted the element of surprise since the recruit wouldn't have expected a Demon like Alastor to be hiding in the forest, searching for a way in.

Alastor waited until the Hellion got closer, and closer, and closer.

The Hellion was barely past puberty. Too bad. Alastor had to take this moment. He stood quickly and shoved the basilisk knife into the soft flesh under the Hellion's jaw. The Hellion never made a sound; he simply died in the forest.

Alastor made quick work of getting the Hellion's uniform off, then he stripped and put on. He took the blade knowing it wouldn't work for him; it was common knowledge that a Hellion's blade was enchanted to only cut for its owner. He had to look the part.

Alastor shivered. His bloodlines didn't run into Hellion territory and he knew nothing about honor and duty. Alastor was a different kind of Demon, his bloodline went to the root. Alastor could never join the Hellion ranks, but he could pretend. He could pretend until he made his way into that castle, killed the half-breed Angel, and took what was his. *Shay*. Alastor would use her as he wished, then sell her, piece by piece, until he'd collected all the money and power that was lost when his skin trade was disrupted.

Two

Jed was used to warding doors so no one could enter his room. He wasn't used to the opposite side of the door being locked so he couldn't exit. He tried the handle again and pulled. It wouldn't budge.

Jed's fingertips tingled as he drew on magic to open the door. He tried unlocking spells, opening spells, and transparency spells, but nothing worked. He paced the suite until he finally stopped next to the bed. Shay was sleeping. She'd been sleeping for more than a day. It had been a rough night with her breaking her leg again. She'd lost a lot of blood. He was sure that she was beyond tired after everything.

Jed bent and touched her forehead, remembering that he'd kept her up longer than he should have that night. Jed couldn't help it. He'd almost lost her. Need built within him as he remembered how he'd bathed the blood off her body, then carried her to the bed and gave her a few good reasons to never sneak off in the night again. There wasn't an inch of her body that he hadn't explored with his mouth, his tongue, his fingers. Desire stirred. He wanted her again. Again and again. Forever.

Shay shifted, rolling onto her stomach and pulling her right leg up. She was naked. The scar along her thigh was all he could see.

Jed lowered himself to the floor and kneeled. He moved his hand over the mark. There was something different about it. He closed his eyes and tried to get a sense of what was going on with the scar. His fingers glowed as he inspected the edges of it. He'd healed her femur; repaired the bone, muscle, and blood vessels. Something wasn't quite right though. The healing magic took, but it was almost as though something was lingering under her skin. Dirt, or a shard of... something. Jed wasn't sure. He wasn't a healer by trade, he simply had magic to help the healing process. Maybe he should consult Teari? The only problem was, he couldn't leave the room.

The sun was rising. Maybe Chel had locked them in here because whatever had spooked Skeele was still lurking in the forests surrounding the castle. Locking them up was a bit overboard. Certainly, they'd be safe within the walls of the castle. They'd be warm at least– winter chill was worsening.

Jed glanced at Shay's face. Chel probably didn't trust Shay to follow directions. Nero was still on the premises, roaming. He'd stood under the window and neighed sadly, calling for Shay. It was strange that the horse knew exactly which window was hers.

Shay sighed in her sleep. The sheet fell, revealing her bare shoulder. Her hair was longer––down the middle of her back. It had grown from one of the many healing spells he'd used.

Jed rubbed his face. He had plenty of questions, but right now no one wanted anything from either of them. He stripped off his clothes and crawled into bed next to Shay. She didn't protest as he dragged her body close to his and wrapped himself around her.

He could stay like this forever with her. Warm, safe, trapped. He'd let his guard down. It was easy, not looking over a shoulder and expecting danger every moment.

Jed pulled Shay's hair aside, revealing her neck. He watched her pulse, inspected her healed skin from the Hellion bite. He pressed his lips there, then across her neck to the sensitive skin behind her ear.

Shay nudged him with her hips. It was barely a movement, but he felt it and took it as an invitation. His free hand drifted down her body, lazily toying with her skin, her breasts, the plane of her stomach, edge of her ribs, the swell of her hips. Shay moaned and pressed against him. He parted her legs and nudged inside of her. He kissed her neck, her shoulder, and when his hand pressed against her lower belly, edging him deeper, her hand wrapped around his wrist and they fell away together.

THREE

NERO NIBBLED AT THE SWEET GRASS THAT GREW ALONG the tree line. A crew was fixing the damaged barn but Nero had no desire to be contained by four walls ever again. He considered drinking from the nearby ponds but the Hellion who'd called him chum left out buckets of water. Nero was glad he wouldn't have to risk a stomach ache.

Nero stood near the Hellion training grounds, watching them train in combat. Something was wrong with Shay. Nero could sense her fatigue. After that night in the barn, the tether connecting them felt stronger, tighter. He wasn't sure why.

When she didn't come to the window, he'd felt disparaged. All he wanted was to see her and make sure she was okay. He'd apologize if he could. He never meant to hurt her. Never in his life would he do that intentionally. She was small and fragile, and he was so much bigger than he used to be. Still, Nero would watch over Shay. Nero would help her like she'd helped him when he was a foal.

He felt much stronger now that the basilisk had removed all the poison from his wound. There was barely an ache as it finished healing overnight.

The Hellion named Chel had threatened to make him leave, but there had been no official order. Nero liked the castle grounds. It was warmer than the forests and the mountains. He'd found a crack in an outcropping of rocks that leaked warm steam. Nero never wanted to return to that hovel. He'd do everything to stay here, close to Shay. This wasn't the Earthen plane. There were too many dangers.

"It's still out there," Klaus said to Tukka. "Whatever Skeele sensed is still here, somewhere."

Nero was listening and wandered closer.

"Keep up the reconnaissance." Tukka crossed his arms and frowned. "We're down three Hellions. We need to replace them."

"Call upon the families for more recruits. They'll be young." Klaus motioned to the recruits, and they switched sparring partners.

Nero nudged Klaus's shoulder, wishing he could speak and tell them he'd help.

"What do you want, beast?" Klaus smiled as he stroked Nero's nose. "You probably don't need to be pet like a puppy."

Nero huffed and nudged him again. He didn't mind the contact, it made him remember the days when everyone pet him. He'd received much less affection since Hell became his home.

"What about the family out there at the chapel?" Tukka motioned to the road. "Whatever's out there could be hunting them."

"Let's hope not." Klaus rubbed his white beard. "If anything happens to that baby, Meg will lose it."

Nero's ears twitched. He didn't realize there was a child so close. Since he had nothing to do, he decided he'd go investigate. Shay needed him but he could help protect the child as well. It was the least he could do for moving in uninvited.

Nero walked away from the Hellions and made his way across the yard. He left hoofprints on the rock path and overgrown grass. Nero avoided the stained dirt where the three Hellions had died. He didn't want to remember that night, what he'd done, or what he'd turned into.

Nero shook his head before glancing up at Shay's window. It was still closed, the curtains pulled. He hoped she'd come out soon.

He passed the courtyard with the dead-looking tree in the center and headed for the main road that led to the graveyard. He'd seen it the night he ran here to find Shay.

Nero took his time, taking in his surroundings, searching for whatever threat was out here. His pace was lazy and slow but he made it to the graveyard faster than he expected.

There was a fence surrounding the chapel and Nero could hear the laughter of a young child. He remembered the joy of seeing children in Lame Deer and wandered closer.

The fence was tall but Nero could still see over it. He was sure he could leap over it if he needed to.

"Oh look, Thrush," a familiar voice said. "It's Nero."

He recognized Noah.

"Horsey," Noah said to the chubby baby in his arms. "Want to pet the horsey?"

"Are you sure that's a horse?" a woman's voice asked.

Nero tilted his head to see a woman with dark hair walking closer. Ah, Nightingale, the mother of the baby. He remembered now. Noah spoke of her when he'd visited Nero for the basilisk therapy.

"Big horsey," Noah said, bouncing the baby in his arms. He stopped near the fence. "How'd you get that tall, Nero? Just a few days ago you were shorter."

Nero huffed and shook his head. He wasn't sure how tall he was, just that he could see over this fence and he was sure he'd never been able to do that before.

"Suppose you can't really tell me." Noah lifted baby Thrush and held him closer. "Horsey. Touch him."

A fat little hand reached out and touched the side of Nero's face. The baby laughed and babbled.

"Does he want a treat?" Nightingale asked, passing a carrot into Thrush's hand, helping him hold it up.

Nero took the carrot–easy and careful like Shay trained him–and chewed it, watching Thrush giggle as he crunched loudly.

Nightingale looked up as a shadow passed overhead. A Hellion was flying, scoping out the grounds. Nero wished he could speak and tell them that something dangerous was in the forest. He watched Nightingale closely and got the sense that whatever it was, should be afraid of her.

The wind was chilly, and baby Thrush was bundled up in a snowsuit. His cheeks were red.

Nightingale rubbed her arms and shivered. "We should get him inside," she said. "It's going to snow tonight."

Noah held Thrush close. "You stay warm tonight, Nero. Visit us again whenever you'd like."

Nero whinnied before turning and wandering toward the road.

As he walked, he heard Nightingale's voice mention *giant* and *Demon horse* and *dangerous*. But, the good thing about being a horse was he didn't have to give two shits about what people said about him.

Snowflakes were falling, leaving stark white dots against Nero's coat. He shook his head as they collected on his eyelashes.

A strange smell wafted from the forest. Nero paused and moved closer. Frozen leaves crunched under his hooves as he searched for the smell. It was familiar, something rotting. He wondered if this was what the Hellions were worried about. He searched and searched. Tree trunks scraped against his sides as he walked through the forest. Some trees bent or snapped off, too close together to accommodate his size.

Finally, he found it. A rotting corpse of a Demon under the leaves. A sense of pride filled Nero. He'd solved their problem and found the smell and the creature the Hellions were wary of. There was no danger after all.

Nero returned to the castle grounds and approached the first Hellion he came across.

He neighed and nodded his head. He walked back and forth, tugging on the Hellion's uniform with his teeth.

"Get away," the Hellion said, stepping back. "Shoo." He gripped his blade.

Nero gave up. This creature wasn't understanding that he had to show him something. He left and went in search of someone who might listen to him. Maybe that Hellion who'd called him chum, or their leader Skeele, or maybe he'd go back and get Noah. Who he really needed was Shay, she'd understand that he was trying to tell them something important.

Four

CHEL LAY in the Hellion recruit barracks, hands behind his head, feet crossed, waiting for the bullshit to start. He'd been awake for hours, waiting for the Commander to come in shouting and dragging him and the rest of the Hellion recruits out of bed. His father had warned him it would be like this. His family was bred to be Hellions but something changed when Lucifer died and the new Queen took over. There was a shift in the edge that drove Hellions to violence. They held back, anticipated, contained their rage for only necessary times. They slept lighter and trained harder. New concepts had been taught like compassion and delayed reaction. In two days Chel would be released on forty-eight hours of leave. He had nowhere else to go besides home.

Chel would never forget when he stepped through the threshold, the familiar sights and sounds of his childhood greeted him with a bittersweet embrace. The air was still heavy with grief, the weight of

599

loss palpable in every corner, especially the kitchen where his mother spent most of her time.

Chel's mother hadn't spoken much during dinner, her eyes hollow with sorrow. She sat in silence, hands clasped tightly in her lap as if trying to hold on to the fragments of her shattered world. She'd been like this since Yelena went missing.

His father was a brooding figure in his favorite lounge chair, radiating an aura of simmering anger, his jaw clenched with unspoken fury. Chel remembered the same Demon from childhood. He hadn't changed a bit.

"Utter bullshit," his father slammed a fork down. "I didn't send my only son off to be a pussy in the ranks." He reached across the table and grabbed Chel by the collar of his uniform. "You listen to me, you smile and nod but deep down understand that mentality will not save a soul. You need to be quick, exact. You need to kill. That is a Hellion's duty."

"Yes, sir," Chel had nodded and stared into his father's red eyes until the moment of rage passed.

There it was. Sparrow, the Hellion Commander, had mentioned the rage that drove previous ages. They were going to be different, better. Sparrow's teaching and guidance was always inspiring, but Chel didn't tell his father that. He finished his dinner and came to the realization that this might be the last time he visited his parents.

Chel's mother stood and began clearing dishes. She left the dusty plate at the setting next to Chel. Yelena's seat. She'd never cleared the place setting after all these years. It was like she was expecting Yelena to come running back home and burst through the door for dinner. She never came, she would never come. Yelena had been gone for years; kidnapped and murdered by wrath-filled Demons.

Chel's gaze shifted to the empty space where Yelena once sat, a void that echoed with the haunting absence of her presence. The ache of her loss weighed heavily on his heart, a reminder of the fragility of life and the cruel whims of fate.

As the evening wore on, Chel found himself grappling with a

revelation that gnawed at the core of his being. His father's violent outbursts and callous disregard for Yelena's death stirred a wellspring of conflicting emotions within him: a potent brew of anger, sadness, and a dawning realization that threatened to shatter his sense of identity.

In a moment of clarity, Chel realized that he could no longer ignore the toxic legacy of his father's behavior. He could not condone the cycle of violence and indifference that had plagued his family for far too long. He was not his father, and he refused to allow himself to become a reflection of the man who had brought so much pain and suffering into their lives.

"Do you have any news of Yelena's body being found?" Chel asked his father.

"Who cares?" his father shouted. "She's gone. Just another damned Demon woman, they make more every day."

"Yelena was more. Your wife is more. Do you not give a fuck about either of them?" Chel challenged the Demon. He spoke of the love and warmth that Yelena had brought into their lives; cozy evenings reading, dancing, picking flowers. The memories were a stark contrast to the darkness that his father's rage had wrought upon their family.

His father's anger boiled over and Chel stood his ground, refusing to back down. "I'm going to be better than you and if I ever have a wife or daughter I will love them more than you have ever loved anything."

"Get out of my fucking hovel with that mouth. You're nothing but a piece of shit. Hellions in my day didn't give a fuck about women or children. You were bred to serve the throne. Wait and see where this new ideology takes you all. You'll be dead in no time, and well deserved. Fuck off." Chel's father stormed off, disappearing to a room in the back of the hovel and slamming the door.

His mother hugged him. "You're a good Demon." There were tears in her eyes. "Yelena would be proud. I'm proud." She was taking off her apron and threw it aside. "I'll be leaving here now."

"I'll take you elsewhere. You can't stay here," Chel said.

She pulled a bag from under the sink. "I have only stayed this long for you, but I don't think you'll be back."

Chel shook his head. "I'll never see him again."

His mother nodded, wiping tears from her face. "There's a place I can go." She was shaking her head. "It's safe. Private."

"Good." Chel reached for the door. "Let's get you out of here."

His mother walked outside and Chel grabbed his gear and belongings. He closed the door to the hovel, taking one last glance at his family home. "Goodbye," he whispered.

Chel turned to face his mother. Walking closer, he wrapped his arm around her narrow shoulders. In that moment, Chel realized that he was not defined by the sins of his father, not bound by the chains of past Hellions. He was a warrior, a protector, and above all a son who refused to let the darkness of his father's legacy extinguish the light of hope that burned within him.

They walked down a dirt path. The sounds of furniture breaking and angry shouting came from the hovel. As they moved on, Chel vowed to honor Yelena's memory by forging a new path; one guided by empathy, tenderness, and the unwavering belief that he could be the change that his family so desperately needed.

The reign of Lucifer was over, the darkness that had infiltrated every corner of Hell was slowly dispersing.

FIVE

SHAY WAS STILL ASLEEP. IT HAD BEEN TOO LONG—SHE'D been sleeping for days. He touched the scar on her thigh. It shined silvery and red. Healing magic lit his fingertips as he attempted to heal it further. Nothing happened.

Jed watched her face, relaxed, unknowing of his worry. He could have done it, erased her memories and sent her back to Montana. He could still do it. She'd been terribly injured twice now, and Jed was sure it wouldn't be the last time. This place was not for humans. The Earthen plane was rebuilding now that the Fast-Zombie War was over. She would be better off without him.

No. He closed his eyes to reset his thoughts. No. Jed promised her. Jed promised himself. He'd do better.

He touched her face, his fingertips still glowing. She slept but nuzzled his palm like a cat.

"Wake up, Shay-baby," Jed whispered. "You need to wake." He tucked blue hair behind her ear.

Nothing.

Jed stood, made his way to the door to their suite and tried to open it.

Nothing.

He scrubbed his head and tugged at his overgrown hair. He needed out of these rooms.

———

Then

Under the cloak of night, a moonless sky painted in inky darkness, Clara clutched Jed tightly to her chest as they fled through the twisting alleyways of the city.

"Don't look in its eyes," Clara whispered.

Jed was barely three. He was old enough to understand the fear in her voice.

"Don't, baby. Look at me."

Jed stopped looking over his mother's shoulder and buried his face in her neck, squeezing his eyes shut.

The cobblestone streets, worn and weathered, echoed with the urgency of Clara's footsteps as she navigated the labyrinth of buildings. Shadows danced on the walls like malevolent specters, a silent reminder of the pursuit.

"It's okay." Clara ran faster. Her footsteps echoed on the cobblestone road. It was dark outside and Jed could barely see a thing.

Jed knew it wasn't okay. He'd seen the monster lurking outside the diner window. His mother hadn't listened to him when he pointed and tried to tell her. He didn't know the exact words to say. But then, they couldn't stay at the diner all night, he knew that.

Clara's hand pressed on Jed's back to hold him in place. Jed's eyes were wide as he clung to her neck, his small fingers twisting in her shirt.

Something growled in the distance, reverberating through the night. Clara stole glances over her shoulders, glimpsing at the dark creature pursuing them. It had red eyes and scaled arms and lurked after them like some type of dog.

Clara turned a corner into a dimly lit alley. The moonlight broke through the clouds, painting fractured patterns on the cobblestones, revealing intricate carving and runes etched into the stones. Jed didn't know how to make the shapes, but he knew they were important.

The door to their apartment was close. Clara moved toward the doorstop wishing she'd taken the time to extend the runes to the door. It was only a few feet, but the Demon was too close. Clara hesitated as the demonic growls drew nearer, their presence palpable in the cool night air.

Clara set Jed on his feet and tucked him behind her. "Hold on to me," she told him. "Keep your eyes closed."

It growled, sounding like a dog or a tiger. Jed wasn't sure. He'd only gotten one good glimpse at it.

"Come on, you bastard," Clara called into the shadows.

Jed wanted to cry, but he was too scared. He could hear the Demons' nails clicking on the cobblestone as it paced.

Clara made a clicking noise, taunting the Demon. She reached in her skirt and pulled out a long hunting knife. With her free hand, she reached back and pressed Jed against her legs.

He squeezed his eyes shut, felt the thud of the creature against Clara's legs as it dove at her.

Clara chanted strange words and the Demon creature yelped like a kicked dog.

Jed opened his eyes. It had stopped attacking. There was blood on the cobblestone and his mother's hand was bloody.

"Inside! Now, baby," Clara rushed him to leave the rune circle. She unlocked the door with her clean hand and pushed him inside. "Stay here for me, baby." She looked him in his eyes. "I'll be back in just a few minutes. Okay?"

Jed nodded as she closed the door and locked it. He waited, sitting on the floor. He didn't know how to tell time, but it felt like he was waiting forever. His belly hurt and he was tired. He didn't like being locked in dark rooms. Jed wanted to shout and cry, wanted to scream for his mother to come back. But he knew that if he did that, the monsters would come. And he didn't want the monsters to come. He didn't want to cause his mother any more trouble.

Jed's eyes were nearly closed when the door opened again. His mother walked in, blood staining her skirts. "Just a moment, baby." She locked the door and walked past him, running the water in the sink, and scrubbing her hands.

He didn't know what she'd been doing, all he knew was that he never wanted to be locked in a dark room again.

SIX

SHAY WASN'T WEARING anything especially revealing but tight jeans, cowboy boots, and a tank top turned nearly every head in the house when she opened the door to that dive bar. This was her last night of freedom–if she survived.

Shay looked over her shoulder one last time before the door closed. There were no strange noises outside, no gunshots, no squealing tires. The dive bar outside of Lame Deer wasn't too far from home but just far enough for her to feel a sense of freedom. Daddy and Momma would be pissed once they found out she'd snuck out her bedroom window and climbed down the porch supports. Hopefully they wouldn't find out. She was angry with them but didn't want to completely disappoint them. What did it matter anyway? Her life would never be what she wanted it to be.

She'd never been to a place like this, but she'd been around rowdy cowboys most of her life. It wasn't much different than the energy of the bull rider shows she'd been too. The only difference was she didn't have Daddy on her hip, nor Momma waiting in the stands. And she was grown, looking to feel something more than disappointment.

Shay kept her chin up and ignored the fluttering in her heart as she walked to the bartender.

"What'll you have, little lady?" the bartender asked.

"Rum and coke." Shay didn't normally drink, but it was the only thing she could think of. It rolled off her tongue nicely, and she figured she could like asking for something other than a fruity drink or plain beer.

She sipped at her drink and watched the bull riders on the television screen. Her eyes drifted down to the zombie warnings streaming across the bottom of the screen. California was overrun and so was the East Coast. Shay was grateful for living in the Midwest. The hell that had broken loose was trickling in.

Her eyes flicked around the room as she sipped at her drink. She sagged against the high-back of her barstool and crossed her legs.

It wasn't long before she was interrupted.

"What's your name, Cowgirl?" a handsome guy asked.

"Shay." She'd planned on lying about her name but when it came down to it, she couldn't. Shay had never been a good liar, she'd much rather tell the truth and move on.

"That's a nice name for a pretty girl." He touched her hair.

Craving the attention, Shay leaned toward his hand and looked down. She wasn't sure what to do exactly, she'd never done this kind of thing before.

"What are you having to drink?" the cowboy asked.

The bartender made a face of trepidation as he poured another rum and coke.

"What's your name?" Shay asked the cowboy. She liked his dark eyes and wide smile, the dimple in his cheek. He talked with a western accent that was hard to place.

"Clyburn." He sipped at his beer.

Shay and Clyburn talked about horses and ranches.

"Are you here alone?" he finally asked.

The bartender's eyes flicked to Shay.

She could tell he was wary of the cowboy, but Shay had come here with a purpose. One last night of fun.

She nodded and threw back the rest of her rum and coke. She motioned for another drink and took money out of her pocket to pay for it.

"No, sweety, I got it." Clyburn touched her hand.

Shay was thinking about the feeling of his fingertips, how they'd feel touching the rest of her skin. She glanced up at him and his pupils widened.

Shay took another sip of her fresh rum and coke, feeling tipsy when someone turned up the jukebox. Southern rock was playing. A few couples had shown up during the night and were dancing.

Clyburn noticed her watching. "Come on." He took her hand and dragged her to the dance floor. Shay had never been dancing with a man before. Suddenly she fully realized how sheltered her life was. No boyfriends, no freedom, nothing–especially now that the apocalypse had arrived. Shay couldn't go on knowing she'd never lived fully; she could die at any moment. A need to experience it all bloomed in her chest. Shay's body moved in rhythm with Clyburn and the music. He touched her hip and she touched his shoulder. His thumb slid under the hem of her shirt, stroking the soft skin of her stomach.

Shay's fingertips stretched up the side of his neck and into his dark hair.

Clyburn pulled her close.

He smelled like liquor and tobacco. Like bales of hay and manly musk.

She toyed with the button of his shirt with her free hand. He tugged her close until their bodies were touching. Her hips gyrated with the music. His thigh slid between hers and pressed against her core. Sweat slid down Shay's back as a hunger grew within her belly.

Clyburn touched her and held her tight and she let him, never having known a man's touch like this before. She liked it. He was strong. His hands felt good. They moved together during the brief silence between songs.

They danced like this until the bar started to empty out and the jukebox music came to an abrupt stop.

"Last call," the bartender shouted.

The spell that had struck Shay broke. She blinked and looked up at Clyburn. His pupils were wide, his lips parted. Shay wanted to kiss him, so... she did.

He tasted like liquor. Fresh and warm. Shay pressed her body to his, closer. She wanted to be closer.

Clyburn pulled away, gripping her hips. "Christ, girl," he swore.

"I don't want to go home." Shay's fingers twisted in his shirt.

He nodded, leading them back to their drinks.

Shay threw back the last of her rum and coke. Clyburn paid the tab then led her out the door.

"I'm parked around back." He gripped her wrist.

Shay felt light, energized. She'd never been this drunk before but all she could think was how she *wasn't* thinking, finally. For once in her life.

Vehicles were leaving as Clyburn led her to a big truck parked in the shadows.

"I don't have a place nearby," Clyburn warned as he pressed her back against the truck and kissed her.

"I don't care," Shay said. She reached for his shirt, working the buttons until she could press her palms against his hard chest.

Clyburn's hands were under her shirt, rubbing and kneading.

Shay felt like she was on fire. Like she was invincible. Like she could live forever.

Clyburn hesitated.

Shay pulled away and noticed the parking lot was empty. There was nothing but darkness and empty cow pasture behind them.

"Here," Shay whispered. "I don't care."

Clyburn pulled away from her, opened the truck, and pulled out a thick blanket. He laid it out in the truck bed then jumped down. His hands returned to her body, his lips to hers. They kissed, and he pulled her against him until they were at the tailgate. Clyburn lifted her. Shay took off her top and he followed.

She traced the ridges of his body, illuminated by moonlight, and reveled in his strength as he jumped into the truck bed and lifted her, bringing her to the blanket.

He was gentle. His mouth licked and bit her skin. He folded her jeans after dragging them down her legs. When he stretched his body over hers, Shay shivered feeling the bulge against her leg.

Clyburn was slow. Too slow. He paid too much attention. It made her sick. This wasn't what Shay wanted. She wanted something quick and dirty, something hard and fast. She wasn't looking for marriage, just a one night stand. Clyburn was turning this into something else. Shay's stomach lurched at the wrongness of it all. She sat up, shoving him off.

"You okay?" Clyburn asked, surprised.

Shay scrambled off the truck and puked into the grass at the edge of the parking lot.

"It's okay." Clyburn was close, holding her hair as the drinks from the bar forced their way out.

Shay heaved until there was nothing left. She sagged against the truck.

Clyburn started rubbing her back, then her hips. "I'm not done," he whispered as he forced her to bend over and took her from behind.

The tailgate of the truck bit into her stomach. This was what Shay wanted. Something disgusting and heartbreaking. Something dirty and erasable.

He finally stopped and pulled out.

"Christ," he muttered. "There's blood." His voice shifted. "I'm sorry."

"It's fine." Shay reached for her clothes and got dressed faster than a fox in a hen house.

"Let me care for you—"

"No." Shay stopped him. "I didn't come here for that."

"What did you come for, little lady?" Clyburn was standing stark naked in the moonlight. He was a spectacle, a nearly perfect man; muscled and tall, dark hair and eyes.

"Forget this ever happened." Shay ran to her car. She was rapidly sobering up. Ignoring the ache between her thighs, she unlocked the driver door.

Clyburn caught up with her, grabbed her arm and turned her. "I don't understand."

"Ain't nothing for you to understand, cowboy." Shay searched his eyes, hoping he'd understand that she wanted nothing else to do with the man.

She left him with his jaw clenching in the dark parking lot.

Shay went home. She climbed the porch railing and opened her bedroom window. She showered the blood off her thighs and hid her dirty clothes.

The next morning, Shay got up and started breakfast like nothing had ever happened. She'd slept three hours.

"You feeling okay, hun?" Momma asked.

"Fine." Shay rubbed her face. "Just didn't sleep good."

"I heard you in the shower. Do you want some tea?"

Shay shook her head and continued cracking eggs into her bowl until she heard heavy, booted footsteps on the porch, Daddy's voice, and someone else's.

"We got a new ranch hand this morning. Lord knows we could use him," Momma said, wiping her hands on a towel. "Let's say hello."

Shay nodded and followed Momma to the screen door. She heard Daddy's voice as he introduced them. Shay looked up as the door closed and her eyes met familiar dark ones.

Clyburn.

Breath caught in her throat. There was a pain behind her ribs. No.

"Nice to meet ya, Shay." Clyburn held out a hand.

Shay didn't want her parents to know what she'd done the night before. She couldn't let them know. Shay shook the familiar hand that was reaching for her. "Nice to meet you, cowboy."

Clyburn smiled. Shay's face was still as her lungs begged for air. She was sure she'd never drag another breath through them again. What in the hell was he doing here?

Daddy started talking about cattle and horses and led Clyburn off the porch. Momma opened the screen door. Wood creaked under Shay's feet as she tried to move.

It wasn't even worth what she'd gone through. Those few minutes with a handsome cowboy in a dive bar parking lot were definitely not worth losing everything. She knew she was going to lose everything. The premonition was overwhelming. A sickening emptiness filled her gut. Shay hated herself more than she hated anything on this planet.

As he walked toward the barn with Nicholas, Clyburn glanced back at her and winked.

———

Now

SHAY WOKE UP SCREAMING.

Jed heard her from the other room and ran in to find her staring blankly at the ceiling. He grabbed her shoulders and shook her until life re-entered her eyes. "Shay-baby, come back."

She focused on Jed's face before whimpering and scrambling onto his lap, her arms and legs gripping him tight.

It took him a moment to wrap his arms around her and rub her back. "It's okay," he murmured over and over again. "You're safe."

He rocked her, thinking about the speck of something that was locked under the scar on her thigh, wondering if maybe that had something to do with her screaming. Maybe it had something to do with the locked door and the sense of danger. He wasn't sure.

Shay's sobs finally ceased and she pressed her forehead against his collarbone. "Something bad happened," she said.

"Yeah." Jed stopped rubbing her back.

"I feel okay."

"You're looking much better than you were the other night."

"Tell me."

Jed took in a deep breath. "There were three Hellion recruits–"

"And Nero."

"Yes, and Nero."

"Is Nero okay?" Shay whispered.

"Nero is good."

There was a moment of silence as Shay plucked at Jed's shirt before she said, "Tell me more."

"The Hellions are dead. You broke your leg... again. It's mostly healed."

Shay's hand brushed over her thigh, feeling the scarred ridge on her skin. "It feels okay."

"Whatever Skeele sensed is still out there. We've been locked in our suite for a few days."

Shay sat up straight and leaned back. "Days?"

Jed searched her eyes, brushing her hair away from her face and cupping her jaw with both hands. "You're really feeling okay? What were you dreaming about?"

Shay's mouth parted, and she licked her bottom lip with the tip of her tongue. "Clyburn."

Jed scowled. "He's dead."

Shay nodded. "I remember. Nero killed him."

Jed wished it had been him. But his weakness was that he didn't know how to transverse realms during that time. He was thankful for Nero and what the horse had done when rescuing Shay. Even if it meant he'd changed into something else.

"The barn was destroyed," Jed continued, his thumb rubbing her skin. "Workers have been fixing it little by little."

"Where has Nero been sleeping?" Shay asked.

"Where ever he wants." Jed motioned to the balcony window. "Sometimes he shows up there."

"That's good. I don't know what I'd do if I couldn't see him."

Jed released Shay's jaw and his hands slid down her neck to her shoulders and he rubbed her arms. "Are you hungry? You have eaten nothing in days."

Shay nodded and moved to crawl off his lap.

Jed stopped her by gripping her thighs. "Promise me you will never go outside alone again."

"That's ridiculous," Shay scoffed. "I can't promise that. I already promised I wouldn't go outside while you're sleeping."

"So you did remember something from the other night." Jed smirked.

SEVEN

ALASTOR COULD HANDLE THE WEAPONS; IT WAS THE FORM of hand-to-hand combat that got him in trouble, got him noticed. The Hellion Commander, Skeele, was watching him from the sidelines. He'd become accustomed to his new name of Dalk and answered when Skeele called him to the sidelines.

"Where did you learn to fight like that?" Skeele asked.

Alastor didn't look directly at him when he replied, "The hovels in the mountains."

"Hm." Skeele rubbed his face. "You're going to need to work harder. An Angel would defeat you in a heartbeat with moves like those." Skeele paused, sniffed the air, and glanced toward the forest.

"Yes, Sir," Alastor noted.

He went back to his sparring partner and wound up on his ass more than a handful of times. Alastor had underestimated Hellion recruit training. He'd lasted for decades with his skin trade but there were weapons and extra hands involved to help with fighting. He'd grown lax in his strength. Alastor promised to work harder. He'd need the strength to get Shay out of the castle.

Alastor had been there nearly a week and learned the daily

agenda. Training, lunch, training, rounding on the royal grounds and nearby graveyard and a few other locations he'd not been privy to. Then more training. Alastor didn't care, he only needed to find where Shay was.

"Hey, Dalk." A Hellion recruit with a stubby nose nodded to him. "You look different than last time I saw you."

Alastor blinked. "Must be this slop." He scooped up a spoonful of gruel and dripped it back into the bowl.

The Hellion laughed and the conversation turned into razzing the terrible meals they got during the week.

"Can't wait for Sunday dinner." The Hellion licked his lips. "Don't know why they only give us the good food once a week."

Alastor ate and considered his next steps. He was fitting in more and more each day. He didn't get too close to the castle and he noticed there was a giant black horse wandering freely. There was something familiar about the creature.

Sunday dinner was a spectacle. It reminded Alastor of the Thanksgiving dinners on the Earthen plane. There were piles of food. A roasted pig, baked turkey, hamburgers, and hot dogs. Fresh vegetables and fruits. Beers and wine. Alastor waited in line to fill his plate and listened to the surrounding conversations.

"Don't know why they don't feed us like this all week."

"Cause you'd be fat."

"My gut would pop from all the beer."

"We'd be slow."

"Shut up."

"Hey, there's pie!"

Alastor ate more than he had in years. As he sipped at the beer, he watched the Hellion recruits around him go back for seconds and thirds. There was a limit of three servings on the alcohol. That was probably an excellent decision, Alastor thought. A barracks full of drunk Hellion recruits would be messy. He sidled up to the drunkest of the Hellion recruits to get some information out of him.

They clinked beer mugs. Alastor sat.

"I heard a rumor that a human was being kept nearby."

The drunk Hellion muttered something about "not in Lucifers day."

"Tragic what Hell has become with a woman on the throne." Alastor sipped at his beer. "Why a human though? Never had one in Hell before. Or at least never had one roaming around freely like a pet." He added a lewd laugh.

"Definitely should be kept in the dungeons and used for other things." The drunk Hellions lips became looser with each word. "She walks around here freely, sometimes with that crossbreed freak."

"I haven't seen them."

"Will do you good to ignore them. Last week they got three of us killed."

"I missed it."

"They got her blood. Got the blood lust and went hunting her. Commander made a spectacle out of it. Snapped their necks and left their bodies for all of us to see."

"Shit." Alastor sipped at his beer. "And yet so many recruits have stayed."

"Not one left," the Hellion recruit slurred.

"Why?"

"We are bred to serve, not think."

"Wouldn't take much to end a human."

"Get yourself on dungeon guard duty and you'll be halfway there." He pointed toward the castle in the distance. "The horse goes to her window at night. Seen it with my own eyes." He poked two fingers toward his eyes. Beer dribbled down his chin.

"What floor is she on?" Alastor asked.

"Watch the horse." The Hellion recruit suddenly fell over, spilling his beer and snoring on the bench.

Alastor walked away from the drunk Hellion and made his way to the window. There were too many tables and bodies and noise. He veered toward the door, taking his drink with him.

There were shadows below an oak tree outside the Hellion

recruit lounge. Alastor sat with his back against the trunk and watched the castle in the distance. The sun had set in Hellsky and the ochre moonglow illuminated the expanse of grass between the training grounds and the castle. It didn't take long for the large black horse to wander by without a care in the world. It stopped to nibble on grass and drink out of a bucket before meandering toward the castle.

Alastor sipped at his beer. That wasn't just a horse, he could tell. There was something wrong with it.

The horse stopped under a row of windows and whinnied, looking up.

Alastor watched the windows for movement. Then, curtains fluttered and a pale face looked out.

There she was.

Hell had changed Shay. She still had the blowtorch blue hair, but she looked paler than when he'd last seen her on the Earthen plane. He remembered the warmth of her skin, the shine in her eyes. She'd had more life than any of the women they'd captured for the skin trades. It was all the strength he contained to leave her alone in that cabin with a bowl of spaghetti, freshly showered. He should have touched her more then. Branded her. Taken her. Never let her leave. Chained her up and kept her for eternity.

Alastor drained his beer and stood. He knew where her window was. He knew she was weakened. Finding her room once he was inside the castle and getting her out would be a cake walk.

EIGHT

Shay stood in a dimly lit cavern, shadows dancing ominously as Chel watched her with eyes like burning coals.

A few days had passed, and Shay had energy to train again. Actually, since leaving the suite her energy levels had increased by leaps and bounds. She felt as though she'd drank a pot of coffee and was ready to run some laps.

The air crackled with anticipation as Chel prepared for their training session.

"Where are the Hellion recruits?" Shay asked warily.

Chel stood to his full height. "They're elsewhere. They won't harm you."

Shay shivered. "Okay." Shay couldn't stop thinking about that night. She needed more time to process the memories. It was strange; everything coming back to her full force, the dreams of Clyburn. It was all too much right now.

"Maybe we should wait until next week," Chel suggested.

"No." Shay shook her head. "No more waiting. I needed fresh air. Been locked up in that room for too long. I feel good."

Jed was lingering nearby, watching them.

"It was for your safety." Chel passed Shay a wooden sword to practice with.

"The threat is gone now?" Shay asked.

"I wouldn't say that. Threats are never absent."

"You're a ray of sunshine, Chel." Shay bent her knees, wincing when pain sliced through her thigh.

"You're not ready."

"I'm ready. Let's just get this over with. Please." Shay gripped the wooden sword and swung it.

Chel jumped back. "Dang, woman."

It went on for another hour, Chel showing Shay how to wield a sword, then a hunting knife. He showed her where to hit an enemy. The throat, the solar plexus, the crotch.

"Listen carefully, Shay," Chel's voice resonated with a gravelly timbre, dripping with the weight of centuries of experience. "In the realm of darkness, survival hinges on mastery of the blade and the art of deception."

With a swift motion, Chel drew forth a wickedly curved blade, its surface glinting malevolently in the dim light of the cave. He tossed it to Shay, who caught it with a determined grip.

Chel's brows rose in surprise. "Good catch."

"Caught plenty of flying shit on the ranch back home," Shay said with a smile. "You should see me with a rope."

"The blade is an extension of your will," Chel instructed, his eyes burning with intensity. "Feel its weight, its balance. Let it become a part of you."

Shay nodded, her muscles tensing with anticipation as she poised herself for the onslaught of Chel's teachings. She'd done plenty of physical activity on the ranch with shooting and horse riding. Her father had taught her how to shoot a bow and wield a knife. The sword was just another tool, another extension of her body. She was simply facing different animals.

"Attack me," Chel commanded, his stance shifting into a defensive position, his eyes gleaming with anticipation.

Without hesitation Shay lunged forward, her movements fluid and graceful as she unleashed as series of strikes. But Chel, with the agility of a serpent, evaded each blow with uncanny precision, his movements a blur of darkness.

"Predictable," Chel's voice echoed with disdain as he countered Shay's attacks with lightning-fast strikes of his own, forcing her to retreat.

Gritting her teeth, Shay pressed on, her determination fueling her every move. She focused on Chel's movements, seeing an opening.

As the duel raged on, Shay's instincts sharpened, her movements becoming more fluid, more instinctual. With each exchange she learned, adapting her tactics to anticipate Chel's elusive maneuvers.

Jed watched quietly on the sidelines.

In a sudden burst of speed, Shay closed the distance between them, her blade flashing in the dim light as she launched a relentless assault. Chel staggered backward, a look of surprise flickering across his Hellion visage.

With a triumphant smirk, Shay pressed on, her strikes raining down upon Chel with unbridled ferocity. In a flurry of motion, she delivered a blow that sent him stumbling backward. Shay's chest heaved with exertion, her leg burned, her eyes blazed with newfound determination. She was more than just a human woman; she was a warrior, forged in the fires of darkness, ready to face whatever challenges lay ahead.

"Bring your head back down out of the clouds, Shay," Chel warned.

Shay blinked and focused on him.

"This was one session. We are far from done." Chel collected the swords and sheathed them. "If you stay in the realm of Hell, you need to keep training."

"Are you going to send me back to the Earthen plane?" she asked.

"No," Jed stepped forward. "He can't tell us to do anything."

Chel made a face. "I can tell you that you're both under curfew. Skeele wants you in your suite at sunset." Chel looked down at Shay. "It's for her safety."

NINE

SHAY FELT HOT. IT CAME ON SUDDENLY. SHE GLANCED AT the roast beef on her plate and wondered if the food was bad. No. Not the food. She tried to take another bite but when the juices hit her tongue she gagged.

Shay moved her napkin to her mouth and spit out the meat so no one could see what she was doing. She folded the napkin and set it next to her plate.

Jed was watching her from across the table. He sipped at a glass of wine, toying with his fork, moving around perfectly seasoned asparagus. His eyes looked away for a second before landing on her face again.

"Okay?" he mouthed, concerned.

Shay shook her head. She wasn't okay. She was ready to blow chunks all over Meg's special family dinner night. The last time someone interrupted family dinner, Meg killed them. Shay's gaze roamed to Meg at the end of the table. She was eating and laughing at something Skeele said. Meg hadn't been in the killing mood since the Deacons released her from the Safe House. She'd actually calmed nearly eighty percent compared to how she was always on edge before. At least that was Shay's assessment of the Queen of Hell. Still, Shay didn't want to puke on the good China.

She pushed her chair back.

Chel turned to her, followed by the rest of the Hellions. Shay didn't want to make a scene, but it appeared it was too late.

"What's wrong?" Chel asked.

She couldn't shake the Hellion. He'd been up her ass since she arrived. They'd grown closer but she could tell by the way he looked at Jed, something wasn't right between the two of them.

"Nothing," Shay replied before standing and walking out of the room. "I'll be right back," she whispered to Meg with a wave.

The Queen of Hell nodded and Shay released a sigh of relief. Tonight wouldn't end with her as a bloodstain on the floor.

Shay pushed open the dining room door and leaned her cheek against the cool stone of the wall.

She heard footsteps, smelled something delectable. The feeling of wanting to vomit was replaced with her mouth watering. She turned and saw a small creature carrying a tray of meat. This time it was prepared for the Hellions. Bloody and raw, barely a sear. She wanted it, could barely control the urge to grab it off the tray.

"Can I have a piece of that?" Shay asked the creature.

It stopped for her and motioned in agreement.

Shay took a slice of the bloody meat and licked it. Amazing. Better than anything she'd ever eaten before. She shoved the slice of meat in her mouth. It was so good. She wanted more. She turned to get another piece but the creature was walking into the dining room. Through the open door, she saw Jed and Chel making their way toward her.

She turned and walked down the hallway as fast as she could. Shay felt better having eaten the nearly raw meat, but she knew that wasn't right. She'd never eaten raw meat before.

"Shay!" Jed called after her. "Wait up."

Crap. Shay started walking away from them.

Footsteps followed. Shay walked faster. "I'm just going to get some fresh air."

"No you're not," Chel warned. "It's past your curfew."

Her heart beat against her ribs. She needed out of here. Shay needed some freedom, needed air and peace. She needed the ochre shine of Hellnight on her skin.

"Just a few minutes," Shay shouted over her shoulder.

The footsteps behind her turned heavy. The men were running.

Something like electricity zipped up her spine. Shay ran. She was close to the door. She could make it. Shay ran faster, arms out and ready to push the door open. She was close. So close.

She made it. She shoved the centuries-old wood and ran into the courtyard, heart thumping and throat aching with dryness.

Sharp pain shot up her leg. It came from her scar. Her leg felt strange, not right. It felt heavier, longer. She stumbled then tripped. Shay held her hands out to catch her as she fell but the courtyard ground was uneven. Her hands slid, torn up by rough rock. She cried out just before she hit her head and knocked herself unconscious.

———

JED COULD BARELY BELIEVE his eyes as Shay's leg flickered. There was something wrong with it. It didn't look like the rest of her body. It was twisted and shaped strangely, but only for a moment before it went back to normal. Like a mirage, like something was messing with his vision.

Chel made a noise of irritation as he kneeled next to Shay and rolled her over. "Fucking woman." His eyes flashed red as he looked at Jed. "What's gotten into her?"

Jed healed Shay's hands first. He didn't want to risk her blood spilling on Meg's land again and risking the Hellions coming after her. He worked fast, watching her shallow breaths. His hands drifted to her jawbone, healing a scrape. Then to the sides of her head.

The urge was there, still. The urge to clear her mind of all this and send her away. The Fast-Zombie War was over. She'd be safe rebuilding on the Earthen plane. He swallowed against a dry throat. Jed could protect her from afar. He could linger nearby and let her live a life without all this darkness. Jed's fingertips tingled with magic.

"What the fuck are you doing?" Chel shoved at Jed's hands. "Don't dig your hole deeper."

Jed moved his hands lower, searching for injuries, and when he found none he lifted her. "Let's get her to the infirmary and send for Teari." He held her limp body close, wanting nothing more than to heal and protect her from whatever was going on inside her body.

Chel held the door open as they walked inside the castle. He paused, glancing across the dry grass as movement caught his eye. There was something shifting in the shadows. It stepped out, into the ochre moonlight.

Nero.

Ten

Nero felt it all happening through the thread that connected him to Shay. He didn't know transforming into the Demon would affect her. He didn't know she'd crave blood and freedom like he did.

Nero shook the dark energy off his hide. The transformation was still new to him. His long black tail and mane were stiff as needles and sharp as razorblades. His veins were giant ropes of obsidian under his skin, twining and swirling like protective armor. He turned into something less.

He had been on the other side of the cemetery. There was something bad lingering over there. Something worse than him. Worse than the creature who'd invaded the royal grounds then went incognito. Nero had gone to investigate.

It was a Demon and it was too close to Thrush. Nero wouldn't risk danger coming that close to Nightingale and Thrush. He was sure Noah could handle himself, could probably protect his family but Nero wouldn't stand down. He'd sensed it and searched for it. No one else had come looking for the danger. It made Nero wonder how strong the Hellion's inherent sense of danger toward the Queen and her land was.

He'd searched Hellforest and found a creature that looked like a cloud. It undulated maniacally, surged toward him and tried to pass. He wouldn't let the creature hurt the little boy who'd pet his snout so curiously. He wouldn't let it get near Shay. Nero had no choice but to transform and defeat it. When it was dead and dropped to the ground like black mist, Nero ate it.

It tasted like licorice and blackberries. And while there were no bones, its cotton-candy texture crunched between his giant teeth and echoed throughout Hellforest.

Only afterwards did he feel the tug from Shay; her unease and nausea, her panic and fear as she ran.

Nero was running toward her, back to the castle. It didn't take him long in this form. When he saw her run into the courtyard from the shadows, he transformed to the Nero she knew. He didn't want to scare her. But then she fell. He watched from a distance, afraid that Chel would cast him out if he saw Nero changing and lingering. The Hellion was overprotective of Shay and the royal grounds. Not as bad as Skeele, but close.

Eleven

"Your leg is still bothering you?" Teari asked.

Shay was sitting on a bed in the infirmary. "It aches sometimes." She touched the stiff sheets.

"Jed is worried about it." Teari held her hands over the scar.

Shay was staring at the ceiling, ignoring the sharp pains that jolted up her leg every few minutes.

"Sometimes?" Teari asked.

"Yes," Shay lied. "Just every now and again." Shay sighed. She didn't want to be in the infirmary. She didn't understand why Teari wouldn't meet her somewhere else. This room was too white. Too pristine. Too cold. There was no smell to it. Shay supposed it was a hygienic measure, she didn't have to enjoy it.

"Were you bit by a Demon?" Teari asked.

Shay shook her head.

"Cut with a Demon blade?" Teari asked.

Shay shook her head again.

Teari made a face.

"What?" Shay asked.

"Jed was right. There's something trapped in this scar."

Shay wanted to tell her about eating the raw meat and enjoying it. She wanted to tell her about running away and her leg feeling changed. It sounded so stupid though. She was human, unlike the beings she was now surrounded with. Her body didn't have magic or the ability to transform. She was sick. That was all. Whatever sickness had infected her was driving her insane.

"Noah," Teari called.

A few minutes passed before Noah appeared in the room.

"Thank you for coming." Teari smiled.

"I'll take a break from searching the ends of Hell for Meg's snacks." He rubbed his face with both hands. "That woman is insufferable."

"Show some compassion," Teari said. "She's under a lot of stress. And she's with child."

Noah took a deep breath and rolled his eyes exaggeratedly. "What do you need?"

"A small Basilisk." Teari smiled.

Noah made a face and shuddered. "Of course." He disappeared.

Teari turned to Shay. "Poor guy doesn't like the creatures."

"Is this going to hurt?" Shay asked.

"No." Teari was watching Shay closely. "Jed said you looked sick at dinner last night. Tell me about that."

Remembering the foul taste of the cooked meat on her plate, Shay swallowed hard. The sensation hadn't hit her today but Shay was wary it would come back again.

"I'm just going to check your stomach and see what's going on." Teari's hands hovered over Shay's skin, from her leg to her hip, over her pelvis, to her stomach, ribcage. She stopped at Shay's center and closed her eyes.

"What do you think–" Shay was about to ask what was wrong but Noah opened the door, carrying a heavy basket. She saw two shadows in the hall outside the door.

Noah thumbed toward the door that was closing. "You got a line out there."

"Who?" Shay asked.

"It's Jed and Chel. They're concerned." Teari moved to the side so Noah could set the basket down near Shay's injured leg.

He opened the flip top and removed the small Basilisk and held it steady, mouth pointed toward Shay's scar.

The Basilisk turned away. It thrashed and whipped its head, trying to escape and having no interest in the Demon venom that was trapped in Shay's scar. This went on for minutes until Noah's hands were thick with slime that dripped on the white floor.

Teari was talking to the creature, trying to encourage it. "You can do it. Right there."

"Maybe you should open it up," Noah suggested.

Shay and Teari looked to a nearby table with neatly arranged tools and surgical blades.

"Don't," Shay flinched. "I'm tired of cuts and wounds and magical healing. Maybe all this is unnecessary."

Shay covered her bare leg. "Get it out of here." She waved at the Basilisk. "Take it back. I don't want to try this." Shay was feeling sick again. The smell of the Basilisk slime made her stomach roil.

"You don't want it to heal you?" Teari asked.

"I don't want my leg cut open again." Shay rubbed the scar through the sheet.

"Even if it fixes you?" Teari asked.

Noah was wrestling the Basilisk to get it in the basket again. He stood, flipping his shaggy hair and wiping his hands on his pants. "Fine with me," he said. "I'd prefer not to have to fetch these blasted things every time someone gets a little Demon poison in them." He scoffed like it was the worst job in the world.

"I'm fine," Shay said. "It's just some lingering pain and a stomach bug. I don't understand why you are all so concerned."

Noah left the room with the Basilisk basket.

Shay threw the rough sheet off her body and got dressed. She didn't care if Teari saw her.

"You should stay here and rest," Teari offered. "I can give you something to help."

"No." Shay shook her head. "I'm going to sleep in my bed." Shay headed for the door. "Thanks for the help, Teari," she said over her shoulder.

Shay shoved the door open, hoping to hit the two men waiting on the other side.

Jed and Chel jumped back.

"Are you okay?" Jed asked.

"Fine." Shay walked past him and headed for the staircase.

The two men looked at each other, wondering if they should follow.

"I'm going to bed." Shay's heavy footsteps echoed as she stomped up the winding staircase.

Shay opened the door to the suite she shared with Jed. The familiar runes and markings were everywhere. Suddenly, it all looked so chaotic. It made her anxious. She wanted just a normal room with normal walls and floors and window casings. Shay didn't want to see that Jed feared her weak humanity at every turn. She was tired of it.

Shay went to the closet and changed her clothes. She put on a dark pair of jeans, a button-down flannel that was soft and worn, then her boots. She grabbed a hunting knife and her pistol.

Shay walked to the balcony, threw open the doors and leaned against the railing. Women had a habit of throwing themselves off the railings here. Someone should probably do something about that.

Nero was waiting below. The drop wasn't far at all. Shay's gaze went to the exterior wall. There were vines and jutting rocks. She might break her neck but she'd climbed worse in Montana. Once she'd scaled a rock wall to the valley below and tied Nicholas's rope around a calf that had fallen. That was at least twice as tall as the distance below the balcony.

Shay threw her leg over the railing and climbed down.

.

Twelve

Teari stood in the infirmary with Jed and Chel.

"I'm going to have to do some research." Teari tapped a finger on her chin, thinking. "Something is off and I'm not sure what it is."

"She's different," Jed said. "Shay was training with Chel and almost sliced him through. She's stronger."

"Strength isn't a bad thing." Teari was searching Jed's face. "There's more?"

Jed tried not to think about how beautiful Teari was, how white her wings were, how he wanted to tell her everything. He assumed that was part of being a royal healer. She was easy to talk to, gave him diarrhea of the mouth. Or maybe it was him, finally spending time with an Angel that didn't include a death match. He wanted it to go on forever.

"After she was injured again, it took her days to wake up. She slept for days," he said.

"She didn't wake up at all?" Teari asked.

Jed's cheeks turned pink as he remembered slipping into her from behind, her soft hand edging him on. He controlled his mouth.

"You healed her just like we did the first time she broke her leg?" Teari asked.

"Yes."

"Something is off." Teari paced the room. "We need to open up the scar. The only problem is, she doesn't want us to."

"We must," Chel said. "We'll have to restrain her."

Jed was shaking his head. "She won't go for that."

"She must be healed," Chel argued.

"She will never forgive us for restraining her. It's not right." Jed was shaking his head. His relationship with Shay had been on shaky ground for a while. They'd both made promises to each other and broken them. He didn't want to lose her and he feared this would be the end of everything.

Jed rubbed his face. His stomach twisted. "I can erase her memory of it."

Chel frowned. "She explicitly told you to never do that."

"She'll leave if she remembers what we have planned." Jed was shaking his head, feeling defeated. "I can't lose her."

The door slammed open and a giant Hellion entered the room. It was Skeele. He looked at Jed. "Do you know where your human is?"

"Sleeping," Jed said.

Skeele made a face. "Klaus just saw her scale the side of the castle and ride off into the forest on Nero's back." Skeele's brows rose. "What are you two going to do about that?"

THIRTEEN

NERO WAS RUNNING. HE WAS FASTER THAN THE WIND. Faster than lighting. Faster than the speed of sound. His speed didn't scare Shay and Nero didn't worry about it frightening her like last time. He was definitely faster than when he'd rescued her at Clyburn's hovel. It felt like electricity was tingling under his skin as he galloped.

Shay's fingers twisted tight in Nero's mane as she held on. Fresh air brushed her face; it was still chilly, but it seemed winter was nearing an end. It smelled like springtime and burning embers. Shay felt alive for the first time in days. The anger and angst flowed off her back as Nero's hooves thudded on the ground. He galloped at a steady beat, a dark song, something archaic and intimidating like the sound of deep drums welcoming a sacrifice. His hoofbeats thrummed against dirt. The dead wandered nearby but never got close. Nothing came close to them.

Shay started telling Nero everything that had been going on. The broken leg, the fighting, Chel training her. She told her oldest friend everything and anything that came to mind.

Nero ran down broken streets. He ran between tall trees and

down empty fields. He made a wide turn when Shay was done emptying her soul of all the chaotic thoughts that had been tormenting her. She felt lighter, freer, having all of that off her mind.

Nero slowed and paced in an empty grocery store parking lot.

Shay sat up straighter. "That felt good, boy." She rubbed Nero's neck.

Nero whinnied joyously. Nothing was better than having Shay back. Nothing. When he became the Crossroads Demon he feared he'd barely ever see her again. Fate had changed that. He was thankful to have her nearby every day.

"I don't know what to do," Shay said. "I'm not sure Jed really wants this. He's distant one minute, overprotective another." Shay shook her head and let her blue hair fly in the wind. "Maybe I should leave? Maybe we aren't meant to be together." Tears were welling behind Shay's eyes as she said it.

Nero weaved off the road and headed for the cemetery. He didn't have the words to help her, but he knew someone who might.

Shay recognized where they were. "It wasn't too long ago that I was here, playing house with Jed and Thrush." Shay took a deep breath and fought the pinching in her heart. It was the closest thing to normalcy they'd experienced. Jed let his guard down. He fell into bed with her every night and didn't hold back. It was just them. No one else. Until it wasn't. It seemed their relationship changed daily. Detours kept arising and driving a wedge between them. Just when Shay thought he was ready, something new caused him to second guess them.

"Hey, Shay." Noah waved from the other side of the fence. "What brings you out here?"

Shay jumped down from Nero's back and walked toward the gate. "I was just out getting some fresh air. I hope you don't mind that we stopped by."

"You're always welcome," a soft voice said.

Shay noticed Nightingale standing on the front stoop. "After everything you've done for our son, never worry about coming to visit."

Shay nodded, tears threatening to fall again. She didn't understand why she was so emotional.

"I know Thrush misses you," Nightingale said.

"Really?" Shay found that hard to believe since they'd only had a few weeks together.

Shay walked past the gate and Noah stayed, talking to Nero.

"Come on," Nightingale motioned for Shay to follow. "He's waking up from his nap."

Shay played on the floor with Thrush. She was sitting cross-legged with the little boy sitting on her lap. They played with wooden blocks. Shay whispered silly things to Thrush until he giggled and knocked the blocks over.

Nightingale was watching her. "Are you okay?" she asked.

Shay shrugged. "I'm not sure. Strange things have been happening and..."

"What kind of strange things?" Nightingale asked as she moved from the couch to the floor and scooted closer.

Shay told herself it wasn't because Nightingale could sense something off in Shay. Nightingale moved closer in a friendly way because she cared. That's what she repeated in her mind.

"I have a scar from my broken leg and Teari and Jed think there's some type of Demon poison stuck in it." Shay was rubbing her thigh.

"Noah told me a little bit about that."

Shay was looking down at the floor. "Last night at dinner... I ate nearly raw meat and liked it."

"That's not so concerning after being surrounded by Demons and half-breeds with blood bonds who drink each other's blood to stay alive. I'd say eating raw meat is the least of your concerns. Or at least it is in my opinion."

Shay laughed lightly. "Okay. My leg felt funny last night. Like it had changed shape."

"What kind of Demon poison is in your leg?" Nightingale asked.

"I don't know."

"Has a Demon injured you?"

"Nero kicked me and broke my leg. Twice. It was an accident."

Nightingale was nodding. "Have you been having nightmares?"

"Not that I can remember."

Nightingale pointed toward the door. "Your horse–"

"Nero. His name is Nero," Shay interrupted. "Sorry."

"He's a Demon. Never seen a horse Demon before. But you're both connected in some way."

Shay told Nightingale the story of how she'd found Nero in the field as a newborn foal covered in stings and barely alive. How she'd nursed him back to life and he had been her best friend ever since.

Nightingale was nodding in understanding as Shay spoke.

"You're both deeply connected. I know little about poisons and healing, but I could search your dreams and try to find some answers for you." Nightingale cleared her throat. "I try not to do it without permission these days. People get mad when I just show up."

Shay thought for a bit, staring out the window at Nero's black form pacing and eating grass. "Maybe that would give us some answers."

FOURTEEN

"Dalk, you're assigned to dungeon duty tonight."

Alastor could barely believe his luck. He didn't even need to sneak into the castle, he was assigned to be there for the week.

Patience was a virtue he rarely possessed but the weeks of impersonating the Hellion recruit Dalk were paying off. All it took was one whisper to his commanding officer that he'd be grateful to be assigned guard duty. And bam, he was assigned. Alastor was floating on cloud nine as he ate dinner with the recruits then prepared to head to the castle. It was late in the evening as Alastor crossed the expanse of grass making his way to the dungeon entrance at the base of the mountain.

There was movement near the entrance. Alastor was far enough away that he could watch it all unfold. Shay arrived on Nero. The horse trotted up to the door and Shay was throwing her leg over the side to get down when the Hellions blasted the door open. They grabbed Shay and dragged her off the horse. She fought as they carried her toward the entrance.

Don't damage my property, Alastor thought, wishing he could scold the Hellion who had his hands on her. He didn't want her bruised up and broken. Not unless it was by his hand.

He kept walking, reaching the lower entrance to the dungeon. He went inside.

Alastor felt cold prickle his skin. He turned to find a wisp of a woman watching him; black hair and ruby red lips. One moment she was there, the next she was gone. Alastor huffed. There was something familiar about her. He itched a scratch on his arm and kept walking.

FIFTEEN

"NO!" SHAY WAS SCREAMING AT THEM. "DON'T touch me!"

"This is to help you," Chel shouted back, baring sharp teeth to scare her into submission.

Shay kicked harder, panicked that they'd dragged her into the castle and down the hall to the infirmary without as much as a hello. It all felt very violating as they'd set her on an exam table and held her down. She'd done nothing wrong.

Jed was quiet as he held Shay's upper body.

"Make them stop, Jed!" Shay's eyes were wide with panic. "Make them stop!" Shay kicked until Chel grabbed her right leg and held it straight.

She swung her left foot around, kicked him in the side of the head and twisted her hips.

"Don't make me hurt you," Chel said.

"You are hurting me!" Shay yelled. "Let go!"

Chel grabbed her left ankle and held it down.

Teari walked closer with a pair of scissors. "I'm going to cut your jeans."

"No!" Shay was trying to twist her body, trying to get free, but Jed and Chel were stronger than her.

Tears streamed down Shay's face. She could feel her heart thrumming against her ribcage. She dragged air into her lungs. Warm breath puffed against her face. The room started spinning.

It sucked knowing that her relationship with Jed was over in this instant. He wasn't protecting her. He was in on their plan to cut her open against her will. Something broke in Shay. Something more than when her mother and father died at the ranch in Montana. It was broken and burning. It would never be the same. *They'd* never be the same.

The rough handling at the door pissed her off. This was worse. They didn't invite her to the infirmary once she'd returned. Chel and Klaus met her at the door and dragged her here. Jed showed up later, swapping places with Klaus. Shay hated that he was here. Hated that she was going to lose every ounce of trust she ever had for the man. She glanced at him while struggling. He was the most handsome man she'd ever met. She was sure his looks let him get away with plenty of shit. Not this time. She'd never trust a beautiful face again.

"This could all be for nothing," Teari warned. "The basilisk treatments have never worked on a human. I could find no record of it."

"We have to try," Jed pressed. "Whatever is stuck in her leg needs out."

"How could you?" Shay turned to Jed, loathing in her eyes. "How could you do this to me?"

Jed's mouth opened like he was going to say something.

Shay screamed as her jeans were cut and ripped.

"I'll make you forget," Jed promised. "You won't remember this." His features were like stone; uncaring.

"I hate you." Shay squeezed her eyes shut and tried to ignore the twisting sensation in her stomach. "Never touch me again."

"I'm sorry," Jed said. "It's for your own good."

Shay went still. Her head hurt but her stomach hurt more than ever. "You're lying to me again." She was looking at Jed. Crushed.

It felt like she was being stabbed through her heart and abdomen at the same time. Shay screamed as the pain in her stomach tightened and pulled. It yanked once, twice, three times and...

Shay disappeared.

Sixteen

Jed, Chel and Teari were staring at the empty cot in the infirmary.

"What just happened?" Chel asked. "Where did she go?" Chel started searching the room. "Shay!" He shoved cots and trays aside trying to find her. "She can't do that." Chel's eyes were like fire as he confronted Teari. "She's a human. She can't just disappear!"

"No. I suppose she can't." Teari set down the scissors she was using to cut Shay's jeans. She looked up at Jed.

"Did you do something to her?" Teari asked. "Did you change her?"

"Never," Jed promised. "I never changed her. I only promised to make her forget this." Both hands stretched through his hair and pulled at the ends as he paced away from the cot. "I only promised to make her forget me. This. To forget any of this ever happened but she wouldn't let me. She forbade me from erasing her memories of me and sending her back to Montana."

Teari crossed her arms and stared at Jed. "You would make her forget? After all she's done? She helped save this realm by standing-in as Queen. She walked into a Safe House so Meg could get out. Shay saved you on the Earthen plane. She's quite possibly the strongest human I've ever met and yet you want to send her away. You want to make her forget? Is she deserving of this?"

"I must. To keep her safe. It's too dangerous here." Jed avoided Chel's gaze as the words came tumbling out of his mouth. The cement he'd used in his mind to keep his face straight while Shay had screamed at him was chipping and falling in chunks.

"I knew I could never trust you with her." Chel's voice was full of disgust.

The dam he'd put up was cracking and within seconds it all came tumbling down. Jed hated that he'd lied to her. Again. He betrayed her. Held her down in the infirmary and told her that he was going to wipe her memories. He wanted to puke. He pressed his hand to his stomach and tried to breathe but he couldn't. Something was blocking his throat. Something was squeezing him from the inside. He'd never felt so empty.

Suddenly heavy footsteps were coming at him. Jed looked up to see Chel's rage filled expression. He leaned back on his knees accepting of his fate. Shay was gone. Jed had no reason to be here. He didn't know it before. He didn't realize how her lack of a presence would affect him. In this moment, he relished the blow that would send him elsewhere. He'd never accepted death so openly in his entire damned life.

Teari was fast when she leapt in Chel's path, humming blade of light drawn and ready.

"Don't," Teari warned Chel.

"We had one job and that was to protect her. Meg is gonna be pissed!" Chel was shouting, his deep voice echoing off the white walls of the infirmary.

"Leave me with him," Teari commanded.

Chel left, slamming the door so hard that wood shattered from the corners of the frame.

Teari turned on Jed. The flat of her foot struck him on the shoulder and he fell back onto the floor. Her mood shifted. Teari was a healer but she was also a warrior. The Archangel Gabriel would have no less as his personal healer.

"Is she dead?" Teari asked, blade ready.

Jed stared.

Teari took a deep breath. "I have had it up to here," she raised her hand above her head, "with you lovesick Angels."

"I'm not an Angel," Jed said.

"No shit. But it seems you've inherited the idiot half." Teari leaned closer to his face. "You have a bond with her. Search for her. Close your eyes and feel her just as closely as you feel her when you're taking her clothes off. Find that tether and follow it. Use a spell if you must."

Jed closed his eyes, his fingers tapped in spell casting. He whispered words that sounded like sunlight and rain and apology. *Her thread was there. Gold twisted with black.* Something wasn't right but she was there. He told Teari everything he saw.

"Is she dead?" Teari asked again.

"She's alive." Jed's eyes flashed open. "But she's not in Hell."

SEVENTEEN

At the Crossroads

IT WAS DARK. One minute Shay was screaming at Jed, the next she was gone, surrounded by night. Her head was spinning. She reached out to steady herself and felt something warm–soft hair. She blinked until her vision cleared and she heard the soft whinny of Nero foot-steps on pea gravel. She no longer smelled woodsmoke or pine.

Nero was nudging her. She took the cue, climbed on his back, and tangled her fingers in Nero's mane.

"Where are we, boy?" she whispered.

Nero's teeth clicked. His only movement was a few steps forward then a few steps back.

Clouds cleared, and the moon illuminated their surroundings. Shay noticed the ochre haze of Hell was gone. The air smelled fresh. The moonlight was milky.

"We're back on the Earthen plane. How did we get here?" she asked Nero.

"Thought you'd never get here," a deep voice said.

Nero turned.

Shay noticed markings on the road underneath them. Tension filled her body. She recognized the runes in a circular shape around them. They were trapped.

The man in front of them was dressed in a black suit. There was a black sports car parked on the side of the road. His shined shoes reflected moonlight.

Shay took in the four roads extending from the crossroads she and Nero were trapped in.

"Never seen a Crossroads Demon as pretty as you," the man said, watching them warily. "Never seen a horse show up either."

Shay wasn't the Crossroads Demon. Nero couldn't talk, though. So Shay decided it was best for her to speak.

"What do you want?" Shay asked.

"A deal." The man rubbed his chin and watched her with dark eyes.

"What kind of deal?"

"Rebuilding after the war has become profitable for our company. I want you to kill my business partner."

"Why?"

"Money my dear."

"I'm not your dear." Shay narrowed her eyes.

"Will you make the deal or not?"

Shay nodded. "Your business partner."

"What do I give you in return?"

Shay's eyes flashed red. The tether that connected her to Nero went taut. The words that came out of her mouth were not of her own volition. They were compelled by the curse of the Crossroads Demon and Nero. "Out of the eater will come something to eat. And out of the strong will come something sweet."

Shay smiled and held out a dusky hand that was unfamiliar to her, one with long necrotic fingernails and a transparent golden ring on her middle finger.

"You want me to give you food?" the businessman asked.

"You said anything. Something sweet. Something to eat. Shake on it." Shay smiled wickedly. "Step into the circle," she taunted.

The businessman stepped forward, his back ramrod straight. He was trying to show calmness, but Shay could hear the rapid fluttering of his heart. Her mouth watered.

He held out a hand. Shay reached down from where she sat on Nero's back, her necrotic index finger scraped the soft inner skin of the businessman's wrist as they shook on it. Etched in darkness, the deal was done.

Nero reared up on his hind legs, hooves in the air. He whinnied, dark and ominous. A promise had been made and now the Crossroads Demon had to take care of business.

"Do you want his information?" the businessman stepped back, giving Nero more room.

"We know it all." Shay stared at the man. "Elias Corchran. Black hair. Fifty-two. Has a wife and three children, now teenagers. He'll be at a stoplight on Green Street in Marksville, Tennessee in eighty-four minutes. He will choke on his own blood after being ejected from the driver seat of his Dodge Ram pickup truck. He'll lay in the road for seven minutes as the EMTs fight traffic to get to him. After he dies you inherit a majority in the construction business you've been growing for ten years. Congratulations, Mr–"

Shay's head tipped as she realized he'd never introduced himself. She didn't need the information, she'd draw it from his soul. "Mr. Fremel. You're about to be a multi-millionaire."

The businessman took a few more steps back. "You know all that from our deal?"

"And more."

Now that the deal was done, Nero and Shay were released from the runes trapping them in the crossroads.

Nero shivered. His spine tingled as the transformation overtook him. He shivered, gnashed his teeth together, tensed his body, and changed. Nero was already huge but in that second he doubled in size, his long black tail and mane becoming stiff as needles and sharp

673

as razorblades. His veins became giant ropes of obsidian, twining and swirling under his skin like protective armor.

"Holy shit," the business man muttered, backstepping as quickly as possible until he got to his car.

Shay changed. She didn't realize it. Her whole person had changed. Vision, form, morals. The poison in her scar allowed her to transform with Nero. They were a packaged deal now, their soul tether closer than ever. She was just as much of the Crossroads Demon as Nero was.

Shay clicked her tongue and Nero took off in the direction of Elias Corchran.

He galloped faster than the moonlight that was spilling over the Earthen plane. On his back, there was nothing but a shadow and a blue blur from Shay's hair.

Shay smiled wide as the crisp, cool air touched her skin and blew her hair behind her in a wave. There was nothing like a horse sprinting across an open plain. Shay remembered this feeling from life on the ranch. She leaned down and touched Nero's stiff mane. The sharp tines curled under her hands, providing grips. She held on tight as Nero ran. She wanted to laugh and shout and whoop into the night air. The thrall of running in the dark, free and unrestricted, filled her with dark energy.

Shay wasn't sure where they started their journey, she only knew the direction of Marksville, Tennessee.

Nero sprinted through forests, down empty roads, through towns and cities as nothing more than a shadow. Streetlights went black as he moved close but flickered back to life as he cleared them.

It felt like only minutes had passed when Nero slowed and Shay saw the sign for Marksville.

An engine revved as a dark blue truck sped down the road. A Dodge Ram. Elias slowed for the stoplight on Green Street. The light flicked to green. He sped up. Nero leapt into the intersection.

Elias saw the giant Demon horse but no one else did. They only saw the crash as he sideswiped the beast, veered to the side, and hit a pole. In a series of unfortunate events, his airbags failed–they had been filled with paper bags by the used car dealership he'd bought the truck from, and his seatbelt failed–the fabric and stitching tearing and releasing under the inertia of his body. Shay's head turned to watch Elias's body fly out the front window. He landed in the street with a sickening crack of bones and squelch of internal organs.

Nero wandered closer.

Blood spurted from Elias's mouth. He couldn't move with twenty-three broken bones including his cervical spine. Sirens blared in the distance. The ambulance company was having a rough night. This accident was one of ten in the past few hours. The crew was exhausted, the driver bleary-eyed as he took a wrong turn, delaying their response time by an extra four minutes. Those four minutes could have meant life. But for Elias, they simply helped sign his death certificate.

Nero backstepped into the shadows of an alley. Shay turned her head, listening to the *thump–thump–thump* as Elias's heartbeat slowed then finally stopped.

The golden rings on Shay and Nero's bodies glimmered with the transfer of power.

"Out of the eater will come something to eat. And out of the strong will come something sweet," Shay whispered the words.

She didn't know when they'd call upon Mr. Fremel to repay their deal. But they would call upon him eventually.

Nero and Shay's bodies shivered with anxious energy. "Let's do it again, boy." A dark smile quirked Shay's lip. She clicked her tongue and kicked her heel against Nero's belly. "Hiya!"

Nero took off. He galloped through forests, across rivers and streams, up rocky hillsides and through mountain valleys. Shay thought the landscape resembled the southern Rockies with the snowcapped mountains.

Nero galloped into a valley clearing with a dark lake. The moon and stars were perfectly reflected, like a dark mirror. Nero bent to

675

take a drink. A tingle ran down both their spines simultaneously and they transformed into their normal appearances.

There was a noise behind them. Shay reached for her weapon only to realize she didn't have one. She never had a chance to collect one before she was summoned out of Hell.

A large form walked toward them. Dark energy permeated from it, shadows curled around its legs and feet. Black feathers dragged against the grass in a continuous *shhhhh* sound. Shay recognized the wings. She recognized the feeling of him. This wasn't the first time they'd met. She knew him before he'd turned into this, helped him. She'd ridden in a car with him, guided him to safety.

It was Sparrow. The Raven King.

Eighteen

Sparrow was staring, moonlight glittered in his eyes. A creature as alluring as Sparrow didn't belong in the valley between mountains. The beauty of nature was nothing compared to him. He was out of place. Or maybe, the scenic valley was out of place with Sparrow standing there.

"What are you doing here?" Shay asked.

"I could ask you the same thing." His head tipped to the side in a quirky movement. "Shay."

"Congratulations, you've remembered my name."

Silence passed.

"Does your Queen know that you're on the Earthen plane with your Demon hanging out? It's so... blasphemous." Sparrow was grinning.

"She's not my Queen." Shay held no alliances in the feud between Sparrow and Meg.

"Then why did you cover for her in that Safe House? The Deacons told me what you did. Impersonated the Queen of Hell. Why would a little human girl do that?" He took one step forward, hands hung unsuspecting at his sides.

Shay stood her ground. "It was the right thing to do."

Sparrow smiled charmingly, showing teeth. He glanced away from her, his focus on Nero. "Never seen a Demon horse before." He looked at her again, taking her in. "Never seen a Demon *human* before. Only recognized the blowtorch blue hair when I saw the blur running across the Earthen plane. Could never forget a human like you."

"We were summoned." Shay crossed her arms and lifted her chin. Sparrow's form was imposing but she was sure he would not hurt her. And Shay sure as shit would not take threats from a man who was quite fucked in the head since the first time she'd met him. Sure he was a King from the Seven Kingdoms of Heaven, that didn't mean his brain was right. Something was twisted in him. Twisted and broken.

"I heard a rumor that a human girl killed an Angel mid-air, which is impressive." Sparrow's wings relaxed.

Shay shrugged.

"And then the bell tolled for the Crossroads Demon pact." Sparrow's chin dipped. "You have blood on your hands now."

"I'm not the only one."

"How did you get in this situation?"

Shay shook her head, blue hair flying. "I don't know."

But she did know, she knew that she had Demon poison in her scar. She would not tell Sparrow that.

"There are rules. Didn't the Deacons tell you?"

"I haven't spoken with any Deacons," Shay said.

"That's probably a good thing given Meg's *situation*. I'm sure if another showed up at her door she'd slaughter them like she did that poor Hellion recruit."

"How do you know about that?" Shay asked. Narrowing her eyes, she noted every tick in his face, every quirk, every flash of teeth.

"Word gets around." Sparrow's hand went to his pocket. He sighed. "So, whose side are you going to choose?"

"That's none of my business," Shay said. The only side she'd chosen was Jed's. Now she wasn't so sure about all that.

"Oh you're too naïve. You must choose a side in a war like this."

"You told the Deacons you'd truced. The war is over."

"The war never ends. And what I said doesn't make a difference to the side you've chosen."

"I didn't choose a side."

"But you're doing Demon work now." Sparrow wagged his finger. "That has to be breaking a rule of some kind. There's never been a human doing the things you've just done."

Shay chuckled. "Have you spent any time on the Earthen plane? Humans can be pretty despicable. The things they can do to each other..." Shay threw her hands in defeat. "It's not by my choice. I didn't make a choice to do this."

"But you refused the choice to fix it."

Shay blinked and closed her mouth. Sparrow knew too much. He shouldn't know what goes on behind closed doors in Hell.

"Who told you that?"

Sparrow motioned to her. "You're clearly here. Your Queen would not have allowed this to continue. We all know Teari has been visiting Meg's realm. It's easy putting the puzzle together. And your reaction solidifies my speculations."

"She's not my Queen. How many times do I need to tell you?"

"Everyone chooses." His head tipped to the side and he blinks. "How's that half-Angel you were tagging around with?" Sparrow held his arms out showing the black, twisting runes. "I might need him to refresh my ink."

"I'm not sure he'll take kindly to you threatening me."

Sparrow laughed, his face turned to the starry night sky until he'd finished, then finally he looked at her again. "I didn't come here to threaten you, Shay. I'm just catching up with an old friend. I'll never forget you and Jed guiding me to safety. You guided me straight to Meg and changed *everything*."

He was suddenly too close to her. In an instant he'd moved and she'd barely seen it. His shadows curled around her feet. Two feathers broke loose of his wings and floated through the air. One landed on her shirt.

Nero made a noise that sounded like a growl, his snout pushing over her shoulder. He was ready to call upon the change if need be.

Sparrow glanced up at Nero. His smile dropped. "You have a leash for that thing?"

"He's a free horse." Shay looped her arm around Nero's head and pet him. "He does what he wants."

Sparrow reached out and grabbed the black feather off Shay's shirt. He twirled it between his fingertips, then slid the soft edge of it against her cheek. "Hold onto this, Shay-baby. It might come in handy one day."

He was standing in her space, his green eyes boring into hers. He smelled good and she could feel the heat from his body. Jed had warned her about Sparrow. Warned her to stay away from him and she was realizing why. The Raven King was a spectacle. He was a black hole that drew you in. Mesmerizing. His voice was like warm whiskey. Shay wanted to touch him. It was hard being this close, hard to look away. He was too handsome. Moreso than that Angel she killed. Moreso than Jed, and she hated to admit that.

Shay wanted to bare her neck in offering. She couldn't control the urge. She closed her eyes and felt Sparrow tuck the feather into the pocket of her jeans. His fingers pressed against her hip.

"Stop what you're doing," Shay warned.

"Be careful, Shay-baby," Sparrow was whispering in her hear. "I'd hate to see Meg pay for what's happening to you."

"My choice," Shay said. "Stop calling me Shay-baby."

When her eyes flashed open, Sparrow was gone and only wisps of black shadows remained. Shay shivered, feeling cold without his warm body next to her.

"Fuck," she shouted to the night.

Nero whinnied in agreement.

Nineteen

Shay woke up in the suite, alone, her body aching. She was exhausted. She felt like she'd been hit by a truck.

Somehow she'd returned to Hell. She didn't remember crossing the Veil or a portal. She rubbed her face and rolled out of bed. Her neck was sore–Sparrow. Shay ran to the bathroom, her hand against the soft skin of her neck. She couldn't feel any scars marking her skin. Shay flicked on the light and leaned toward the mirror, checking her skin. She released a breath when she didn't see any bite marks.

Shay had never known Sparrow like that. The dude was a nutcase last time she was in his presence. But that Sparrow... it was no surprise Meg had fallen so hard for him. Shay thought about the scars on Jed's neck from Meg and his reaction to her having bitten him. Shay wondered if she'd feel the same about Sparrow's bite, pissed off but enchanted.

She wandered the suite. Jed wasn't there. Her skin ached and prickled. Shay rubbed her arms trying to quell the sensation. Her shoulder brushed against the doorway and it worsened. Shay paused and touched the doorway again. Her skin prickled like a thousand ants were crawling on her.

The runes.

Shay found a sponge in the kitchenette, wet it, and began scrubbing the suite. She started with the largest rune on the floor by the door. With every one that she erased, the prickling of her skin eased. She scooped up the lines of salt and threw them down the sink. Shay scrubbed the walls. She took a knife, then a marker to the doorways and damaged Jed's intricately drawn and carved markings.

When she was done, the room looked less chaotic and Shay felt like she could finally breathe. Her skin calmed and felt warm. She turned when the door opened.

Shay wasn't sure how she was going to react to seeing Jed again after he'd held her down in the infirmary. She wanted to slap him for promising to erase her memories. She wanted to kiss him because she'd missed him. Something melted in her when she saw him. It always did. She was drawn to him just as badly as he was drawn to her.

He looked tired, his hair falling loose from where it was tied behind his neck.

"You're back." Jed closed the door and stood unmoving. "Where did you go?"

Shay shook her head. "I... I don't know."

"What happened?"

She brushed salt off her arm before walking to the sink and washing her arms under the tap.

"Where have you been, Shay?" Jed asked again.

"I said, I don't know." Her back was to him. She turned.

"Were you in Hell? A different plane? How did you disappear like that?" His eyes were searching her face for truth, for something to hold on to. Nothing was right between them anymore. "Tell me, Shay." He rubbed his face, startled when he noticed the changes to the suite.

"No. No, no, no." Jed turned, taking in the bare walls and scratched door frames. "What did you do?" he shouted.

"They were making me sick." Shay crossed her arms.

"How? You're human. There's nothing supernatural about you. You're not an Angel or a Demon. How could they make you sick?"

Shay scratched her thigh absently. It hurt. His true thoughts were coming out. She was nothing special. Just a human. She'd saved his life battling an Angel on the Earthen plane but that wasn't enough for him. She was nothing special in his eyes.

"Where's my marker?" Jed started searching the kitchen drawers.

"Gone." Shay felt no remorse over what she'd done.

"Where are they?" Jed was rifling through drawers, panicked. "I had a whole bunch."

"I threw them out the window."

Jed stilled. "Why would you do that?"

"Hurts like a bitch, doesn't it?" Shay's face twisted, her chin trembled. "Losing all your trust in someone you thought you loved." She felt tears burning her eyes.

"You never said you loved me."

"Would that even make a difference?" Shay asked. "Would *love* have stopped you from lying to me? From holding me down so they could cut me open?"

Jed was staring, his eyes bleary. He already hated himself. Hearing the accusation from her lips made it worse; made it real. All he'd ever wanted was some normalcy.

"Shay," Jed said. "You are not yourself."

"Maybe I *like* it," she bit back through clenched teeth. "Maybe I enjoy not being weaker than everyone around me."

Tension filled the room. The energy was vibrating. Shay's heart beat against her ribs. She wanted to touch him. She moved closer. Her hands slid up his chest and around his neck, her fingers twisting in his hair. She kissed him, gently at first, exploring his body while they were both angry and on edge.

He pulled back. "You said you hated me."

Shay kissed him again, harder this time; punishing.

Jed matched her. His tongue entered her mouth and twined with hers.

She pulled away, out of breath, lips swollen and aching. "You lied to me."

"You told me to never touch you again," Jed reminded her.

"Well... now that you're standing in front of me looking like you do..." Her eyes wandered up and down, taking him all in. "Clearly you're feeling miserable about what you did to me." His hair was tousled, his shirt torn. He obviously hadn't slept since she disappeared. If anything he'd been razing Hell trying to find her.

That's what she told herself. He'd searched everywhere for her. She searched his eyes and found torment staring back at her.

Shay's hands moved over his shirt and tore it down the center. Her lips never left his. Her palms pressed against his hot skin, feeling the ridges and planes of his body.

Jed's hands were in her hair, holding her as he kissed her deeply, his tongue working against hers, his teeth nipping at her lips.

Shay's hands went to the waist of his pants and tugged, knuckles brushing against hot skin. She felt him tense.

Jed moaned into her mouth. His fingers pressed against her skull in silent plea.

She unbuttoned. Unzipped.

"Fuck," Jed murmured as he kicked his pants off. He stiffened.

"Don't," Shay begged. "Don't freeze up on me. I can't stand it." She reached down and took him in her hand, stroking, squeezing lightly.

Jed shuddered and closed his eyes as his hands trailed down her neck, down her chest to press against her breasts. He gripped her waist and lifted her.

Shay's legs wrapped around his waist and she held onto his shoulders as he moved to the couch. He lowered her feet to the ground, tearing her shirt like she'd done to him, but faster, harder, jerking her body. The thrill was electric, the heat burning.

"Christ." Shay was kicking off her boots and pulling her pants down. She shoved Jed until he fell back on the couch, looking up at her.

Shay blinked, wanting to remember this moment with him, looking up at her like she was an Angel, like she was something more than human. A shiver ran up her spine as she gazed at his body, hard and waiting for her.

"From this moment on," Shay said as she straddled him, "you promise me. Never hold me down against my will again." She licked his mouth and lifted her hips, her hand between them, touching his hardness; moving up and down, painfully slow.

Jed hissed, sucking in a breath. "You're going to kill me."

"I might." Shay smirked. "Promise."

"Never again." His gaze was dark, true.

Jed whispered something that sounded like ice clinking in a whiskey glass. Her underwear fell away. His fingers brushed down her body, taking in every curve before dipping between her legs and stroking her.

Shay let out a shaky breath, her hands moving to his shoulders to steady herself. "Oh, God..." Shay moaned as he pressed his finger between her folds. She shuddered as he circled.

Shay kissed his neck, his collarbone, the soft skin below his ear. She was so close. His fingers moved away and Jed gripped her hips and lowered her body against his. In a slick movement, he pressed inside her. Her body stilled at the ache.

"You always wait too long." Shay leaned back as she adjusted, slowly taking his length and thickness into her body. "We should do this twice a day, every day."

Jed smirked, palms rubbing over her nipples, his hips pressed up. "I'm trying to be better than the Hellions."

"I'm not asking for blood." Shay bit her lip as he rubbed against her inner walls.

"You just want my body?" His hands moved to her hips again and squeezed. He held her still against him and sat up straight, focusing on the door behind Shay's shoulder.

The movement was right. Shay moaned, her mouth went to his

collarbone. She licked and kissed and sucked as he dragged against her. She wanted to answer him but she couldn't think straight.

"Someone is here."

"Let them wait." Shay shifted her hips, forcing him deeper and moaning with pleasure.

There was a loud thud as the door to the suite blasted open.

Twenty

Alastor entered Shay's suite easily with one solid kick to the door, surprised that there were no protection spells or fancy locks. He chuckled to himself with how easy it was and laughed louder when he saw Shay and that half-breed fucking on the couch.

He'd never seen her naked when they were at the camp. For the one moment in his life he'd given her privacy in the cabin shower. He shouldn't have.

Shay was a prize to look at; all smooth skin, curves, and muscle. The long, blue hair did it though. She was small compared to Demon females, this would be easy.

Jed chanted a spell and they were clothed again. He scrambled forward and shoved Shay behind him.

"Exactly who I was looking for," Alastor said. "We meet again." He showed sharp teeth and glared.

"You're dead," Jed said, his fingertips sparking as he drew energy.

"Wrong." Alastor looked to Shay and smiled. "You both have a debt to pay."

Alastor went after Jed, blade drawn and malice on his face.

The men fought, but the space was too small. Fists flew. Walls cracked. Furniture was turned to toothpicks as Jed blasted Alastor with battle magic. Nothing stopped the Demon. His Hellion uniform was ripped. His arm was bleeding.

The air crackled with tension as Jed and Alastor locked eyes, each prepared to do whatever it took to emerge victorious in this deadly game.

Shay stood between them, her presence a tantalizing prize coveted by Alastor, her eyes reflecting a mixture of fear and determination as she braced herself.

With a flick of his wrist, Jed summoned tendrils of arcane energy, crackling with raw power, to encircle Shay protectively. His eyes blazed with determination as he prepared to defend her against the malevolent force that threatened to tear her from his grasp. She'd only just returned, he needed more time to make it right between them, to show her that he'd do better.

Alastor was a creature of darkness and deceit; he grinned wickedly as he brandished a basilisk tooth knife, its jagged edges glinting ominously in the subdued light of the suite. With a predatory gleam in his eyes, he advanced toward Shay, his intentions clear as he sought to claim her for his own dark purposes.

The air filled with the clash of magic and malice as Jed and Alastor engaged in a deadly dance of power and peril. Spells crackled through the air, weaving intricate patterns of light and shadow as they clashed with thunderous force. The tendrils slammed into Alastor's chest, throwing him back and cracking a wall. As plaster showered the room, Alastor sprang to his feet and launched himself at Jed, knife ready.

Alastor's movements were swift and unpredictable as he dodged Jed's attacks with uncanny agility. With each strike of the basilisk tooth knife, he carved through the protective barriers that Jed summoned, inching closer to his prize.

Shay was caught in the crossfire. She was trying to get to the bedroom to get her pistol or hunting knife but every time she made a move, the fighting men blocked her. She picked up a broken chair leg and held it like a batter at the box, ready for action. She watched as the two men collided with terrifying ferocity. Her heart ached with fear for Jed's safety.

The room smelled of dust and sweat and blood as the chaos continued. Energy flew from Jed's hands, hit the window, and broke it. Shay ducked to avoid the spray of glass.

Jed tripped on a piece of broken table.

Alastor seized his opportunity, took the moment to leap forward, arm raised, Basilisk tooth blade ready. With swift and decisive blow, the knife found its mark with deadly precision. The blade sunk in Jed's chest, the tip landing directly into his heart.

"No!" Shay screamed as she ran toward Jed. "No, no, no!" He didn't move. Never took a final breath. He wasn't struggling. Something wasn't right.

Alastor seized his opportunity, picking up the chair leg and advancing on Shay.

Something hit Shay in the back of the head. All she saw was a bright light then darkness. She didn't even feel Alastor dragging her across the floor then throwing her over his shoulder.

The room fell silent as Jed finally took his last breath and it echoed amongst the debris.

Twenty-One

Shay couldn't move. She was strapped to a table, thick leather wrapped around her wrists and ankles. Coarse wood scraped her back as she struggled to get free. Shay dragged air into her lungs, did her best to ignore the sharp pull of pain in her ribs.

Footsteps came closer; hollow sounding. Heavy. She recognized the large man, the scruffy beard, the shadows that seemed to shift on his face.

Alastor.

"You're dead." Shay's eyes went wide, terrified. "I watched you die."

Alastor laughed, deep and booming from down in his chest. "I am very hard to kill, Shay."

He was touching her bare ankle. Shay's heart was thrumming in her chest. She was wearing nothing. "Stop," she said.

Alastor's hand stopped mid-calf and he twisted her leg so he could see all of the scar along her thigh. His eyes traced the ragged red edge of it.

"Oh, dear, little human." He sniffed her leg. "This is something different." His large hand circled just above her knee, holding her leg

697

still as he touched the raised scar with his free hand. Nails drifted over her skin drawing goose bumps. Dark eyes met hers.

"Let me go," Shay said, tugging at the leather binding her wrists. "You killed him!" Shay could barely process everything that was happening. The last thing she saw was Alastor stabbing Jed and a pool of blood.

Alastor chuckled. "Doubt he's dead. That knife can't kill a half-breed like him," he shook his head and clicked his tongue. "It only incapacitated him long enough for me to get away with my prize."

Alastor's fingers rubbed soft skin. "No. No, I don't think I will let you go. You and that half-breed Angel cost me everything. And now you're going to pay me back for eons worth of work." He exhaled loudly. "So much was lost when you all got in the mix. You cannot imagine what you disrupted."

"I don't have any money." Shay struggled, this time shifting her feet against the straps holding her ankles.

Alastor laughed, his deep voice echoing throughout the walls of the hovel. "You won't be paying me back in money." He squeezed her scarred thigh.

"I have nothing," Shay said, watching him warily.

He smiled and it was devious.

Alastor reached for the metal handle of a fire poker. The end was red-hot. It wasn't a poker, Shay realized. It was a brand like the one her daddy used to mark the cows that belonged to the ranch. Shay knew exactly what that was. Alastor was going to mark her as his and judging from the shape of the rune, she would have a very hard time escaping him.

"This way, you'll always come back to me." Alastor's eyes reflected the flame in the fireplace as he searched her bare body for the right place to burn her.

TWENTY-TWO

NERO FELT A TUG ALONG THE THREAD THAT CONNECTED to Shay. Something was wrong. She was frightened and hurt. Nero moved to his feet and paced under her window.

He whinnied, loud. Then again louder. She didn't come to the window.

He stomped his hooves and snorted.

More fear tore down the thread. She was terrified. He rose on his hind legs and slammed his front hooves down on the outer wall of the castle. Shards of stone flew into the air, rocks fell around him.

It was moments like this that he wished he could speak. He whinnied louder, his eyes wide.

Shay never came.

Nero had been on the royal grounds long enough to know where certain people were during the day. He ran to the Hellion training grounds to find Skeele and Chel. Those two were the most protective of Shay.

Nero galloped, his heavy body leaving deep hoofprints in the field and kicking up clumps of grass.

Nero interrupted Skeele as he spoke to three rows of Hellions. He ran right between them, blocking Skeele with his gigantic body.

"Get out of here." Skeele shoved at Nero.

Nero nickered and huffed.

The Hellion Commander was becoming more annoyed as Nero tried to get his attention and communicate that something was wrong. Skeele kept pushing the horse away and baring sharp teeth. Skeele was reaching for his blade.

"Come here, Nero," Chel interrupted.

"Get that damned creature off the training grounds. I'll cast him off this land if he can't control himself," Skeele threatened.

Chel made a clucking sound and motioned for Nero to follow.

"You're going to get your ass tossed out of here, beast." Chel crossed his arms and stared.

Nero's eyes were wide as he dragged his head toward the castle over and over again.

"Is it Shay?" Chel asked.

Nero whinnied loudly.

"Show me."

Nero ran toward the castle in the burning caves. Chel ran, keeping a steady pace behind him.

Nero motioned toward Shay's window with his muzzle. He snowed his teeth and widened his eyes.

Chel rubbed his chin. "I'm going inside."

Chel made his way to the door of the castle. He ran down the hall that led to the winding stairway. Then up he went, taking three steps at a time. Something wasn't right. He sniffed the air. Someone who didn't belong had been here.

Heavy footsteps echoed behind him.

Chel turned to see Skeele running up the stairs.

"What happened?" Skeele asked.

"Something is not right," Chel gripped his blade.

"Meg!" Skeele ran for Meg's room.

Chel followed. He was sure the problem wasn't Meg, but he had a duty to protect her first. Meg's wing was undamaged.

Skeele shoved Meg's bedroom door open.

Chel saw her sitting on the balcony, whistling to a yellow songbird. He left Skeele and ran down the opposite end of the hall.

He was right. The door to Shay and Jed's suite was broken to pieces and strewn across the floor.

"Shay?" Chel called. Unease filled his gut. This was very bad. He'd been in this suite enough to know that runes were missing. Jed was so neurotic he'd marked every wall, every door and window. There was less magic here than before.

"Shay? Are you here?" Chel asked. He could hear Nero making noise below the window.

Furniture was broken. There were holes in the walls. Chel followed the worst of the damage. There was blood everywhere. Chel held a hand to his face, fought the desire to lick it off the floorboards. He found the cause of all the gore.

Jed was lying in a pool of blood, a Basilisk tooth blade jabbed through his chest.

"Fuck." Chel ran to Jed and pulled out the blade of Basilisk tooth. He hadn't seen one of those since he was a child.

Once the bone was out, Jed's eyes flickered open. The milky dullness cleared. The wound in his chest began healing from a quickly whispered charm.

"What the fuck was that?" Jed's voice croaked.

Chel inspected the weapon in his hand. "Something old." He tucked the blade in his pocket for later inspection. "Something I've only heard about in fairytales."

"Hell has fairytales?" Jed quipped.

Chel shrugged. "Where's Shay?" He snapped as he began searching the bedroom. He tore the sheets off the bed, flipped the mattress, pulled down the curtains. He slammed open the door to the closet then the bathroom.

"She's not here," Jed confessed. "Someone took her."

"Are you sure it was someone? Or was it the poison?" Chel asked.

"No. No." Jed held up a hand as he moved slowly to stand. "It was Demon dressed as a Hellion. We've come across him before on the Earthen plane. I killed him months ago." Jed shook his head. "How is he still alive? How was he a Hellion recruit?"

"How did you kill him?" Chel asked.

Energy crackled from Jed's fingertips. "Archaic light."

Chel released a cold snicker. "If that Demon did not die by light, he must die by fire." Chel headed for the doorway. "You didn't kill him the first time and now he has found his way back to you and taken Shay. Is that what you're telling me?"

Jed was collecting weapons, changing his torn shirt, and slinging his bag of supplies over his shoulder as he replied, "It appears so."

"Perfect." Chel led Jed down the hall. "It's been a while since I killed something." He cracked his knuckles. "We will hunt it."

———

CHEL WAS CONVERSING with Skeele and the other Hellions as Jed selected another blade from the wall of weapons in the Hellion lounge.

There was a loud knock on the door and Teari let herself in.

The warriors and Jed turned to face her.

"She has Crossroads Demon poison in her." Teari's face was perfectly still as she tried to explain the seriousness of the situation. "Nero has it on his hoofs just like any other Crossroads Demon would have on their claws. It's just like the injury he had on his flank that we had to heal with the basilisk."

"So heal her," Chel said.

Teari shook her head. "It's not that easy. The basilisk doesn't take to humans, we saw that. And her wound is closed. There is poison trapped in the scar tissue."

"Cut it out. That's what you wanted to do before," Skeele said, glaring like he had no time for this side-quest.

Teari was shaking her head. "That was before I knew what it was. It could spread if we cut wrong. Then it would go throughout her body. If it's in the scar tissue, then it's contained for the most part. If it gets into her blood, we have a bigger problem."

"But she is not the same. She's not right," Jed said.

"You could have her like this, with a little darkness she can control most of the time. Or she could turn into something completely different," Teari explained. "Right now, she's still Shay. She might get called off to do some Crossroads Demon work with Nero, but it's still Shay deep down. If that poison gets released into her whole body, we have no idea what she'll turn into or if she'll survive. You could lose her. Forever."

The realization hit Jed like a freight train. His breath hitched. He'd imagined freeing Shay from this nightmare. It seemed slightly innocent if by his hands, on his terms. Jed would have control over saying goodbye. That false dream would come to a quick end. Jed didn't like the feeling of having no control. He'd spent too much of his life without control.

Jed flexed his fists.

Teari's gaze fell to the motion.

"Where is she?" Teari asked. "I have to speak with her."

"That's going to be kinda hard," Jed said. "She's been kidnapped."

"By whom?" Teari walked closer to the men, searching their faces, unafraid to challenge them. "Who took her?"

"A Demon named Alastor," Chel said.

Teari paled as she glanced to Jed and he didn't like what he saw in the depths of her irises. "You're going to get her?"

"Yes," Jed tucked the knife in his belt. "We're leaving now."

Nero was waiting at the door as Jed and Chel exited. Skeele wouldn't risk sending any more Hellions. Meg was with child and that put her at risk. He didn't want to let Chel go, but the Hellion argued until Skeele gave in.

"Of course you're here," Chel said to Nero. "Let's go."

Jed reached out as Nero nuzzled his shoulder, urging him on. "Thanks, boy."

The trio left the royal grounds, headed to find Shay and kill the Demon who took her.

Twenty-Three

TEARI STOOD BEFORE KING GABRIEL. SHE HAD RETURNED to the Seven Kingdoms of Heaven. Something wasn't sitting right in her gut. She'd worked hard to figure out what was afflicting Shay and combined with Meg's pregnancy, the demands from both realms were draining her. She needed guidance.

Gabriel was one of the original Archangels, one of the few surviving that Meg hadn't killed. He was also Meg's father.

Gabriel raised overgrown brows as Teari approached him, smelling like brimstone. Gabriel recognized it.

"What?" he asked.

"Something strange is happening in Hell." Teari sat with Gabriel and poured herself a glass of water from the tray in front of her.

"Something strange is always happening there since Meg took over." Gabriel scratched his beard absently.

Teari took a long drink and collected her thoughts. "Have you heard of a Demon called Alastor?"

Gabriel's enormous form stilled for the slightest instant. "Perhaps."

"I'm trying to decide if I should involve the Deacons."

709

"That's not your call," Gabriel reminded her. "Meg hates when they meddle."

Teari tapped long fingers against the glass. "A human is involved."

Gabriel looked bored. "They better get it to a Safe House."

"This human is not dead. It's the one from Meg's trial."

Gabriel had been there for Meg's tribunal with the Deacons. "They didn't seem to care about her months ago. She's harmless."

Blue eyes searched her face. Gabriel was the most neutral of all the Archangels but he knew if the others got wind of a human still traipsing around Hell, that would give the Deacons and the Seven Kingdoms of Heaven another reason to meddle with Meg.

Gabriel sighed. "We've only had a few blissful months of silence on all realms."

"It was wonderful." Teari pushed the glass away, her stomach feeling queasy. "So you know Alastor?"

Gabriel nodded, solemnly.

"Who is he?"

"Clea's brother."

Dread filled Teari. If Alastor was Clea's brother, that meant Alastor was Meg's uncle. She probably didn't even know. He could challenge her for the throne.

Clea couldn't take the throne because she was a ghost but she could forewarn her daughter.

"I must inform her," Teari said as she stood.

Gabriel grabbed her wrist. "Leave it alone."

"But she's your daughter."

Gabriel shook his head. "I know."

A million terrible scenarios were running through Teari's mind. Meg had killed Lucifer in a moment of rage and unexpectedly took the throne of Hell. No one had challenged Meg, yet. None of the Archangels were happy with Meg taking the throne. The Deacons seemed impassive, as usual. The inhabitants of Hell were under control, as much as wild Demons and the dead could be controlled.

But now Alastor was close enough to kidnap someone from inside the castle. This was a change that Teari never saw coming.

"I need air," Teari said as she launched from her chair and ran out of Gabriel's house. She ran past freshly painted walls, workers cleaning windows, art that had been on display for eons. She shoved open the newly constructed door that had been replaced after the Fast-Zombie War. Fresh air hit her face as she ran down the steps of the porch. White wings burst from her back and Teari took to the air like an uncaged lion. She flew straight up, until the sun burned her face. She turned, gazing down. From this distance she could see the Raven King's lands and the glittering of Babylon. She didn't know where to go or who could help.

Teari held up her hands, remembering a time when she didn't have any, when she'd been bitten by the dead and nearly died, and Meg *saved* her. She owed a debt to Meg. A life debt. She wasn't sure what Alastor had planned but Teari knew that the balance between realms was fickle and delicate and this was the first time in ages that they'd found peace.

Teari tilted her body, positioning herself to divebomb to the nearby forest. She dropped from the sky like an eagle and landed near Sparrow's old cabin on Gabriel's land.

The door was unlocked. Teari let herself in and the memories flooded her, memories of the time when Sparrow was Gabriel's Legion Commander. A time before he'd gone to Hell to do his time as a Hellion to clear his family's curse before he'd been let loose upon the Earthen plane as a shadow to cause unbalance and chaos. It had all changed so much. Teari paced the cabin. She couldn't do much. Yes, she was an Archangel's daughter, but she'd joined Gabriel's kingdom. Her father was no ally. She rubbed her face. She and the Raven King had been friends long ago. They'd been on the same team. Teari needed a friend like Sparrow again. She gazed at the long forgotten bookshelf lined with books about birds. The only problem was, Sparrow was not the man he used to be and Teari doubted he'd help his archenemy. But maybe... maybe if there was something in it for him.

TWENTY-FOUR

CHEL WAS POINTING TO A DROP OF BLOOD ON THE ROAD. "She's bleeding." He sniffed. "This way."

Jed didn't need to track her the way Chel was. He'd whispered a spell that showed him the direction Alastor was travelling.

Chel watched the wisps of Alastor moving through time. The Demon was carrying Shay over his shoulder and running. Shay looked like a child in comparison. The Demon was fast and strong but Chel wasn't scared. He'd kill the Demon in a heartbeat. He swore he wouldn't let the male darkness that ended his sister's life reach Shay. At least this time there was no surprise, they had a trail to follow.

"Showoff," Chel grumbled as the wisps of magic disappeared.

"Where is he going?" Jed asked.

"Probably the mountains." Chel waved ahead of them. "It's far." Chel glanced at Jed, judgingly. "Would be easier if you could move faster." He held out his arms. "I could carry you."

"Not on your life, buddy."

Jed pulled his spell book from a pocket and flipped through the pages, looking for something that might help them. He'd become better with his magic these past few months. There was a time when he'd have to pull out the spell book daily. Now it was rare, but he kept it on him.

Nero kept nudging Jed's shoulder. Every so often the horse would gallop ahead of the men and look back expectantly, like they were going far too slow for Nero's liking. Nero would huff and paw at the road, urging them to move faster. Finally, Nero stopped in front of Jed and when Jed tried to sidestep, Nero nudged him with his flank.

"What's gotten into you, boy?" Jed reached out and raked his hand over Nero's shoulder.

"Not one for signals are ya, man?" Chel asked. "Not surprised."

Jed threw him a confused look.

"Nero wants you on his back. We'll move a lot faster if you ride him."

"It's been a while." Jed jumped, threw a leg over Nero's back, and gripped his mane.

Nero shook his head and whinnied what sounded like an exasperated "*finally.*"

"I think he wants you to hold on." Chel chuckled as he took two steps then launched himself into the air.

Nero neighed wildly before tipping his head down and taking off.

Jed startled, nearly fell, before he leaned forward and held on for dear life. Wind whipped his face. Jed had never ridden a horse or any beast that moved as fast as Nero. The rescue crew of three moved much faster this way. Chel flew overhead, his strong bat-like wings propelling him through the air. Nero held back with how fast he wanted to run. He knew Jed wasn't used to his speed and didn't want to lose the man. But he was fast, so fast Chel laughed from the sky as he beat his wings. It was a race like never before. Wings beating, hooves clomping. The pair of Demons beat the air and the road like it was their playground. The sound of it sent creatures of Hell scattering to avoid them.

Chel's face split into a childlike grin. Nero showed his teeth and flared his nostrils with the reminiscent memory of freedom running through the mountains on the Earthen plane. It was electric. The feeling of being a savior was like nothing else.

TWENTY-FIVE

ALASTOR PRESSED THE RED-HOT BRANDING POKER TO Shay's hip. Her skin sizzled and smoked.

Shay screamed at the top of her lungs. Skin along her wrists and ankles tore as she surged against the leather bindings. Tears fell from her cheeks. She wanted nothing more than to escape but she was trapped, tied to this shitty table like a hog for butchering.

"That's lovely. Scream for me." Alastor was enjoying this too much. "You'll scream later too." He was staring at the vee of her thighs. "You'll scream every day for me."

"You're a fucking pig." Shay spit on him and tried to wiggle away from the scorching pain of the branding tool.

Alastor slapped one massive hand down on her pelvis to hold her in place. He was a giant to her. His hand spanned her from hipbone to hipbone as he braced her. "We're almost finished." He licked his lips. "Want this to burn you good and deep so you never forget what you cost me."

The branding hurt worse than anything, worse than breaking her leg. There was something about the smell of singed skin and the bone deep pain that sent Shay over the edge. She knocked her head against the table, trying to focus elsewhere but it just hurt so damn bad. Her hands curled into fists, still pulling against the restraints.

When it finally stopped, Shay's body ached. Tears soaked her hair. Metal clanged as Alastor tossed the branding tool aside and scrutinized his work.

The mark on Shay's hip was bright red. Blood dripped down her hip. Alastor swiped a finger across her skin, collecting the blood, and brought it to his lips.

"Mmmmm." Alastor closed his eyes as he tasted her blood. "Wow." His eyes flashed open and Shay could see the red return. Shadows danced across his cheekbones. He shook a finger at her. "Never thought you'd taste like that. Familiar. Human... but there's something else there."

Something flashed across his face; control.

Shay was looking at the brand on her hip wishing it would heal. She wasn't sure she'd be able to walk if she ever got free. She was sure he'd branded her bone.

Shay turned, feeling something sharp against her thigh. She tried to move her leg but Alastor gripped it, twisting, the tip of his knife circling her scar.

"What is this?" Alastor tapped on the disfigured skin. He seemed genuinely curious.

"I broke my leg. The bone was sticking through." Shay's words came out staccato and breathy as she fought the pain from her deeply burnt skin.

"You didn't have this on the earthen plane." Alastor pressed the point of his knife against the raised skin. "I would have noticed."

"Don't." Shay's eyes were wide, remembering how Chel and Jed had held her down and tried to cut it open. "Please. Just leave it alone. Haven't you done enough to me today?"

Alastor rubbed his thumb absently over the scar on her thigh as he stared at her face. "Someone hurt you here, didn't they?"

"You did."

A nauseating smile spread across Alastor's lips. "I'll do more," he promised.

Shay felt sick. Bile rose in the back of her throat. She squeezed her eyes shut and tried to ignore the twisting sensation in her stomach. "Don't touch me. Please, just stop."

Her head hurt and her stomach hurt. It felt like she was being stabbed. Shay screamed as the pain in her stomach tightened and pulled. It yanked once, twice, three times and...

Shay disappeared.

Alastor's hand thumped against the table in the absence of Shay's thigh.

"Interesting," Alastor said as he touched the leather straps which once held her in place.

Alastor crossed the hovel to return the knife to the chopping block in the kitchen. Then he made himself a sandwich and waited for her to come back.

Twenty-Six

The strange thing about riding a Demon horse is that they might be called for a Crossroads deal at any time. Jed learned this the hard way. One moment he was riding like the devil, wind chapping his face and the next he was on the ground with road rash to his ass.

"Fuck," Jed shouted as he rolled.

Chel's giant boots landed heavy on the crumbling asphalt. He was bent over in laughter, gripping his knees. "You should have seen your sorry hide tumbling down the road."

Jed groaned as he made it to his feet and checked his bag to make sure nothing fell out. He whispered a spell that fixed his torn pants.

"Guess we're walking again." Chel held out his hands. "Or I can take you to the sky." He winked.

"Never," Jed sneered as he secured his pack and headed toward a dirt road. "Just, stop asking."

They had been traveling on foot for half the day when a pub became visible in the distance. Shrouded by long-limbed pine trees, and pushed back from the dirt path they were following, Jed was eager to find a place to rest for a few minutes. Chel was eager to test the alliance of the lesser Demons of Hell.

"Let's see if they know anything." Chel motioned toward the pub. "It will give us a better idea of how many of Alastor's friends we'll be up against when we find him." Chel cracked his knuckles. "Ready to pick a fight?"

"I could kill something." Jed followed the Hellion.

They entered the squat establishment and the chatter of Hellspeak stopped. Only their footsteps were heard as Chel and Jed crossed the room to the seating area of the bar.

There were strange Demons everywhere, creatures like Jed had never seen in his life–only in books. And then some he'd never seen even in the books of the Peabody Library. The one behind the bar was squat and wide, his skin the color of pea soup.

Chel approached the bartender. "I'm looking for a Demon."

"Got plenty of 'em." The bartender waved his hand motioning to the full tables.

"A specific one. He might have been traveling with a human." Chel gripped his Hellion blade just in case anyone needed clarification of what he was.

The bartender's eyes flashed up from cleaning a mug. "You're traveling with a human."

"Not quite." Jed clicked his tongue as he sat and waved extra friendly at a Demon that resembled a bat–just the face, no wings. "Only half human." He winked.

The bat-faced Demon's eyes went wide before his face twisted in disgust.

"Don't toy with the locals," Chel warned Jed under his breath before turning back to the bartender. "His name is Alastor. We have it on good intel that he crossed through these parts."

The bartender's gaze spanned his patrons. The air was heavy with unspoken words. Seemed everyone had something to say but no one was saying it.

"Two ale and bread and cheese." Chel ordered.

"I'll say, Alastor is a right snake." Jed spit on the ground.

No one moved.

"That's not quite an insult here." Chel's voice was hushed. "You need to channel something a bit different."

Jed winked. "Hope we find that fluffy unicorn."

"More archaic," Chel whispered.

"Ah right," Jed had to channel ancient books he'd read at Peabody Library, "sheep-biting clotpole."

Three Demons shoved their chairs back and stood.

"There ya go." Chel took a swig of his ale. "Think it was involving the sheep that did it."

Jed's fingertips tingled with magic.

Chel pulled his blade; it hummed to life and glowed.

The bartender scraped a dish across the counter and set down two mugs, the ale sloshing.

Chel reached over and took a mug, sipping from it gently before downing the entire thing in one gulp.

Jed sat and broke the bread. He ate leisurely as Chel fought with the three Demons who had stood. Every so often he'd send a blast of power and knock someone over.

By the time Chel was done fighting, half the pub was empty and Jed had eaten most of the bread and cheese.

"Now," Chel turned to the bartender, "tell me about Alastor."

"He hasn't been around for decades," the bartender said. "Just showed up a few weeks ago and rumor has it he was carrying a woman back to his hovel. She looked human."

"What color was her hair?" Chel asked.

"Blue," the bartender replied.

Chel left coins on the bar to pay for their food.

"Do you need directions to his hovel?" the bartender asked.

"Already know where it is," Jed said as they left.

The surrounding forest was quiet as Jed and Chel made their way to the mountain path.

"There is little allegiance," Chel said.

"You gained that from one bar fight?" Jed asked.

"Most of the Demons left, that tells me all I need to know." Chel looked toward Jed. "And what in the heck is a clotpole?"

Jed shrugged. "Don't know. Read it in a book once."

TWENTY-SEVEN

AT THE CROSSROADS

SHAY HAD NEVER BEEN HAPPIER to see Nero or to be on the Earthen plane and out of that hovel in Hell. She just wished she had some clothes. Nero's head jerked up, blocking her nakedness from the man who'd called them to the crossroads. He looked hopeful and guilty. Typical.

Shay's eyes narrowed on the man. "Give me your shirt."

He leaned to the side and his eyes went straight to her naked breasts.

"Now!" Shay shouted.

The man startled and started unbuttoning his shirt. He tossed it to her.

Shay put the shirt on and refocused on the man as she was doing the buttons. Thankfully the guy was tall and the shirt went well below her hips. She hissed as the fabric touched the burn. She had hoped to find underwear or pants but decided she wasn't going to be able to deal with the rubbing on her hip.

"What do you want?" Shay snapped with the tilt of her head.

There was something warm coming down the tether from Nero. Soothing. Calming. Shay didn't know how all of this worked, she'd narrowly escaped Alastor cutting her open and she needed to figure out a way to escape him.

"I need to make a deal," the shirtless man said.

Shay was calming. As long as she was here, making this deal, she was free. Her fingers tangled in Nero's mane.

"You want someone dead?" Shay asked. "It's always the same with you."

"No," the man corrected. "I'll do the killing. I want immortality."

Nero's ears twitched. He wasn't so sure immortality was a deal they could make. Shay waited for a sign from Nero.

Nero shook his head and huffed.

"Can't do it," Shay said. "No deal."

The shirtless man crossed his arms. Shay noticed the tattoos that ran down his shoulders and across his neck. He looked like a biker or a gang member or someone who did bad deeds.

"I want my wife gone," he finally said.

The images came to Shay–memories of his life, the past, the future, and the woman he wanted gone. There were children. Of course, always children involved. Men rarely considered what the loss of a mother would do to the children. But judging from this man, he didn't care.

Nero nodded in agreement with the pact.

"Your deal is accepted. Out of the eater will come something to eat. And out of the strong will come something sweet." The gold jewelry shined as the deal was accepted.

Nero walked out of the trapping runes that were drawn in the crossroads.

The man's eyes widened. "You're doing it now?"

"Of course," Shay replied.

"Can you give me time to say goodbye?" he asked.

"It doesn't work like that." Shay shook her head. "We have places to go, deals to be made. It happens now."

———

THE JOB WAS DONE.

Shay shook leaves from her leg and she gazed at their work. She hated this.

"Nero," Shay's voice was low, "let's run fast."

Nero whinnied, high stepped a few times, then took off.

Shay's skin tingled. Her spine arched as she pressed herself into the wind and held her arms wide. She didn't care about falling off. She knew Nero would never knock her down but she also would do anything to not return to Alastor.

Nero ran faster. They passed cities and towns, valleys, and streams. Nero finally stopped at the lake in the mountain valley, where they'd stopped before. Spring flowers had erupted from the soil, their petals closed to the moonlight.

Shadows moved. It was too familiar for Shay to ignore.

"Are you following me?" Shay snapped.

"It's that hair. Draws me like a moth to a flame." Sparrow gazed at her lazily from under a large oak tree. "I heard a rumor."

"I bet." Shay got off Nero's back, limped when pain sprung from her hip.

"Heard you'd been kidnapped, but here you are. Free as a bird. Killing and making deals on the Earthen plane." His eyes focused on her limp.

Shay held on to Nero for support, unable to put full weight on her leg.

"What do you want, Raven King?" Shay snapped.

"Show me." He motioned to her hip.

"Why?"

"I want to help."

Shay snickered. "I will not owe a debt to you."

"Have you asked your Queen for help?" One dark brow rose on Sparrow's handsome face.

"She doesn't know. Or at least, I'm not sure if she knows."

"Hm." He pointed, thoughtful with her response. "Show me."

Shay lifted the hem of the man's button-down shirt she was wearing and revealed the brand that Alastor had burned into her body.

Sparrow sank to his haunches to get a good look at the blistering skin in the moonlight. "Looks like it hurts." Sparrow stood, rubbing his chin. "The Demon that took you, is he planning to kill you?"

"Just torture. Eons of torture." Shay shivered with the confession. "We busted up his skin trade ring he had going. Now he wants me to pay for all the money he's lost out on. Jed killed him but it didn't stick." Shay rubbed her face in exhaustion. "He was selling kids and women. He's kidnapped me once already, right before we found you in California."

"Your soul will be worth more than money. Your Queen should know that your soul has been stolen."

"You care about my soul?" Shay asked. "It hasn't been stolen. He simply kidnapped me. He's kidnapped me before. I'll get away. Jed will kill him, again."

"You killed an Angel. The Seven Kingdoms of Heaven will want retribution."

"Wonderful."

"They're waiting. Patiently. A soul like yours is valuable."

"I don't care." Shay exhaled. "Also, I'm not dead. My soul is mine. None of ya'll get to lay claim to it." Shay was pointing and there was an edge to her voice. She'd had enough with everyone telling her what to do and when to do it. She'd never lived by the rules of Heaven and Hell and she wasn't about to.

Sparrow nodded, a strange look on his face as he backed into the shadows.

Shay felt the tug in her stomach. It was coming. They were done with their deal making and now she was going to be pulled back to Alastor's hovel. She didn't want to go.

"Help me," Shay whispered to Nero, begged, despair in her voice. "I can't go back to that Demon. You saved me before, boy." She was stroking his cheek. "I need you to find me. I can't go back to him. Alastor is going to torture me."

Sparrow had never left the shadows he'd backed into. He heard Shay's every word. The pain in her voice. Sparrow lacked compassion for most, but Shay didn't deserve this. She'd helped him once. Before he could think longer on the situation, he returned to Heaven in a flash.

Twenty-Eight

Shay landed on her hip when she appeared in Alastor's hovel and her knees gave out from the shock of it all. She cried out in pain, wishing she'd had the forethought to land differently. She hissed and rolled to her stomach, scrambling to stand. Shay got to her knees before a hand was tangling in her hair, pulling her up.

"I've missed you," Alastor said as he pulled her to stand. "What's this?" His hand gripped the collar of her shirt and pulled until two of the buttons popped off.

"You want me naked on the Earthen plane? Imagine what the men there would do." Shay glared at Alastor. She could feel his hot breath on her face as she stared into his dark eyes.

Shay knew she needed to do something different. She wasn't going to be a victim in this. She was stronger and Chel had taught her to fight. Shay needed to manipulate him just like she'd done that night in the dive bar where she'd met Clyburn.

"You used to be nicer to me," Shay reminded Alastor. "At that camp. You made those men stop trying to hurt me. You made me dinner." She searched his eyes and relaxed her face, tried her best to play the innocent fawn.

Alastor stilled as he stared down at her. "And then you burned down my camp and tried to kill me." He shoved her away.

Shay stumbled over a chair that was behind her but was able to stay upright. She glanced toward the door, wondering if she could beat him to it.

"Sit down," he warned. "Don't even think about it. This is your home now. I've marked you, you're mine. You will always re-appear where I am."

Shay's hip burned as he spoke.

"Where were you? Humans can't disappear like that." He sniffed the air. "You smell like the Earthen plane. Like blood and hate." His eyes glimmered with hope that she'd turned just as dark as him since she'd found her home in Hell.

"I follow the Crossroads Demon. I don't know how or why. It just started happening. I can't control it." Shay winced as Alastor threatened to move closer.

Alastor lay his large hands on the table and pointed. "You go to do Crossroads Demon work, then you come back to me." He jabbed the aged table with this index finger. "There's nothing else." He stood to his full height. "Do you understand? Don't linger."

Shay's heart was beating against her ribs. She didn't want to be scared but Alastor was like a drill Sargent and she didn't want to wind up dead by his hands. She glanced at the door one last time and let all of her hope of escape flutter away.

"I understand," Shay said.

———

WEEKS PASSED and Shay wondered why no one had come to find her. Maybe they'd all decided she wasn't worth saving. She knew she'd upset everyone with sneaking out and refusing to let them cut open her scar. But leaving her at the mercy of a Demon was cruel.

She tried to stay strong but the fact that she was alone was tearing her apart.

Alastor always walked the line of barely hospitable and hostile. Sometimes he left for days at a time, returning tired and grumpy. Other days he puttered around the hovel, in and out of his office, making phone calls and dealing deals. He reminded her of a businessman. But then, Alastor *was* a business man. He'd run a human trafficking business between realms for ages. Shay watched him and eavesdropped on every conversation as she did the chores he demanded. Sometimes he simply wanted her to sit and stare, unmoving like a statue. She was bored to tears on those days.

Alastor had given her a room. There was no door and it was across the hall from his, but she had a small bed and a shelf for clothing. He allowed her to shower and eat what she wanted. It was a very confounding situation. He'd threatened her with a lifetime of pain yet treated her like a houseguest most days.

There were nights when he'd come home raging like the Demon that he was. He'd slam doors and punch walls. He'd threaten her, grab at her skin, and promise to do terrible things to her. Shay fought back. She always did. She was puny next to him but she wasn't going to go down without a fight.

"What are you going to do, feeble human?" Alastor's voice was thick with contempt. "I should rip you to shreds."

"What a waste of risking your life to find me then." Shay smirked.

He slapped the scarred brand on her hip and she cried out, scrambling away from him. "I didn't risk shit. That was the simplest task I ever experienced. Getting into the castle was nothing. The Queen of Hell is *weak*. Lucifer would have never allowed that to happen."

She was tempted to stand up for Meg. To tell Alastor that Meg was pregnant, not weak. But Shay was smarter than that. She kept her mouth shut. "You're a fucking bastard," she spat back.

"You have barely broken the surface of what I am." Alastor jabbed a finger to his chest. "You know nothing."

Shay had scratched herself on the table as she scrambled to get away from him and her arm began to bleed.

Alastor's eyes zeroed in on the small drip sliding down her arm. He picked up a chair and slammed it over the table. "Get out of my face and clean yourself," he shouted, throwing the splintered pieces of chair at her.

He didn't have to tell her twice. Shay ran to the bathroom and locked herself inside. She pressed a cloth to her arm until the bleeding stopped, wondering why it had caused such a visceral reaction from him. Then Shay remembered the Hellions who'd come after her for her blood, the way Skeele and Queen Meg acted around each other's blood, and the Hellions drinking from glasses of blood. All these weeks she'd been trapped with him he never took her blood, but always avoided it.

Shay showered then went to her room. The hovel was quiet. Either Alastor had found something to occupy his time or he'd left. Or maybe he was asleep. She took it as time to prepare. Shay dressed then began her nightly exercises. She wasn't going to be weakened by being locked up in this place. She did sit-ups until her stomach ached, pushups until her arms felt like jelly, and lunges until her thighs burned. She'd done this nearly every night, readying herself.

Later, as she lay in bed, thinking about ways to escape, the twinge of pain started in her belly. It was familiar now. Shay sat up and put on her boots. She'd been sleeping fully clothed since Alastor allowed her clothing again. She didn't want any surprises being half dressed. The pain in her stomach intensified; pulled once, twice, three times. Shay disappeared, drawn to whatever crossroads pact was calling her. She smiled inwardly at the thought of seeing Nero again.

Twenty-Nine

Jed was starting to feel the fatigue of walking through Hellscape. He glanced up at Chel only to find the Hellion lowering himself to the ground and walking next to Jed, wings tucked tightly against his back.

"We can stop to rest," Chel suggested.

"I can't leave Shay alone with that scum any longer than necessary." Jed noticed he was breathing heavy–it felt like a boulder was crushing him from above.

"If Nero is on Crossroads Demon work, then Shay is with him," Chel reminded. "We have time until Nero returns."

Jed's face twisted. "Something is not right. He's been gone too long. Would a Crossroads Demon be called away for this long?"

The air felt thick. The gravity of Hell pressed down on his bones. The ochre sun lingered in the sky for an obtrusive amount of time.

Jed paused, rested his hand against a tree trunk. He wiped sweat from his brow. How much time had passed? He wasn't sure. Everything looked familiar and different.

"Have we been here before?" Jed asked.

Chel walked in a tight circle and rubbed his head. "It does look familiar."

Jed crouched and inspected the path just like the Crow men had done. He scanned the ground. "There are no footprints ahead. Old ones behind." He focused, realized their old footprints had filled with dirt and leaves as though days had passed and they hadn't just walked there. "Look," he motioned to Chel.

"Fucking A." Chel pulled his blade, ready to fight.

"Who are you going after?" Jed asked.

"Those bastards at the pub. It was them. I know it."

Static sparked from Jed's fingertips. "Let me try something." He pulled the notebook from his pocket and searched through it for a moment.

"Have you encountered something like this before?" Jed asked.

"Never." Chel was fuming.

"Heard any rumors about this? Is time repeating? What is this we are stuck in? I think time is moving very slowly."

Chel paced, thinking. His arm brushed against a tree, dust fell. Chel stopped moving and felt stiffness in his joints. "It's..."

Chel remained still, slowed his breathing. Dust collected on his shoulders and shoes. He looked up at Jed who was deep in thought reading spells, searching for something to help them out of this, now covered in a layer of white dust. It fluttered away from the pages as he turned them.

"I know of this. It's a potion to slow us. Walking slower and slower on the same path." Chel replaced his blade. "Even if we get back to the pub, much time will have passed." He wiped the white dust off his arm. "We must keep moving before we turn to stone. We must return to the pub and destroy the mother potion."

"How long have we been like this?" Jed tucked his notebook in a pocket.

"If the dust is settling on us, too long. Days. Maybe longer."

The men walked, eager to move, and they noticed that the shadows passing over them were not a bird in the sky but the coming and going of night. They took five footsteps and two nights came and went, maybe longer. It was hard to discern in the state they were in. So much could be missed in a blink.

"I must get to Shay." Jed walked faster but the potion worked in a way that made him continue to move slow. It was a slow rot concoction, one that caused the men to dwindle and wane. It wanted him to stop and rest and turn to stone and decay under the ochre Hellsky. They would never make it back to the pub. It was impossible. They'd be moss covered stone before they got there; joints arthritic and unmoving, minds slowed to molasses. And so, the rescuers needed their own saving.

THIRTY

AT THE CROSSROADS

SPARROW DREW a rune in the dirt and called upon the Crossroads Demon. He shouldn't have meddled, especially since he despised others meddling. It was a task usually reserved for the Deacons but they seemed to have turned a blind eye to the situation. Sparrow crossed his arms and flexed his wings. He shouldn't have had them visible on the Earthen plane, but he was standing in the middle of nowhere and the night breeze felt heavenly between his feathers. He tipped his neck to the side just so until it cracked. He needed more time away. Rebuilding his kingdom was a giant pain in the ass. After the Fast-Zombie War and the Basilisk visit, he barely had any of his own people. Sparrow took his father's throne only to be designated the weakest in the Seven Kingdoms of Heaven. It was embarrassing but utterly no fault of his own. He simply needed to build it up. There were plenty of souls to go around.

His thoughts went to the Demon who had taken Shay. Sparrow could work with that creature to secure souls. Kings before him had done it. No one rose to power without doing some dastardly deeds. No one was pure. Sparrow certainly wasn't. His angelic wholesomeness had been burned out of him by curses and lies and deception.

Nero and Shay arrived with a *crack* and walked closer, confined to the circle of runes he'd drawn.

"I want to make a deal." The night breeze disrupted the way the black feathers laid at the arch of his wings. It made him look disheveled.

"It seems kinda wrong. You're an Angel. A King. Aren't there rules against making deals with Demons?"

Sparrow shrugged. "I don't really care. You're not really a Demon." His eyes narrowed as he noticed her torn clothing, more marks on her arms and legs, and her bandaged arm with drying blood. Sparrow's mouth watered. He swallowed the urge back. "Your boyfriend hasn't found you yet?"

Shay bit her lip, held back tears. She'd cried enough for Jed to find her. But it had been weeks. Something happened to him. She figured he was probably dead. Or he left her. She had never felt more alone.

Shay tipped her chin up. "I don't know where he is."

"That's too bad. I heard a rumor that he's missing." Sparrow's features were impassive.

Tears welled behind Shay's eyes but she refused to let them fall. Daddy raised her to be stronger than this. She was a cowgirl through and through. Daddy taught her to survive the apocalypse if she were all alone; this was nothing. Shay rotated her shoulders and straightened her back.

"You hear a lot of rumors. Now. What do you want?" Shay asked.

Nero whinnied and bobbed his head in agreement.

"A deal against a Demon," Sparrow said.

"We need more details than that."

"Against a Demon who deals in flesh." Sparrow cocked an eyebrow.

"Be more specific."

Sparrow sat in the thick grass and motioned across from him. "Sit with me. Negotiate."

"I don't have time for this." Shay shivered, feeling a chill pass under her skin. She and Nero were getting annoyed with the lack of details.

"You want time for this. Negotiation. Every moment you are here with me, you are not with your captor."

"How heroic of you," Shay said as she swung her leg and climbed down from Nero's back. "I guess this torture is better than the alternative." Shay sat at the edge of the circular rune. Nero lay next to her, facing Sparrow. "Negotiate." She waved her arms open in anticipation like she was accepting a hug from a friend.

Sparrow tapped his chin. "A deal against a Demon who deals in flesh." He paused again, toying.

"I only know of one at the moment."

"You might meet more, soon. If I make a deal with a Crossroads Demon, what will you take from me?" Sparrow asked.

"It is unknown," Shay replied as Nero watched the conversation closely. "Out of the eater will come something to eat. And out of the strong will come something sweet." Shay sighed. "You will be eaten."

Sparrow made a face that indicated the threat didn't sound too terrible and perhaps he'd received worse threats. "To be eaten doesn't mean I must die."

"I don't make the rules, I just live by them." Shay reached to the side and patted Nero absently. "But the others, they have only made a one sided deal, they didn't negotiate for what we would take."

"Their loss," Sparrow said with a smirk. "You can consume something else from me."

"Possibly," Shay said.

"You know, most of these deals you make are simply a transfer of souls. One soul for another. There is balance in the Crossroads deal."

Shay nodded. "It's true."

Sparrow smiled, brought out all the charm until he saw the hitch in her breath. He could indulge, mar her morals, and draw her away from Jed. It would be easy to seduce her. It always was easy to seduce humans. Sparrow released a breath. No, he liked her and that shade of blue hair, but Shay was not his type. Her hair wasn't black, her skin not covered in ink, there was no scar over her heart, and he didn't have the burning desire to stab her so she'd be consumed with revenge and obsessed with him. No, he wouldn't try and seduce her. Shay was someone he needed on his side. She'd have to learn how to walk the tightrope and balance her loyalty to the Queen of Hell and the Raven King.

Shay's soul was the equivalent of diamonds and rubies and piles of gold, and Sparrow was going to find a way to make it his.

THIRTY-ONE

"PUT THIS ON," ALASTOR SAID AS HE STOOD IN THE doorway to Shay's room. He tossed a bag on the floor and checked his watch. "We are leaving in one hour."

"We?" Shay's throat felt dry. She hadn't left the hovel except to go on Crossroads Demon missions. Alastor hadn't been happy that she was gone so long on the last Crossroads deal. It was a gift from the Raven King. One she'd never mention to Alastor. She wasn't sure why Sparrow was so interested in her all of a sudden.

"Get ready." Alastor turned on his heel, crossed the hallway to his room, and closed the door.

Shay moved from the bed and opened the bag. There was a dress inside. She brought it to the bathroom, showered, and slipped the garment on.

The dress was black with rhinestones and had a slit up the thigh, all the way to her hip, showing the rune Alastor had branded her with. She wished she could twist up her hair but she had nothing here. Shay stared at herself in the mirror. In a dress like this, she wasn't sure what to expect. She wished she had makeup. No, change that. She was glad she didn't have makeup. She should rub dirt on her body and wreck her hair and make herself look like a pig in a dress. Whatever Alastor was up to, she didn't want to participate willingly.

Shay opened the bathroom door. Alastor was standing there in a black suit. Waiting.

Shay held her breath and stepped to the side. "Why am I wearing this?" she asked.

"We have a party to attend." Alastor waved her toward the door.

"I don't have any shoes."

"You won't need them."

Shay swallowed hard and her mind traveled at warp speed, imagining scenarios. The split in her dress showed a lot of leg as she walked quickly to keep up with Alastor. She stepped past the threshold to the hovel and paused, taking a deep breath. She had nearly forgotten how the ochre sky glowed, how everything looked so shadowed.

"Come on," Alastor ordered as he walked toward a Jeep.

"You have a car?" Shay asked.

Alastor opened the passenger door and waited. "Most inhabitants of Hell do. We aren't so uncultured, human." He glanced down at her. "I borrowed it." His tone was clipped.

Shay got in the passenger seat and Alastor shoved the door closed before walking around the Jeep and getting in the driver seat.

Shay rubbed her feet on the floor mat, cleaning them of dirt from the walk to the Jeep.

Alastor drove crumbling roads through the mountain. Everything looked unfamiliar yet vaguely familiar. Shay had been told that Hell was nothing more than a dark reflection of the Earthen plane. Maybe she'd been through these mountains before. Shay worried at what awaited her. She never hoped for the Crossroads pact to call her away, but tonight she did. She didn't want to face whatever Alastor had planned.

Shay fidgeted with a rhinestone on her dress and shifted in her seat to relieve the pressure off her branded hip. It ached. She glanced at Alastor. He was focused on the road, the shadows of his face churning as though he were deep in thought. Shay recognized it as the mask of a man preparing to make deals. He warned she'd repay him.

Shay glanced out the window. She wanted to run. She didn't want to repay him with her flesh. Sadness flooded her chest as she thought about Jed and why he hadn't come to find her.

Alastor turned down a long driveway that ended at a black mansion pressed into the forest. There were other vehicles and a steady stream of Demons and strange creatures walking inside. He parked the Jeep and got out.

Alastor opened the passenger side door and waited.

Shay didn't move.

"Get out," he warned.

She shook her head.

Alastor snapped his fingers and the brand on her hip burned like it was new again.

Vehicles filled the parking area. People–no, Demons-walked to the grand front entrance dressed in suits and dresses. Although, Shay noticed, she saw more suits than dresses and wondered why. She'd seen very few Demon females in her time.

The Demon party resembled a gathering of the rich and famous on the Earthen plane, Shay supposed, since she'd never been to a party like that before; she had only seen them on TV and in the movies.

Small creatures carried trays with champagne and food. She tried not to stare at the Demons of all shapes and sizes. Horns and leathered skin met formal suits and dresses. Many turned to watch when Alastor entered with Shay following close behind.

Shay looked down at her bare feet and felt underdressed.

There was conversation, but it sounded strange to Shay's ears. Hellspeak. They were conversing in Hellspeak, a completely different language. She wouldn't have a clue what they were discussing. Shay watched Alastor's facial features to try and guess what he was saying as he greeted a tall Demon with goat-like horns and a white beard. The Demon scrutinized her, an eerie smile on his face. Their Hells-peak sounded garbled and wicked. Goat horns licked his lips with a split tongue.

A shiver tore down Shay's spine. They were watching her, judging. Some walked around her like she was cattle ripe for bidding.

She closed her eyes and wished for that sharp feeling in her gut to pull her away.

It never came.

Someone touched her arm. Shay glanced from the corner of her eye and saw a black nail dragging down her skin. She looked up to a giant Demon with black horns and black claws. He wore a suit with diamond studded lapels.

"We match, don't you think?" the Demon said in English.

"I don't think so," Shay replied, taking a step away, toward Alastor.

A warm arm wrapped around Shay's waist and held on tight.

Alastor said something to the Demon with the diamond lapels that sounded like a joking threat. He squeezed Shay against him.

Shay went stiff. She didn't want Alastor's hands on her. She glanced at the door. Alastor pressed her against him again and sipped at his champagne.

———

THE PARTY WENT ON ENTIRELY TOO long in Shay's opinion. She was glad to be away from the leering gazes and strange fingers stroking her arms like they were testing the thickness of her skin.

"Thank you for finally leaving," Shay said sarcastically as Alastor opened the door to the Jeep.

"I should have stayed. We were taking preliminary bids," Alastor replied.

"On what?"

"You." He smirked darkly. "You're going to help me get the skin trades up and running again. Remember?"

Shay sighed and leaned against the car door. She had to find a way to escape before something terrible happened to her. She needed to escape and find Jed. She was sure no one else would look for him. He'd spend most of his life as a loner; it seemed he never created lasting friendships with anyone. Shay figured that was why their relationship was so touch and go.

"Stop thinking of him," Alastor warned. "You are mine now."

"I don't belong to anyone."

Alastor snapped his fingers and the brand burned.

Shay hissed in pain. "Fine. Ok. Whatever."

Alastor was smirking as he drove, like he had a secret. Like he knew everything.

"What?" Shay demanded.

"I paid some friends to poison them." He checked his watch like he was late for a date. "They're probably turned to stone by now. It's been long enough."

Shay's worse fear had come true. Jed was probably dead and it was Alastor's doing. "You are a fucking bastard," she seethed with all the venom she could muster.

Thirty-Two

At the Crossroads

"What's wrong, boy?" Shay asked as she absently rubbed circles on Nero's shoulder.

He turned his head to look at her, his eyes glassy.

"Are you sad?" Shay asked. "I'm sad too." She leaned forward to lay across his neck. "I'm so lonely and scared."

Nero whinnied something forlorn and gnashed his teeth together. He sent emotion down the tether that bound them, hoping she might understand why he hadn't attempted to save her yet. It was too dangerous; they'd die without Jed and the Hellion.

Shay stilled for a moment as she processed.

"Have you been searching for Jed?"

Nero wagged his head in a yes motion.

"Stop looking," Shay warned. "He's dead. Alastor had him poisoned. Said he's turned to stone. It's just me and you now."

Nero looked away. Although the sound of having Shay to himself was exquisite, he knew it wasn't right. They both needed Jed to make

757

it through this. Nero pawed the ground with a front hoof. He wasn't so sure Jed was gone.

At the desolate crossroads where the boundary between the mortal realm and the abysmal depths blurred, Shay was caught between two worlds, her presence a haunting reminder of the fragile balance between light and darkness.

The air crackled with an ominous energy as the figure approached the crossroads, their steps hesitant yet filled with a sense of desperate determination. They bore the weight of something heavy upon their shoulders, their gaze haunted by the specter of tragedy that loomed over their existence.

It was a Deacon.

Nero backed up.

Shay tensed.

Deacons were the gatekeepers of balance between the Seven Kingdoms of Heaven, the Earthen plane, and Hell. Why did one summon Shay and Nero?

"What is it that you seek, Deacon?" Shay asked.

The Deacon hesitated, their gaze flickering with uncertainty before they spoke, voice tinged with a mixture of power and desperation.

"No one can know that I'm here," the Deacon said.

Shay nodded. "Is that your deal?"

"No." the Deacon folded his hands. "This deal will be a great burden for both of us."

The Deacon kept looking over his shoulder and to the desert beyond. He'd drawn them to a crossroads in the middle of nowhere. They could see for miles even with only moonlight.

"There is a great darkness coming," the Deacon warned.

"That sounds like a warning, not a deal. Why did you call me here?" Shay didn't want to return to Alastor but she didn't want her time wasted by this creature.

The Deacon paused and closed his eyes, finding calm and choosing his words carefully. "The deal is, you must take the children to safety and tell no one where they are. You must hide them until Clea's prophecy comes to fruition."

"What children?"

The Deacon held up a finger. "They are not born yet. When the time comes, you will know. You must agree to this now, before it's too late."

"What are you wishing to give me?" Shay asked, knowing that what the Crossroads Demon would take was not negotiable and typically unknown.

"I will give my life. Sooner rather than later."

Shay searched his face. He was so plain there was no way she'd be able to tell who he was, but that was the way of the Deacons. They looked the same, sounded the same. They could blend into a crowd and never be seen again. Once he left, Shay knew they'd have a hard time finding him again.

The rings on Nero's ear and Shay's hand shimmered with agreement.

Shay held out her hand and the Deacon reached forward to shake on the deal.

"Why here?" Shay asked. "Why not come to me in Hell?"

"This is God's land," the Deacon said. "I needed witness that I tried to prevent what was coming. God must know we tried." His hands shook.

Shay wasn't sure why she'd become the resident babysitter in Hell. First Thrush and now this. But she wouldn't let children suffer; couldn't.

The Deacon nodded then backed away. There was no portal in the desert, no water, nothing. The Deacon just walked away across the sand until his figure wavered like a mirage and eventually disappeared.

"Whatever that was all about, I hope you're there to help me." Shay rubbed Nero's neck.

He huffed and scraped his hoof over the markings on the ground, releasing them. Shay was grateful she didn't have to kill anyone tonight.

"Run, boy," Shay whispered.

Nero took off, only stopping when he reached their valley.

Sparrow didn't appear from the shadows near the valley like before. There was only the hushed lapping of lake water, the gentle song of crickets, the warm summer breeze. Perhaps the Deacon scared him off?

"I don't want to go back," Shay said to Nero, rubbing her cheek against his neck.

The brand on her hip didn't listen. She returned to the hovel with a sickening feeling in her gut that had nothing to do with the travel from the Earthen plane to Hell.

Thirty-Three

Alastor was waiting, dressed in a black suit, hair styled, and smelling like fresh brimstone.

"Put this on," Alastor said as he tossed Shay a garment. This was becoming too familiar. Twice now: the same motion, the same orders.

Shay rubbed thin fabric between her fingertips. She started to make her way to the bathroom.

"No," Alastor said, "here, now. Put it on. We're late."

Shay didn't want to get naked in front of the Demon. He'd seen everything she had to offer before but it was a precarious position to be in. She took off her shirt, dropped it to the floor and pulled the garment over her head. It was another dress, this one shorter than before; silver, and with another slit up the hip. She shimmied her pants off and stood with her spine straight for Alastor's inspection, the scar on her thigh visible for all to see.

Alastor circled her. He was too close, his breath sifting across her skin. He had a knife, always carried one now. Something old. He pressed it against the scar on her thigh.

"We still haven't talked about this."

"Leave it alone." Shay met his gaze. "Please," she said through gritted teeth as memories of people she'd considered friends held her down to cut it open.

"My associates are going to want answers. They don't want skin with ugly scars like this." He pressed the tip of the knife to the jagged disfigurement. "I should cut it off."

He was too close and probably heard Shay swallow hard at the mention of what he'd like to do.

"Your *associates* should be happy with what they get." Shay's skin felt tight and she wanted nothing more than to go to sleep after crying on Nero's shoulder for the past hour.

"They bring the money to help pay off your debt. I'll bring them what they wish." Alastor removed the knife tip from her skin and secured the blade under his suit jacket. "Let's go."

As much of a bastard as Alastor was, he held the door for her as they exited the hovel. He opened the passenger door of the Jeep and waited for her to sit before closing it. He treated her as equal parts something precious and something despised.

Alastor took the same route to the black mansion in the woods. They were much later than last time, the only ones crossing the parking pad and walking to the giant glass door.

All heads turned when Alastor entered and stepped to the side. Some Demons licked their lips, nearly all stared. Shay felt naked in the thin, revealing dress.

Alastor led Shay down a hallway with a winding stairwell with black marble and deep red carpet. He stopped in what looked like a dining room with three pedestals. Two women were standing on the pedestals, each wearing a dress similar to Shay's. They had shoes.

"Get up there," Alastor ordered.

Shay walked, silently in her bare feet, and stepped up onto the pedestal in the middle. She met the gazes of the other women. They were young, beautiful and... human.

A sickening feeling tore at Shay's stomach as Alastor walked closer, looking like the predator that he was.

"What are you doing?" Shay asked. "Humans aren't supposed to be in this realm."

"But look at you here. Now, shut up." Alastor walked around the other women first, inspecting and nodding approval. "These ladies might be able to teach you a few things about being on display for the bidders."

Neither said a word; they both faced forward, dead-eyed grins on their faces when Alastor tested their resilience by touching their skin, their hair, their breasts. He licked their shoulders and smelled them loudly.

Shay shivered, disgusted.

"Don't do that, Shay," Alastor warned. "Be still, like these ones." There was a knock on the door to the room. "Be grateful that you're alive and I don't let these Demons do what they want." Alastor flashed a fiery gaze before he went and opened the door. "You are a delicacy to them. They'd eat you whole."

The Demons entered the room, taking seats in the chairs surrounding the pedestals.

Shay realized what was happening. This was an auction. She swallowed hard and tipped her chin up. She focused on the wall in the distance and did her best to hide her fear. She was looking for an escape but soon realized she'd never get out of this room with all the Demons that filled it.

Garbled speech echoed in her ears as the Demons chatted in Hellspeak.

Shay closed her eyes, only opening them again when she heard Alastor's voice. He started auctioning off the girl on the left first. Hands rose, money was promised. Shay watched the girl pose demurely, making eye contact with the Demons raising flags and the ones who'd placed bets prior. She was edging them to pay more and more until it was finally over. Something similar happened to the girl on her right. Flags raised in eager bidding. The girl posed like a model for a fashion shoot, engaging the crowd.

And then it was Shay's turn. Alastor was standing close, touching her hair and making comments that she couldn't understand. Alastor's hand reached for her face, his index finger and thumb forcing her lips into a smile.

The crowd laughed.

Shay forced a smile and froze her chin to stop it from quivering. Too many flags were raised. Alastor was talking fast in their language. She didn't know what the garbled speech meant, but there was a joking tone and laughter from the crowd as he clearly said things about her.

Someone pointed to Shay's thigh.

Alastor's hand smoothed over her leg, rubbing it. Shay hated that she found his touch comforting, possibly even grounding. She hated him but she knew no one, knew nothing. She told herself that he'd treat her kindly, that he wouldn't let the others hurt her. It was an inner mantra of lies that kept her standing on two feet. She was afraid she'd collapse if she focused on all the terrible things that were going to happen to her. She blinked back a tear and prayed Daddy never got wind of this. He'd be so disappointed to see how far she'd fallen after all he'd taught her to stay alive.

When the auction was over, the Demons filed out of the room. The girls stood, waiting.

Alastor handed glasses of champagne to the other two and dismissed them to a door at the back of the room. He had two glasses of champagne in his hands as he approached Shay.

"Well, the bidding didn't get as high as I would have liked, but it's a good start." He moved the flutes to one hand and reached up, offering his free hand to support Shay as she stepped down from the pedestal.

"Cheers." He handed her champagne.

Shay hesitated, her heart beating wildly against her ribs. She had the slight feeling that she might faint.

"Drink it," Alastor ordered. "It will take the edge off."

The last time Shay had champagne, she was celebrating Meg's release at the castle. That was the night Jed danced with her and kissed her for all to see, claiming her. The sweet smell of the champagne brought it all crashing back. It seemed like forever ago. And now he was dead.

She threw her head back and downed the entire glass in two swallows.

Alastor was sipping at his flute, brows raised. "Should I be impressed or concerned?"

"Fuck right off." Shay threw the flute on the floor and watched it shatter against the marble tiles.

Shay's head felt foggy.

"I expected you to nurse that for a bit. Guess we'll head to the next stop."

Shay stumbled. "What are you talking about?"

Alastor grabbed her upper arm to steady her. "It's time to deliver you to the highest bidder." He checked his watch. "Paid a premium price for five hours. Better get you there before the drugs wear off."

Shay's vision blurred. The bastard had drugged her. She slapped at him as she stumbled to keep up with his pace. Shay tripped once and Alastor lifted her off her feet, carrying her. She could feel the cool air on her ass cheeks as her dress stretched against his arms. But Shay didn't care because her body felt warm and her lower abdomen filled with an ache that she needed to satisfy.

Shay didn't see the Demons watching Alastor carry her out of the black mansion with envy. They licked their lips and touched themselves. They reached for her and Alastor growled like the wild beast he was to keep them at a distance.

He tucked Shay into the passenger seat of the Jeep, buckled her seatbelt, and closed the door.

Her figure was slouched in the front seat as he got behind the wheel and started driving away. He calculated how long the drugs might last, since Shay unexpectedly downed all of them in one swallow. She was supposed to sip demurely, like a lady, so the drugs would enter her system slowly. Alastor glanced at her, the scar on her thigh illumined by moonlight. Her skirt was cinched around her waist, leaving nothing to the imagination. Alastor smirked to himself, glad that he'd arranged the death of her boyfriend. The trash didn't deserve her. Alastor decided, when she was done making him money, he'd keep her. He'd always wanted to. Alastor had caught the change in her demeanor when he'd touched her scarred thigh during the auction. She'd calmed, her heart rate had slowed, she trusted him. Not much but enough to make a difference.

He touched her leg again now as he drove.

Shay startled and mumbled, her foggy mind trying to make sense of where she was.

Shay noticed the hand on her leg and looked up. "How much did you get for me?"

"Not nearly as much as you need to pay your debt to me," Alastor replied with a smirk. "But it's a start."

Shay made a noise deep in her throat.

"Don't worry, he'll be gentle with you." Alastor squeezed Shay's leg and chuckled coldly.

Rage filled Shay's bones. She had nothing left to lose. Shay lurched forward, grabbed the steering wheel, and jerked it to the side as hard as she could.

The Jeep veered off the crumbling mountain road. It rolled, over and over and over as it fell to the ravine below.

Thirty-Four

At the Crossroads

Shay never felt the familiar tug in her gut as she was called to the crossroads. She arrived aching, dirty, covered in blood, and her dress torn. Rolling onto the ground as though she fell from the sky, she stopped abruptly as she hit the edge of the crossroads summoning rune.

"What the fuck happened to you?" Sparrow asked.

"It was a car accident." Shay adjusted her dress.

"Is that blood?" he asked.

"It's not mine," Shay replied as she searched her body for injuries and rolled to sit up.

"That's not reassuring."

"I might have some bruises. Good thing I was wearing my seat-belt." Shay smiled weakly as she leaned against Nero for support.

"Wash that blood off," Sparrow demanded.

"I don't see a nice little bathroom anywhere around here so this is what you get." Shay held her sore arm and thought about sitting down.

"Over there." Sparrow was pointing to the lake.

"I can't leave the circle," Shay reminded him.

"Make a deal with me and leave it." Sparrow smirked.

"Fine. What do you want?" she asked.

Sparrow toyed with the edge of his wings. "I need the feather of a night owl. Just one or two will do."

Shay's eyes narrowed. "What exactly is a *night owl*?"

"It's related to the snowy owl. I'm sure you can figure it out." Sparrow's brow rose. "Are you going to leave the circle?"

"You want the feathers now?" Shay asked.

"Nah, later." It was a riddle she needed to solve, and Sparrow knew it would take time. He wasn't in a rush. He needed time for everything to fall into place.

Nero's ears twitched in agreement and Shay felt the golden ring on her hand surge with excitement.

"Fine." Shay held out a dusky hand with long necrotic fingernails. She shivered as she saw it, something grotesque and cursed. She blinked and her hand returned to normal.

Sparrow didn't seem bothered as he shook on the deal.

"See, that wasn't so hard." Sparrow moved to the side as Shay left the rune circle, Nero close behind her. "Next we work on the big deal." He spread is arms wide. "It's gonna be huge."

"Uh-huh." Shay said absently as she crouched near the lake and washed the blood off her arms with cold water.

Sparrow leaned back, crossing his long legs in front of him and propping himself up with his elbows. He looked too relaxed. But Shay was sure the Raven King didn't have much to fear with the power she could feel radiating off him.

Shay left the pond, Nero close behind her. They settled on the tall grass near Sparrow.

Nero folded his legs to lay down and snacked on the Earthen

plane grass, taking special interest in the purple flowers. He closed his eyes as he chewed, savoring the flavor of spring time.

Shay tore long pieces from their roots and began braiding them. Her arms were sore and her ribs ached. Shay wasn't sure how many times the Jeep had rolled after she pulled the wheel. She'd been pulled away before it stopped. She hoped Alastor was dead.

Shay leaned back, her head resting on Nero's flank as he ate.

"Did you call me here just to hang out?" Shay asked.

"We made a deal and we have another deal to discuss."

"Ah, yes, the Demon." Her deft fingers braided another cluster of grass blades.

"I want the Demon." Sparrow's voice was without inflection.

"And my payment?" Shay asked. "Nero's? This is a huge request. Usually people just want someone killed. You're asking for an entire being."

Something sparked in her mind. Jed.

"Ask," Sparrow replied.

"Jed is dead. Alastor had him killed."

Sparrow frowned. "Are you sure?"

"When a Demon such as Alastor tells me he paid his little Demon buddies to kill my boyfriend, I believe him."

"But do you believe that Jed's actually dead?"

Shay shrugged and swallowed back tears.

"You love him?" Sparrow asked.

"I'm mad at him for not doing the right thing so many times. But yes, I love him. I can forgive him for the things we need to work on together."

Sparrow was silent for a long while before he said, "You know when souls die they go to Meg's plane. They go to a Safe House for sorting or repenting. For deciding where their final resting place will be. Heaven or Hell or the Astral plane."

"So he's still in Hell if he's dead?"

Sparrow cleared his throat. "There's one more piece to the puzzle. Since he's half angel, he could go elsewhere, he could not actually die." Sparrow was watching her. "Did Jed tell you who his father is? That little detail might make a difference."

Shay shook her head. "Do you know?" she asked.

"I don't." Sparrow lay back, threading his fingers behind his head and watching the stars twinkle above them in the night.

"You have power," Shay said. "You can do things, make deals of your own." She sighed. "I need you to find Jed for me. Whatever is left of him."

"I want the Demon to be compelled to follow my every order." Sparrow moved an arm, plucking at the grass.

"You want a Demon slave?" Shay asked. "For how long?"

"Forever."

"And you'll do what I asked?" Shay was wary. She knew better than to trust the Raven King but this was imperative.

"Yes."

Shay looked at Nero and a silent agreement of the proposed deal passed between them. She scooted closer to Sparrow and held out her hand. "Deal."

"Deal." Sparrow shook her hand, his grip harder than before, a shine in his eyes. "One last thing." Sparrow jerked her closer until she could feel his breath on her face. "I find Jed, I get something from you."

Shay's eyes searched his face. She was beginning to realize that deals with the Raven King would never end. She was being pulled into his tangled web and this was probably why Jed had tried to hide her from Sparrow when they were searching for him in California. The Raven King was nothing more than a deadly spider lying in wait. There was so much about Heaven and Hell that Shay didn't know. She was ignorant to the way things worked, but she knew one thing: she loved Jed and she needed to know where he was, she needed to know if he could be brought back like Nightingale. She'd do anything. He was all she had, after all.

"What else do you want?" Shay asked.

"Your soul is mine when you die."

Shay swallowed hard. Nero whinnied behind her and moved to his feet. He was pawing at the ground and wagging his head.

"Tell your Demon horse to move back," Sparrow warned.

Shay held out her free hand, urging Nero to keep his distance.

"Your soul?" Sparrow repeated.

"Yes."

His grip was too tight, the bones of her fingers rubbed.

"Are you ever going to tell me this Demon's name or do I have to figure that out myself?" Shay asked.

"Alastor." Sparrow smiled.

THIRTY-FIVE

ALASTOR WAS BANDAGING HIS ARM WHEN SHAY APPEARED in the hovel. Just like he'd promised, she always came back to him.

"I should destroy you," he snorted. "You nearly got us fucking killed." His voice was too calm for what she'd done.

Shay said nothing, simply stood still as a statue in her torn dress that was coated in dirt and blood.

"Are you injured?" Alastor asked.

"I didn't think you'd care." Shay's body was sore all over, the deal with Sparrow fresh in her mind.

He was scanning her as he spoke. "I'm not sure you realize how much you've cost me with your little attempt to kill us both." Alastor threw down a rag and stood. "We missed your appointment. I had to make promises that I couldn't afford. I had to make the other girls do double duty." He glanced at his watch. "You've been gone for hours."

Shay shrugged. "When they call at the crossroads, I must go."

"We'll have to fix that."

Shay felt weary after all she'd been through the past evening. She stumbled to the table where Alastor was standing, dragged a chair out and sat.

"I didn't say you could sit," Alastor sneered. "Get up."

Shay took a deep breath. "I literally can't." She held her hand up and showed that it was shaking.

Alastor was fuming as he went to the kitchen and opened the fridge. He slammed the glass on the countertop as he took out orange juice and filled it.

Shay closed her eyes for just a moment, afraid she'd fall asleep and then he'd do something terrible to her. She opened her eyes again as footsteps neared.

Alastor was close. "Drink this."

Shay stared at the glass. She didn't want to drink it, but she was hungry and tired, and she feared what Alastor would do if she disobeyed him again.

Shay slowly sipped at the juice. "You have oranges in Hell?"

"We have more than you know." He waited, standing entirely too close to her, smelling like a bonfire and whiskey and dried blood.

Shay felt better as the juice settled in her stomach. When she set the glass on the table, Alastor took it away and washed it.

He was standing near the sink, clothing rumpled, hair a mess, looking completely opposite the well-dressed Demon who'd started the night. Alastor's hands gripped the countertop like he was waiting for something.

"What?" Shay asked. "You want to punish me? I'd rather be dead than sold to a Demon. I'd do it again. *I'll do it again.*" She pointed at him. "I can promise..." Shay's tongue felt too big for her mouth and her mind went fuzzy. It was the same way she felt at the black mansion after Alastor had drugged her.

He smiled.

Shay should have known better. She'd never accept food or drink from him again. She kicked the chair back and stood, wobbly on her feet.

"I told you that you'd pay off your debt." He pushed away from the counter. "One way or another."

Shay shook her head to chase away the fog, felt her body go loose.

Heat flooded her limbs. That itch in her lower belly ached, begged to be sated.

No. No. Shay tried to tell herself. *It's the drugs. It's not you. It's not him.*

The problem was, she didn't protest as he lifted her. She didn't move her arm as he draped it over his neck.

"I told myself I wouldn't test these goods until after. But since you're so intent on killing yourself and me, I'll do it now, before it's too late." Alastor's voice was smooth as silk, dark as night, sharp as the blade he kept under his suit jacket.

Shay heard the sound of a door being kicked open–her room didn't have a door. They were in his room.

She closed her eyes and tried to right her brain, tried to talk herself awake and into the right mind. Nothing worked. Heat flowed through her veins as the drugs spread.

Alastor settled her on the bed and tugged her body until she lay in the center. He kicked off his fancy shoes and undid his tie, tossing it toward the pillows.

Shay could only watch, groggy, and limbs heavy as cement.

He kicked off his pants, tossed his suit jacket and tore the buttons on his shirt, leaving it open. Alastor was a Demon, but his body was hard and muscled like a bodybuilder; tall but not too bulky. The hollows and planes of his body were on full display.

Shay looked away. She didn't want to see him, didn't want to see what he was going to do to her. She focused on the dark wood of the furniture, the black sheets, the red satin pillows. Anything but him.

The bed dipped as he crawled. She felt his tongue on her ankle. Felt his hand wrap around and tug her leg to the side. A small noise escaped her throat.

Alastor chuckled as he continued to climb up her body. "You're so small," he whispered against her thigh. "Those bastards at the auction would have torn you apart."

"Go away," Shay forced out.

"You smell like the Earthen plane. Like true sunshine. Yellow and crisp." He ran his lips across her unscarred thigh. "Always have. Guess that's what makes you so valuable. You don't smell like Hell. Not entirely at least. Just a little bit right here." He licked her scar. "And here." He grabbed a strand of her long blue hair and tugged.

He reached for her dress and tore it up from the hem. "You've cost me so much money."

Shay fought her muscles, tried to get her legs to move.

"Don't fight me, Shay." His tongue was on her belly, licking upward. "It will be easier this way. You'll understand punishment and behave." He tore her dress further until it was shredded.

Underneath the haze of the drugs, Shay's body was panicking. She didn't want Alastor to touch her like this. Didn't want to come to the full realization that she was nothing but commercial flesh to the Demons of Hell now.

If she could puke she would.

Alastor grabbed the tie from where he'd thrown it near the pillows. He was straddling her hips and she could see the bulge under his boxers. He took her arm and wrapped the tie around her wrist, forming a loose knot. He slid the tie up her arm and tightened it.

He was reaching for the nightstand. Shay heard the clank of metal and glass. She summoned enough energy to turn her head and watch as he prepared a needle and vial.

"No," Shay forced out.

Alastor sat back, trapping Shay underneath him. He bent, his face too close to hers. Warm breath brushed her neck as his arm pressed across her collarbone. She couldn't move, could barely breathe. He stretched her arm out with the tie, tightened it more, then slapped the crook of her arm.

"There we go." Alastor was whispering something in Hellspeak as the glass clanged.

Then, she felt a pinch and opened her eyes to see red liquid fill the vial. Alastor was taking her blood.

When Alastor pulled the needle out, he was greedy, pressing his lips to the crook of her arm as it bled, sucking and licking until the puncture wound clotted, leaving a bruise on her pale skin. Shay's arm ached from how tightly he'd tied her arm. She tried to wiggle her fingers, but all she could feel was pins and needles from lack of blood in her arm... and his mouth. It was hot and soft and made that burning in her pelvis ignite. She hated it. All of it. Everything. The betrayal of her body, even though it was the drugs.

Alastor stretched to set the needle on the nightstand, his forearm finally releasing her chest so she could take a full breath. Shay was still pinned underneath him as he straddled her and held up the vial of blood.

"I told myself I wouldn't do this again." He glanced at her, licked his lips before throwing back the vial and drinking her blood. "Ah," Alastor groaned as he pressed the heel of his hand against his forehead. He threw the vial and it broke against the wall.

Shay had to admit, there was something sexy watching the Demon fall apart because of her. Alastor was always in control. Always. But it seemed once he swallowed her blood, he lost it. His eyes glazed over, his hips rocked like someone was riding him, his hands stretched into his hair, and there were drops of blood on his lips. This went on for a few minutes and Shay could only watch wide-eyed, feeling like she was at a male strip club and getting the lap dance of the century. Her blood burned, her body ached. She wanted him to touch her but hated him, never wanted to be in his presence ever again.

But then, Alastor's body went limp. His shoulders slumped and he fell to the side.

He'd fallen asleep in a drugged haze.

Shay exhaled a breath, more thankful than she'd ever been in her entire life as Alastor's still body lay next to hers, his mouth against her shoulder. She lay motionless until the drugs wore off and she could move her body. Little by little she shifted so as not to wake Alastor. She loosened the tie from her arm and flexed her fingers until the blood began flowing.

Shay scooted, inch by inch toward the edge of the mattress. Alastor shifted. Shay went still.

"Where do you think you're going?" he grabbed her wrist and pulled it toward his mouth. His eyes fluttered closed.

Shay was still as stone, waiting. His mouth on her wrist was all she could feel. His lips felt nothing like Jed's.

Warm tears dripped down Shay's face and into her hair. For the first time since Alastor had told her that Jed was dead, she cried. As silently as she could muster, the tears flowed and soaked her hair and the blanket under her head. All these days she'd tried not to think about how she'd lost everyone. Daddy, Momma, her home, and now Jed. Sure their relationship hadn't been easy, especially lately, but they had each other and he'd promised to do better. At least he was trying and so was she.

A stomach full of drugged blood kept Alastor asleep for the night. The Demon didn't notice the second time when Shay slipped her hand from his and edged herself away from him until her feet touch the floor. She stood at the foot of the bed, her gaze spanning the room, looking for something that could be of use. There was nothing. Whatever weapons Alastor had in the hovel, they weren't here.

Shay made her way toward the door, wiped her eyes, and left the room holding the tattered edges of her dress together.

THIRTY-SIX

NERO COULDN'T FIND JED OR CHEL. LAST HE'D SEEN THEM they were on the road and Nero had been called to make a deal on the Earthen plane. He'd searched the area where he'd left Jed but there was no one, only the infrequent Demon or dead soul wandering.

Nero needed help and there was only one place he could go. He galloped full speed ahead toward the castle. Head down and hooves beating the road, he ran past mountains and valleys and Demon towns. He passed Safe Houses filled with Deacons and freshly dead souls repenting. He passed hordes of zombies who'd missed their chance to repent and were stuck and rotting in Hell. He passed familiar roads and towns until he could finally see the castle in the burning caves.

Nero slowed at the driveway and the Hellions let him pass. He went to the courtyard and whinnied loudly, hoping someone would come out as he called over and over again.

The sun was coming up and Nero was getting antsy. He went to the large wooden door and kicked at it, neighing louder and more frequently. He kicked so hard splinters of wood popped off the door and littered the courtyard.

It finally opened.

The Hellion named Klaus was there, white beard and horns and looking extra grumpy.

Nero waved his head and snapped his teeth.

Klaus said something in Hellspeak. Unfortunately Nero couldn't speak that language either. He stomped his hooves and wagged his head toward the driveway, bit at Klaus's shirt and tried to drag him.

"Nah, don't do that beast." Klaus pushed his nose away. "Let me get the boss."

Nero paced the courtyard as he waited for the Hellions to return.

When he heard voices behind him, Nero turned to see a group of people. The Hellion Commander Skeele was there standing protectively close to Meg.

"What's with the horse?" Meg asked.

"He's acting strange," Klaus replied, tugging on his shirt. "Tried to tug me down the road."

Skeele stepped closer to Nero and held out a hand. "What's the problem? Where are Jed and Chel?"

Nero whinnied, wagged his head toward the road again. He trotted in a circle and tried to get them to follow but the Hellions and their Queen wouldn't budge.

"He's trying to tell us something," Meg said. "Something must've happened."

"Nero wouldn't leave Shay," Skeele said as he rubbed his chin.

Nero nickered and bobbed his head toward the road but they weren't understanding a thing.

"I think he wants us to go with him," Meg finally said.

Yes! Yes! Nero reared up the tiniest bit and whinnied with joy before turning away and galloping down the driveway. He paused to turn. No one was following.

Nero's only conclusion was that this group was too stupid to understand. Idiots, just staring. Had they never seen an animal trying to tell them something? Had they never watched Lassie? Nero had in the early days when Shay was nursing him back to life and Daddy and Momma let her bring him into the farmhouse. If people could understand a dog why couldn't they understand him?

Nero galloped back toward everyone and stared. Communication was getting him nowhere. They were idiots as far as he was concerned. This was pointless.

"He wants someone to go," Meg said, pointing down the road. She walked closer to Nero and touched his shoulder. "Show me."

Nero stared for a moment into her eyes then turned, leading her away.

"You can't go," Skeele said as he strode to Meg's side.

"Someone has to," Meg said. "I ordered that Shay not be harmed and look what's happened. She's been kidnapped and you only allowed a skeleton crew to go find her."

Skeele stepped in front of Meg to stop her. "You can't go in your condition." He motioned to her abdomen. "You are staying here. They can figure it out."

"Send more Hellions," Meg said.

"No. They stay here to protect you." Skeele crossed his arms, holding his ground.

Meg mimicked his stance. "We owe it to Shay. She stood in for me when I was imprisoned; she put her life on the line for me. For us."

"And how do you think Shay would feel if something happened to you after she risked her life to save you?" Skeele asked.

Nero looked at Meg. She was pregnant. No, this wouldn't do. Nero wouldn't bring the pregnant Queen of Hell on a rescue mission.

Nero whinnied a goodbye and galloped away. He needed help but Queen Meg and her Hellion Commander were too much drama for him to deal with. He shook his head in disgust. He missed the simpleness of life on the ranch when the greatest dilemma was Momma asking the ranch hands what they wanted for dinner and they muttered on and on about fried chicken and grilled steak and macaroni and cheese until she gave up and just made whatever she felt like. She always gave Nero a plate in secret on the back porch while everyone else was gathered around the dinner table. Yes, he missed the simple days.

Nero heard the beating of wings as Hellions took to the sky following him. He didn't bother to look up and see who it was.

Nero and Shay had gotten through plenty in their lives, this was just one more hurdle. Nero didn't need the others. He'd figure this out himself, just like when he hunted down Clyburn and killed him.

THIRTY-SEVEN

MORNING BROUGHT SHAME FROM ONLY ONE OF THE parties. It wasn't Alastor. He was looking thoughtful as he chewed his breakfast and drank his coffee.

Shay had cooked for him, not because she wanted to but because it was expected of her.

Shay was sore and tired and felt as though she'd participated in something dirty and disgraceful. It wasn't by choice, but she felt shameful.

Alastor was vibrant and filled with energy. She assumed it had something to do with the blood he'd ingested. The shadows that lingered on his face were set and calm, revealing a Demon that some might consider handsome. He was freshly showered and had combed back his dark hair. He'd dressed in a black suit and looked ready to head out to business meetings for the day.

"I have a better plan now." Alastor wagged his fork in Shay's direction. "Now that I've tasted the goods." He winked and the shadows on his face darkened.

The interaction looked very much like a business proposition and Shay was sure Alastor had more than enough experience to con someone into agreeing with him.

Shay set her fork down, feeling disgusted.

"I think I'd like to keep you for myself. There are other things we can sell." He was focused on the bruise in the crook of her arm. "Your blood will replenish but other things won't." His dark eyes roamed over her as she stood to clear her dishes. "One of them could hurt you once they got a taste and then you'd be no use to me dead."

Shay washed her dishes in the sink and thought about how she might be able to kill Alastor. There were plenty of knives for cooking. She scanned the drawers wondering where he'd pulled the drugs from last night.

———

SHAY DIDN'T EXPECT it when Alastor left for the entire day. She was alone. Shay occupied her time with sleeping and snooping. She searched every drawer in the hovel, every closet. She found a book with runes and strange writing in Alastor's room. In his bathroom she found baggies of white powder behind the mirror. She took one and hid it in her pocket.

"What are you doing in here?" Alastor's voice said from behind her.

Shay stilled. "Cleaning." She turned with a cloth in her hand and pretended to wipe down the countertop.

"You're not the maid." Alastor was watching her warily.

"I was bored."

Alastor's brow rose and his lips tipped up. "If you're bored, there's plenty we can do."

"Not that bored." She moved to escape the bathroom but his big body blocked her.

"This is a good a place as any." He pointed to the counter. "Sit."

"I'd rather leave. I'm tired." Shay stepped to the side. She heard the clang of metal and glass and looked toward his hand. He wanted blood.

"You can sleep after."

"No."

"Sit." His gaze was threatening. "Sit or I will make you sit."

Shay watched him warily. He no doubt had been wheeling and dealing all day long. He probably made some promises that he now had to deliver on them.

"I don't like this," Shay warned as she backed up, her back hitting the ledge of the counter.

"Doesn't matter." Alastor washed his hands in the sink and dried them on a clean towel from the shelf. It was a very human thing to do, almost clinical. And while Shay appreciated it, she still didn't like it.

"Sit. Now." Alastor demanded, his deep voice rising a few octaves.

Shay slid up on the counter and waited.

He didn't use a tie this time, he had a long piece of elastic which he knotted above her elbow.

Shay noticed four glass vials as she tried to ignore the pinch of the elastic.

"Don't move." Alastor positioned his body between her legs and leaned forward, crowding her. He pulled Shay's arm straight before sticking her with the needle.

Alastor filled the vials, hesitated for a moment before unknotting the elastic. He didn't have a bandage. Shay felt his mouth on her arm, his hot tongue on the spot where he'd punctured her skin.

Shay thought of Meg and Skeele and their blood bond. She closed her eyes. Shay didn't want that, definitely not with Alastor. She leaned away and considered a future in which she pretended to enjoy this and him and what he'd make her do. Shay couldn't see it.

His heat left her and Shay opened her eyes. Alastor had walked into his bedroom and retrieved a package.

"Put this on." He collected the vials of blood and tucked them into a leather case. "We have another party tonight."

Shay slid off the counter, feeling wobbly. She gripped the edge of the counter and steadied herself before taking the package and heading to her bathroom.

The dress was black, again, with a swirling embroidered pattern that looked like vines. It was sleeveless with a high neck, a slit to her hip that showed his brand marked on her skin.

Shay waited in the living room of the hovel until Alastor appeared at the front door. Apparently he'd left her alone while she readied herself.

"Do I get shoes tonight?" Shay asked.

"No." Alastor motioned for her to move. He led her to a different black Jeep. She was sure the other one was totaled after she'd made him drive it off the road and down the ravine. "Get in the back." Alastor's lips were pressed in a line. "I'd much rather have you in the front where I can see you, but I don't trust you after last time."

He drove to the black mansion again. There was a line of Demons entering. Alastor parked and got Shay out. She hissed as the sharp rocks from the driveway tore at her bare feet.

"I'll carry you." It was a command not an offer. "Can't have you bleeding all over the floor."

Alastor lifted Shay like she weighed nothing. She didn't want to touch him but for fear of falling, stretched an arm across his shoulders and gripped his suite jacket. He stopped just before the path turned smooth and set her down.

Shay flinched as the sharp rocks cut into her feet.

"Changed my mind," Alastor whispered. "You'll see why. Stay next to me, don't wander."

Since Alastor was considerably much taller than Shay, she had to skip to keep up with his stride and that only deepened the cuts on her feet. When they reached the steps to the black mansion, Shay was leaving bloody footprints everywhere she went.

It didn't take long to see what Alastor's plan was. There was no shame when the Demons at the party bent to swipe at her bloody footprints and taste. Shay was reminded of that brutal night in the barn when the Hellion recruits had come for her. She scanned the party. There had to be a hundred Demons packed in to the mansion. There was no saving her here. She moved closer to Alastor and he smirked as he chatted with two male Demons, glancing at her from the corner of his eye.

Alastor paraded Shay into every room, and in every room she left bloodied footprints. It felt very deliberate to Shay and she didn't like the feeling she got as some of the Demons bent to the floor and licked her blood like dogs. There were growls and howls and moans of delight. All made her considerably uncomfortable.

Worse was when one of the Demons licked her heel and she shrieked in surprise. Alastor dragged her away from the one who'd done it and threatened the Demon in Hellspeak.

By the time they reached the dining room, the bleeding had stopped. Coagulated gobs of blood trickled to nothing. Alastor brought her into the empty dining room and like last time, there were pedestals in the center of the room.

"Up." Alastor motioned for Shay to take the pedestal in the middle.

"You said you weren't going to do this again." Shay reminded him.

He patted his jacket pocket and Shay heard the *tink* of glass. "We're not selling you, just your blood. And now that they got a taste, they'll bid higher."

Alastor went to the door at the far end of the room and came back with two young women, the same as last time. They smiled at her. They were far too relaxed and Shay wondered if they'd been drugged like Alastor had done to her before. But, they were upright and walking and seemed in control of their bodies.

"Don't judge," the girl in red said. "Some of us like the auction and the thrill afterwards."

The girl to Shay's left clicked her tongue. "Some of us enjoy it quite a lot. Have you let him have you yet?" She tipped her chin toward Alastor. "That's the one I'd want."

Shay stared at Alastor as he opened the door and let the guests take their seats.

"Never," Shay replied to the girls. "Not over my dead body."

"So you won't mind if I offer myself to him?" the one in red asked.

"I don't care what he does." Shay held her head high as Alastor headed back toward the pedestals where the girls stood on display.

The girls stopped talking once Alastor got within earshot. He was working the crowd, chatting up the customers. Shay didn't understand any of it since he chose Hellspeak again. The whole night had been garbled speech that made her ears ache. She understood the laughs and the jeers and when Alastor took a protective stance when some got out of hand. The rest of it was gibberish.

The auction was enthusiastic for the other two girls. But when Alastor held up the vials of blood, the room went wild.

There was roaring, keening, screaming, growling coming from the throats of the Demons in the seats. Some stood and shouted, all throwing their offers for more and more money at Alastor.

Shay glanced to him, a wide smile spread on his face, his chest puffed and he stood tall, reveling in the mounds of money the Demons were willing to pay him for a vial of Shay's blood. It sickened her.

When the auction was over, Alastor escorted Shay to the back room with the other girls.

He slapped her on the ass as she walked through the threshold. "Got a prime price for these." He held the vials, ready to distribute to their rightful owners.

The girls were watching her as Alastor closed the door.

"Is there a way out?" Shay asked, searching the room.

"It's a closet," the one in red said. "There's no way out."

"We searched it already. Alastor wouldn't risk putting us in an unsecure room," the other girl said, toying with her blonde hair.

Shay stared at them both, unbelieving. They didn't seem afraid or angry at all.

"You aren't here against your will?" Shay asked.

The blonde shook her head. "Don't judge me. Just because I don't desire the boys of the Earthen plane."

Shay blinked hard. Before she met Jed, she didn't know there was anything else besides the Earthen plane, and she'd never called it that. Just planet earth or home. To know that there were people who knew about Hell and Demons blew her mind. She never thought she'd lived a sheltered life, but the more she saw, the more she decided she must have.

"Not everyone is a princess," the one in the red dress said. "Before the Zombie War, I was a mess. Stripping for five-dollar bills just to put food on the table." She stretched and spun in a circle, showing off her dress. "Now I get pampered every week."

The door opened. Alastor called, "Red, let's go."

"Toodles," she said as she waved at Shay and the blonde before leaving.

The blonde was fixing her hair. "Take Alastor for a ride. You know what they say..."

"I certainly don't," Shay replied.

"Once you go Demon, you never go back." She was standing by the door as it opened and winked at Shay as she left.

Shay paced the room. She was definitely not going to *go Demon*. The thought made her gag, no matter how nice Alastor ever treated her, he'd kidnapped her and killed her boyfriend. If she went anything with a Demon, it would be to kill him.

Alastor left Shay in the room alone long enough for her to get nervous about what was going on and if he'd ever come back. She paced the small room. Sat, stood, paced some more. She leaned against the walls and listened for voices. She ran her hands over the plaster panels and pressed, searching for hidden doors. There was nothing.

When the door finally opened, Alastor was leaning against the frame like he could barely stand.

"What the fuck?" Shay snapped at him. "I've been in here forever."

Alastor's eyes were half-lidded as he motioned for her to follow. His movements were slow, relaxed, very unlike his usual demeanor.

The mansion was empty. Small creatures were cleaning and rearranging as Alastor led her to the front door. They left; the Jeep they'd arrived in was the only vehicle remaining.

Shay stopped at the sharp rocks and glanced to where the Jeep was parked. She considered walking at a snail's pace to prevent the rocks from cutting up her feet.

Alastor noticed. He lifted her without warning and held her close. "You made some good money tonight." He smelled like whiskey and smoke.

Shay turned away as the heat of his breath brushed her cheek.

"You were such a good girl. I should get you a present." He stopped at the Jeep and opened the door.

"I don't need a present. I need to be let the fuck out of this situation." She squeaked as he tossed her onto the seat.

Alastor slammed the door closed and walked to the driver side. "You pay the debts you owe," he said as he got in and started the vehicle.

"Should you be driving?" Shay asked from the backseat. "You smell like a dive bar."

"I'm fine." The Jeep jerked as he hit the brake at an awkward moment then hit the curb.

"You're going to kill us." Shay buckled her seatbelt.

Alastor shrugged. "No different than you."

Shay spent the ride through the mountains gripping the doorhandle and pressing herself against the seat, bracing for impact.

When Alastor parked at the hovel, he let her out and said, "See, not a blemish on your hide." His dark gaze drifted over her.

Shay ran inside to the bathroom and locked the door. She washed the dried blood off her feet and showered the sweat off her back and tried to figure a way out of this mess she was in.

Thirty-Eight

Nero was pissed. Steam rose from his nostrils as he galloped. There was only one more place he could go for help. The chapel in the graveyard.

Nero whinnied as he galloped, like a firetruck with sirens blaring. He paced at the fence, stomping the grass and dirt until the door opened. The morning sun was coming over the treetops but the graveyard still had a coating of fog over the grass.

Noah was wearing pajama pants with no shirt and carrying a cup of coffee. "What's all the racket about?" he hollered to Nero. "You got a Demon foot up your ass or are you just happy to see me?" Noah flinched as his bare feet hit the wet grass. He walked closer and opened the gate.

Nero moved to enter the fenced yard but he was too big to fit through the gate opening.

"Back up big boy." Noah held up a hand motioning for him to reverse. "What brings you by at the crack of early-as-fuck-dawn? You're going to wake Thrush sounding off like that."

Nero went still. He felt stupid for coming here. The baby... Noah couldn't come with him, he had a family to protect.

"Cat got your tongue?" Noah asked, sipping at his coffee with raised brows.

"Ah, Nero," Nightingale's light voice called out from the stoop.

Nero felt more stupid. What was he doing here? Why did he think these people could help him? Noah and Nightingale were technically ghosts but something drew him here.

Noah's eyes narrowed on the Demon horse. "You're supposed to be on a mission to rescue Shay. What're you doing here?"

Nero whinnied as though the noise told the entire story, everything he couldn't say with words.

Noah pressed his lips together and tipped his head with a few nods, like he understood every stuttered sound that left Nero's throat. But then he said, "Got no clue, buddy. Not a frickin' clue."

Nightingale slipped in front of Noah and held her hand out.

Nero hesitated. He knew the dead Angel woman had been brought back from elsewhere. He'd heard enough conversations about Nightingale visiting people in their dreams, he'd heard about her defeating the Nightjar to save her little boy, Thrush. Nightingale had an energy and power that caused Nero to take a step back. He could sense she was something *different*.

"I won't hurt you, Nero." Nightingale whistled a light trill. She sounded like a bird. "Touch me and I'll see what I can understand from you."

Nero hesitated, but he didn't have much of a choice, time was running out. He set his snout in her palm.

Noah's lips pressed together and his expression elicited a sense that this was bullshit.

Nero looked away from Noah and focused on Nightingale. Her eyes were closed, her face flexed in concentration.

Nightingale's hand fell away and Nero felt hopeless for a moment, anticipating nothing.

"He's lost them," Nightingale said. "He can't find Jed or Chel but he knows where Shay is. He just needs help. This Demon he's up against is strong." She pet Nero's cheek. "He doesn't want to hurt Shay again."

Noah made a face of agreement.

"Give me a minute." Nightingale's hand left Nero and she closed her eyes. "Some get really mad when I do this so you'll have to apologize for me."

Nero looked to Noah for an explanation but the man was staring into his coffee cup. "Meg wants me to fetch her pancakes," he muttered. "Christ, I just want one morning to drink my coffee in peace."

Nightingale's eyes flashed open. "Jed and Chel are in Hell. I'm not sure where, but their minds are... *slowed*." Nightingale took a deep breath. "You need to find them before it's too late, Nero."

Nero nodded his head silently, his mane flying in the morning sun.

"Thrush is awake." Nightingale was watching Nero warily. "We can't go with you but I know you will find them. You can do this Nero. You're a Crossroads Demon, you haven't even realized half of your power."

Nero nickered lightly as he turned to gallop away. He'd learned one thing from all of his recent interactions, these people weren't much help at all and Shay deserved better.

You haven't even realized half of your power. Nero wondered what Nightingale had meant.

Thirty-Nine

There was music playing. Shay recognized it as Michael Jackson's Smooth Criminal. Alastor was drunk. Wasted. He was stumbling through the kitchen searching the cabinets, bobbing along to the beat of the music.

"Ah. Shay-baby. There you are." He danced over to her, moonwalk and all. It was ridiculous how well he danced.

"Don't call me that." The only people allowed to call her Shay-baby were Daddy and Jed and they were both dead. Thanks to Demons.

"Don't be so cruel." He was swaying, moving to the beat of the song. If Shay didn't dislike him so much she might find it endearing. "Come on." He grabbed her hips and pulled her closer.

"Don't touch me." Shay slapped at his chest. His fingers brushed the brand on her hip and Shay hissed in shock.

"Look at us. We could take over the world together. You've done so well as my pet. You could be more. Like the others. You might like it."

He kept touching her; hands on her waist, pulling her closer, rubbing himself against her.

Shay slapped him across the face. Hard.

"You fucking bitch!" Alastor shouted. His eyes were black as pitch and filled with rage.

Shay stood her ground. "I told you to stop."

"After all this time, all these weeks. I've given you everything." His hands were pinching her hips as she struggled to back away from him. "So much more than all the others. I've never allowed them the freedoms you have. I treated you better."

"No!" Shay shouted back. "You've taken everything from me. You ruined my life. I hate you. I hate everything that you are and what you've done to me." Shay was filled with rage. "You and your kind have killed everyone that I love." Shay was shaking and she could barely think straight.

"You want me to treat you like shit, treat you like cattle? Like a dog? I can do that." He backhanded her.

Shay wasn't ready for it, and her vision turned red as she flew across the room and hit the wall. She could barely move.

Alastor was on her before she could stand. He grabbed a handful of blue hair and dragged her up. "Your blood is enough." He dragged her to his bedroom and threw her on the bed. "If this is what you want, this is what you get."

Blood dripped into Shay's left eye. Her mind felt fuzzy and she figured she'd cut herself when she hit the wall. She rolled, tried to crawl off the bed but Alastor came back with rope. He tied her wrists and ankles, pulling the rope tight to the bedframe.

"You're a bastard," Shay said, fighting him and losing. He was too big and too strong.

"I embrace it."

Shay tried to kick at him with her knees but Alastor held her leg down, his grip painful on her right leg. His thumb touched the scar there.

"I have a feeling you've a demon inside you also, little human. That's the only conclusion I can come to with this scar and that Crossroads Demon connection." Alastor was staring for minutes before he released her and moved to the table near the bed. Glass and metal clinked together.

He took her blood, vials and vials until she felt dizzy and weak and she couldn't fight him when his mouth touched her arm and licked and licked and licked until it clotted. When he was done, she could see the bulge in his groin through half-lidded eyes and feared what would come next.

If she had her pistol she'd shoot him. If she had a lasso of rope she'd choke him. She couldn't do any of that in her current state.

Alastor didn't touch her again. Thank God. He was a bastard but at least he had some type of morals that stopped him from touching her below the belt.

He was lounging across the room where he'd stumbled onto a dressing bench. Shay swallowed hard as she watched him, inebriated and high on blood. He slid off the bench near the closet and rolled onto his back, hands in his hair as he watched the ceiling. He was imagining someone was there, touching him, groping him, riding him. It was indecent. Shay turned away and focused on the rope that tied her wrists. She tried tugging but the knot only got tighter. She scooted up, hoping to get to the knot with her teeth, but the ropes at her ankles tightened.

Shay stretched her fingers, trying to reach the ends of the rope or loosen the knot. She tried until her arms and back ached and she fell asleep.

In the morning, Alastor left the bathroom with a towel wrapped low around his waist and made his way to the closet. He'd taken a handful of phone calls since he scraped himself off the floor. He'd taken more of Shay's blood as soon as he woke up and threatened to be back soon.

Shay eavesdropped on his phone calls. He was selling her blood and getting more money than he would have for her body.

It went on for days. More vials of blood than Shay could count. She wished for a Crossroads Demon call just so she could escape the bedroom and the needle Alastor kept sticking in her veins.

Shay soon found herself sleeping more than she was awake. The pinch of the needle barely triggered her to open her eyes. Her mouth was dry, and she'd never been so thirsty. Her eyes felt like sand had been rubbed in them. Shay's arms and legs felt like lead; moving was too much effort. Alastor hadn't given her more than a bite of bread and a sip of water since he'd started draining her. She was weak, wasting away.

"You want what?" Alastor's deep voice pulled Shay from slumber. "No. That's not part of the deal...." Alastor was staring at her as he talked into the phone. "I won't offer that." He was making a face, his brow creased. "How much?" There was a long silence as he pinched the bridge of his nose before looking at her again. "Fine. It's a deal but if you do anything more than take her blood, I'll kill you myself."

Shay closed her eyes, not caring what the deal was. She felt the bed shift as Alastor sat next to her. He touched her hair, then her torn shirt.

"It wasn't supposed to be like this."

"Fuck off," Shay croaked.

Alastor gripped her chin and forced Shay to look at him. "I wanted more from you."

Shay glared, unfeeling, too tired to say anything.

"I had better plans. The other girls..." he was searching her dull eyes, "aren't as valuable as you." He licked his lips. "Don't taste as sweet..."

Shay thought Alastor was trying to confess something but his words tumbled then jumbled then turned into Hellspeak and she could no longer understand him. It didn't matter, the more time she spent in Hell the harder it was to figure out the rules that governed this place. Just like the human world, there was sin and evilness, little accountability, few laws that mattered. Shay decided all the realms were pretty much a cluster fuck. The scar on her thigh ached right down to the bone. Shay worried that the lack of blood might weaken her leg. She didn't have anyone to heal her out here in the wilderness of Hell. If something happened–heck, if this got any worse–she was good as dead.

FORTY

NERO GALLOPED THROUGH HELLSCAPE. HE RAN PATHS
down to dirt between the trees, trampled grass, searched every scrap
of land he came across. He couldn't find Jed or the Hellion.

They were here. He could feel it in his center. They were here in
the echoes of the leaves when the wind blew and the movement of
shadows from the corner of his eye. Some strange magic had them
trapped. Their shadows disappeared like morning mist. He could
smell them. He saw their nearly dirt-filled footprints and traces of
their travels; scuff marks in the soil, broken branches, and then all
trace of them stopped and there was nothing. Hellforest and its paths
became quiet as fresh fallen snow and just as secretive. The only thing
Nero found was a large rock that looked out of place. The Demons
and Nero had curled a path around it in both directions.

Nero huffed in frustration as another sunset appeared. He'd been
searching for Jed and the Hellion for days and weeks. He'd been back
from making the deal on the Earthen plane with one desire; to save
Shay. But he couldn't do it alone. He needed help. He needed Jed's
magic and the Hellion's strength. He wouldn't risk hurting her
again. The incident at the barn was enough to haunt him forever.

When those young Hellions came for Shay, hunting her, Nero had injured her while fighting with them. No, Nero wouldn't go for that again. He needed help to ensure that Shay was safe and saved.

Nero stopped at a meandering path that led to a pub. They had been here, long ago. There were traces of the men. Nero stood in the path and watched the Demons come and go from the front door. He wondered if Jed and the Hellion were in there. Nero's head tracked back and forth slowly as he made the decision. The golden chain strung from his ear to his throat jingled as his head moved. He walked closer, judging the size of the door, sure that he could make it through.

The door opened as a Demon walked through and didn't close all the way. He moved forward, leaving hoofprints in the path. He nudged the door with his snout until it opened, then walked through.

Nero had to dip his head under the threshold of the door and squeeze his flank to get inside, but it was worth the look on all the Demons' faces. Nero knew horses didn't walk into pubs. They didn't walk into many places like he just had but he didn't care. Nero wasn't a normal horse and too much was on the line for animal politeness.

All heads turned.

Clop. Clop. Clop. Nero's footsteps echoed on the hard floor as he neared the bar. He wasn't sure who to approach, but the Demon on the other side of the bar looked authoritative. Nero walked right up, shoved the barstools aside with this big body, tilted his head, and stared at the Demon bartender with one large black eye.

"What do you want horse?" the bartender asked.

Nero huffed.

The bartender stared.

The pub was silent.

Nero nickered. He couldn't speak otherwise so he tried a variety of noises that he could make with this throat.

"Are ya looking for food?" the bartender asked.

Nero huffed.

The bartender filled a mug with beer and set it in front of Nero, then set a brick of cheese next to the mug.

Nero sniffed. He'd tried beer. The ranch hands would give it to him on the Fourth of July and Christmas, late at night when Nicholas and the rest of the family were asleep. Meanwhile, the ranch hands were awake with loneliness wandering the ranch all thoughtful and depressed. Nero knew what beer tasted and smelled like, and what the bartender had set in front of him was not right. There was a murky scent. Nero's eyes blew wide as he realized what had happened.

It was poisoned!

Nero hit the mug with his snout. Beer spilled and the murky scent spread. Nero whinnied a noise that was filled with *rage*.

He slammed his front hooves on the bar top, splintering the wood. He shivered, felt the quiver of electricity under his skin. He shivered harder, gnashed his teeth together, tensed his body, and *changed*. Nero was already huge but in that second he doubled in size, his long black tail and mane becoming stiff as needles and sharp as razorblades. His veins became giant ropes of obsidian, twining and swirling under his skin like protective armor. The hunger was the worst part.

Nero was a thrashing beast in a small box. He broke everything wooden, everything with bones. His hooves were sharp, stabbing and cutting, his legs a power to be reckoned with. He blocked the door so none of the Demons could escape. When they charged, he killed them. When they jabbed their weapons at him, he killed them. When they looked at him, he killed them.

And when he was done destroying, he ate them. The sound of their bones crunching between his teeth echoed through Hellscape like a lightning storm. The only thing that remained of the pub was bloodstains and splintered timber. He came across a smoky glass jar that smelled like the poison from the beer and cheese. Something clicked in Nero's throat, a strange power he'd never called upon. He whinnied something wrath-filled and fire came out, burning the jar of potion, flames licking the blood soaked floorboards.

He huffed and cleared his throat, shook until the shiver returned his body to something less frightening.

He roamed from what was left of the pub as it turned to ash, stopping at the end of the path and turning his ears, searching for the sound of Jed's voice. He heard the deep timbre in the distance and galloped toward it.

FORTY-ONE

LAYERS OF ROCK DUST HAD SOLIDIFIED ON THE MEN. THEY resembled a strange formation of granite dropped by a glacier as it passed the Hellscape eons ago. Pitted and stained green with forest mildew, the men had been trapped for far too long but not as long as one might think. The potion had accelerated their solidification. They didn't know but their thoughts had become as slow as their movements and they'd turned to stone unknowingly.

But then, everything suddenly shifted. Rock crumbled and fell away from the men. Jed felt the fog lift from his mind and the weight lift from his shoulders.

Chel's wings no longer dragged as though weighed down by bricks. He flexed the bat-like appendages and groaned. "I feel like I've been sleeping under a mountain."

"Something's changed," Jed said, turning to Chel and stretching his hands in front of him.

"The mother potion has been wasted. Something's coming," Chel said, turning to glance behind them as the ground shook.

Jed kicked a lump of stone. No. The realization came to him that they never made it to the pub. They hadn't made it more than a few hundred feet before becoming encased in stone. He wasn't sure how much time had passed. How much time they'd missed. How long had Shay been left with Alastor...

Nero's happy whinny echoed.

"Finally." Jed rubbed his face as the fog cleared.

Nero was running toward them.

"Where have you been?" Chel asked the horse. "We've been waiting for you to come back for ages."

Nero was bobbing his head and huffed. He jerked his head in the direction of the hovel in the mountains and nudged Jed to get moving.

"We're not going back to the pub to confront them?" Chel asked.

Nero hollered, showing his teeth and stomping. He rubbed his flank against Jed, urging him to climb up.

Jed jumped, muscles weak from disuse, and he almost didn't make it onto Nero's back. His legs ached as he stretched and pulled himself straight.

Chel leapt to launch himself into the air but he stumbled and fell down on one knee. "How long were we trapped in rock?" Chel asked. "My wings can barely hold me."

"Too long." Jed wrapped his hands in Nero's mane, fingers feeling numb from weeks without motion. "You want me to carry you?" Jed asked with a smirk.

"I'd rather crawl." Chel stood and launched himself into the air. He flew, lopsided for a few beats until he had enough force to right himself.

Jed laughed from the path where Nero galloped.

FORTY-TWO

*"THEY'RE COMING FOR YOU," THE DARK HAIRED WOMAN
said in Shay's dream.*

*"Who?" Shay no longer believed anyone was going to help her. She
was in a bad place. A terrible place that no human would ever come
back from.*

*Cold hands touched her face. "Hang on for just a little bit longer."
Dark eyes searched hers. "Please, Shay."*

———

SHAY WAS BEING LIFTED. Her arms ached but they were no
longer tied down. She was wearing something new, a dress, the black
one. Alastor had changed her clothing.

"You've sold me," she mumbled. "I'm going to die here."

"No," Alastor's voice was stern, "this is part of your repayment.
Krelp has clear instructions to only feed, nothing more. He's very
wealthy and is paying a prime price for you."

"You suck," was all Shay could muster to say to him.

A sly smile crossed Alastor's face. "Perhaps I do, but the other girls don't think I'm so bad."

"They're stupid." Shay wanted to walk but she couldn't find the energy to struggle and get out of his arms. "You've done something to them."

"I gave them money and freedom," Alastor said.

"Your skin trades are not freedom. I remember the chains and the tents where you kept me the first time."

Alastor didn't reply.

They were at another mansion, black brick with three stories. Alastor carried Shay inside and a butler of sorts escorted them down hallways and stairs before pointing to a closed door. "He's expecting you."

Alastor stepped forward, easing Shay through the doorway.

Shay heard the scuttling sound of claws on hardwood, the *shhhhh*-sweep of wings dragging.

"Finally," a gravelly voice said. "Put her there."

A wet sound filled the air as Krelp licked his chops, eager.

Shay saw the lair in slow blinks, too tired to keep her heavy eyes open. She wondered if Alastor had drugged her again or if she was weak from being drained of blood daily.

"Put her there. Put her there!" Krelp clambered. Wings and limbs lobbed across the floor.

Alastor paused. "We have a deal," he reminded Krelp as he hesitated to lay Shay on the table.

"Yes, yes. Yes. Just a taste. Just a feast on the skin." Hands were rubbing together.

"No feasting on the skin!" Alastor shouted.

"Yes. No skin. No skin." Krelp was close to the table, he rapped on the wood with his fist. "Put her here. Give me what I paid for."

"Money first." Alastor held Shay, refusing to put her down.

Krelp began muttering in Hellspeak then reached in his pocket and pulled out a sack of coins. He slammed it on the table. "I'm hungry. Give her to me."

Shay's eyes fluttered open as Alastor set her down on the table and helped Krelp with the bindings to hold her in place. Then he left.

In the dimly lit chamber of the Demon's lair, Shay found herself bound and helpless, her heart pounding with fear as she awaited her grim fate. This was the end. She could feel it. Alastor had threatened the Demon but it was a malevolent creature hungry for blood. That was easy to see.

The air hung heavy with the stench of decay as the Demon approached, its form cloaked in shadows that seemed to writhe and twist with a sinister energy. Krelp's eyes glowed with an unholy light, fixated on Shay with an insatiable hunger that sent shivers down her spine. The creature was malformed with extra limbs that draped on the ground, boneless and limp.

Shay's breath caught in her throat as the Demon drew closer, its taloned fingers reaching out to brush against her skin with a chilling touch. She recoiled, the cold tendrils of fear wrapping around her heart like icy chains.

"You are mine now," the Demon hissed, its voice a guttural rasp that sent a panicked shiver downs Shay's spine. "Your blood will sustain me, human."

Shay's heart raced with panic as she struggled against her bindings, her mind racing with desperate thoughts. The chains that bound her were unyielding, their iron grip a cruel reminder of her captivity and all that she'd lost.

She prayed to be called away by the Crossroads but at the same time she feared Alastor's reaction if she fucked this up for him. She regretted making him angry. Look at where that had gotten her. Shay's skin crawled as she watched Krelp drooling over her.

Krelp ran his fingers along her skin, muttering in Hellspeak, his tongue lolling between his lips. He began licking her wrist slowly, then moved up her arm, tasting, probing for thick veins to feed from.

"He's used these ones already." Krelp's tongue pressed on the veins in her inner elbow. He licked up to her shoulder. She saw the gleam of a knife as he slid it under her dress and cut the fabric. "Mmmm. You taste like the Earthen plane. Like forbidden fruit." His tongue lathed over her collarbone.

Shay's body began trembling uncontrollably.

"Are you cold, my sweet?"

Shay slammed her eyes closed, thankful that he'd stopped licking her for a moment. "Yes," she replied, hoping to distract him.

"Let me light the fire. Don't want your blood turning to ice. I like it warm like soup."

Krelp slumped away, crossing the lair and starting a fire in the fireplace. The heat helped but didn't make the situation any better.

"There, my sweet." He'd returned to her side too quickly. His taloned fingers toyed with the pieces of her dress that he'd cut. He began licking her again, starting at her shoulder. Soon fingers were in her hair and he jerked her head to the side, revealing the smooth skin of Shay's neck.

"Yes. Yes. The sweet blood comes from here." A hand pressed against the vee of her thighs. "And here. Which would you have me feed from, my sweet?"

"Up here," Shay whispered, disgusted with the thought of him near another part of her body.

As the Demon prepared to sink its fangs into shay's flesh, a surge of defiance welled within her. With a trembling voice she summoned every ounce of courage she possessed, refusing to surrender to the darkness that threatened to consume her.

"You will not touch me," Shay declared, her voice trembling yet defiant. "I am not your prey."

The Demon only laughed, a cruel and mocking sound that echoed through the chamber like a death knell. With a swift motion, it seized Shay's wrist, its talons piercing her skin as it prepared to feed.

In that moment of desperation, Shay closed her eyes and tried to summon a glimmer of hope amidst the despair that threatened to engulf her. She refused to give in, clung to the belief that somehow, someway, she would find a way to escape this.

Krelp bit her, hard, and there was nothing nice about it.

Shay cried out as his fangs stabbed into her neck. She struggled against the bindings.

Krelp's taloned hand moved to her neck and held her steady.

Shay's body felt colder than ever; the heat of the fire did nothing to melt the ice in her veins. Krelp's grip tightened on the base of her neck as he fed.

He finally pulled away, blood smearing his lips. His eyes were big and black, and he seemed to grow before her.

"More," Krelp said, his taloned fingers roving her body, searching. The knife appeared again and he began cutting her dress. Slice by slice he exposed more of her body. Licking his lips, he bit her in other places; her wrist, her ankle, her stomach, her hip. He paused at the scar on her thigh.

"This is for me. This is mine." His knife pressed against the scar.

"No! No!" Shay screamed. "Don't touch me." She screamed as loud as she could, hoping someone would hear her. She was so afraid that Krelp would cut open the scar and release the Demon poison, afraid it would forever change her. And... deep down, she was afraid she'd lose her connection to Nero if it was gone.

Shay screamed louder.

FORTY-THREE

PAIN RIPPLED DOWN THE TETHER THAT CONNECTED SHAY and Nero. Shay was terrified and in pain. Something bad was happening.

Nero's eyes blew wide, his whinny sounding like a roar as he put his head down and ran faster.

Chel couldn't keep pace from the sky. His batlike wings whipped harder and harder through Hellsky but he was getting further and further behind. All he could do was follow the shaking of the trees as Nero blasted past them.

"Whoa. Whoa!" Jed shouted, doing his best to hang on to Nero as he sped lighting fast through the forest then the winding mountain roads. The horse was moving so fast he was feeling queasy. "Don't drop me," Jed said.

Nero didn't slow, he only moved faster. His hooves pounded into the ground, dirt and leaves flying into the air leaving a cloud of debris in his wake.

Nero felt Shay scream again. The tether drew him in a different direction. Not towards the Demon's hovel in the mountains.

He galloped through winding mountain roads, up and up until a

827

dirt road led to a clearing and a black brick mansion loomed before them.

Nero slammed his front hooves on the door to the mansion and it blew open. Wood and brick shattered. Nero neighed and it sounded like a roar.

Shay's screams echoed through the mansion. Nero followed the sound. Somewhere along the way, Jed had fallen off his back.

Chel landed outside the black mansion. He was running, pausing only to help Jed to his feet and follow Nero. Chel's Hellion blade was drawn as he entered.

Jed was close behind, his fingertips spurting lightning. He heard Shay's screams.

"Shay!" Jed shouted.

Then the deluge began. Lesser Demons began coming through the doors of the mansion.

Nero was near the stairwell, fighting off a handful of small, bird-like creatures.

Chel and Jed fought clusters of Demons.

Chel's blade cut through them like butter. Jed's magic slayed the ones that missed the blade and the ones Nero's hooves hadn't stomped to death. They met at the stairwell and began running down. They could hear Shay's screams and other strange noises.

"Shay!" Jed shouted again.

They followed the sound of her shrieks; she was close, but there were so many doors in this dungeon. Nero and Chel and Jed began kicking open every door they came across.

On the last one, Nero slammed his hooves on a door and it crumpled under his weight.

Jed stormed into the room, his aura blazing blue, arcane energy streaming from his fingertips.

Shay was there.

Jed recognized Alastor immediately. He was fighting with a deformed Demon that had blood on his mouth.

Alastor was standing next to Shay, protectively. She was tied down, bleeding, pale, her clothing ripped to shreds.

"Kill them!" Shay shouted.

She didn't have to ask twice.

Jed went for Alastor.

Chel went for Krelp.

Nero went for Shay, and he bit at the ropes holding her until they broke and she could sit up. Shay cried, wrapped her arms around Nero's neck and held on as he dragged her to her feet. Nero nickered lightly and licked her hands.

Krelp was stronger now that he had fresh blood in his gut. He moved quick, sidestepping and spinning away from Chel's blade. His taloned fingers swept out to scratch at Chel's body. Chel took his time, unfamiliar with this Demon and what powers he could have.

The room was crammed with furniture and trinkets, which Krelp took advantage of, using lamps and chairs as weapons against Chel. His dragging extra appendages found life and the Demon suddenly had five arms.

Chel guarded his head, ducked behind a couch to figure out a plan as the barrage of items flew past him and into the couch.

Energy crackled from Jed's fingertips. As he whispered a spell that sounded like ink and bone on parchment, tendrils of energy came from his hands and wrapped around Alastor.

They'd fought before, and Alastor didn't forget. He aimed well, aimed for Jed's hands and mouth as he ran toward Jed, punching. Alastor pulled the knife from under his jacket and cut Jed on the wrist.

Magic sputtered with the injury to his left arm.

Alastor shook his knife at Jed. "You won't defeat me again."

Jed smirked as the wound on his wrist healed with a quick charm. Sparks and energy intensified, wrapping around Alastor's body.

Alastor had his own weapons and he was more powerful than anyone in the room realized. But that's what happens when your father was Lucifer and your birthright was chaos and darkness, primed for eons. Alastor chanted in Hellspeak and the ground under their feet opened up. Just like at the campground on the Earthen plane, lesser Demons and strange creatures began crawling out. Cockroaches and spiders and black beetles swarmed Jed and Chel, biting and scratching, bringing chaos and destruction.

Nero slammed his front hooves on the table where Shay had been bound, splintering the wood. Shay dropped to the ground under Nero, covering her face. Slivers and splinters took to the air, stabbing through the lesser Demons. Nero shivered, felt the quiver of electricity under his skin. He shivered harder, gnashed his teeth together, tensed his body, and *changed*. Nero doubled in size, his long black tail and mane became stiff and sharp as razorblades. His veins, ropes of obsidian, twined and swirled under his skin like protective armor.

Shay changed forms too and Jed saw her like that for the first time. His eyes blew wide as he took her in. She was tall, hair so blue, eyes darker than night. She wasn't a terrifying Demon like her horse, no, she was a warrior; intimidating and absolutely stunning.

Lesser Demons grappled at Jed's legs like cockroaches. He cast a spell to disperse them.

Alastor got the upper hand, swinging a chair at his head. Jed kneeled to the ground, stunned.

Shay was closest to Krelp and killed him like she'd trained her whole life to do so. Her hand wrapped around his voluminous neck, squeezing until his spine broke. She threw the body on the floor. Silent communication went to Nero.

Nero opened his mouth, roared, and flames came out, setting Krelp's body on fire.

Jed's mouth went dry as he watched. It was a disruption he didn't need. He'd have to do better when Shay was around and they were entombed in battle. Alastor launched himself at Jed, wrapping around his legs and dragging Jed down until he dropped. Jed's head hit the ground, arcane energy swirling around his body as he used a wind-like force to throw Alastor away. Jed rose to his feet, blood dripping down the side of his head. Alastor was running toward him again.

"Clotpole!" Chel shouted.

It was a distraction and a secret communication. Chel tossed the basilisk tooth knife to Jed then launched himself at Alastor's legs, dragging him to the ground.

Jed caught the blade, gripped it tightly in his palm, ran, and leapt to Alastor's falling body. He dropped to a knee and jabbed the blade into Alastor's heart, just as the Demon had done to him weeks ago.

Alastor went still. The creatures stopped coming from the hole in the ground.

"Burn it all," Shay said with an angry growl.

Nero opened his mouth to comply, whinnied something that sounded like curse words and an oath upon the mansion and creatures that lived within the structure. Fire lit the room.

FORTY-FOUR

A SHIVER OF ELECTRICITY RAN DOWN SHAY'S SPINE AT THE exact moment it ran down Nero's. They both transformed back to normal.

"Kill him with fire," Shay said.

Flames lit Alastor's clothing as the basilisk tooth blade in his heart kept him immobile.

"We must leave or we'll die here also," Chel was urging the group toward the door. They ran down the hall and up the winding stairs, finding their way out of the black mansion.

They ran down the grand entry stairs, no longer being followed by lesser Demons or spiders or cockroaches.

They stopped to catch their breath.

"You came for me," Shay couldn't hide the glimmer in her eyes.

Nero whinnied a response that sounded like, "what did you expect us to do, leave you?"

Chel laughed, wrapped his arms around Shay and lifted her, spinning her. "We would have made it sooner if your boyfriend hadn't been picking fights in the pub."

Shay giggled as Chel set her on her feet. "That doesn't sound like the Jed I know."

She turned to kiss Jed and fall into his arms, but as she stepped toward him she noticed he looked awfully pale, too much blood was dripping from the side of his head and the cuts on his body.

Jed gave a little smirk. "Sorry about that–"

He dropped to the ground, a knife stuck under his shoulder blade.

"No! No, no, no, no..." Shay was scrambling to Jed's lifeless body, She dropped to her knees trying to roll him.. "No! I just got you back." She gripped the blade. "It's Alastor's. He always carried it on him."

"Leave it," Chel warned. "He'll bleed out if you remove it."

Nero was nudging Shay's shoulder. "Help me move him. I can't lift him."

"I'll fly him back," Chel said as he lifted Jed's limp body.

"No, Nero is faster." Shay patted Nero's back.

"With both of you?" Chel asked.

"Yes." Shay was certain. "He could carry a hundred people and be faster than you." She paused for a split second. "Don't take that personal."

Chel draped Jed's body over Nero's back.

Shay climbed up and held onto Jed and Nero's mane. She clicked her tongue. "Go fast!"

Nero took off with a thunderbolt.

FORTY-FIVE

NERO WAS FASTER THAN LIGHTNING, FASTER THAN THE speed of light, faster than a black hole. Trees bent away from him before he passed them, hoofprints appeared in the soil before his gallop hit the ground. The ground in the distance shook before the black blur passed. Demons gaped, wondering what it was.

Chel took to the sky but all he saw was a blur, the shudder of the forest, the sound of thunder in the distance. Then nothing. He flew as fast as he could but he'd never keep up.

Shay held onto Jed. Blood soaked their clothing. Alastor's knife was embedded so deep in his back, it never moved with the force of Nero's gallop.

Shay leaned down, her upper body covering Jed's protectively as Nero ran. She whispered things to him, wished she could whisper a spell to keep him alive just as he'd done for her, but Shay didn't have magic like Jed. She had her words though.

"I have loved you since the moment I saw you at that Casino in Lame Deer and you dropped your French toast when you saw me. I have never felt this for anyone." Shay was gazing at his face. "I thought I'd never see you again after the Casino was under siege, but I did. You found me. You found me and charmed my parents and helped me when they died." Tears were streaming down her face. She wiped them away. "Please don't die. Please. Stay with me."

Shay's fingers stretched into his hair, tangled and tugging like she was trying to pull him back from death by the strands. Her leg wrapped around his, holding him tightly to Nero's side. She wouldn't let him fall. No matter how much he disappointed her, no matter how badly he'd hurt her with his fluttering back and forth. Shay wouldn't let him fall and she prayed that he'd notice and see the light and make the change within his own heart. Because Shay couldn't watch him die.

Blue hair fluttered like waves. The Hellions saw the blue blur before they saw the dark stallion. They smelled the blood before they saw Nero's passengers.

Skeele was waiting at the doors to the castle in the burning mountains, worried that something dark was coming for Meg. He was always overprotective. Always watching the doors and the perimeter.

Nero skidded to a stop.

Shay leapt off Nero's back, threadbare dress blowing in the wind. "Jed needs the infirmary. Can you get Teari?" There was panic in her voice, tears dried on her face, blood dried on her arms.

Skeele was no idiot. He realized the severity of the situation once he saw Shay was freed and Jed's bleeding body on Nero's back.

"Move him," Skeele ordered the nearby Hellions.

Klaus and Tukka were quick to gently move Jed and carry him into the castle.

Shay tried to follow them but Skeele held up a hand, stopping her.

"Where is Chel?" Skeele asked.

Shay pointed to the sky. "He's on his way."

"You left him behind?" Skeele asked.

"No. We were simply faster than him." Shay moved toward the door.

"How much faster?" Skeele asked.

But Shay had gone inside and the only one to greet Skeele's gaze was Nero, who was smirking and huffed with pride.

———

TEARI NEVER PANICKED when she saw the blood and the knife. She took one look at Jed and began healing him. She removed the knife and cast it aside saying, "at least there was no poison in this blade." She stitched Jed's back then went to work on the hundreds of tiny bites on his arms and legs from the spiders and roaches and beetles and Demons.

Shay's hand never left Jed, she stroked his dirty and disheveled hair and whispered in his ear to *hold on* and *come back* and *stay*. At least he was still breathing, although shallow and slow. She wanted to kiss him, wanted to see the color of his eyes and pink flush his cheeks with life; she'd waited so long. She'd been too long without him and this was torture.

Chel was waiting in the corner of the room, trying not to be disruptive to Teari. He'd cleaned his wounds and bandaged them the best he could all the while muttering about how Meg needed her own healer and needed to stop borrowing her father's.

After some time, Chel pulled Shay from Jed's side and began washing and bandaging her wounds. He found the bitemarks from Krelp, and the bruises on her inner elbows from where Alastor had drained her.

"Will you be okay?" Chel asked Shay, holding her arms out straight, his voice low, his eyes focused on the bites. "Did he hurt you in other ways?" Chel paused before clarifying, "Do you need to be alone with the healer?"

Shay shook her head. "I'm fine. I just want him to wake." She glanced at Jed as Teari was covering him with a sheet, tucking it around his shoulders.

Teari washed her hands at the sink before approaching Chel and Shay.

"He just needs rest," Teari said. "He'll be fine. But you, there's something we need to take a look at."

Shay went still, afraid that Chel had told Teari about her transforming with Nero during the fight in the dungeon of the black mansion. She didn't want Teari to know. After all, Shay was simply a human who shouldn't be able to do things like that.

"You have a new wound," Teari was pointing to Shay's hip.

Shay had barely noticed that the dress was not much more than shreds. Krelp had cut it up and now it hung off her body in strips and threads, threatening to fall the rest of the way apart.

"Go get her some clothing," Teari told Chel.

He nodded and left he infirmary.

Teari motioned to the cot next to Jed's. "Sit. Show me."

Shay climbed onto the cot and leaned to the side, showing Teari the brand on her hip. "Alastor did it. The... the Demon who took me. He said that I would always return to him. It's never healed."

"Does it hurt?" Teari asked, examining the mark, probing Shay's tender skin but never touching the rune directly.

"It hurts less than it used to." Shay looked away, focused on anything in the room besides the ugly mark on her hip.

"It smells rotten. I think it's infected." Teari's hand hovered over the red edges and burned black skin. "The rune, I've never seen it before."

Teari pulled a curtain around them. "Remove that torn dress," she said, handing Shay a white gown from the bedside table. "Let me get a few things while you change."

Shay removed the strips of dress and found more bite marks from Krelp. Her hands shook as she realized how much worse the situation could have been. Even though Alastor was a bastard he'd come in the room when Shay started screaming. He was the one to stop Krelp from feasting on her whole body. It was the last redeeming moment the Demon had before he died. Shay shivered as she draped the gown over herself and lay back on the cot.

Teari returned with a tray of cloths and tins. She set the tray down and sat on the edge of the bed. "This is probably going to hurt," she warned.

Shay nodded. Nothing had hurt as much as Alastor telling her Jed was dead. Shay was certain she could take anything now. Teari could cut off her leg and Shay was certain she'd barely feel it.

Teari set a warm cloth on the brand for a few moments, then dabbed it dry. She held her hands over the mark, trying to heal it, but nothing happened.

"Just as I feared," Teari said. "My healing magic won't work on this Demon-made thing. We'll have to stick with poultices and clean dressings."

Teari layered the brand with a thick coat of minty smelling salve. She wrapped Shay's hip in a clean bandage then began inspecting her other wounds. Chel had done a decent job cleaning them. Teari's eyes kept falling on the scar on her thigh.

"Leave it alone," Shay finally said. "It's part of me now."

Teari frowned. "I wish I could have helped you with that."

"It doesn't matter anymore."

Teari cleaned up and opened the curtain. "I'm headed back to Gabriel's realm. I can come back in a few days."

"And Jed?" Shay asked.

"He'll wake up when he's ready." Teari paused and it seemed like she wanted to say more but she didn't.

Teari left and Shay heard voices outside the infirmary doors.

Shay slipped off the cot and padded over to Jed. She pulled back his sheet and crawled into bed next to him. Her fingers traced the scars on his chest, old and new.

"Stay," she whispered in his ear and kissed his jaw.

Jed twitched. His arm tightened around her. His voice sounded like nothing more than a breath but Shay heard Jed loud and clear. "*Stunning.*"

She smiled as she tucked herself against Jed, her head nestled on his shoulder. And she promised herself, maybe this time she wouldn't go outside alone in the dark. This time she might listen and if she listened, she prayed Jed would too.

FORTY-SIX

JED WAS SOMEWHERE DARK AND WARM. HE DIDN'T remember the knife going in his back, he only recalled the sickening feeling of dropping at Shay's feet before he could kiss her and let her know she was everything to him. He missed Shay terribly; her smell, her softness... everything. Jed had just gotten her back and she was gone again, slipped through his fingertips. He had to find her.

Jed wasn't exactly sure where he was. There was fog, the familiar train station that he and his mother used to travel the Northeast. He stood near a wooden bench, waiting, unsure if he was waiting for the train or something else. He scrutinized the sky, the tracks, the steps behind him. There was nothing, until there was a familiar voice.

"Baby," Clara said, "where have you been all this time?"

Jed's chest filled with emotion. Last time he'd seen his mother, he was floating in the ocean ready to give up on life.

"What are you doing here?" she asked again.

"I got hurt," he motioned to his back, "during a fight with a Demon."

"Let me look." Her voice was soft and concerned. He felt her touch on his shoulders.

"It appears you've been stabbed," Clara was stepping around him, her hand never leaving him. "Must've been a sly creature to get past you."

Jed nodded. "It was." Emotion swelled. "Am I dead?"

Clara shook her head. "No, baby, you're somewhere in between." She searched his face. "You're not supposed to be here but let's not waste this time together. What troubles you?"

His mother always had the answer to everything, when he was a child and then again when he'd see her in dreams or near death experiences.

He paused for too long, couldn't find the words to explain what he'd been going through.

Clara smiled, somehow she knew. "Did you meet a nice girl?"

Jed's chin trembled and the noise that came out of his throat sounded like a cry and a laugh. He covered his face, realizing he'd lost her in death. Unexpectedly, ironically, he'd been the one to die in the end.

Warm hands pulled at his wrists. "Baby, tell me about her. Is she pretty? Strong? Tell me everything."

Jed looked up to Clara's warm smile. He wiped his face. "She's beautiful. Long blue hair."

"Blue?" Clara smiled wide. "To match your aura?" Her hands outlined the glowing blue aura that surrounded him. "Have you protected her?"

Jed was silent for a moment as he chose his words. "She protected me. Once she killed an Angel that had the upper hand. She dragged me to safety. She saved me."

"I knew she'd be strong."

"But she's so small. So... human." Jed didn't like saying the phrase like a flaw but he didn't know another way.

"I was small compared to you as a man." Clara motioned to his height. "Much smaller than you are now and I did just fine." Clara took his hands and dragged him to the bench, forcing him to sit. "Tell me more."

"She is a bit defiant. She's gotten hurt."

Clara waved the concern away. "Think back to all we lived through and how many times you helped bandage me up. It's not uncommon for humans to get hurt. The scars show we *lived*. That's all anyone wants, to live. What's her name?"

"Shay." Jed squeezed Clara's hands. "I wish you were alive to meet her."

"She sounds lovely. And you seem hesitant about something."

"We saved her from a Demon... again."

"*We*? You're making friends? Wonderful. I always wanted you to have friends but it was too dangerous. Keep going." Clara smiled, eager to hear more.

"I'm afraid that she'll get hurt again and again. I just want to keep her safe. I think the best way to keep her safe is to keep my distance."

Clara was shaking her head. "Baby, enjoy the time you get with Shay and stop keeping her at arm's length. I didn't keep you alive all those years so you could live half a life."

Jed nodded, solemn, understanding.

The blare of a train horn interrupted them. Clara stood. "It's my time to go."

Jed stood and she hugged him tightly, not wanting to let go. Clara rose up on her toes and kissed his cheek.

"Baby, I love you. You're going to wake up soon. Go *live*."

Jed was beaming as Clara stepped onto the empty train. The doors closed and it pulled away from the station.

———

Now

Jed opened his eyes. Shay was there, asleep, her leg thrown over his and her chin tucked against his chest. He took a deep breath, inhaling the scent of her. His body ached but he'd never felt better than with Shay next to him. She made a soft sound in her sleep.

Jed twisted his body to face her, felt the stitches in his back pulling. He touched her face, tucked the strands of blue behind her ear. His fingertips traced her neck, paused on the scars from where the Demon had fed. He pulled the sheet back and found more on her arms. He moved the thin gown she was wearing and saw marks on her legs. If the Demon bastard wasn't already dead, he'd kill the beast over and over again for marking her skin.

Shay's eyes flashed open. "You're awake," she murmured.

Jed kissed her, gently, savoring the softness of Shay's lips and her taste. Her body pressed against his and her small hands roamed over his shoulders and chest and back.

"Does it hurt?" she asked, her fingertips moving over the bandage on his back.

"Not even close to how much it hurt nearly losing you." He leaned back, searching her eyes. "Did they hurt you? I don't want to scare you or hurt you more."

"Teari said the bite marks would go away eventually." She gazed into his eyes, feeling warm all over. "You won't hurt me." She slid her leg over his, up his hip, and pulled him closer. "I don't want to hurt you."

Jed smiled. "Never." He was toying with the knot at the closure of her gown before he tugged it loose. "I want you like never before."

Shay's hands slid into his hair and tugged him closer for a kiss. Jed's hand slid the gown aside and their mouths opened, tongues tangled in a kiss that had been too long in the waiting.

Jed's free hand roamed her body, cupped her breasts, his thumb pressing over her pebbled nipple. Shay moaned and threw her head back. Jed kissed down her neck, sucking and licking along her clavicle, her chest, until he reached her breast with his mouth. He sucked as his hand roved over her hip, squeezed her backside before deft fingers trailed to her front and down to the vee of her thighs.

Jed shifted to brace himself above her and tugged Shay's body under his. She squealed, pressed her breasts upward for him to suck and kiss. He paused and she whined with the loss of his warm mouth on her body.

"It's not too much is it? Too fast?" Jed's fingers were pressed against her core.

"Never," Shay whispered before glancing at the door. "Someone might come in."

Jed whispered a spell that sounded like satin sheets dragging against each other, and the door locked. "No one will enter," he promised.

Shay kissed him again, pressing herself upwards so his fingers slid further between her legs. "Please," she begged. "Please, don't stop."

Jed's forehead dropped against hers as he pushed his fingers inside, stretching her, readying her.

Shay's hips moved to the same motion. Her hands gripped his hair, pulling him in for a deep kiss. He felt good, too good. He always did. She felt his length and hardness against her thigh. Shay reached down and took him in her hand, stroking.

"Fuck," Jed moaned, breaking their kiss. "I never want to stop."

"Don't stop." Shay moved her leg, making space for him. Jed's fingers left her. He shifted and Shay felt his thickness begin to stretch her.

They moved together slowly, so slow Shay thought she might die from the pleasure of it. Jed kissed her everywhere; lips, skin, breasts. Shay moaned softly when Jed ground his hips against hers. He held her close, one hand under her hips and one behind her back, crushing her to him, never letting go.

Tears stung Shay's eyes as her arms tightened around him. "Never let me go," she whispered. "Please."

"Heaven and Hell will have to fight me for you. I'll never let go. You're mine. Forever," Jed promised with a searing kiss that tore at her soul. Jed's hips jerked and tension swelled inside Shay. They rode into oblivion together.

FORTY-SEVEN

Sparrow stood outside the door of a burning mansion. The air was filled with smoke and ash, smelled like fresh cinders. He sent shadows under the door to smother the smoke and flame before kicking the door open.

He searched the burning ruins, held the walls and ceiling up with shadows until he was able to find what he was looking for.

Alastor was half burned with a knife in his heart. If the Raven King had been any later, the Demon would be dead. Sparrow's shadows smothered the flames on Alastor's clothing and skin. He reached down and pulled the knife out of Alastor's chest, tucked it into his leathers and waited.

Alastor's eyes fluttered open and the wound slowly closed. He stared up at Sparrow.

"What have you done?" Alastor asked.

"Saved your life." Sparrow paced, ash and ichor collecting on the feathers of his wings that dragged on the floor. "I suggest getting to your feet so we can leave this place before it collapses." Sparrow was inspecting Krelp's charred remains.

"Where is Shay?" Alastor asked.

"Not here." Sparrow waited for the Demon to move.

"I will burn all of Hellscape until I find her. Is that what you want, Raven King?"

"I will drain you to a husk." Sparrow threatened.

"Try," Alastor challenged.

"Get fucked," Sparrow said.

"I'd like to but you kidnapped my girl."

"She is not your girl. Erase her memory from your mind." Sparrow crossed his arms, gripping the basilisk blade in his right hand.

Alastor tipped his head. "Whose girl is she then?" He leaned forward, his brow wrinkled as he searched Sparrow's face for an answer. "If she's not my girl, whose girl is she?"

"The Nephilim. Leave them alone. You are mine now."

Alastor's eyes went wide as he read between the lines. Then he threw his head back and laughed out loud like a coyote at midnight who'd found fresh meat. "You? You! Fucking sick. Just like your father. The apple doesn't fall far from the tree. I have to say, Raven King, I didn't expect this from you but I'm not surprised in the least bit." He sat, crossed his leg over his knee and asked, "What do you want? How many?"

"As many as I can get."

"Nah." Alastor shook his head. "That's not how this works."

Sparrow palmed the basilisk tooth knife. "I could impale you with this again and you can continue on in stasis with nothing. I pulled this from your blackened heart. You owe me a life debt. I don't need to make a deal. *You do*!"

Sparrow slammed the tip of the basilisk blade into the wooden table. "Eighty percent."

Alastor shook his head. "Nah. I can't run this on twenty percent. I need the funds. Thirty percent."

"Sixty."

The Demon and the Raven King went back and forth with numbers and values until Sparrow began to get annoyed.

"Your father only wanted five percent," Alastor revealed.

"I am not my father."

"Remiel was a greedy bastard. Heard that Queen Meg drained him dry." Alastor prodded.

"I'm not here to talk about *your* Queen." Sparrow's features went blank.

Alastor chuckled. He'd heard rumors about the fated Meg and Sparrow and their epic downfall. Seems the Raven King was still butthurt over it all.

"I killed her once already. I'd do it again. She is nothing." Sparrow picked up the basilisk tooth knife. "I'll kill you in a heartbeat if you don't remain on topic." Shadows pooled around his feet with the threat.

Alastor was rubbing his temples, wishing he'd taken Shay like he'd wanted to all those weeks. Now it was too late. He'd never taste her like he desired. This was a game he was quickly losing.

"Fifty fifty," Alastor finally said.

"Deal." Sparrow led the Demon out of the crumbling mansion, stopping once they were outside its doors and the whispers of Hellnight greeted them.

"Now." Sparrow stepped closer. "Recall the rune you branded into Shay."

Alastor's eyes lit with fire.

"You think I'd forget? Remove it."

"I need her here." Alastor licked his lips.

"Fuck that. Remove it remotely." Sparrow spun the basilisk blade between his fingers with the intent of smashing it into Alastor's skull if he didn't comply. He'd hate to lose all those souls but Shay was worth more. Combined, Sparrow would be the most powerful King in the Seven Kingdoms of Heaven. More powerful than Gabriel, Meg's father, more powerful than Babylon or the Deacons.

A sudden tick quirked Sparrow's cheek and he thought he heard the call of a barn owl in the night. He ignored it.

Alastor glared, then stood tall, adjusting his burnt suit, and rubbing a hand over his newly scarred face. He needed a healer; he couldn't be walking around looking like a melting marshmallow. He had skin to trade and a partner to keep happy. Alastor grinned inwardly; things were looking up with a King from the Seven Kingdoms of Heaven on his side.

No, he wouldn't fix his face, Alastor finally decided. He'd leave the scars as a reminder to what distraction brings.

FORTY-EIGHT

"Something bad is coming to this place," Teari warned Meg and Skeele.

"How do you know?" Meg asked. "Plenty of bad omens have been delivered to me. They've never been right, completely. This is Hell, bad shit happens."

Teari clasped her hands and focused on Meg. "You all need to be on high alert."

"Just fucking tell me what the deal is, Teari," Meg said.

"I can't say." Teari's face was impassive.

"Bullshit." Meg was fidgeting. "Tell me or get the fuck out."

Teari's brows rose. "Are you serious?"

"I'll cast you out of my realm–"

Teari's face twisted. "I'll file this under you're probably hangry." She glanced to Skeele. "Feed her will you?"

And then Teari was gone, having stepped through the portal and gone back to Gabriel's realm in Heaven.

Skeele turned to Meg, "Was that necessary?"

Meg sighed and ran hands through her hair. "She'll forgive me, she always does."

Skeele stared.

"Fine. Fine! I'll send her a letter or something apologizing."

"Hell is a large realm," Skeele reminded Meg. "Intel is important no matter who it comes from."

"What have the Hellions reported?" Meg asked.

"The problems are relatively mild compared to what went on here during Lucifer's reign." Skeele was looking away from Meg.

"Tell me the truth." Meg's eyes narrowed on him.

Skeele led her away. "Not here."

FORTY-NINE

Meg purchased the Peabody Library after speaking with Jed and deciding on a place where Jed and Shay could hide. There was too much risk in Hell for them to stay.

Meg was rich on the Earthen plane. Her mother had left her a boatload of money and since she didn't spend much time there, purchasing a foreclosed library was the perfect expenditure. The structure had good bones, the walls solid, good plumbing, and power. It was pre-warded from the time Declan lived there. Iron-strong wards guarded every entrance, heck even the sidewalk had wards carved underneath the cement.

Peabody Library was a sanctuary now. It would remain boarded and warded so Jed and Shay could live in safety and seclusion. And Nero. There was plenty of room for Nero.

——————

"Stay out of trouble," Chel warned, hugging Shay goodbye.

"If I find trouble, you'll be the first Hellion I call," Shay promised.

Chel turned to Jed, slapping him on the back. "You're still a piece of shit." Jed's eyes widened as Chel grabbed a handful of shirt and yanked him closer, hugging him like an old friend. "But I guess you'll do. Take care of her."

"I always will," Jed promised, a chill passing through him when Chel stepped away.

"See ya around, clotpole." Chel waved before walking back to his post near the castle gates.

"I'm not comfortable with you *poofing* these two back and forth between Hell and the Earthen plane," Skeele grumbled as he crossed his arms.

Nero whinnied expectantly.

"No," Meg warned the stallion. "You can cross the Veil on your own. Meet us at the library."

Nero huffed and stomped the dirt at Meg's audacity. He didn't want Shay out of his sight on the Earthen plane, but he knew how to get there, *fast*. Nero grinned, tipped his head down and readied himself, eager to beat Meg at her own game of traveling faster than the speed of light.

"You want to come too?" Meg held out her hand and wiggled her fingers in Skeele's direction. "Freshly fed means I'm *uber* powerful right now. Come on."

"Fine." Skeele stomped closer, grumbling in Hellspeak. He lowered his voice and murmured something to Meg, calling her *Night Owl* as he kissed her neck and whispered dark promises in her ear, making Meg close her eyes and moan like she'd eaten chocolate cake.

"Dare ya," Meg said as she stared him down. "I'll even call you Kal." She winked. "We can get shrimp in the panhandle."

Recognition sparked as Shay took Meg's hand, ready to travel in her swift and violent manner of *poofing* from place to place.

"Okay," Meg smirked at the three. "Don't let go, this is gonna be fast." She closed her eyes and... *poof!*

Shay wobbled, feeling dizzy and nauseous. She leaned against

Meg, knowing Meg didn't like to be touched. Something must've changed in the queen because instead of pulling away, Meg gripped Shay to steady her.

Shay's fingers grabbed two feathers and just before she pulled them out, her knee bent and she dropped to the ground. Meg went with her and never felt the sting of feathers being pulled out of her wing.

"I'm sorry," Shay said with a flustered giggle, gripping her scarred thigh. "It's this leg, didn't heal right. I think the travel between realms hit me too hard." She looked up at Meg. "Are you okay?"

"I'm fine." Meg smiled but her eyes narrowed on Shay. Meg let go. "I can't lift you." She touched her swollen belly then motioned to Skeele.

Shay realized it was hard for Meg to admit she couldn't do something. Shay had that same problem sometimes.

The Hellion lifted Shay to her feet like she weighed nothing. Jed was there to take Shay into his arms and steady her; he didn't see when Shay tucked the feathers of the Night Owl into her pocket.

No one did.

FIFTY

A HORSE IN A LIBRARY... IT SOUNDED RIDICULOUS BUT Nero didn't give two shits about what people would think. He liked the sound his hooves made on the wooden floor, liked the sound on tile even better. Jed had built him a real bed in one of the rooms near where he and Shay slept. It was better than matted straw or fresh grass. Horses didn't typically sleep on mattresses or have a private room with four walls and a bathroom. But Nero did. The tub was filled with fresh water every night. Nero took to the change as though he'd always lived inside like a human.

Nero never trotted fast in the library, he took his time, he went *slow*. The hallways were wide and the rooms large. When he was wandering between the stacks of books he was careful not to tip them over by rubbing his sides against them. He stayed in the middle and gazed at the rows of books that smelled like they just might be a tasty snack. A tunnel led to the river where Nero could stretch his legs and graze in the moonlight.

There were runes of protection drawn on the walls and the doorframes but they were far enough away that they didn't make Shay's skin itch and feel tight. Whatever she'd felt in the suite at the castle in the burning caves, she wasn't feeling it here.

Jed was relaxed, like the days at the graveyard chapel. The creases had left his face and he didn't seem so stuck in his own head. He was quick to talk and kiss and touch. He was quick to fall into bed without a second thought, touching Shay like she was all he'd ever wanted, like she was a goddess he worshipped.

They spent their days reading and lounging. They built a rooftop garden, shielded from the nearby city. Peabody library looked abandoned and was warded to appear so. Nobody would know from the outside looking in that a Demon horse, a Demon poison-stained girl, and a half-breed Angel sought refuge in the old library.

Jed and Shay and Nero lived in peace. No one knew where they were besides Meg and Skeele. Jed didn't care to leave the safety of the library any more than to walk by the river in the moonlight with Nero.

They spent their days reading, sleeping, and playing board games from before Shay was born. She got really good at cards and betting and hiding her reactions if she had a good hand or a shit hand.

Shay was leaning against Jed, both immersed in a book, enjoying the silence of the library and the warmth of each other's bodies. Suddenly, Shay's pupils went black and a shiver tore up her spine.

"What was that?" Jed asked, turning toward her.

"Nothing," Shay said.

Shay and Nero made eye contact. The horse was resting near the lit fireplace like a dog. A deal had snapped into place. The only one waiting for delivery was Sparrow's.

That fuck resurrected Alastor.

"Jed, baby?" Shay inched closer. "Have you ever thought about which one of the Archangels fathered you?"

"Yes."

"Do you know who it is? It might come in handy in the future." She tucked blue hair behind her ear and tried her best to look innocent.

Jed was searching her eyes. He was so tired of running and hiding and being back in Peabody library was the most peaceful he'd felt since the first time he'd lived here. He missed his friend Declan and many memories had flooded him walking through the familiar doors. The rooms where he'd learned to harness his magic seemed haunted now.

Jed stood and walked away. He explored the alphabetical markers on stacks until he came across a familiar book about Archangels.

Jed returned to the table where they'd been reading. Shay's bare legs were hanging over the arms of a wooden chair.

"My mother told me once. Only once." Jed was flipping the pages, smoothing his fingers over ages old script and parchment. His fingertips made a sweeping sound, like the dragging of Angel wing feathers. He stopped on the Archangel Michael. He tapped his finger on the page. "This one. She seemed afraid to say his name out loud but she was already dead so he couldn't do anything to her."

"She came to you as a ghost?" Shay asked.

Jed nodded, remembering the flooded boat and how he'd barely made it back to shore. He'd be at the bottom of the sea if she hadn't come to him. He wanted to tell Shay that Clara had come to him when he was unconscious, after Alastor had stabbed him but he would wait for another time to tell her that story.

Shay shifted in her seat, curling her legs underneath her and leaning close. Blue hair fell on Jed's arm. "Your father is the Archangel Michael."

Shay's leg scar burned. Her stomach ached. She felt that familiar tug. "We're about to be pulled to the Crossroads," she warned Jed.

"Okay." He kissed her quickly. "Be safe." He searched her face, wanting to be there to protect her, afraid that she'd get hurt. He finally accepted that she'd never be completely safe and he'd relish whatever time he was allowed to have with her. "I want to come with you."

"I must go with Nero."

Jed nodded knowingly, accepting.

"Make us dinner?" Shay asked as the tugging in her stomach became more intense.

"What do you want?" Jed asked.

"French toast. Extra bacon. Hot coffee." Shay smiled before she was wrenched away to the Crossroads.

-The End-

Preview of Veil of Shadows Book 11 [Untitled and Unedited]

Note from the author: Veil of Shadows Books 11+ will jump to the future, one where there is a war, tragedy, enemies to lovers, second chance romance. It's time for Sparrow's redemption...

Reminder: this is a preview of an unedited work in progress, names may change, scenes may change, plotting may change during editing. Below is just a rough draft of the next book for your enjoyment. Make sure you're following my website/blog to get more chapter previews and announcements.

Chapter 1

Nightingale has found me in a dream. I want to tell her she promised to stop. I'm sitting on a soggy dock, feet dangling in cool, dark water. I'm watching the loons floating in the morning mist. Nightingale is running toward me. Running on water, arms out, terrified look on her face. The loons scramble away, their wings flapping against the water as they soar low. I want to yell at Nightingale for ruining my fucking peace. But, this must be something serious because she hasn't come to me in a dream like this in years.

"What is it?" I ask.

"Wake up, Meg." She's shaking my shoulders. "Get up! Get up now! They're storming the castle. Wake up you must save your children!" she screams in my face.

My eyes flash open.

I sit up in bed, smell acrid creosote. It's familiar but too intense, too fresh. The window is open, no birds chirp, no owls hoot. There's fresh smoke, the hammering of stone, shouting.

Skeele shifts, moving closer. Someone howls, there's footsteps in the hallway.

"Wake up!" I yell to Skeele, launching myself out of bed.

He's on his feet, naked, ready to fight. A spec of dried blood on his lip. There's no slow morning stretches with our limbs rubbing together, savoring the memories and ache of last night.

"Clothes." I throw him a pair of pants and shirt.

"The babies." His eyes are wide, terrified. "Get them." Skeele's shirt gets caught on his horns, he tugs hard, tearing it in a rush.

He calls them babies still but they are much older, too old to be called babies, they're teenagers now but he's never stopped. I guess compared to him they will always appear to be babies. Young, innocent, his. Something he never thought he'd have. Bred to serve the throne, he took on so much more.

I grab clothes and throw them on. I get my bag, my blade, and weapons, they've been ready to go since Teari warned me of something terrible coming years ago. I threatened to kick her out of my realm for it because she didn't give me details, she just had a feeling, a premonition. She was right and I'm thankful she told me. Otherwise I wouldn't have a bugout bag packed and ready, and a plan.

"Here." Skeele tosses me the jar of Snowy Owl feathers from my bedside.

Poof. I leave the room.

"Children," I whisper shaking them awake. "Wake up right now."

Remington launches up straight with a deep intake of breath. Rue is quieter, green eyes flash open, her arms jerk to the sides, gripping the sheets. "Are we going to die?" she asks.

"Get moving." I throw her blankets back and don't answer her question. I can't answer her question because fear is more than a flood threatening to overtake my body, it's a tsunami, an earthquake, something thoroughly consuming that clogs my throat and traps my words.

This is not new. I have been attacked by evil before, but that was when my world was small. The stakes are higher than ever now. I couldn't protect the seed in my womb then, but now... now I could lose everything I didn't think I deserved. Fate has been cruel and unfair but I don't have time to dwell on it now.

Remington and Rue scramble out of bed, and when they smell the smoke that seeps under their door and hear the commotion echoing in the hall, they move quickly and meet me in their closet.

"Get clothes," I say. "Boots, knives, leather jackets and pants."

They listen. They listen because Teari warned me thirteen years ago that something was coming, something bad and every day since we've prepared.

Clea arrives, wisps of white swirl into her ethereal form. "Let me say goodbye," Clea's voice breaks through before she's fully formed. "I must say goodbye to them."

My mother's lips are deep red, her transparent skin a ghastly white, but, she doesn't scare them. This is all they know of their grandmother. She died the day I was born so it is all I know of her as well.

"Hurry, Clea," I warn, collecting more clothing and tucking knives into Rue's pockets.

"Oh, children," her form turns solid, "be safe." She hugs them

871

together, one on each arm, hugged so tight they might complain that they can't breathe but instead they hug her back just as fiercely.

"What have you seen?" I ask Clea, tossing a pack to Remington. He straps it on and pulls the clips tight.

"Demons from the mountains. Bugs and snakes and roaches." Clea shivers with disgust. "The dark force is strong, familiar."

"Did you see a face?" I ask, helping Rue tighten her pack.

"Not yet," Clea says. "I had to stop and say goodbye, I'll go back."

"Be careful," I warn.

"Hide them well," Clea says with a warm smile, patting each child on a cheek then pinching them. "I wish you could take my bones so I could go with you and have more time. Our women are cursed with losing children."

"They won't be lost," I say. "They'll be in hiding."

Clea nods and straightens her back. "Hurry." She turns toward the door. "Something is coming."

I nod. "Help the Hellions. Skeele is in charge while I'm gone."

I take Rue's hand then Remington's. *Poof*–we're gone.

Chapter 2

Alastor trekked from his hovel in the mountains to the black lakes of Hell's Adirondacks. He had one goal, to secure a Basilisk. He didn't have a castle to defend, yet, but he'd need the creature to get there.

Alastor drove to Old Forge, taking Interstate-81 but avoiding all of Pennsylvania. He passed herds of the walking dead, a smirk crossing his face as he counted them and calculated how large his army would become.

Alastor turned off the exit toward Interstate-481 north, then turned on Interstate-90 east. He passed farmland and dense forests. He saw signs for the Safe House nearby. He made a mental note to have those taken down. They wouldn't be a factor much longer. Alastor merged onto 365 E and veered off onto Eastern Rock Rd. The Jeep jostled across the busted parking lot. He turned onto Moose River Road and drove past old houses and grocery stores. The Black River roared from nearby, the waters turbid and angry and the slick serpentine backs of the basilisk swim.

There were spawning.

He stood on a giant rock, planning his next move. There were plenty of ways to fish for a basilisk.

Alastor jumped down to lower rocks and made his way toward the shallow pool of baby basilisk.

A giant head rose from the surface of the river, watching. Rows of sharp teeth and a warning hiss.

"Come on ya slimy, bitch," Alastor said, pulling a knife from his belt.

He crouched, reaching into the pool of babies. The mother swam closer, teeth bared. Alastor reached into the water and grabbed a small one. The creature squealed ear-piercingly. Alastor cut it in half and tossed the body back into the water, turning it a murky red. The mother moved closer, jaws gnashing, threatening. It didn't scare Alastor, he had a plan. Alastor jumped in the dark water and made quick work of slaughtering the baby basilisk. Within minutes, he was saturated in bloody river water. Alastor rubbed the pieces of basilisk on his body, dipped his head and coated his hair and clothing in their blood. He bathed, rubbing their blood on his arms and neck.

The mother basilisk slithered closer, confused. Her children dead but Alastor smelling just like them. Being a creature of darkness, she followed the Demon who smelled like her children because if he smelled like her children, then he must be one, the only one, and she would protect him until the very end.

Alastor tucked pieces of bleeding basilisk into his pockets so the smell remained fresh. He emerged from the river, covered in blood and bits of flesh and bone. He walked back to his Jeep, smiling as the mother basilisk followed him. A menacing shadow at his back.

Chapter 3

Meg

Peabody Library is dark. I wish I could have sent warning that I'd be coming, when we arrive, it sets off every ward in the in the building. Hm. After all these years Jed would ward his home against me, after I bought it for him. Typical Jed. The horse shows up to investigate first.

A shallow whinny greets us.

"Nero," I say. "Come clear this rune." I motion to the circle that's trapping us.

Nero shakes his head in a firm response of "no."

The damn horse is trained not to trust me. Perfect. I can't blame Jed and Shay, I've gotten them in plenty of trouble over the years. The probably don't want any surprises.

"Then go get Shay," I say. "And hurry."

Before the giant black stallion gets himself turned around, footsteps echo down the hall.

"Meg?" Shay's voice shouts.

"Shhh," Jed shushes her.

"Come free us," I holler. "I don't have much time." I do my best

874

to hide the panic in my voice. I have to get out of here, return to Hell and defend the castle.

"What shit-fuckery did you bring us this time?" Jed asks, turning the corner around a bookshelf, he stops short when he sees the children behind me. His eyes blow wide, knowing. "What's happening?" He moves closer but doesn't clear the rune of chalk on the floor.

"The castle in the burning caves is under attack." I shift on my feet, eager to get out of the circle in the middle of the room. I feel too exposed like this. Trapped with my children.

"You mean *your* throne is under attack?" Shay clarifies.

I nod. I don't want to admit it. I never wanted the throne it was part of the price for killing my grandfather, Lucifer.

Jed takes a few quick steps forward and scuffs his boot over the chalk on the floor.

I take a deep breath, and step away, dragging the children with me. I go to Shay. She helped me many years ago with a search and rescue, then again when I was imprisoned with the Deacons, she impersonated me to keep the throne of Hell safe.

"Wait," I say. "One more thing." I drop my bag off my shoulder, unzip it and pull out the jar of snowy owl feathers. "Put this somewhere safe."

Shay reaches for the jar. It's small, not much more than a jelly jar. Etched glass, a stainless steel lid. These are the remains of my dead daughter, Elise. I swallow hard, tamping down emotion afraid that this night might leave me with three jars of feathers and no children.

There. I have left everything that I care about in Peabody library. Everything I never thought I'd have, I've left in the hands of others. It's a terrible feeling, leaving trust with others. Something that took me a long time to adjust to.

Chapter

Shay took the jar of mottled white and brown feathers, blinked and she was immediately transported back to a memory from a Crossroads Demon deal.

The air crackled with an ominous energy as the figure approached the crossroads, their steps hesitant yet filled with a sense of desperate determination. They bore the weight of something heavy upon their shoulders, their gaze haunted by the specter of tragedy that loomed over their existence.

It was a Deacon.

Nero backed up.

Shay tensed.

Deacons were the gatekeepers of balance between the Seven Kingdoms of Heaven, the Earthen plane and Hell. Why did one summon Shay and Nero?

"What is it that you seek, Deacon?" Shay asked.

The Deacon hesitated, their gaze flickering with uncertainty before they spoke, voice tinged with a mixture of power and desperation.

"No one can know that I'm here," the Deacon said.

Shay nodded. "Is that your deal?"

"No." the Deacon folded his hands. "This deal will be a great burden for both of us."

The Deacon kept looking over his shoulder and to the desert beyond. He'd drawn them to a crossroads in the middle of nowhere. They could see for miles even with only moonlight.

"There is a great darkness coming," the Deacon warned.

"That sounds like a warning, not a deal. Why did you call me here?" Shay didn't want to return to Alastor but she didn't want her time wasted by this creature.

The Deacon paused and closed his eyes, finding calm and choosing his words carefully. "The deal is, you must take the children to safety and tell no one where they are. You must hide them until Clea's prophecy comes to fruition."

"What children?"

The Deacon held up a finger. "They are not born yet. When the time comes, you will know. You must agree to this now, before it's too late."

"What are you wishing to give me?" Shay asked, knowing that what the Crossroads Demon would take was not negotiable and typically unknown.

"I will give my life. Sooner rather than later."

Shay blinked again before glancing at Nero. His ear twitched with recognition.

"They'll be safe her. We won't let anything happen to them," Shay said.

Meg nodded, and Shay noticed the slight quiver in her bottom lip. Meg wouldn't fall apart though, she never did, always kept her feelings in check unless it was anger. She wasn't afraid to let her anger out, but love, that was a feeling Meg kept under wraps and Shay could understand why. Meg had let her love escape once, she'd loved the Raven King and he nearly killed her. He ruined her, wrecked her, left others to clean up what was left of her broken heart and bleeding body. Meg was right to have trust issues. Last time she trusted someone heart and soul, she'd nearly died. Shay would never forget the moment Jed arrived covered in blood and panicking that they'd die in Hell with Meg gone.

Shay focused on the children standing behind Meg. They seemed despondent, didn't show a spec of fear. They'd never been to the Peabody library, never been to the Earthen plane as far as Shay knew. Shay and Jed had met them multiple times during holidays and Sunday dinners that Meg held. Shay and Jed attended, both having no other family and feeling compelled since Meg bought the library and let them live there. The children knew Jed and Shay and Nero, but that was about it.

Shay reached out to Rue first and hugged her. She gripped

Remington's shoulder and gave him a little shake as a greeting and a promise.

"We'll take good care of them, for as long as you need," Shay promised.

Rue didn't say a word but Shay noticed the slight tremble of her bottom lip, exactly like her mother. She'd have to learn how to hide that better. The girl swiped at long dark hair that had fallen across her eyes.

Jed was there, taking Remington aside and whispering to him, no doubt warning him of the Earthen plane and what the boy could and could not do while he was here.

Shay shook Meg's shoulder, "If you've got to burn it all to the ground, then let it *burn*."

A chill passed through Meg as Shay's eyes flashed black. It was a side-effect of the Demon poison Shay had trapped in a scar. She was tethered to the Crossroads Demon Nero, her horse. As a result, Shay had the ability to transform into something wraithlike.

Shay tipped the jar to the side, watched the feathers drift, and realized that they looked very much like Meg's wings.

Meg nodded.

Shay hugged her, worried that Meg might fail. No. No Shay wouldn't let that thought out into the wild. Never wanted it to become true. Meg was the strongest person Shay had ever met. Shay squeezed Meg tight, easy not to pinch her wings.

"Burn it all, Meg," Shay whispered in her ear. "You are formidable."

Meg wiped her eyes, she wanted to tell the children goodbye again but she'd been here too long. She needed to go back.

Meg raised a hand, gaze meeting her children's as she waved goodbye to them. She'd never prayed but at that moment, she did, and she prayed that it wouldn't be the last time she ever saw them.

Poof – Meg returned to Hell.

About the Author

M. R. Pritchard delves into the profound clash between good and evil, the mystical realms of gods and monsters, and the intricate transformations of ordinary people into beings of immense power. Her gripping narratives often unfold within the haunting backdrop of apocalyptic or post-apocalyptic landscapes, offering a unique blend of suspense and wonder.

M. R. Pritchard is a two-time Kindle Scout winning author, her short story "Glitch" has been featured in the 2017 winter edition of THE FIRST LINE literary journal. Her short story "Moon Lord" has been featured in Chronicle Worlds: Half Way Home (Part of the Future Chronicles) and will be time capsuled on the moon on the Lunar Codex in 2024.

Visit her website MRPritchard.com and Subscribe. You'll get subscriber only content, deleted scenes, updates, special previews of new projects, and book deals.

ALSO BY M. R. PRITCHARD

Other Books by M. R. Pritchard

Science Fiction/post-apocalyptic:

The Phoenix Project

The Reformation

Revelation

Inception

Origins

Resurrection

The Phoenix Project Compendium Edition

The Safest City on Earth

The Man Who Fell to Earth

Heartbeat

Asteroid Riders Series

Moon Lord

Collector of Space Junk and Rebellious Dreams

Steampunk:

Tick of a Clockwork Heart

Dark Fantasy:

Veil of Shadows Series:

Sparrow Man

Nightingale Girl

Scarecrow

Raven King

Nightjar

Night Owl

Etched in Darkness

Embrace the Night

Shadows of Destiny

Midnight Serenade

Thread the Bone

Fantasy/Fairy Tale Love Story/Romance:

Muse

Forgotten Princess Duology

Midsummer Night's Dream: A Game of Thrones

Poetry/Short Stories

Consequence of Gravity

Milton Keynes UK
Ingram Content Group UK Ltd.
UKHW040734141124
451073UK00006BA/109

9 781957 709598